pride before a fall

MARY SMYTHE

Quills & Quartos
PUBLISHING

Edited by Debra Anne Watson and Mary McLaughlin

Cover by Hoja Design

ISBN 978-1-956613-41-4 (ebook) and 978-1-956613-42-1 (paperback)

To MawMaw, who would have been tickled pink to see me published. I miss you.

ONE

Fitzwilliam Darcy jerked his drifting gaze back to the pages of his book, scolding himself internally for his lack of self-control. How absurd! He had not been so relentlessly preoccupied by anything—or anyone, as was presently the case—since he had been a boy and first discovered the wonders of reading. Then, as in the present instance, his focus had entirely shifted to his new occupation and left him with little attention for anything else, greatly frustrating his parents, or his governess, whenever he was required to do something other than absorb himself in an adventurous tale or fascinating history.

Currently, it was Darcy himself who was frustrated by his inability to shake his fixation. Frustrated because the object of it was not an innocent pastime or necessary business, but rather a young lady. He had never before been thus infatuated, at least not beyond an appreciation of her appearance or vague consideration of her suitability, and he had not expected the experience to be so...absorbing. As hackneyed as it sounded—and he would never admit such to his cousin Fitzwilliam lest he be mocked incessantly for the remainder of his days—Darcy could now understand why all the poets were so enthused. If he had possessed their talent for waxing lyrical, he would have written an ode to Miss Elizabeth Bennet's fine eyes with the same sort of besotted passion as Shakespeare, but, perhaps fortunately for all, iambic pentameter was not his forte.

Oh, but the feelings which crafted such words were there, Darcy no longer had any doubt. This, however, was the bedrock of his problem, because he could never marry her. Elizabeth —*no, Miss Elizabeth Bennet*, he reminded himself sternly lest he lose his head and refer to her out loud in an informal fashion— was, herself, the most delightful creature he had ever had the fortune to behold. She was beautiful, of course, with dark, tightly spiralling curls, bright and curious green eyes feathered with delicate lashes, and a most becomingly warm complexion. One long ringlet was tangled about her first finger, gently abused while she...

Darcy was startled to realise that he had been staring at Miss Elizabeth again where she sat, curled comfortably in an armchair on the other side of the library with an open tome in her lap, and tore his eyes away. He had entirely lost count of how many times this loss of control had occurred in the past twenty minutes, but he knew that the number was high.

At any rate, Darcy reminded himself, he would not be in half so much trouble was she simply pretty; oh no, it was much more dire than that. Miss Elizabeth Bennet was also witty and quick, with a tongue that often left lesser men bemused by her cleverness. Her opinions, while not always in agreement with his own, were fascinating and defended with cheerful spirit, making her the most interesting object for conversation Darcy had encountered in some time. And, unlike other young ladies who excelled in the art of wounding with words, her commentary tended towards playful teasing—a decided mark in her favour. Darcy detested the subtle, cruel sparring so common amongst *le bon ton*, considering it petty and ridiculous. Miss Elizabeth apparently recognised that she need not descend to such paltry attacks to capture his interest, and it was a refreshing change.

Even had Darcy not noticed this kind levity in Miss Elizabeth's wordplay, her devotion to her elder sister—only recently recovered from a bad cold and able to venture downstairs since falling ill at the dinner table earlier in the week—would have spoken for her. In a show of sisterly care and consolation for the ailing Miss Bennet, Miss Elizabeth had walked three miles through dirt and muck to tend to her personally, rather than leaving her to the indifferent care of Bingley's sisters. Though he would not wish Georgiana to make such an exhibition, the sentiment behind the act was an admirable one he would be pleased for his own sister to emulate.

But, no matter how beguiling, enchantingly clever, or warmly kind Miss Elizabeth proved to be, he could never marry her. Her dowry was essentially nonexistent and, worse, her closest connexions were an embarrassment. The lack of funds he could, perhaps, overlook, but her mother and younger sisters...no, he could never countenance such in-laws. Compounding their personal sins of atrocious behaviour, the Bennets were also, apparently, kin to tradespeople. Mr Bennet's family had been landed for generations, according to Miss Bingley's ill-natured gossip, but Mrs Bennet was the daughter of a country attorney and sister to a man who lived within the shadow of his own warehouses. It was not to be borne, even for a pair of the finest eyes he had ever seen and witty banter that challenged him most delightfully.

The lure of Miss Elizabeth Bennet drew his eyes to her form again as a palpable longing overcame Darcy. She seemed not to notice that she was the object of his abstraction as she casually flipped a page, her own gaze riveted to the book resting propped against her folded knees. Her delicate slippers, a deep, forbidden red which matched the tiny, embroidered flowers sprinkled across the muslin of her day gown, rested upon the carpet beside her armchair while her stocking feet hid beneath her skirts. Her head was tilted to one side and rested against the ruddy leather of her seat, one hand palmed against her cheek as her fingers idly played with the loose curls at her temple, and her body remained comfortably still while her eyes trailed down the script in front of her. She was close to the fireplace and, as a result, the skin of the side of her face, chest, and arm closest to it was flushed a warm pink, highlighting a dusting of freckles that cascaded downward.

I must get out of here.

Miss Elizabeth jolted and looked up at him when he made an agonised growl deep in his throat and closed his own book with a loud thud. Her eyes were slightly widened in surprise, a brow arched, as he stood and tossed the leather-bound volume onto the small table beside his own chair. Typically, he would take the time to put it back in its place upon the bookshelf if he did not intend to carry it away with him, but in that moment, it was critical that he absent himself from Elizabeth's—*Miss Elizabeth Bennet's!*—company before he did anything foolish. Like speak to her. Flirt with her. Pull her into his arms and—

With a bow that was more of a jerk of the head than the graceful mark of respect the lady deserved, Darcy spun about towards the door and fled from the library as if his backside were on fire. Considering how flushed he felt, it might very well be.

I will go for a ride to cool off—yes, that will do. Anything to get myself out from under the same roof as Elizab— Miss Elizabeth Bennet!

An hour or so after his escape from the torturous temptation of the siren known as Miss Elizabeth Bennet, Darcy felt more at ease upon the back of his mount. Blackthorne was a young stallion yet and somewhat unpredictable but served most adequately as a distraction from thoughts of fine eyes and teasing smiles. If Darcy allowed his mind to wander too much towards illicit topics, his horse might take it upon himself to misbehave, as was his inclination whenever given the opportunity. He had brought Blackthorne with him to Netherfield Park to continue their training as he was still too temperamental for casual riding in London parks and his head groom at Pemberley was struggling to command the wilful beast. Despite all these myriad faults, Darcy was fond of Blackthorne; he was strong, fast, and devoted once his loyalty had been earned, much like his master. They understood one another, even if the stallion tended towards the mischievous.

They had been riding the fields surrounding Netherfield for the past three-quarters of an hour and so Darcy steered his mount back in the direction of the stables, slowing their pace to a trot as they approached the smooth, if autumn-browned, lawn of the manor. Both horse and rider were showing signs of fatigue and discomfort from the sharp coldness of the day, so it was time to return to their individual lodgings for the warming care of servants.

Darcy raised his gaze to look towards their destination and, as his heart seized most strongly, tightened his grip on the reins. Blackthorne responded by rearing up off his front legs a few inches, though Darcy easily kept his seat and leant forwards to pat his steed's neck in silent apology. His eyes, however, were fixed upon two slowly strolling figures in the near distance—those of Miss Elizabeth Bennet and her sister. They had, it seemed, decided to take a walk in the fresh, if frigid, air and were making slow circuits about the shrivelled rose garden, arm in arm.

It was not like Darcy to be indecisive, but for a moment he struggled with whether he should continue on his course and inevitably meet up with the ladies or turn Blackthorne round and bolt away. The latter idea he determined was ridiculous—they were young gentlewomen, not highwaymen bent on violent robbery—and so steeled himself to meet Miss Elizabeth with outward equanimity. She would never know that he roiled with irrepressible feelings for her inside.

Darcy inhaled deeply and then expelled the breath in a frosty cloud. Taking the reins more determinedly into his grip, he steered Blackthorne towards the low hedge that outlined the decorative garden space surrounding Netherfield Park's manor house and nudged him in the flanks to encourage a burst of speed. The stallion responded as commanded and sped up into a full gallop. When he reached the leafy barrier between himself and his goal, Blackthorne reared up his front legs, sprung forwards from his back and leapt smoothly over the obstacle with powerful grace. His hooves beat upon the hardened ground on the other side without error and the black beast slowed to a more comfortable trot.

"Well done," Darcy complimented, bending to stroke Blackthorne's neck. The stallion shook his mane in response as if to say, 'you expected otherwise?' This incurred an amused smirk from his master.

The soft smattering of distant applause drew Darcy's attention back to the pair of ladies, now only a few yards ahead of him and quickly growing closer. The two Miss Bennets had paused in their promenade to watch Darcy and his own exercise partner perform their jump and, apparently, approved of his athletic skill. Though it was irrational, and though clearing the obstacle had been little more than a necessary act to achieve his goal of reaching the house without going all the way round the expansive lawn to the front drive, he could not help but feel a swell of masculine pride that he had impressed the lady who had so impressed him. There was nothing quite like appearing capable in the eyes of a woman worthy of being pleased.

Miss Elizabeth leant towards her sister to speak—something he could not hear from so far away—but her eyes were sparkling in his direction. He could see the vivid splash of green fixed upon him, watched as they followed his own movements, and Darcy was filled with a sudden daring desire to repeat his success.

Sitting up straighter in the saddle, Darcy tugged back on Blackthorne's reins to turn him about towards the shrubbery which had brought him such victory. He kicked his horse into faster motion and, just before the stallion raised his legs to make his second jump, pressed his torso low against his mount's neck.

They cleared it again with the same ease and agility as the last attempt and landed nimbly in the taller grass on the other side.

He turned Blackthorne about again once they had achieved enough distance to build the right momentum and looked to the figures of the ladies over yonder. They were in the same spot, their indistinct hands coming together in a demure clap that he could not hear over the heavy breathing of his horse, still watching. Sufficiently encouraged, Darcy once more kicked Blackthorne in the sides to drive him forwards.

Darcy kept his eyes trained on Miss Elizabeth as he spurred Blackthorne onward, his heart pitter-pattering to the rapid rhythm of his mount's hoof beats. She was getting clearer as he approached, still observing him, and their gazes connected.

His mind affixed elsewhere, he did not see the startled pheasant rise from the tall grass until it was too late. The panic of the frightened bird transferred to Blackthorne, and the horse reared back so sharply that Darcy was unable to keep his seat. As gravity claimed him, he heard a pair of terrified shrieks cut the cold air.

Then there was blackness.

TWO

"Jane, go back to the house and fetch help!" Elizabeth cried, lowering the hands she had cupped over her gaping mouth when she had seen Mr Darcy thrown from his horse. It had happened so quickly that all Elizabeth had been able to do was scream, painfully impotent to do anything else more helpful, when he had taken his fall. Conversely, the same moment had seemed to stretch long as Mr Darcy had made his terrifying descent, only colliding with the hard-packed earth after a torturously extended time.

It had all started so innocently, only to end in potential tragedy. Elizabeth had coaxed Jane out into the gardens for a bit of fresh air, feeling that even the biting November chill would be beneficial after being trapped in a stiflingly hot sick-room for so many days together, and they had been doing lazy circuits through the winding paths of dead roses for a quarter of an hour. Their conversation had been similarly commonplace—with Elizabeth teasing Jane about the obvious devotion of Mr Bingley—until Jane spotted Mr Darcy riding in the near distance and had taken the opportunity to shift to a less mortifying subject.

"He is a fine horseman, is he not?" Jane observed, nodding

to the dark figure perched upon the back of a great black beast as they both hurtled across the field ahead of them.

Elizabeth looked to Mr Darcy then and admitted, somewhat grudgingly, that her sister was correct; the gentleman had as good a seat as any she had seen, and his ability to handle his spirited mount was impressive. “But then, there never has been anything deficient in his abilities—only his manners.”

Jane smiled at Elizabeth in a way that reminded the latter strongly of their father. It was a sardonic little smirk, softened by the sweetness of her elder sister’s face, and it conveyed a certain gentle smugness. “I have heard from some sources that Mr Darcy has been paying you a great deal of attention since we arrived at Netherfield. Surely you think his manners improved by now.”

“Attention? To me?” Elizabeth accompanied her disdainful incredulity with an unladylike scoff from the back of her throat. “Who told you such nonsense?”

“Miss Bingley mentioned it during a visit to my bedchamber,” Jane replied, stopping in place and looking towards the distant field where Mr Darcy and his horse were slowing their pace. “She did not seem...pleased, but I am sure she meant no offence.”

Elizabeth halted and allowed her gaze to trail after Mr Darcy. “I am sure. Miss Bingley need not concern herself with Mr Darcy’s so-called attentions because she is entirely wrong about them. I am certain that he detests the very sight of me. He only ever speaks to me to point out my imperfections and bask in his own superiority. Why, just this morning, we spent an entire half an hour in the library together and he said not one word to me! Far from his manners improving, I believe they are getting worse. He at least acknowledged my existence when he called me ‘not handsome enough to tempt him’.”

“I can see you have some strong feelings for him,” Jane teased.

“I most certainly do!” Elizabeth confessed. “I cannot abide him! He is insulting, above his company, haughty, rude, and abominably smug. I very much look forward to returning home tomorrow to spare myself his vexing company."

As Mr Darcy raced towards them on his steed and took the hedge between himself and the lawn upon which the ladies stood, Jane raised her hands and began to clap for his show of athleticism. Elizabeth copied the gesture, both to disguise her uncharitable feelings towards the approaching gentleman and in honest praise; she was no horsewoman herself, but she had always admired the power and agility required to keep one's seat upon an unruly animal. Besides, there was something rather dashing about a tall man with broad shoulders riding with abandon across an open field or leaping an obstacle.

Elizabeth continued to watch Mr Darcy as he turned away from them, swerving his horse about in a semicircle to ride off in the opposite direction. They had jumped the hedge once more, landing with agile grace in the tall grass on the other side, the gentleman laying practically flat against his steed as they had bounded through the crisp air. She clapped again, her kid gloves slapping softly against one another each time her palms collided, and followed Mr Darcy's progress as he turned back for another pass.

"He is handsome, is he not?"

Elizabeth startled at Jane's non-sequitur, but kept her regard trained on Mr Darcy; he was then racing towards them at the greatest speed yet, crouched upon his horse's back as if ready to spring over the obstacle himself. His face was turned upwards and focused upon his goal—no, slightly higher, as if he were looking directly at them. Well, of course he would wish to show off to an audience! Men such as the superior Mr Darcy could not help themselves when an opportunity for display arose.

When Jane nudged Elizabeth with her elbow, a common signal between them that she was awaiting an answer, the younger sister responded with a sigh. "I suppose he is, though he is rendered far less attractive by his arrogance. Why are you suddenly Mr Darcy's champion, Jane?"

"Miss Bingley's comment made me think—" Whatever Jane had been about to say was cut off by a sharp gasp and her hands flew up to cup her face. "Oh my goodness!"

The sudden alarm in Jane's pitch echoed Elizabeth's as calamity unfolded before them. Mr Darcy's inattention to his task had cost him greatly when a startled bird rose out of the tall grass and frightened his mount into rearing backwards. Though he grappled valiantly to remain seated, the effort proved fruitless and Mr Darcy found himself a helpless victim to the pull of gravity. A moment later, he had plunged into the overgrown field and out of Elizabeth's line of sight. His traitorous horse then scampered away in the direction of the stables, leaving his master felled upon the hard ground.

As warned most sternly by the Almighty, it seemed that pride truly did goeth before a fall.

"Jane!" Elizabeth called out for a second time, whipping about to face her stunned sister as she, herself, returned to the present. Jane was still staring dazedly into the distance where they had last seen Mr Darcy and so Elizabeth grasped her sister's elbow and gave it a shake. Finally recalling her senses, Jane looked to Elizabeth as the latter repeated, "Go to the house. Get help. I shall see if I can assist Mr Darcy."

"Y-Yes, of course," replied Jane, her arm sliding easily free of Elizabeth's hold as she quickly fled towards the manor entrance closest to them.

The shriek of hinges and Jane's voice raised in alarm rang in Elizabeth's ear as she gathered fistfuls of her skirt and raised her hem out of the way of her ankles, baring her boots and the lower portion of her stocking-clad legs to the frigid November air. She scarcely felt the sting of coming winter, however, as she raced forwards as rapidly as her feet would take her.

The distance was nothing to a young lady accustomed to frequent walks, and Elizabeth was at the hedge faster than many would have been capable. She was forced to pause at her obstacle as the line of cultivated bushes was waist high, requiring additional manoeuvring to bypass. She placed both hands upon the flattened top and leant forward, her heaving breaths rising about her like a cloud of smoke, to pinpoint the precise location of Mr Darcy.

There he was, a yard or so to her left, lying flat on his back in a tuft of grass. His hat had flown off elsewhere and was not in evidence, allowing Elizabeth a decent view of his face. She saw no blood, nor anything yet more gruesome, but his eyes were closed, and he was perfectly still as if unconscious. *Or...*

Elizabeth dispelled the horrifying thoughts swirling in her brain and set to determining how best to reach Mr Darcy. The hedge was, in one way, easier to climb than a tree, being much shorter than what she was accustomed to. However, it was a dense collection of delicate, leafy branches and provided no easy foothold for her to boost herself up and over. Additionally, her heavy skirts were cumbersome to her task; she could not simply stretch her leg over, nor could she leap it.

There was nothing for it; she must go through. While her dress was a disadvantage to climbing, it was a boon for her new plan, as it would protect her skin from the clawing branches. She was able to spread the hedge apart at the nearly invisible seam between two individual shrubs and bully her way through, albeit clumsily and with much damage to both her clothing and the plants. Elizabeth hoped that Mr Bingley would be more concerned for his friend's health than that of his boundary line.

Elizabeth squawked as she finally fell through to the other side, her skirts still caught up on the partially naked limbs of that wretched hedge. She jerked them free with impatience and scurried towards where Mr Darcy lay prone upon the ground.

She collapsed next to him and, with no consideration to the propriety of it, untied the crimson ribbons of her bonnet and allowed the impeding article to tumble down her back and into the field. Elizabeth then bent and, bracing her palms upon Mr Darcy's torso, pressed her newly bare ear to his chest where one would expect to hear the thud of a young man's heart.

Elizabeth expelled a gasp of relief on hearing its beat, and raised her head, sitting back on the knees folded beneath her. She sought Mr Darcy's face with her eyes and examined him more closely than she had been previously able, tracing the aristocratic features which made him so unfairly handsome with her gaze. His brow, which she only just realised must be usually creased, for it was smooth and relaxed now, sported no visible bruise nor trace of blood. His nose, likewise, appeared undamaged and as straight as ever above his slightly parted lips. She could not see his neck beneath the layers of his great coat, shirt, and cravat, but his jaw was strong and cleanly shaven, excepting the thick growth of sideburns trailing upwards into his mop of curly hair.

Elizabeth felt strangely anxious as she bent over him, searching for damage, and finding only that he was even more well favoured than she had supposed from polite distance. If only he was as attractive on the inside as he was outwardly, he would have made an excellent husband.

Her embarrassment at that thought flared up into a burning flush and she shoved it away to focus on the matter at hand. Mr Darcy could marry no one if he died in the middle of a field. Elizabeth rose onto her knees and awkwardly walked upon them so that she could settle herself at his head, slumping back down once she was in a better position to observe it at closer proximity. She leant forwards again, her fingers delving into his curls to probe for injury beneath his hair.

A slight hiss from her patient indicated that she had found one and she drew back, looking first to her gloved fingertips for splotches of red—she found none—and then to Mr Darcy's face. His eyes were still closed, but the lashes were fluttering as if fighting to pry his lids apart. His mouth, previously slackened, was now twisted into a grimace and his eyebrows furrowed together at their central point. He was in pain.

"Mr Darcy?" Elizabeth spoke softly, mindful of the headache he would surely be experiencing when he woke. "Mr Darcy, can you hear me?"

"...izib..."

Elizabeth moved closer, one hand resting just above where she had heard his heart; it was suddenly restive under her palm. A disobedient ringlet, one which was a frequent source of irritation to her, slipped free of the knot at the back of her head and bobbed between them. It tickled Mr Darcy's face along the line of his cheekbone, raising further response from him; he flinched slightly at the sensation.

"Mr Darcy?" Elizabeth reached up with the hand that was not bracing her against Mr Darcy's torso to brush against the single curl of his own which rested upon his forehead. His expression relaxed and he tilted his head towards her exploring fingertips.

"...beth..."

Like watching the sun rise over the crest of the horizon, Mr Darcy's eyelids slowly lifted until his smoky grey irises were visible to her. They remained glazed, yet also sharply focused upon her face. She was embarrassed by this scrutiny, but forced herself to say, "Sir, you have been in an accident. How do you feel?"

Elizabeth felt movement down by her side and then a gentle tug upon the long, spiralling curl which was dangling between them. Dropping her eyes only, she witnessed Mr Darcy's gloved fingers stroking it in an almost reverent fashion. "Elizabeth?"

Elizabeth's gaze jerked towards Mr Darcy's face at the whispered use of her given name. No man had ever spoken to her so informally before and, though she assumed it was a symptom of his addled mind in the wake of his fall, it created a surge of bashfulness within her.

"Elizabeth," he repeated, softly slurring the syllables. Before she could say anything in response—not that anything occurred to her—Mr Darcy craned his neck upward and closed the short distance between them to press his lips against hers. When he withdrew, he finished, "Dearest...loveliest Elizabeth...be my wife."

And then he fainted.

Elizabeth was frozen in place in the wake of Mr Darcy's befuddled declaration. *Did he truly just...?*

"Lizzy?"

Startled from her paralysis, Elizabeth scrambled backwards and away from the prone gentleman in her care and looked to where she had heard the voice originate. Jane stood just over the line of hedges, Mr Bingley at her shoulder, and both were staring at her in the utmost astonishment. She could reciprocate that feeling.

A loud, affected screech jolted all three of them from their moment of stupefaction and suddenly Miss Bingley was there also, looming over the line of manicured shrubs with an exaggerated expression of deepest despair. "Mr Darcy! Oh, Mr Darcy—what am I to do?" She swooned into her brother's arms as a troupe of footmen and stable grooms deftly vaulted the hedge and bent down to assist Mr Darcy. In the chaos that followed, the impromptu marriage proposal was blessedly forgotten.

THREE

Knock, knock, knock.

Darcy suppressed his inclination to groan in agony as the sound of someone begging entrance to his chambers reverberated about the interior of his skull. He reclined his head back onto his deeply stacked pillows and gritted his teeth as the resultant throbbing threatened to overwhelm him. More than four-and-twenty hours since his mortifying fall, and he was still suffering from it.

"Shall I send them away, sir?"

Darcy began to shake his head in the negative but regretted the motion at once. Instead, without shifting any portion of his body in the direction of his valet, he made the effort to reply verbally. "Only if it is Miss Bingley again." The lady had made several transparent efforts to tend to him as one might an invalid, likely sensing an opportunity to pounce while her prey was lamed, but thankfully Bailey's presence had prevented any impropriety.

The sound of Bailey's retreating footsteps could be heard softly treading in the direction of the door and then the gentle rattle and turning of a knob. "It is Mr Bingley, sir."

"Invite him in." Darcy carefully turned his head, rotating it slowly against his pillow, as his friend strode into the room and approached his bedside.

Bingley was smiling, of course, though his joviality appeared to be tempered by a measure of concern. "How are you feeling, old man? Still suffering from a headache?"

Grimacing, Darcy allowed that it was so. "I feel as if four-and-twenty families are dancing a reel inside my head."

"It is no wonder after the fall you took yesterday! And you still do not recall the accident?"

A few watery images—tall grass, dampness, blurry clouds, a pair of fine eyes widened in horror—skittered across his mind's eye, but none clear enough to be deciphered with any accuracy. The local apothecary, Mr Jones, had reassured Darcy that some memory loss was to be expected from such a bump to the head, but it was still discomfiting to know that he was missing a piece of time. Witness testimony had filled in all necessary blanks, though it was not the same as knowing the events for himself. What if he had said or done something mortifying in his addled state? Darcy could only hope that such had not occurred and that his reputation was as free from blemish as his mind was from the details of his accident.

"The last thing I remember is Blackthorne rearing up because some blasted bird spooked him."

Cursed horse. In his current state, Darcy was tempted to let the beast out to pasture and refuse to ride him ever again, but rationally he knew he would forgive his wild mount eventually, and probably sooner than he should. Blackthorne had a talent for grovelling when he knew his master was displeased with him that always seemed to purchase him absolution, if not from Darcy himself then from Georgiana.

"So, you..." Bingley paused, his eyes flicking to where Bailey stood off to the side, awaiting his master's pleasure. He coughed and lowered his voice to a rasping whisper. "You cannot remember what happened afterwards?"

"No, I recall nothing before waking in my bed sometime later." Aside from the comely figure of Miss Elizabeth Bennet curled up with a book before the fireplace sometime prior to the incident, though Darcy could not say as much. He shifted and his bedclothes rustled beneath him. Bingley was looking unusually grim, his initial smile melted into a more neutral line. Darcy's concerns over having embarrassed himself in his unguarded state flared back into existence. "Why? Did something happen?"

"Well…you see…" Bingley's gaze darted towards Bailey.

Darcy's anxiety rose precipitously. Bingley never hesitated to speak freely before, regardless of how much caution a subject deserved, or who might overhear it. Darcy himself had admonished Bingley more than once to be mindful of his words with varied results, so whatever he was not saying must be so delicate —or so mortifying—that it prompted even his sense of discretion.

"Leave us, Bailey. I shall ring if you are needed."

Darcy returned his scrutiny to Bingley, his face hardening into its familiar stony countenance and his voice taking on an implacable tone. "What is this about?"

After so many years of acquaintance and then friendship, Darcy knew such a command would stop Bingley from hedging further. After a deep breath that ended in a heavy exhale, Bingley blurted, "You proposed to Miss Elizabeth after you fell."

"I what—?"

Darcy bolted upright with a quickness that was not recommended for one suffering from a severe migraine, resulting in a loud groan of agony and an almost immediate return to his previously prone position.

Bingley leapt to his friend's aid. "Shall I summon Bailey to return?"

Darcy used the hand that was not grasping at his forehead to wave him away. "I did what?"

"You proposed to her, right there on the ground at her feet," Bingley said. "She and her sister saw your accident, and while Miss Bennet went for help, Miss Elizabeth ran to check on you. While she was tending you, you woke and asked her to be your wife before falling unconscious again."

Darcy could feel a deep, offended rage heating up inside him. He had thought that she, of all women, would be different, too good, too moral, to try and entrap him while he was unable to defend himself. Instead, she was just the same as her grasping, scheming, money-hungry mother, only even more dangerous because she hid her intentions behind a pair of fine eyes and beguiling kindness! He would not become her victim, no matter how much she attracted his wandering gaze.

"And I suppose she told you this?" he spat once his anger had boiled high enough to spew out of him. Darcy could feel his teeth baring into a feral sneer, his brows drawn together into a scowl, and directed this terrible expression at the messenger who had brought him the crushing news that his Elizabeth was not what she had seemed.

Instead of flinching away, Bingley returned Darcy's expression in kind. It was quite alarming to see Bingley so fierce, and Darcy might have reacted to the change in his friend had he not already been so furious himself. "No, as a matter of fact, I witnessed it myself. You said 'Elizabeth, be my wife', or something very like it, and then kissed her. Or kissed her first...I do not recall which, but it matters not. Miss Bennet was right beside me throughout."

Darcy's rage melted into astonishment. In his enfeebled state, had he willingly ensnared himself in her trap?

"And...and I suppose that her father wishes to speak to me about this?" Darcy surmised, rather weakly.

Bingley crossed his arms over his chest. "You continue to do Miss Elizabeth a great disservice. Though she could have pressed for more, she graciously released you from any obligation due to your...altered state. She further requested that I not mention this to anyone, not even her father, to prevent the situation from getting any more out of hand. Far from trying to catch you, Miss Elizabeth has been nothing but generous considering the circumstances."

Darcy slumped back into the plush of his bedding, almost entirely disregarding the throbbing stab of pain created by this motion. Far from being less than he had believed, Elizabeth turned out to be even more perfect than he had originally thought. His heart began to pound, the rhythm repeated in dull thuds within his cranium, as the recognition of her true benevolence and integrity unleashed the feelings he had been desperately attempting to repress since her arrival at Netherfield.

I am in love with Elizabeth Bennet.

"And that brings me to what I really came here to discuss with you," Bingley said after a long stretch of pondering silence. Darcy, his face slackened in wonder, turned to face his unusually serious friend. "I know that Miss Elizabeth has released you, but will you stand by the proposal?"

It had not taken all night for Darcy to decide on his course of action, but the excruciating pounding in his head had not abated in time for him to render a more formal proposal forthwith. In fact, by the time Bingley had paid his visit to Darcy's guest chambers to question him about his further intentions, the Bennet sisters had already returned to Longbourn and the bosom of their family, escorted thither immediately after church services on Sunday as had been the agreement prior to the events of Saturday. Thus, after recuperating for the remainder of the Lord's Day and attending to necessary business on Monday—including an express letter to his solicitor in town to request a marriage settlement written up post haste and another to Mrs Reynolds at Pemberley with instructions to retrieve his grandmother Darcy's ring from the vault in his study—Tuesday was determined as the best opportunity to visit the estimable lady to whom he would more officially offer his hand.

Bingley had graciously agreed to accompany his friend to Longbourn for moral support, which Darcy recognised as a transparent ploy to pay a visit to the elder sister. It seemed that the Bingleys as a rule were almost entirely lacking in subtlety, no matter how much they believed they excelled at it. At least Bingley also had an invitation to issue for an upcoming ball at Netherfield to legitimise his part in the excursion.

"Do you know what you are going to say?" Bingley asked as their horses plodded along the muddy lane.

Darcy was astride Blackthorne, despite his mount's recent dishonourable behaviour, and keeping him tightly reined in, lest another unexpected fright and fall finish his master off. The stallion hung his head low as they walked at a slow pace, and Darcy suspected that he felt guilty—or perhaps petulant—over his transgression.

"I thought I would begin by thanking her for rendering aid after my accident," Darcy replied, "and then declare how much I ardently admire and love her."

"A good start, I think. Dare I hope there is more to it than that?"

"Of course." Darcy dipped his head so that a sharp shaft of sunlight was not so directly stabbing him in the eye. Most of his aches and pains had resolved themselves with rest and powders from Mr Jones, but his migraine would occasionally flare back up under the right stimuli, and strong light was foremost amongst these instigators. He tipped the brim of his beaver to increase the amount of shade it provided. "Once I have assured her of the violence of my affections, I will relate to her the steadiness of them by detailing my struggles in regard to the comparative disparities of our ranks, fortunes, and general importance in the world. It will be a degradation to me, of course, but Miss Elizabeth with her kindness, integrity, and beauty will be worth the hassle created by my relatives and higher society. She will not doubt for a moment that I—what is the matter, Bingley?"

Darcy, belatedly realising that his friend had stopped in the middle of the road some yards back, turned Blackthorne round to enquire as to why their progression had suddenly halted.

Bingley was sitting straight up in his saddle as if petrified, his eyebrows raised so high as to be hidden beneath the brim of his hat and his mouth slackened in what Darcy interpreted as horror. "Are you daft, man? You are not actually going to say that to Miss Elizabeth, are you?"

"Why should I not? I would think a woman such as Miss Elizabeth, one who comes from a lowly upbringing and with barely a penny to her name, would appreciate how I have overcome numerous scruples which have, until now, prevented my forming any serious design on her. She is a rational creature and will surely be honoured by how much I have had to consider to make her an offer."

"You cannot say those things in a marriage proposal! Not unless you are hoping the lady will reject you." A look of appalled understanding came over Bingley as he further accused, "Is that it? You hope she will refuse you so that you do not have to marry her after all? If that be the case, I must say—"

"Of course not!" Darcy retorted, cutting off whatever offensive thing his friend was about to say next. Really! Bingley thought so little of him that he could misunderstand Darcy's intentions so thoroughly? "Were that the case, I could simply leave well enough alone. Miss Elizabeth has already offered me a graceful exit, and all I need do is accept it, were that my inclination. I would not propose marriage to a lady with the intention of making her hate me enough to reject my suit. What sort of heartless scoundrel do you take me for?"

Though it was difficult to discern in the shadow of Bingley's beaver, Darcy thought he saw his friend flush at the admonition. In a more conciliatory tone, Bingley asked, "Then why say such insulting things if you intend her to accept your offer?"

"A woman like Miss Elizabeth Bennet would be a fool to reject an honourable proposal from a man ten times her consequence, no matter how it was delivered."

"I will not dispute that," Bingley grudgingly admitted, "but there is no cause to abuse her while simultaneously declaring your undying love and devotion. She would become confused, at best, and more likely very angry as any rational creature naturally would. No one wishes to be told that they are inferior to another, even—perhaps especially—when it is true. And to demean her family, whom she has shown overt fondness for, would only compound the sin, and she would despise you for it."

Darcy had not considered it in those terms. He had expected that his declaration of love and adulation would be bolstered by the struggle he had overcome to deliver it. However, Bingley made a fair point regarding the delicate nature of their comparative worth in the eyes of society; Darcy was, against all measures weighed by the *ton*, the more eminent person between the pair of them, but it did not necessarily follow that Elizabeth was without worth. She was lively, witty, and charming in a way that his own personality lacked and, therefore, more likeable. Beyond these superficial qualities of temperament, she was also innately kind, generous, patient, honourable, loyal, and honest—all proved just in the past week she had spent at Netherfield tending her sister and, more telling, by her integrity in the face of what had to have been a tempting opportunity. Her refusal to entrap him in a marriage that she must have supposed he would not want due to their social disparity only reinforced his belief in her considerable goodness and suitability as a wife. Were it not for the material trappings of a judgmental society, Darcy would have been happy to take Elizabeth to wife for the sheer pleasure of it.

Further, Darcy felt that in matters concerning the fairer sex, he must concede authority to Bingley, who had had more infatuations than Darcy had servants—at least in his London establishment. He was far more familiar with the ways of flattery, having been forced to develop them of a necessity due to his status as the son of a tradesman. Had he not been more amiable than Darcy generally bothered to be, he would not have been accepted anywhere, and his hunt for a proper wife would have been over before it had begun.

"Very well," Darcy said at length, having pondered his friend's argument before responding. "What do you suggest?"

The tension in Bingley's shoulders eased and he nudged his horse into motion again with a kick of his heels into her flanks. "Make no mention of Miss Elizabeth's status—you are a gentleman, she is a gentleman's daughter, so in that sense you are equals."

"Go on."

"Secondly, do not insult her family. It is quite apparent that both Miss Elizabeth and her elder sister are aware of their faults—you can see it in the way they try to improve their manners at social occasions. To point it out directly would be mortifying to her."

The contrast between the two eldest daughters and the rest of their immediate relations was stark, so Darcy could easily concede that this must be the case. "Very well. Anything else?"

"Yes. Finally, do not focus on any of the reasons that you should not marry Miss Elizabeth, but instead emphasise those that make you want to. Make her feel not as if you are condescending to ask, but rather that she is granting you the honour of her acceptance."

Darcy frowned and raised an objection. "I am not inclined to flattery. She surely could not expect me to rejoice in the inferiority of her connexions."

"No, of course not, but is there anything to gain by insulting her? There is honesty in your affection for her, is there not?"

"Of course there is!"

"Then do not slight her for things that she cannot help!" Bingley raised his voice a touch to be heard over Darcy's interruption. "I assure you that she is not unaware of the disparity between you, nor is she ignorant of the honour your proposal grants her. To belabour the point is crude and ungentlemanly."

Darcy's jaw tightened at Bingley's recrimination. He had been trained since he was a small lad in short pants in all aspects of gentlemanly behaviour and prided himself on being one in all circumstances. It shamed him that he had not considered that the mode of his declaration might be considered otherwise by the object of it.

"Very well, I concede the point."

"Most excellent, my friend!" Bingley praised as the outskirts of the inconsequential town of Meryton appeared round the bend in the road. "Oh, and one last piece of advice. Do not scowl at her when you make your offer. Women prefer a more friendly aspect."

FOUR

"...do you...not agree, Cousin...Cousin Elizabeth?"

Elizabeth's tolerance for the sweaty, wheezing man jogging at her side was growing rather short. She and Jane had been returned from Netherfield Park for only a single day before the nasty surprise of Mr Collins had shown up at Longbourn's doorstep, aided and abetted by her father's inclination to tease their mother by withholding the announcement of his imminent arrival until the last possible moment. A scant few hours after Mr Bennet had informed them of Mr Collins's visit over the family breakfast table, there he was—tall, heavy, oily, and pungent. Elizabeth was beginning to think that, despite the awkwardness she had left behind, she might have preferred to stay at Netherfield after all, and avoid the loquacious parson.

They—Elizabeth, her sisters, and Mr Collins—were presently on their way to Meryton to call on their aunt Philips, having had nothing to do at home but listen to their cousin rattle away about Lady Catherine de Bourgh and the tidiness of his parsonage in Kent. After suffering many hours already of this suffocating diatribe, it had been agreed upon by all the younger Bennets—including Jane, who would only admit to a sudden longing for fresh air—that a trip to their aunt's home was in order.

Most unfortunately, Mrs Bennet had determined that Mr Collins would make an admirable escort for her daughters, and Elizabeth in particular. They all moaned over the intrusion, some more discreetly than others, but it was Elizabeth herself who was most downtrodden by this turn of events. Not only was she clearly Mr Collins's second choice for a bride—knowledge which engendered no small amount of indignation whenever he offered her a 'delicate compliment' that was often a backwards one—but the man was tedious. Even Mr Darcy with his haughty airs had been a better conversationalist.

Elizabeth's thoughts of the stern gentleman from Derbyshire cost her some of the concentration required to walk straight and so she stumbled over the tread of a wagon wheel which was deeply entrenched in the dirt road. This gave Mr Collins the opportunity to offer his assistance, which came in the form of unsolicited advice from Lady Catherine.

"Miss Elizabeth! Do be careful lest you injure yourself. Lady Catherine says that a lady had best walk slowly and pay much attention to where her feet lead her, or she shall surely face calamity. She is so gracious, often instructing the young women of my parish in proper deportment whenever she so happens to—"

"Yes, thank you, Mr Collins," Elizabeth interrupted what was sure to be another long speech about that venerable lady's so-called virtues, most of which seemed to be the ability to stick her nose where it was not wanted or needed. Without so much as a hand from Mr Collins—which, in his excitement to exalt his patroness, he had forgotten to even offer—Elizabeth straightened herself and readjusted her skirts into a more proper configuration. Alas, her hem was muddy once again; if only the Netherfield party could see her most recent dishevelment.

Only Jane's quiet enquiry from up ahead where she walked with Mary—"Are you well, Lizzy?"—prevented the fiery burn of embarrassment from overtaking her entirely. Thankfully, it proved to be enough of a distraction to allow Elizabeth to regain her composure as she spoke over the ramblings of Mr Collins to reassure her sisters that she was no worse for wear from her stumble. Jane and Mary then proceeded on their way, hurrying more quickly to catch up with Kitty and Lydia, who were already crossing into the town lane. This left Elizabeth to the sole company of their cousin.

While Mr Collins continued to pontificate about the proper way to walk—'neither too quickly, nor too slowly'—Elizabeth allowed her mind to drift into that area she had been attempting to keep it away from all morning, the one which had occupied much of her time for the past two days since Mr Darcy's most unhappy accident. She was positive that he would never have rendered a proposal to someone like herself had he not just suffered a knock to the head, but it was impossible to strike his words, spoken to her with such desperate feeling, such tenderness, from her memory.

"Dearest...loveliest Elizabeth...be my wife."

She had been able to feel each syllable against her lips as he had withdrawn from that soft kiss only moments before issuing his declaration. Sometimes, Elizabeth wondered if she had actually tasted them, as absurd as that seemed. It was not every day that a lady received an offer of marriage, and even rarer still to be proposed to under the set of circumstances which had led Mr Darcy to his addled request for her hand. Something in the way he had looked at her, the warm timbre of his voice, or perhaps that kiss—the only one she had yet to receive in her twenty years—had lingered within her and created an obsessive fascination.

Of course, Elizabeth stood by her initial decision to relieve him of his obligation without any doubts whatsoever. Not only was he clearly not in possession of his wits at the time of his impromptu request, but other memories of Mr Darcy's cold snub at the assembly were equally strong. *Tolerable, indeed!* He would surely be comforted once Mr Bingley assured him that Elizabeth had no intentions of ensnaring him for herself, as she certainly could. With only his most loyal friend and her dearest sister as witnesses to the event, it was easy enough to simply pretend it had never happened, and such was what Elizabeth was endeavouring to do—erase the event from her mind entirely. She hoped that Mr Darcy recognised how close he had come to ruin and, in his gratitude, might now think better of lowly country girls than he had previously. It was exceedingly doubtful that he would have been so fortunate had Miss Bingley been the one to tend to him in the aftermath of his accident.

"Perhaps I should have insisted more strongly last night after dinner in regard to reading Fordyce." Elizabeth's focus was reclaimed by Mr Collins's haughty sniff of derision and she raised her eyes to look ahead of them. There, loitering in front of the milliner's shop, were her youngest sisters, flirting with a pair of unknown males, one of whom sported the vibrant red coat of a militiaman.

Elizabeth suppressed the urge to sigh lest it give Mr Collins permission to castigate further. She secretly agreed with his opinion that the younger girls were wild and unchecked and could certainly use a firmer hand—but she was not about to admit such to a man whose inclination to judge them all by Kitty and Lydia's poor behaviour was obvious. Though it could not be supposed that the derision of his acquaintance in Kent would be felt fifty miles yonder in Hertfordshire, it still would not be acceptable to allow him to spread rumours anywhere.

Luckily, Jane and Mary were with them, and their more demure behaviour would keep Kitty and Lydia at least somewhat in check. Elizabeth would certainly lend her assistance once they drew close enough as well.

"Lizzy, Lizzy! Come and meet Mr Wickham—he is come to join the militia."

Lydia was flapping her hand in a wildly beckoning manner to encourage Elizabeth to join their gathering. All four of her sisters were present and clustered about the pair of young men, both exceptionally handsome, and behaving with varying levels of decorum. The one in red she recognised belatedly as Mr Denny, a relatively new acquaintance they had met when the regiment had recently quartered themselves in Meryton, but the other in blue was a stranger—one with a rather dashing smile. When this gentleman, reported to be Mr Wickham, turned to greet her with a flash of perfectly straight white teeth, Elizabeth felt a shy warmth suffuse her cheeks.

Lieutenant Denny performed the office of introductions between herself and Mr Wickham—Mr Collins conveniently forgotten by all present, despite his incessant prattle—and from there, the newest addition to their neighbourhood proved himself to be everything amiable—a direct contrast to the dour Mr Darcy. Mr Wickham wanted only regimentals to make him completely charming, as he already laid claim to all the best parts of beauty, a fine countenance, a good figure, and very pleasing address. He was also ready to converse with them at length, though he remained perfectly correct and unassuming all the while. There was much to be admired in Mr Wickham.

"Your sisters have invited me to your aunt's card party tomorrow evening. Shall I attend?" Mr Wickham's query was rendered teasing by the curl of his lips and the angle of his head.

"Of course!" Elizabeth responded immediately and with enthusiasm. She very much wished to see this gentleman again, and an early engagement was best. Her aunt Philips's penchant for having the officers over for social gatherings was finally showing some benefit for her as well as Kitty and Lydia. "They are not grand affairs, but I suppose most of us enjoy a simple evening of supper and cards now and again."

Mr Wickham confessed that she was right. "But, as I have not had a word from—Mrs Philips, is it?—your aunt herself, I am somewhat tentative in accepting, and I suppose require your reassurance that my presence will not be unwelcome."

"No, certainly not! My aunt is exceedingly fond of company, and I dare say another officer will present no undue burden on her arrangements. She has often been known to say, 'the more the merrier'."

"If you are certain..." Mr Wickham winked at her. "For you, I shall be there."

Elizabeth nibbled at the lower portion of her lip and restrained herself from saying anything in response, as to accept his overture for her own sake specifically would have been improper. Instead, she changed the subject. "I suppose, now that you are joining the militia, we shall have the privilege of your company through the winter, sir?"

While the whole party was still standing and talking together agreeably, the Bennet sisters found themselves cheerfully hailed from a short distance away. Elizabeth looked away from Mr Wickham momentarily to discover the source, and felt any merriment she had been experiencing in her new friend's company wither away like a bloom felled by frost. Mr Bingley was astride his grey mare and coming towards them from the outskirts of Meryton, waving and grinning at the lot of them, and behind him was the looming dark form of Mr Darcy. The pair of them were approaching with purpose and, unless she intended to be unforgivably rude, Elizabeth was stuck where she was. Every happy thought of an evening spent in Mr Wickham's company faded into the background of her mind as Mr Darcy drew ever nearer.

"Good morning to you, ladies!" cried Mr Bingley as he dismounted his steed with a joyful hop. His gaze immediately found Jane and he declared, "We were just on our way to Longbourn to ask after your health, were we not, Darcy?"

Mr Darcy did not respond verbally, but did offer a slight nod of acknowledgment before pulling his horse up short and climbing down himself. He turned to face the group and his eyes searched each face until he found Elizabeth's, where his attention remained thereafter.

Elizabeth was thrust into turmoil as soon as she became the sole focus of Mr Darcy's intense stare, but she refused to look away. No matter how her insides churned, or how her face heated, she would not be cowed by that look. What could he possibly want from her in any event? Had Mr Bingley not informed him that she was no threat to him? Had he come to confirm it for himself? Well, once she was afforded her first opportunity to do so, she would be sure to comfort him on that score in a manner he would not question or misinterpret!

"And this is Mr Wickham! He will be joining the militia soon, and will look very handsome in his regimentals, I am sure."

At this enthusiastic introduction by Lydia, Mr Darcy's gaze, which had been steadily affixed to her own, suddenly widened and tore away to flick just slightly to Elizabeth's left where Mr Wickham was standing. Startled, Elizabeth followed his movement to see their dashing new acquaintance nod tersely to Mr Darcy, his face absolutely ashen. She whipped her eyes back to Mr Darcy, whose own countenance was taking on an unusual hue as well, though his was brightening to an unhealthy red. Neither man spoke to the other, but their reactions said much.

After a long stretch of tense silence between them, Mr Wickham coughed lightly from the back of his throat and attempted a polite greeting, though his voice sounded strained to Elizabeth's ear. "Darcy, it has been a long time. How is your sister?"

At this, Mr Darcy's jaw tightened and his brow furrowed into a hateful glare at this conversational opening. Instead of replying to Mr Wickham with some assurance of Miss Darcy's continuing good health, he cut the other man by turning his face away and not deigning to give an answer at all! Elizabeth could not help the slight gasp which escaped her lips, nor the widening of her eyes as she bore witness to this unpardonable rudeness.

After dismissing the clearly mortified Mr Wickham so summarily, Mr Darcy returned his attention to Elizabeth, his face only slightly softening its scowl. "Miss Elizabeth, would you do me the honour of allowing me to escort you back to Longbourn?"

Of all the nerve—!

Elizabeth opened her mouth to refuse, to flay him with the

sharp end of her tongue, but before she could so much as gather the words she wished to fling in his unfairly handsome face, Jane spoke up and replied to Mr Bingley's earlier words about calling at Longbourn. "Oh yes, thank you, Mr Bingley, that would be lovely."

Thus, all Elizabeth could do was close her mouth, turn on her heel and begin walking towards home. *Insufferable man!* She would take much pleasure in reassuring him that he was the last man in the world she could ever be prevailed upon to marry.

When Elizabeth stalked away from their gaggle of associates, Darcy reached automatically for the reins of his horse and prepared to follow her, all unsavoury thoughts of Wickham dissipating as the need to catch up with his target usurped them. Without even deigning to glance in that scoundrel's direction, Darcy raised a foot off the ground so that he might begin his pursuit.

Before he could take so much as a single step in Elizabeth's direction, Darcy found himself stumbling to reassert his footing when a heavy weight collided with him from behind. He glared at the back of the offender, a black-clad parson, as the oaf scuttled past him.

"I do beg your pardon—excuse me," the parson offered over his shoulder as he picked up speed and began jogging down the street. "Cousin Elizabeth! Do slow your pace and wait for me to catch up. A young lady such as yourself should not be walking alone! As a clergyman, it is my duty and honour to see to your protection and my patroness..."

'Cousin Elizabeth?' What manner of fresh hell is this?

"I apologise for our cousin, sir." Darcy turned his head to observe Jane Bennet at his elbow, her expression placid save for the slight reddening of her cheeks, no doubt a symptom of the cold. "Mr Collins is very…eager, and I am sure did not intend to be rude."

Darcy could feel his lip beginning to curl, but straightened it lest his impassive expression be marred by the disdain he felt for the bumbling man. Up ahead, the buffoon was trailing just behind Elizabeth, who seemed to be paying him as little mind as she was able, and still jabbering away about something that could not be clearly understood from a distance. Whatever he had to say, there was a lot of it. "Not at all."

Thus, instead of creating an opportunity to speak to Elizabeth on their walk to Longbourn, Darcy was relegated to lingering with the rest of the group as they followed behind the leading pair. He kept his eyes trained upon his Elizabeth and Mr Collins as they narrowed the distance incrementally each passing minute. Though the lady seemed obviously disinclined to favour the parson's company, it was clear to Darcy that the odious man considered himself her suitor. *Not much competition there, I would wager.*

Mr Collins notwithstanding, a much greater danger lay in the blackguard they had left behind. *Wickham, blast him!* Where had he even come from? Had he somehow known that Darcy would be in Hertfordshire and scurried thither to torment him? Worse, he had been interacting with Elizabeth before Darcy had even arrived on the scene and, if the charming smile she had worn when he had first spotted her and the offended air she had adopted after he had spurned his 'old friend' were any indication, he had already taken to wooing her. No doubt, Wickham intended to seduce Elizabeth as he had so many others, and it now fell to Darcy to protect her from that.

But how much should I reveal? Once they were engaged, Darcy could simply forbid her from speaking to Wickham or remaining in his presence. However, knowing the often contrary nature of his beloved, Darcy internally scolded himself that such a simple solution would not be enough; part of Elizabeth's irresistible allure was her ability to think for herself. If she should decide that Darcy was being high-handed in denying her

Wickham's company, she might behave opposite to the manner Darcy intended and seek the man out. Or, at the very least, fail to heed his warnings with any seriousness of purpose.

No, he would have to reveal something of their previous dealings, but it remained to be determined how much. Darcy sighed as it occurred to him that nothing less than the entire, absolute truth would do; to tell her of their childhood differences would make him seem petty, those from university would be similarly regarded, their financial transactions might hold some sway, but none of these would have the desired impact. He would have to tell her about Georgiana. Darcy would not make the same mistake again of keeping too much to himself, not when the safety of another lady he cared for was at stake.

One day, and Darcy could feel it approaching quickly, he would have to deal with that scoundrel in a more permanent manner. But first, he needed to create a new opportunity for a private conversation with Elizabeth. Turning his head to his right, where his friend was flirting with the eldest Miss Bennet, Darcy took the liberty of interrupting them. "Bingley, might I have a word?"

FIVE

"Leave it to me, Mr Darcy," Miss Bennet reassured Darcy in a low, conspiratorial voice that would not carry to the ears of her next youngest sister as they finally crossed through the brick archway which denoted Longbourn's drive. Up ahead of them by several yards was Elizabeth, her arms safely tucked behind her and away from Mr Collins, with her back turned to them most studiously.

Though Darcy had never considered Miss Bennet as a potential partner in his scheme to engage himself to Elizabeth, he was grateful for her contribution to his cause. "I thank you."

Miss Bennet, attached to Bingley's other side, dipped her head so that she could look at Darcy more directly. Her lovely face had lost not a whit of serenity, but her words held caution. "You are most welcome, sir, but I must warn you that Lizzy might be somewhat...surprised by your proposal. In addition, though my dear sister is everything lovely and delightful, she often holds strong opinions which are difficult to overcome. Please be patient when you speak to her."

Bingley, though he actually said nothing, grinned at him with sunny smugness. He clearly felt his earlier advice in regard to the mode of Darcy's declaration was verified by Miss Bennet's sagely genteel guidance.

Darcy ignored his friend and nodded acquiescence to Miss Bennet's strategy. "I shall endeavour to do so."

"Thank you." Miss Bennet then turned from Darcy and directed her survey to where her sister was presently being ushered into the house by Mr Collins. "Lizzy!"

Elizabeth pivoted her head about to regard the elder Miss Bennet. Ignoring the parson's bowing and scraping entreaties for her to cross the threshold to the indoors ahead of him, she responded, "Yes?"

"Mr Bingley and I intend to take a turn about the lawn. Would you please accompany us?"

Elizabeth's eyes darted quickly to Darcy and then away again. "But we have only just returned."

"Mr Bingley has expressed a wish to see the hermitage."

Darcy found himself both wary and secretly admiring of Miss Bennet's capability to deceive so seamlessly. He supposed, however, that it was made easier by strict adherence to truth; Bingley had, in fact, requested to see the hermitage, if only in the context of assisting Darcy with his plan. Still, subterfuge made him uncomfortable and, were he not so impatient to speak to Elizabeth without the intrusive company of Mr Collins —to say nothing of Mrs Bennet and the younger girls—he would have much preferred to do without it.

"I dare say I could do with a bit more fresh air," Mr Collins announced, as the small party of conspirators had guessed he might. "It is the particular recommendation of my patroness that I spend as much time per day out of doors as possible, and I am sure she would heartily approve, even in the winter months."

Darcy withheld the compulsion to point out that it was, in fact, still autumn until the following month and left Miss Bennet in charge of directing the conversation; she had done so ably thus far. In this instance, she took advantage of Mr Collins's pause—one required to refill his lungs and not at all a cessation of his speech altogether—to entreat him, "Sir, I was hoping that you would inform my mother as to our whereabouts. I am sure she will be most grateful."

"Well..."

"And there will, of course, be tea and refreshments in the parlour."

Mr Collins perked up at the implication of victuals, and he hurriedly bowed to Elizabeth to dismiss himself from her presence. Truly, Miss Bennet's delicate guidance was more effective than all of Miss Bingley's machinations; her target never even realised that he was being manipulated to ends other than his own and cheerfully obeyed her every whim. An impressive skill when used for good rather than evil. "In that case, how can I refuse? I shall be inside, dear cousin, awaiting you."

Elizabeth muttered something which Mr Collins did not hear as he had already turned and disappeared into the house. Darcy's lips quirked upwards on one side as he witnessed her faint sigh as soon as the parson was gone.

Now was Darcy's chance to enact his part. While Miss Bennet had been setting their scenario into motion, the gentlemen had handed over the care of their steeds to a groom who led them away to the stables, leaving each now free to escort a lady. Darcy strode to Elizabeth and offered his elbow to her.

Though her jaw was clenched and she huffed in exasperation, Elizabeth hesitated only a single long second before placing her hand within the crook of his arm. He led her away from the house and towards the little wilderness on one side of the lawn which Miss Bennet had assured him would afford them a certain amount of privacy. By design, Bingley and the elder sister lagged behind by several paces and then diverted themselves to the aforementioned hermitage, which was within sight but not hearing of Darcy's intended destination.

Elizabeth, clever girl that she was, recognised the plot at once. "I suppose you have orchestrated this rendezvous to discuss what happened after your accident the other day?"

"You have correctly ascertained my intent. I beg you forgive me for the subterfuge, but it was necessary to speak to you in relative privacy."

Though her expression puckered into one of grudging acceptance, she admitted readily enough, "I suppose you are right."

"Miss Elizabeth—"

"Before you say anything," Elizabeth interrupted, stopping suddenly in place. Darcy staggered to a halt as well and adjusted the angle of his body so that it was turned three quarters in her direction. "I want you to know that I was completely in earnest when I told Mr Bingley that I would not enforce your proposal —you could not have been in your right mind, and it would be very wrong of me to hold you to a promise that you never intended to make."

"Miss Elizabeth—"

She shook her head vehemently and then affixed him with her eyes, bringing his words to a stuttering conclusion before he had had a chance to say more than her name. "I pray you allow me to finish. Truly, sir, you may rest easy knowing that I will neither force you into marriage nor bring a suit against you for breach of promise. So long as only Jane and Mr Bingley are aware of the situation aside from ourselves—and I presume that you trust your friend as much as I trust my dearest sister—I can see no reason to trap ourselves in a union which must bring misery to both of us. I am no threat to you and hope that we may continue on as if your proposal never happened."

Throughout her rather impassioned monologue, Darcy's mouth continuously twitched at both corners. Elizabeth was truly a jewel among women. One who, simply on principle, would not hold a man to his misspoken word. "May I speak now?"

Elizabeth nodded once, indicating that he may proceed.

"Miss Elizabeth—Elizabeth,"—he indulged himself for the first time in speaking her Christian name aloud rather than by her polite title—"far from asking you to release me from my proposal, I have come to renew it."

"I...I beg your pardon?"

Darcy chuckled at her disbelief—how charming it was that she considered herself so beneath him that she could not believe her good fortune in receiving a proper offer—and hurried to assuage her. "Your integrity and honesty in the wake of my accident have greatly impressed me, leading me to offer my hand more formally for your acceptance. I had not intended..." Darcy trailed off for a moment, recalling Bingley's words of admonishment on the subject of his former struggles, and redirected the course of his statement. "That is, I have admired you for many weeks now, and my feelings will no longer be repressed. I love you and wish to make you my wife."

For several heartbeats, only the wind whistling through the empty branches of the wooded area at their backs could be heard. Darcy waited for Elizabeth's answer, exercising that patience which Miss Bennet had cautioned him to take, as she collected her faculties enough to give it. *I have struck her dumb with surprise!*

Elizabeth closed her mouth, which had been hanging slightly agape since he had rendered his proposal, and swallowed. "I..." She seemed to lose her train of thought, then began again, "I...no."

Darcy parted his own lips to respond with his satisfaction, but stopped once her answer seeped properly into his brain. "Did you say 'no'?"

"I did," Elizabeth agreed, blinking at him rapidly. "I thank you for standing so honourably by your previous offer, but I must decline."

Bewilderment delayed Darcy's response for a lagging stretch. "And this is all the reply I am to expect?"

"I do not know what else you wish me to say, Mr Darcy. You have followed the dictates of your conscience and made your offer again, and I have declined it. Honestly, considering what I said to you before you did so, it was all rather unnecessary. I am not inclined to marry you and I am absolutely certain that you do not wish to marry me."

"But I told you I loved you!" Darcy countered, a hot prickle of humiliated indignation rising up the back of his neck. "Does that mean nothing to you?"

Elizabeth had a rebuttal of her own ready. "I thank you for your attempt at flattery, but I prefer sincerity."

"But I do—!" Darcy cut his words off at the quick, realising that his turbulent emotions of the moment were revealing themselves at a loud volume. He took a deep breath in through his nose, released it through his mouth, and willed the simmering anger within to calm. With his voice more properly modulated, he tried again. "Elizabeth, I spoke the truth when I said that I loved you. It has been many weeks now, almost since the start of our acquaintance, that I have felt a great esteem and regard for you."

"Oh?" Elizabeth tilted her head, incredulous. "The start of our acquaintance? Pray allow me to refresh your memory. On the night we were first in company with one another, not even properly introduced yet, you declined an opportunity to dance with me because I was not 'tolerable enough to tempt you' and you were 'in no humour to give consequence to young ladies who had been slighted by other men,' or something to that effect. After that, at each event in which we were in company with one another, you proceeded to glare at me with this same contempt and speak most rudely. That is, whenever you would condescend to speak at all. Was I supposed to think you were admiring me?"

As a matter of fact, he *had* been admiring her. Apparently, it had not seemed that way to the object of this admiration. "I... forgive me, I do not recall saying any such thing."

"You said it to Mr Bingley, and I suspect intentionally within my hearing, as he was coaxing you to dance."

Oh. Of course, I remember now. Darcy had been in such a sour mood that night, rendered such by a most painful headache that was only exacerbated by the loud music and clouds of mixed perfumes of the dance hall, that he had unleashed an insult which could not be misunderstood by either Bingley or the target of his magnanimous aid. He had not actually seen the lady in question, but it had apparently been Elizabeth whom he had snubbed; the irony contained within this moment tasted strong and bitter.

"I had not realised that I insulted you," Darcy said, finding himself the recipient of Elizabeth's dubious expression. "I only wanted Bingley to cease pestering me about dancing. Had I actually looked at you, I would never have said such a thing. I apologise most humbly for wounding your vanity, madam."

Elizabeth's ire seemed to be fading, her features easing into confusion as if she could not quite bring herself to believe him. "Is that true?"

"Yes. You are a very beautiful woman, Elizabeth, as I am sure you are well aware." Darcy was not accustomed to offering up such explicit compliments, even when they were true, and so he spoke this one at a softened tone which laid bare the bashfulness he felt.

His love appeared to be experiencing a similar reaction as her cheeks reddened and her regard darted away from his face to rest upon the dead grass. "And the staring?"

"Do you not study the things you find aesthetically pleasing?"

The colour in her face deepened to the hue of a fresh apple. "I suppose I do, but I had genuinely thought you were looking at me to find fault."

Darcy took a step nearer to her and bent his head so that he was looking her more directly in the eye. "Never."

Elizabeth met his gaze momentarily, her expression riddled with embarrassment and anxiety, before she turned away and walked deeper into the brush. Darcy allowed her the escape as he could empathise with the intensity of what she must be feeling; he himself felt ready to climb out of his skin with restlessness.

Once she was several paces away, and perhaps a safer

emotional distance as well, Elizabeth spun on her heel again and faced him. "I am still not quite reconciled to what you are telling me, Mr Darcy. Shall I be frank?"

Though wary of what she might say next, Darcy entreated, "Please do."

"Since you have been in the neighbourhood, you have treated everyone I have ever known—myself, my neighbours and, most especially, my family—with contempt, seeming to consider them beneath your notice." Elizabeth paused as if to give him leave to object, but he did not—what she said was true. "I must ask if this is your real reason for not wishing an alliance between us before now. Are you truly prepared to be connected to a family who are themselves connected to trade? Will you be willing to overlook their silly behaviour and allow me to visit them?"

Darcy straightened his spine, something he often did when fighting the urge to squirm with either irritation or discomfort. He was warding off the latter in this instance. "I am, though you must realise that there will have to be some…boundaries, particularly whilst we stay in town."

Elizabeth's annoyance returned as indicated by the flare in her eyes and the thrust of her lower jaw. "So you intend to hide them from your elevated circle, is that it?"

His sigh heavy with exasperation, Darcy said, "Not exactly, no, but do you truly believe that your mother and younger sisters will ever be refined enough to mingle in society? Their behaviour is immature at best and entirely boorish at worst. Much as you love them, you must see this. Your elder sister is most welcome in our home at any time, but there will have to be limitations for the rest, at least during the Season. My sister is not yet out, but eventually she shall need to marry—as will our own children one day—and we cannot allow the Bennets to damage her chances at a good match."

Darcy winced at the cessation of his speech as Bingley's warnings and recriminations assaulted him from his memory. He had at least attempted to leave his objections to her family out of his proposal, but Elizabeth would force the issue. Was Darcy still an ungentlemanly churl for responding to her own unladylike frankness? Most likely.

"You forget yourself, sir," Elizabeth countered, a sharp chill in her tone. "I have not yet accepted any proposal you have offered, and am currently not inclined to do so. Quite to the contrary, I have refused you. Please check your presumption in regard to *our* home and *our* children."

"Elizabeth." Darcy moved towards where she stood apart from him. Her eyes narrowed slightly at, he assumed, his further presumption of using her Christian name. "Forgive me. It pains me to offend you, but I have certain obligations which must be met, and it would be impossible to do so if your relations carry on in town in the wild, unabashed way that I have seen them do here. I am not suggesting that you be forbidden from seeing them, or that they never be invited to either Darcy House or Pemberley, only that we exercise precautions where they are introduced and when. I am attempting to be reasonable and asking you to do the same."

Elizabeth wrapped her arms about her middle, preventing Darcy from reaching out to take her hands. "It will only be necessary if I accept your offer which, as I have stated multiple times, I am not inclined to do."

Darcy could feel his insides knotting up as disappointment, kept at bay during the ongoing battle between them, radiated throughout his being. "And so this is your final answer? You will not..." He could not say it aloud; his throat had closed in upon the final words which would mark the end to all of his hopes, short-lived as they were.

Elizabeth's sharp gaze perused his features, searching for something. Darcy knew that she would only find the ugly results of her rejection. Anger, self-castigation, and the deepest melancholy he had ever experienced. He could not even bring himself to hide them, though he hoped he might rally his composure before facing Bingley again.

Almost as if from a long way away, Elizabeth quietly interrupted Darcy's attempts to collect himself with a question. "Do you really wish to marry me?"

Startled, Darcy's answer popped free of his mouth before he could even consider it. "Yes. I love you."

In retrospect, as a gentleman, he probably should have taken her rejection stoically and dismissed himself from her presence, but he could not help himself in the moment, nor could he help the pleading in his tone.

Their gazes mingled during the pause which ensued following Darcy's final appeal. Elizabeth studied him carefully and Darcy left his expression open so that she could do so as he awaited her verdict.

At length, with still a hint of wariness in her eyes, she spoke. "I am still not entirely convinced that we would suit, and I am rather insulted by some of the things you have said. However," she paused to sigh, her shoulders drooping as her breath was exhaled, "considering some of the...other things"—here her cheeks flared into that lovely apple red shade once more—"we have spoken of, I am willing to retract my absolute refusal and reconsider it. If you will give me some time, I will think on my answer and provide it to you at a later date."

Darcy felt some of the tension in his gut unclench. Elizabeth had not accepted him, not yet, but no longer was she giving him an unequivocal 'no', either. "How much time do you require?"

She shrugged. "I do not yet know, sir. It is not the kind of decision one makes in an instant, though I am sure you would wish to have your answer as soon as possible. Is this not so?"

Darcy allowed that it was and further resisted the urge to point out that most women did, in fact, make their decision immediately. "Bingley intends to announce a ball, to be held next Tuesday the twenty-sixth, which is exactly a week from today. Do you think you could have your answer by then?"

"Yes, I think so."

"Then I shall anticipate your response for the evening of the ball." Darcy gently tugged at the elbow nearest to him so that she might unravel the tangle of her arms about her waist. Elizabeth allowed him to do so and he slid his fingers down the length of her forearm to clasp her gloved hand. He stared at the knot of their fingers, his thumb slowly stroking the back of her knuckles, as he quietly entreated, "I would also ask that you reserve the first and supper sets for me, if you are amenable."

Elizabeth nodded again. When she found her voice, she spoke so softly as to be nearly unintelligible to his hearing. "Yes, I would be honoured."

SIX

What am I doing? Have I entirely lost my senses to be considering this man's offer?

When Elizabeth had seen Mr Darcy in Meryton, she had been positive that he only wanted an affirmation that she would not seek his hand and had therefore no suspicion at all that he would instead offer it to her again. Her first instinct to refuse him had somehow been handily rebuffed, and now she was caught in the purgatory of considering his proposal.

Elizabeth remained vexed with Mr Darcy's poor attitude and the high-handed stipulations on how her family was to be treated, but his declaration of steady affection for her had stayed her hand in rejecting him entirely. Even more so, the dejection on his face in the wake of her refusal had touched her. Mr Darcy had appeared so earnest, so shy as he had expounded upon his feelings for her—feelings she had had no inkling of until he had confessed them aloud—that Elizabeth feared she had simply misunderstood him all this time.

His explanation regarding the infamous snub from the assembly had reinforced the notion that Elizabeth had not properly comprehended this complex man before. It had never once occurred to her that Mr Darcy had not actually looked at her before cutting her. Now that she thought back, his eyes did seem to have skimmed over her head at that important moment rather than fixing themselves decidedly upon her. If he was telling the truth—and if there was one thing about Mr Darcy that she had recognised properly, it was his penchant for telling the plain truth—this meant he had not been insulting her and, in actuality, had verily insulted no one at all. The fact that he still should not have said anything so incendiary at a public gathering was not in dispute, but it had apparently not been his intent to cause offence to anyone in particular.

With everything settled between them—or at least settled upon settling at a later date—Elizabeth self-consciously tugged her hand from his and waved it towards the house. "Shall we go in for tea, Mr Darcy?"

"Just a moment more," he replied, halting her footsteps before she could even take them. He was looking down at her with that familiar, intense stare that she now knew carried no hint of censure, and she felt her skin tingle. "There is one more subject I would like to speak to you about, and that is Mr Wickham."

Elizabeth frowned at Mr Darcy as her suspicions rose, but she determined that he be allowed his say; there was clearly some history between the two men and, if she wished to begin giving this dour gentleman more benefit of the doubt, she had best start here and allow him the opportunity to explain his side of it. "I confess I did notice a certain coldness in your greeting earlier. Is that what you wish to discuss?"

"Yes." Mr Darcy took a deep breath and began, "I know not how well acquainted with him you are, but Mr Wickham was the son of a very respectable man..."

Though Elizabeth's initial inclination had been to take Mr Darcy's explanation with a grain of salt, she found herself growing increasingly appalled at the seemingly charming Mr Wickham's long history of excesses. Gambling, seductions, petty crimes! It seemed that the handsome new officer was nothing short of a rake. And to have disdained the generosity of his patron, the elder Mr Darcy, only to then squander a small fortune was abominable! It had not occurred to Elizabeth before, but such wild behaviour certainly explained why a man of his age was only just now starting in the militia as a lieutenant rather than already being distinguished at a higher rank. At least he had declined the position intended for him as a clergyman; the people of Kympton should be most grateful that Mr Darcy had denied him the post when he had come begging for it after spending his four thousand pounds.

"Last summer," Mr Darcy's voice cracked at this point, as if strained, "he was again most painfully obtruded on my notice. I must now mention a circumstance which I would wish to forget myself, and which no obligation less than the present should induce me to unfold to any human being. Having said this much, I feel no doubt of your secrecy. My sister, who is more than ten years my junior..."

If Elizabeth had been disturbed by Mr Darcy's relation of events as pertaining to Mr Wickham's greed and selfishness before, she was absolutely horrified now. To think that such a man, one who would prey upon the innocent affections of a young girl and attempt a clandestine elopement for her fortune, was walking about in their midst! She must warn her father, her sisters—they should not be laid open to the whims of an opportunistic villain.

"I would not wish you to become a target of Wickham's machinations whilst he is in the neighbourhood. Should he become aware of my feelings for you, it is a surety that he will attempt to turn your head and involve you in the kind of disgrace that would prevent any reputable gentleman from marrying you. I should like to see you spared that." Mr Darcy concluded his rendition very quietly, his head bowed to stare at the ground as if seeing nothing.

Elizabeth did not doubt Mr Darcy's story; not only had he offered to show her documentation related to their financial dealings, but only a simpleton would implicate his own sister in a tale which would sully her reputation. Mr Darcy, for all his perceived faults, could not be accused of lacking intelligence or awareness of the world about him. He was correct in that she would never reveal a word to anyone about what he had told her, but it was still a great risk—one might even consider it an unnecessary one—to say anything in regards to Miss Darcy's misadventure. Further, there was truth in all his looks, particularly the abashed set of his drooping shoulders and the way his eyes would not meet hers. He clearly blamed himself for these events, and Elizabeth felt a stab of pity for the soul who took so much of other people's sins upon himself.

Stepping nearer slowly, tentatively, Elizabeth raised a hand from where it had been resting lax at her side and tugged upon the cuff of Mr Darcy's sleeve. The minute spasm of his features indicated that she had surprised him, and he lifted his chin so that he was looking at her, his eyes moving upwards to connect with her gaze.

Once she had gained his attention, Elizabeth reassured him, her voice low and soothing. "You must not blame yourself, sir. Others are culpable. You could not have known, after so many years of separation, that Mr Wickham was a threat. It was owing to your quickness that Miss Darcy was saved. Do not punish yourself over the things you could not help."

"If I had only gone with her from the first, instead of remaining in London, he never would have..."

As Elizabeth continued to stare into his eyes, she noted an uptick in the tempo of her heartbeat. Somehow, seeing Mr Darcy so chastened, so accepting of guilt which did not truly belong to him, made him seem more human than before. He clearly did not think himself so infallible as she had once accused him of. "There is no sense in dwelling on that which has already occurred. The lesson has been learnt and it is time to forgive yourself for any minor part you may have played. You should take up some of my philosophy—remember the past only as it gives you pleasure."

A small, yet authentic, smile appeared on Mr Darcy's lips and Elizabeth's impractical heart beat with even more fervour.

He was so very handsome when his features were softened in something other than his perpetual scowl. "Thank you, Elizabeth. I shall do my best to heed your advice."

"See that you do," Elizabeth quipped with a touch of her usual humour, partly to retain that attractive smile and partly to cover her own burgeoning discomfort in relation to it. She released the hold she had on his sleeve and took a long step back from him. "I believe, sir, that we are due in the parlour for tea. I am grown quite cold standing about out here."

But Mr Darcy appeared to have something else to say. He relaxed his jaw and parted his lips to speak, but all he was able to project from them was a single word—"Elizabeth"—before the wailing screech of Mrs Bennet rent the air and disturbed the tranquillity of the frigid garden. "Jane! Lizzy! Come inside before you catch your death of cold!"

Elizabeth flashed Mr Darcy a smirk, a silent 'did I not tell you so?' as he closed his mouth and abandoned whatever it was he had intended to say.

To his credit, he did not make any disparaging remarks about her uncouth mother, nor did his expression betray any of the impatience he must have felt at her interruption, but rather he offered her his arm and a simple, "Shall we?"

Elizabeth accepted his escort this time without an ounce of hesitation. "We shall."

As Darcy led Elizabeth towards the house where her mother was chiding Miss Bennet in near hysterics about loitering outside in the cold, he intentionally adopted a slow pace so that he could regain the equilibrium he had lost in the retelling of George Wickham's many and various sins. It would never become easier, it seemed, to reflect upon the worst of what that blackguard had done and his own culpability in the events.

Darcy glanced at Elizabeth and calmed somewhat. Her defence of him had been both unexpected and soothing to his conscience, though of course he would likely never absolve himself completely. But at least she seemed to believe his recitation and would, thus, not fall prey to Wickham's poisoned tongue; Elizabeth was now better protected against that scoundrel's charms than Georgiana had been. Given even half a chance, Darcy was certain that Wickham—who could not have possibly missed the attention Darcy had paid to Elizabeth in Meryton when their parties had converged—would set his beloved against him and cause untold damage to his already fragile suit with lies.

No, it seemed as if Elizabeth would be turned from him by his own merits alone. How could he have misread her so completely? Had he even attempted to discern her feelings at all, or had he simply assumed that she must regard him favourably because he had wished it? Her teasing commentary at Netherfield had seemed flirtation at the time, but perhaps her playful tone had been disguising barbs intended to wound him and he, besotted idiot that he was, had not noticed. Darcy generally prided himself on his discernment, particularly in regard to the scheming arts and machinations of the fairer sex, but it appeared he had seen only that which he had wanted to see in Elizabeth's manner towards himself. To think that she had not released him initially in a show of selflessness, but rather because of her intense dislike for his presence!

In a way, it was almost more impressive a gesture than he had first given her credit for. A woman who would reject a man she simply did not care for, regardless of his status and fortune, was a rare gem, indeed. Elizabeth had to well know that Darcy could give her everything her heart desired if she would only accept his proposal, yet she had not. Not yet. If he could not change her terrible first impression of him, she possibly never would. Darcy was determined to earn Elizabeth's good opinion and then hope for a better response to his offer than she had heretofore given.

And is it worth it? Another sly glance at her profile, a glimpse of that same naughty ringlet he had been enamoured of since the beginning of their acquaintance bouncing playfully in the breeze, decided him immediately. A woman worthy of being pleased was deserving of the effort. Moreover, once he had achieved his aim—if he even could; he prayed that it was not too late—the reward would be that much greater. To think that he would actually know that his wife cared for him and not his wealth or status...it was a boon he had never thought to expect considering his position in life. Darcy had previously only hoped for a woman whom he could tolerate—he flinched slightly as that word entered his mind; he would never use it again without a sense of burning shame—like his father had before him. Incredibly, he had the opportunity for so much more than he could have reasonably predicted from life. If he could make Elizabeth love him, he truly would have everything a man could desire.

With these thoughts tumbling through his mind, Darcy halted their progression towards the house, earning him a raised brow from his beloved. Mrs Bennet had since ushered her eldest daughter and this same said daughter's suitor into the warm indoors and had, apparently, forgotten her second child for the moment. Overlooking this lack of motherly concern for Elizabeth's health, Darcy took advantage of this favourable circumstance to make a request. "Elizabeth, it occurs to me that we do not know each other as we should. If I wish to obtain your acceptance of my hand, and you hope for an informed decision, it would be best to spend more time in one another's company. Would you grant me the honour of calling on you between now and the ball?"

Elizabeth's lips parted with apparent surprise. She hesitated to answer. "I suppose that is fair, though I beg you would not do so with the object of pressuring me for an answer. May I have your word?"

"Of course."

"Then, yes, you may call on me," she said. "Though perhaps it would be better to conduct our meetings away from my mother, lest she gain expectations that may not be fulfilled."

Darcy felt the slap of Elizabeth's reminder that she might never accept his hand, but it was a fair concern. "My intentions are what she would wish. She would make no incorrect assumptions."

"Perhaps not," Elizabeth allowed, with some asperity, "but if I ultimately decide against you, I shall never hear the end of my mother's lamentations on the subject. Thus, I would prefer a certain amount of discretion lest I be forced to join a nunnery!"

The theatrical turn of this tease was amusing to Darcy and he chuckled, though inside his heart squeezed painfully. Elizabeth must not think there was much chance of her changing her mind if she were conscious of tempering Mrs Bennet's expectations.

He must not have hidden this thought as well as he generally did, for Elizabeth's expression softened into one of sympathetic chagrin. "I apologise, sir, that was unkind. You must realise I cannot pretend there is not a chance of us parting ways permanently, that would be dishonest and cruel. However, I admit that our acquaintance, such as it is, has been flawed thus far and would benefit from an improved understanding of one another. Knowing you better can only be to our mutual benefit, so I am amenable to your...your attentions, and I suppose there is only one proper venue for you to show them. Rather than risking both of our reputations with secret rendezvous, you must, of course, come to Longbourn for your business. I only ask that you not be too overt in front of my mother, or she will become unbearable for us both."

An image of Mrs Bennet screeching and crowing about Bingley's attentions to Miss Bennet filtered into Darcy's mind and he recognised the reasonableness of Elizabeth's request. He would not wish to be the object of her mother's ill-mannered exclamations and unsubtle hints.

"Lizzy! Come inside at once, Mr Collins is asking for you!"

"Coming, Mama!"

Darcy extended his arm for her to take. She did, and they

began walking towards the house once more. Leaning closer so that he might speak at a volume which did not carry, Darcy asked, only half seriously, "I do not suppose I have a rival to contend with?"

Elizabeth shuddered at the suggestion. "I should say not! I think I can safely promise you that I shall never marry my cousin."

"It is a great comfort to know that I am not the absolute last man in the world you could be prevailed upon to marry."

SEVEN

In the sitting room, Mrs Bennet fussed and fluttered even after the entire walking party had been safely ensconced inside; she wailed at the top of her voice about her 'lovely Jane's' delicate health and how no one gave proper consideration to her poor nerves. Darcy thought it rather rich that a woman who would allow—if not orchestrate, as he suspected she had—this same daughter to ride three miles on horseback on a day which ominously threatened rain should now claim to be overcome by the notion of her child catching a chill. Never mind that the only clouds in the sky this particular morning were still some ways in the distance and the weather was fair, if rather crisp, as one could generally expect in late autumn. And she had not once mentioned Elizabeth's well-being, he noted rather grimly. It was only for his beloved's sake that Darcy restrained himself from scowling at Mrs Bennet and her single-minded theatrics.

Darcy allowed Elizabeth to precede him in selecting a chair so that he might have the benefit of choosing one next to her. It had been too much to hope that she might claim a sofa which the both of them could share, but she did not thwart him by planting herself between a pair of sisters, either. Only slightly in her wake, Darcy contented himself with the proximity she would graciously allow, which was not so very far, and placed him within touching range of her should he be so bold as to make the attempt.

They were gratefully accepting cups of hot tea from Mary when Mrs Bennet's attention shifted to Elizabeth at last. "It is about time you came in from the cold, Lizzy," she scolded with a sour pucker to her mouth. Mrs Bennet then glanced at Mr Collins, who was bowing deeply to the latecomers—and, most especially, to his lovely cousin Elizabeth—and softened her tone. "My Lizzy is excessively fond of the outdoors, Mr Collins. I understand that you keep a large garden at your parsonage?"

The clergyman straightened from his bow, yet still seemed oddly slouched at the shoulders. "Oh yes, indeed, Mrs Bennet! My patroness, Lady Catherine de Bourgh," Mr Collins glanced at Darcy, a smug and also somehow simpering curve upon his lips, as if he wished the newest amongst them to recognise the grandiosity of his connexion, "most fervently recommended that I keep an extensive garden at my humble abode. 'Mr Collins,' she said, 'there is no greater benefit to one's health and productivity than a garden. It is most important for a clergyman in your position...'"

Lady Catherine! Darcy hissed slightly when a steaming trickle of tea splashed over the side of his cup and onto the back of his hand, burning the skin between his thumb and forefinger. Thankfully, he had been able to save the remainder—and his lap—from overturning completely. Had Mr Collins just invoked the name of his meddlesome aunt?

This newest information posed a potential stumbling block for Darcy. For most of his life Lady Catherine had advocated—commanded, really—for himself and her daughter, Anne, to marry. His own mother had hinted that the match was pleasing to her before her death some ten years ago, but since adolescence, Darcy had abhorred the idea. Anne herself was not wholly objectionable with regard to her connexions, status, and fortune, but the same epidemic which had taken Lady Anne Darcy had weakened his cousin into something wraith-like and irritable. Darcy did not blame poor Anne for an ongoing ailment she could not help, but neither did he have any inclination to take her for his wife upon sympathy alone. Anne would probably expire naturally in the next few years without even the intervention of childbirth to precipitate it. Attempting to bring forth an heir would only curtail his cousin's already dismally short life expectancy, and Darcy would not have that on his conscience.

None of Darcy's arguments in favour of Anne's well-being, however, had ever dissuaded her mother from scheming the match, and Lady Catherine was only becoming more persistent. With Mr Collins, her pet parson, in residence at Longbourn and presumably willing to report any and all activities therein to his aunt—and most especially those which would impact her ladyship directly—Darcy would have to be more cautious in his wooing of Elizabeth than he had expected. Mrs Bennet, whom one must presume would be a friend to his alliance with Elizabeth, was a minor obstacle in comparison.

Happily, Mr Collins seemed as yet ignorant of Darcy's connexion to Lady Catherine, and he prayed most fervently that it would remain that way. Had he been aware that Darcy was, in fact, Lady Catherine's nephew, the one slated to marry Anne, Mr Collins would surely have grovelled at his feet after nearly knocking him down in Meryton earlier. Darcy would make sure that he remained unaware and warn Elizabeth of a possible problem before taking his leave. He would also make a point of cautioning Bingley lest his voluble friend, who had heard many unflattering stories of Lady Catherine, accidentally let something slip.

"Are you well, sir?"

Darting his eyes to his right, Darcy observed Elizabeth looking directly at him with an inquisitive brow raised. Mr Collins prattled on in the background, regurgitating what sounded like Lady Catherine's words verbatim in relation to the subject of gardens and horticulture—something he highly doubted his aunt had much true knowledge of, but knew she likely spoke on with great authority nonetheless—and the rest of the room seemed inattentive to their quiet tête-à-tête.

"I am," he assured her, also in a low register that would not carry to the others in the parlour. With the cautious hope that he had mistaken Mr Collins, he murmured, "Your cousin mentioned a Lady Catherine. Tell me, does he refer to the mistress of Rosings Park?"

"He does," Elizabeth confirmed, leaning minutely closer to him. He caught the subtle whiff of lavender from her hair as the air about her shifted with her movement. "Do you know her?"

"She is my aunt on my mother's side. I presume that Mr Collins is the new rector she has lately assigned to Hunsford?"

Both of Elizabeth's brows were now raised in apparent surprise. Truly, the coincidence was rather astounding. "He informed us that he took orders at Easter and was appointed his position soon thereafter."

Well, that certainly explained it. Darcy had paid his annual Easter visit to Lady Catherine, stayed for the minimum number of days, and then returned to London as quickly as his team of horses could convey him thither. Old Mr Brayden, the wizened cleric who had been in possession of the living at Hunsford for most of Darcy's life, had been on his deathbed then, and his curate had delivered the sermon on the holy day he had been present for. Mr Brayden had died the following month and Lady Catherine had, apparently, filled his vacancy with Mr Collins.

Darcy marvelled at the happenstance which would not only place Elizabeth's cousin under the authority of his autocratic aunt, but also bring the pair of them separately to Hertfordshire to court the same woman. As to Mr Collins himself, it was truly no wonder that Lady Catherine would employ the toadying, sycophantic gudgeon as her clergyman. Mr Collins was exactly the type of man his aunt preferred: stupid, easily led about, and unquestioningly reverent towards her. She had outdone herself in this instance.

"I think it best that we keep my—" Darcy glanced quickly

at Mr Collins, who had yet to halt his soliloquy venerating his patroness— "interest in you from your cousin's notice."

"And why is that?" Elizabeth's eyes were trained upon his and there was a slight furrow between them as if she expected to be offended by his answer.

Darcy inched closer, mostly because he wished to and not merely for the purpose of secrecy. "Because my aunt has declared that I am to marry her daughter, my cousin Anne, and Mr Collins seems likely to inform her of my intentions should they be made known to him. It also seems imperative that he not know of my connexion to Lady Catherine at all if we can help it."

Elizabeth drew back, her eyes narrowed. "If you are engaged to your cousin then why did you only this morning make an offer to me?"

"I am not engaged to my cousin, no more than you are engaged to yours." Darcy nodded to Mr Collins, and Elizabeth's gaze followed his movement before returning to his face. "Lady Catherine is not accustomed to brooking disappointment, however, and so she continues to consider it a settled thing, no matter what I say on the subject. I suspect that she will not subside until I am actually married to another woman."

"Then what is the risk of Mr Collins telling her?"

Darcy huffed indignantly, though not at Elizabeth's question. "Because she will be insufferable about it and stir up as much trouble as she can. It would be better, regardless of how things turn out between us," he swallowed hard to clear the strain from his throat, "if she remains ignorant of my intentions towards you. She is most persistent when displeased."

"But how can she—"

"Do you not think so, Cousin Elizabeth?"

They looked, in tandem, towards the very man they had been plotting against, neither aware of what should be said in response to Mr Collins's query. "I apologise, Mr Collins, I was not attending," Elizabeth said. "Mr Darcy was asking me a question, and I am afraid I could not help answering."

Mr Collins did not even spare Darcy a glance as he continued to stare at Elizabeth with greedy eyes. Darcy's jaw clenched as he realised that the pompous toad's gaze was aligned with a point lower than her face. "No apologies are necessary."

Before Mr Collins could begin on another topic—or, worse, continue with the same threadbare one—Darcy spoke up. "Bingley, did you not have an announcement?"

"Hm?" Bingley looked up from his conversation with Miss Bennet, his expression uncomprehending.

"The ball?" Darcy prodded. "You said on the ride over that you hoped to issue an invitation on this visit."

"Oh! Yes, quite right." Bingley sprung to his feet, tugging at the lapels of his blue coat. As he surveyed the room, looking fondly at each of the faces individually, he proclaimed, "On Tuesday next, I shall be hosting a ball at Netherfield. Can I hope that you will all be in attendance?"

The room erupted into deafening squeals even before Bingley had finished speaking. These were largely emanating from the corner in which the youngest girls were seated, but Mrs Bennet was nearly as overcome as her boisterous offspring.

"How wonderful! Did you hear, Jane? A ball! We thank you so much for inviting us, Mr Bingley—Jane, thank the man for his invitation."

Miss Bennet, contrary to her mother's reaction, seemed unsurprised by the news of Bingley's upcoming soiree, and Darcy assumed that his friend must have shared the intelligence with her during their garden stroll. Undoubtedly, Bingley had also secured whichever dances he preferred with her, as Darcy had done with Elizabeth. With the faintest hint of pink staining her cheeks, Miss Bennet thanked Bingley in a demure way which her mother seemed incapable of.

"Not at all," Bingley replied. In a formal manner, he requested, "May I take this opportunity to secure your hand for the first two dances?"

Before the lady could say anything in response, Mrs Bennet again interjected where she was not wanted or needed. "Why, of course she will be most happy to reserve those dances for you, Mr Bingley! Are you not, Jane? Oh! How wonderful an evening it shall be! We are always eager to spend time in the company of our dear friends."

While Mrs Bennet blathered on, Darcy could just make out a quieter, more polite acceptance of Bingley's request from Miss Bennet herself. The pair then settled back into a conversation between only themselves and seemingly ignored Mrs Bennet's prolonged raptures thereafter.

A quick peek at Elizabeth revealed that she, unlike her elder sister, was more visibly suffering from the mortification wrought by their mother's effusions. Darcy wished that he could reassure her, but remembered her injunctions against making obvious overtures in front of Mrs Bennet. And, of course, the dullard Mr Collins was also present; should he make the connexion between Darcy and his beloved patroness, there would be much to report if excessive attention was paid to Elizabeth. Thus, Darcy held himself in check and clenched the hand which longed to reach out and stroke her cheek into a fist.

Even had Darcy truly intended to soothe his beloved, Mr Collins just then regained control of the conversation by clearing his throat loudly. Mrs Bennet quieted her enthusiasm immediately and, with hopeful eyes, turned to her husband's cousin. "I am by no means of the opinion, I assure you," said he, though no one had accused him of anything to the contrary, "that a ball of this kind, given by a young man of character, to respectable people, can have any evil tendency; and I am so far from objecting to dance myself that I shall hope to be honoured with the hands of all my fair cousins in the course of the evening, and I take this opportunity of soliciting yours, Miss Elizabeth, for the first two dances especially."

Mrs Bennet, again, jumped in to accept the overtures of a suitor on behalf of one of her daughters. "There now, Lizzy! You shall have a partner for the first set, too. What an honour to be so singled out! Thank you, Mr Collins."

Darcy was rigid with offence at Mrs Bennet's audacity. He

would leave it to Elizabeth to correct the assumptions of her kin, though he longed to stake his claim personally.

When it was finally her turn to speak, Elizabeth addressed Mr Collins directly. "Forgive me, sir, but I am afraid that I cannot accept your hand for the dances in question as they are already engaged elsewhere." She flicked her eyes in Darcy's direction, a pinkness glowing in her cheeks as she gave him a private look and small smile before returning to Mr Collins. "I can reserve another set for you, if you would like."

A palpable hush filled the parlour until Mr Collins broke it with a condescending chuckle. "You are most amusing with your little jokes, my dear cousin. Truly, your wit and vivacity are a treasure—when utilised in the appropriate setting—and I am sure will be greatly appreciated when...well, on that point I think it best to be silent for now. In the meantime, I shall look forward with great anticipation to leading you onto the dance floor for the first set."

Elizabeth looked, somehow, even more offended than Darcy felt with her expression slackened in incredulous outrage. She opened her mouth to retort, paused to clench her eyes shut as if gathering her patience, and then replied to Mr Collins in a tone calmer than Darcy himself could have managed. "Forgive me if I have led you to believe that I speak in jest, sir, but I am in earnest. The first two dances belong to another."

"Oh, Lizzy!" Mrs Bennet cried. "Do not be ridiculous! Who could have asked you, pray? Only the people in this room are even privy to the information that there is to be a ball at all. No, you will accept Mr Collins, thank him for singling you out amongst your sisters and open the ball with him. I insist."

Yet again, the irritation Darcy felt was mirrored in Elizabeth's features as she reiterated her refusal for a third time. "I cannot, Mama, as I have already said. I shall not break my word."

"You try my patience, you stubborn girl! Who could have possibly—?"

"It was I."

Darcy felt the weight of the entire parlour's scrutiny transfer from Elizabeth to himself as soon as his words were free from his throat. He had not consciously decided to interject, but they had burst from him in a fit of indignation upon witnessing the prolonged disrespect to his beloved. Darcy was unaccustomed to having his word questioned, and it grated on him that Elizabeth should suffer the disbelief of her most stubbornly ridiculous kin; it was not to be borne a second longer.

"You?" Mrs Bennet's responding tone was incredulous.

"Indeed," affirmed Darcy, firmly and with no hesitation. "I have requested Miss Elizabeth's hand for the dances in question and she has honoured me with her acceptance."

Mrs Bennet flicked her sceptical gaze back and forth repeatedly between her second daughter—now blushing bright red and staring at her lap—and Darcy. When neither disputed the facts nor proclaimed it all a silly jest, Mrs Bennet acceded to the truth presented to her. And, though Darcy could not be certain, calculation seemed to be warming within her eyes.

"I see. Very well, Mr Collins," she spoke to the parson, but Mrs Bennet's scrutiny remained hungrily affixed upon Darcy, "I suppose you shall have to request a different set with Lizzy. Mary can dance the first with you."

"But—" Mr Collins, still looking stupidly about, seemed ready to argue again.

"Why not the supper set with Elizabeth?" Mrs Bennet suggested, at last redirecting her regard to the object of her statement. "Then you might have company through the meal."

Mr Collins was looking quite petulant, glaring at Darcy with his jowls crumpled into a frown. "I suppose that would be acceptable..."

"I am afraid that will not do either, Mrs Bennet," Darcy interrupted. His initial plan to leave the orchestration of this farce to Elizabeth had already been set aside, so it seemed only natural to stake his claim as far as it would go. He only hoped that his beloved would not be excessively cross with him for creating the kind of overt display she had specifically asked him to avoid since he was saving her from being prominently linked in the neighbourhood to Mr Collins instead. Elizabeth, he noted from his periphery, was watching the proceedings with a grim aspect, but as she made no move to take back the reins of conversation Darcy supposed that she must recognise the benefits, as well. "Miss Elizabeth has granted me that set also."

The spark of calculation Darcy had previously noted in Mrs Bennet's eyes flared into an inferno at this new information. Thankfully, she seemed too stunned to begin another round of hysterics.

Mr Collins continued to protest, but Mrs Bennet was now Darcy's advocate over the comparatively penniless clergyman. Mr Collins was thus forced to be satisfied with dancing the first with Miss Mary, the second with Miss Elizabeth and the third with Miss Bennet; the two youngest girls would be attended to later in the evening but were not secured for specific sets.

It seemed that few in the room—save Mrs Bennet who verily glowed at the newly discovered prospect of not one, but two, beaus apparently interested in her second daughter—were especially happy with the results of this conversation, but it would have to do. Elizabeth would, by necessity, be forced to succumb to a dance with her odious cousin, but she could at least avoid giving him prominent sets; Miss Mary appeared antagonistic towards the concept of dancing at all; Miss Bennet seemed somewhat vexed at the ongoing dispute, though it was difficult to tell for sure; Bingley was attempting to soothe Miss Bennet's disquiet; the younger girls complained that they had no partners secured for the first set; and Mr Collins, of course, carried on with his long-winded complaints no matter how pointless they were at this juncture.

Shortly thereafter, it was time for the visiting gentlemen to take their leave as they had already stayed well beyond the allotted time for a polite call. Darcy rose, caught Bingley's attention and they both bid their farewells.

At Mrs Bennet's insistence, Elizabeth and Jane saw their suitors to the door. They had only just crossed the threshold from the parlour into the corridor when Mr Darcy, rather abruptly, made an enquiry. "Before we depart, I had hoped to speak to your father about Mr Wickham. I wish him to know that he is not to be trusted."

Elizabeth applied to the housekeeper who was walking towards the group with the gentlemen's overcoats draped across her arms. "Hill, is Papa in his book-room?"

"No. The master rode out to speak to one of the tenants this morning. Smith, I think. He said not to expect him back till this afternoon."

Naturally, Mr Bennet would be unavailable one of the few days a visitor had an interest in seeing him. Had Elizabeth not known it to be impossible, she might have even accused her dear papa of orchestrating his absence just to be difficult. The thought brought a small quirk to her lips and an indulgent huff of annoyance.

"Shall I call on you tomorrow, then?" As he softly breathed this request into her ear, Elizabeth was startled to realise that Mr Darcy was much closer to her person than she had perceived. She turned her regard to him to find his head bent low, the tips of their noses only a scant few inches divided from one another, and she felt a blush instantly heat her cheeks. He was staring at her again, which only made their unexpected proximity more unnerving.

Elizabeth took a shuffling step back, putting a more comfortable amount of space between them, and banished the pleasant fluttering in her stomach by reminding herself that she was out of sorts with him. "My mother is much more aware of your interests than I had wished."

"It could not be helped, Elizabeth. You must see that," Mr Darcy admonished, gently, in return.

He is right, of course. She had greatly underestimated Mr Collins's enthusiasm for his own pursuit of her hand, and it had not occurred to her that he might, in front of company, stake his claim for her first two dances. If Elizabeth could be flattered by his eager compliment, she would have been, but one could not help being a touch disgusted by his 'delicate attentions', as he called them. His person was objectionable enough with his suspect hygiene and wandering eyes, but it was Mr Collins's demeanour which truly offended. One could tell by his air alone that he was secure in the success of his suit regardless of how little encouragement he received from the object of it. It would have been a greater compliment had Mr Collins taken the hint and turned his intentions elsewhere—preferably away from the ladies of Longbourn altogether.

Elizabeth felt strong sympathy for her sister Mary, who was now stuck with Mr Collins as a partner for the first set, since both of her elder sisters were already engaged elsewhere. When Mrs Bennet had proclaimed acquiescence to the scheme without even consulting her third daughter for approval, the expression on Mary's face had been angry but unsurprised. Elizabeth was unsure if this was a consequence of being saddled with Mr Collins in particular, or just being forced to dance in general, which Mary avoided more studiously even than Mr Darcy. Her poor, often overlooked sister was to be pitied regardless. She would make sure to speak to Mary this evening before bed to ascertain her actual feelings on the matter and try to comfort her where she could.

In the present, however, Mr Darcy was owed a concession.

Elizabeth sighed. "I suppose I must, considering Mr Collins unintentionally cornered us. I am merely cross because I know my mother will be insufferable about you now, and I shall never experience another moment's peace."

"Unless you accept my proposal and allow me to take you away to Pemberley. Derbyshire is an enticingly long distance away." Mr Darcy's words and affect were both flat, rather suspiciously so, and it occurred to Elizabeth that he had dared to make a joke at the expense of their strangely convoluted situation.

When she laughed, it was in a rather startled burst. Feeling quite suddenly more playful, Elizabeth teased him back. “I see your plan now, sir! But I shall not be swayed so easily. Come tomorrow, for you will have your work cut out for you still.”

“I accept your challenge most cheerfully, madam.” Mr Darcy’s rejoinder was accompanied by a smile which Elizabeth thought most sly, indeed, and unfairly charming. “And I shall have to come in any event because I did not have the opportunity to yet speak to your father. Do you expect him to be available to visitors tomorrow?”

As Mr Bennet was famously sedentary and rarely left his book-room for anything other than meals and urgent estate business Elizabeth could see no impediment to Mr Darcy’s plan. “I do, indeed.”

“Very well,” said Mr Darcy, standing erect at his full height as Hill put herself forwards to present him with his coat, hat, and gloves. Mr Bingley was already dressed for the outdoors and saying his final farewells to Jane. “I shall come tomorrow. I greatly anticipate it, Miss Elizabeth.”

After an awkward kiss to the back of Elizabeth’s hand and a mumbled goodbye, the gentlemen finally left. Elizabeth and Jane waved from the doorway as the pair of them trotted back up the lane towards Netherfield, leaving their ladies in similar yet quite different states of agitation.

The rest of the morning and afternoon were, indeed, as trying to Elizabeth’s patience as she had expected them to be. Her mother was at least more quietly exultant than her second daughter had given her credit for, perhaps in an attempt to avoid offending Mr Collins. Though Mrs Bennet did not say so directly, it was clear to Elizabeth that she was hedging her bets; a man such as Mr Darcy might show interest in the short term and then ultimately never make an offer, whereas a cousin and more modestly wealthy catch such as Mr Collins was, in the matron’s mind, a sure thing. Had Elizabeth told her mother that Mr Darcy had, in fact, already made her an offer twice, she was certain that Mrs Bennet would have thrown over Mr Collins's suit entirely. As Elizabeth herself remained unsure as to how favourably she would ultimately respond to said offer, it was better to keep that information to herself for the present.

Mr Collins was still pouting over being thwarted by Mr Darcy's claim upon her first dances and had been full of many complaints in relation to that insult. Elizabeth was at least mildly surprised by this as, even considering Mr Collins's ignorance as to Mr Darcy's connexion to the revered Lady Catherine de Bourgh, it was still clear to anyone that Mr Darcy was Mr Collins's superior in every way. His manners, the cut and obvious expense of his clothing, as well as his association with the wealthy Mr Bingley were all apparent.

These things did not impress Mr Collins, it seemed, though it was Elizabeth's conjecture that the buffoon was more oblivious than intentionally dismissive. He likely would not have noticed Mr Darcy at all had his rival not presented a stumbling block to his own pursuit of Elizabeth. Mr Collins had, she recalled with some guilty amusement, been so insensible of Mr Darcy's person that he had practically knocked the Derbyshire gentleman down in the middle of a dusty street just that very morning. Mr Darcy's expression in the wake of such an offence made a diverting image, one Elizabeth was inclined to tarry on; she had never seen him so discomposed before and his bug-eyed incredulity would not be easily forgotten.

Elizabeth banished Mr Darcy and his comical outrage to the far corner of her thoughts and refocused her concentration on the flaws of her other unwanted suitor. Mr Collins's petulance made him even less desirable a companion than before, which Elizabeth would have denied as a possibility had she not experienced it. Even Mary, who generally had more patience for the clergyman than the rest of them, had eventually dismissed herself to practise the pianoforte in the music room to avoid listening to their cousin's thinly veiled diatribes against 'some gentlemen' who were 'so rude as to pursue a lady when he was not wanted'. The irony of his complaints was lost on no one except himself. Neither was the implied insult to poor Mary, his assigned partner for the contested dances.

When Mr Bennet had returned home from his business and the family had collected to dine, he made the situation, if anything, worse by prodding Mr Collins to repeat his woes over soup so that he might laugh at his cousin's foolishness. Elizabeth nearly groaned, while Kitty and Lydia actually did. Mr Collins, of course, noticed none of the impatient looks he was receiving from the ladies, although he feigned unhappiness, naturally, to Mr Bennet's request to elaborate on the details.

"It must be gratifying to be so popular, Lizzy," Mr Bennet commented later over the main course. Elizabeth, for fear of getting Mr Collins started again on another excruciating soliloquy, had merely glared at her father and sawed more ferociously at her meat. This show of ill-humour only made Mr Bennet laugh heartily at her expense.

Finally, it was time to go to bed—after yet another arduous conversation in the parlour featuring her mother gushing over the ball and everything they need do to prepare for it, as well as more of Mr Collins's threadbare complaints—and Elizabeth trudged up the staircase with her sisters. Mary, Kitty, and Lydia clearly did not thank her for bringing so much irritating strife into their household, muttering darkly amongst themselves as they separated to their individual bedrooms for the evening, but at least Jane was sympathetic. When Mary's door closed with decidedly more force than usual, Elizabeth sighed and bid her remaining sisters a goodnight; she would have to speak to Mary upon the morrow, it seemed.

Jane, the dear heart that she was, offered to come to Elizabeth's room to discuss the happenings of the day, but Elizabeth was entirely too exhausted and frustrated to tolerate anyone's company but her own. She appreciated Jane's concern but declined with a hug and they both adjourned to their own chambers.

Elizabeth performed her nightly ablutions by rote as the

events of the day swirled about in her head on an unending rotation. *To think that Mr Darcy considers himself in love with me!* Enough to not only renew but also persist in his proposals. It was really quite absurd, when one stopped to think about it, but so it was. Elizabeth would have dismissed any and all thoughts of accepting him already had other portions of their conversation not swayed her, ever so slightly, in his favour.

It had not occurred to her, for instance, that his horrible insult at the assembly had not actually been intended for her. Elizabeth had been entirely certain that he had looked at her immediately before delivering his set down, yet he claimed that such was not the case and that he had not properly laid eyes upon her until later.

Is Mr Darcy speaking the truth? Or revising our personal history to achieve his aim of drawing me into marriage? But no, that made no rational sense. *If he is prevaricating and he genuinely considers me merely 'tolerable', then why would he wish to marry me at all?*

Further, his expression had been so surprised, shocked even, when she had laid her accusation at his feet that Elizabeth felt he must have been sincere in his explanation. It still did not entirely excuse him, for it was most ungentlemanly to say such things about any woman, even when he had aimed his insult at no one in particular, and Mr Darcy was wrong to do so. In such a public place, he should have been more circumspect and kept his ugly words to himself.

If I am inclined to believe him regarding his initial slight, should I then accept all of Mr Darcy's assertions as true? He had been much in earnest when warning her away from Mr Wickham and, more than that, positively anxious that she believe him. And who would spread untrue and damaging rumours about their own sister? No, it must be true. She would make sure to reveal all to her father, even if Mr Darcy failed to do so upon the morrow. Only Miss Darcy's identity must be obscured in the retelling.

And all of this consideration of Mr Darcy's honesty

brought her full circle back to his supposed feelings for her. He claimed to be in love with her, wanted to marry her, but he was so taciturn and haughty. She had had absolutely no inkling of his great attraction to her until he had come out and said so that very day, despite his initial proposal and the tender nature of his kiss. *Will he always be so cold and unreadable until pushed to be otherwise?*

Remembering the soft warmth of his lips against hers made Elizabeth burn from the roots of her hair to the tips of her toes. She had never been kissed before, as was good and proper for an unmarried maiden, but had wondered from time to time what it might be like. It was more moist than she had expected, certainly, but also more...just more. There was no adequate way to describe the sensation of being so close to a man, feeling the heat of his breath against her cheek and the scent of his shaving soap in her nose. And then there was still something yet more intangible in the tingle which had suffused her when Mr Darcy had leant in...and...

Elizabeth shook herself to banish these improper musings from her mind. They lingered, however, and she got up to pace away the confusion stirred up within her. *Is it a point in Mr Darcy's favour that I cannot forget his kiss? Or am I merely wanton and desiring of any man's carnal attentions?*

An image of Mr Collins rose within her consciousness, simpering at her in that oily way of his and waggling his fingers at her, and her question was thus answered; no, Mr Darcy was not interchangeable with just anyone. It still remained to be seen if he was the only gentleman who could inspire such attraction—and attraction it must be, she admitted reluctantly to herself—in her, but at least she held some standards.

With this consideration in mind, the only thing Elizabeth reasonably could do about the situation was allow Mr Darcy his opportunity to woo her. She still felt dubious over the validity of his devotion to her, wondered if perhaps his mind had not been permanently addled by his accident somehow, but she could not dismiss him entirely. Not just yet.

Elizabeth huffed the flame of her candle out of existence and climbed back into bed, determined to put all thoughts of Mr Darcy and his unfathomable feelings and motivations away for the night. It was not so easily done, however, and she drifted off some hours later still puzzling over what she should do.

EIGHT

The following day, Mr Darcy did not visit Longbourn. It was not his fault, however, as even Elizabeth could fairly admit, considering the heavy rain which had been falling steadily since sometime in the early morning hours before dawn. It would be folly for anyone to venture out in such a downpour just to go visiting their neighbours. Elizabeth insisted to herself that she was not disappointed in the slightest by his absence but still glowered at the sodden landscape with impatience.

There was much discussion amongst the Bennets as to whether or not they should attend Mrs Philips's card party in the evening. The younger girls were so adamant about going—no doubt wishing to flirt with the officers in attendance and eager to escape their cousin in the crowd—that the rest were eventually convinced to go. Thankfully, the precipitation abated right about the noon hour and the roads were allowed to dry somewhat in the weak autumn sunlight. At five o'clock precisely, the carriage was ordered, all but Mr Bennet climbed into it, and they carefully traversed the single mile which would take them to Meryton.

When they arrived at the Philipses' home, they found it

bustling inside. Many of their acquaintances were not in attendance due to the aftereffects of the poor weather, but the officers were all quartered within the town and it was no difficulty for them to traverse the muddy lanes when refreshments and society were freely offered. As soon as the Bennet party crossed the threshold, the two youngest disappeared instantly into the sea of red whilst the rest dispersed more sedately to mingle.

After a spot of tea, the card tables were placed and the guests called to order to play. Elizabeth sat down to a lottery game so that she might keep Lydia more contained while Jane settled at a separate table with Kitty in a prearranged manoeuvre to keep the girls apart for at least a short while. They were generally less troublesome when not together—at least Kitty was; Lydia benefited from more focused attention—and the elder sisters had designed this tactic when Lydia had come out in society as a way to curb some of their more outlandish impulses. Whenever it seemed that the pair of them were on the verge of getting into mischief and it was possible to prevent it, Elizabeth and Jane divided and conquered. Tonight's card party had been rife with temptation for the girls and, once their giggling and squealing had reached a fever pitch, Elizabeth had signalled to Jane that it was time to counter it.

Thus, Elizabeth was distracted when Mr Wickham walked up to their table and asked, "May I join you?"

Startled from the hissing scold she was issuing to a pouting Lydia, Elizabeth turned. Mr Darcy's accusations against this man were ringing in her ears when she opened her mouth to refuse as politely as possible, only to be superseded by Lydia. "Oh! Yes, sit next to me, Mr Wickham."

Elizabeth threw a sharp glare at her youngest sister, but Lydia took no notice, the entirety of her focus attuned to displaying herself to advantage for Mr Wickham's sake. She appeared embarrassingly bold with her chest thrust out and her lashes flapping suggestively. Elizabeth jabbed her sister in the side with the point of her elbow and Lydia's coquetry crumpled into petulance.

Mr Wickham flashed the younger Bennet girl a dashing smile and then turned his attention completely to the elder before taking his seat, not by Lydia, but by Elizabeth. He seemed to either not notice or to simply ignore all the signs that he was not welcomed there. "Miss Elizabeth, I am most enchanted to see you again. I have thought of you often since our meeting yesterday."

Despite her better knowledge of this man's proclivities, Elizabeth felt her cheeks tingle in response. Being reportedly despicable did not lessen any of Mr Wickham's physical charms, of which he had many. Of all the gentlemen she had ever been in company with, only Mr Darcy could arguably be considered more attractive than the gallant before her. With his blond hair styled in a carefully crafted wave and his vivid blue eyes twinkling mischievously in the warm candlelight, he was an Adonis amidst his peers. Had she not become privy to his more vicious propensities, Elizabeth feared that she might have been entirely taken in by this dangerously handsome officer.

Elizabeth muttered some kind of demurral to Mr Wickham's flattery and, knowing it was too late to alter the situation more to her liking, dropped her eyes to the spot where the dealer was piling cards up before her. In the back of her mind, she knew that this action, coupled with her persistent flush, must appear to Mr Wickham as a bashful reaction to his advances, but it could not be helped. Elizabeth would avoid engaging him in conversation if she could, wary of encouraging further flirtation. Mr Darcy would not like it—though why she should care about his opinion on the matter, Elizabeth chose not to consider too closely—and she would be a simpleton indeed if she allowed some silly fancy for Mr Wickham's pleasing countenance to place her in a position to be imposed upon.

Lydia was happy to draw Mr Wickham's notice to herself as soon as Elizabeth declaimed her share in it, which was a mixed blessing. Mr Wickham might be distracted from his target—and, considering Mr Darcy's rather obvious staring in the street the day before, Elizabeth was quite certain that a target was what she was at this juncture—but now Lydia was exposed to the snake's poisonous allure. There seemed quite a danger of the pair of them continuing on so, as Lydia was a most determined talker, but thankfully she soon grew too much interested in the game and her attention wandered to making bets and exclaiming after prizes.

This presented another opening for Mr Wickham to ply his charm to Elizabeth, who determinedly followed her youngest sister's example and focused on the game as much as possible. She responded politely to his enquiries regarding her health, that of her family, commentary about the neighbourhood and the damp weather of the morning, but Mr Wickham could draw nothing more than general opinions from Elizabeth. A certain stiffness in his air after some minutes at this pursuit convinced her that Mr Wickham was growing a mite frustrated at her lack of response to him and she was tempted to giggle at his expense, though she held it inside admirably.

Finally, Mr Wickham hit upon a subject which could not but wrestle her attention to him at last. "And how far is Netherfield to Meryton?"

Elizabeth felt unaccountably startled by this question, though it was the most natural thing in the world for Mr Wickham to reference the temporary dwelling of his only acquaintance outside of the militia in all of Hertfordshire. Additionally, it made sense that he would eventually lead them into a conversation about Mr Darcy, no doubt in an attempt to discredit him somehow. It had been naive of her to expect that Mr Wickham might give up so easily just because she had given him no encouragement thus far.

Affecting nonchalance, Elizabeth answered simply, "About two miles, sir."

"And," Mr Wickham hesitated, no doubt in a show of false anxiety adopted for the benefit of his audience, "how long has Mr Darcy been staying there?"

"About a month," said Elizabeth, hoping that this was the closure of the subject.

Mr Wickham, however, was not to be deterred. With a quick glance about the table to make sure that all were absorbed in playing, he elaborated. "He is a man of very large property in Derbyshire. A noble estate which brings in a clear ten thousand per annum. You could not have met with a person more capable of giving you certain information than myself; for I have been connected with his family in a particular manner from my infancy."

"Oh?" Elizabeth replied automatically, then flinched as she belatedly realised that she had given Mr Wickham an opening to carry on with whatever tale he intended to feed her.

"You may well be surprised," though she had never intimated any such thing, "at such an assertion, after seeing, as you probably might, the very cold manner of our meeting yesterday. Are you very much acquainted with Mr Darcy?"

There was considerable weight to Mr Wickham's question, and she could feel him watching her intently. Elizabeth shivered and pulled her wrap more tightly about herself as though someone had dropped ice down the back of her gown. "As much as I ever wish to be," she said with some asperity. "I have spent four days in the same house with him, and I think him very disagreeable."

There. Perhaps if Mr Wickham thinks I dislike Mr Darcy, he will desist in his defamation. Elizabeth pointedly looked down at her cards and pretended to be considering her next move.

Alas, he was far from finished. "I have no right to give *my* opinion..."

"And on and on he went, without any reference to the truth or the propriety of revealing such delicate, personal information on such a short acquaintance! I was really quite ashamed of him," Elizabeth complained, insensible of the loud, grating noise of her brush being pulled through her hair with greater than necessary force.

"And are you sure everything he said was false?" Jane asked, seated primly upon the edge of Elizabeth's bed with a tight, disconcerted expression across her lovely face. "Not that I think Mr Darcy capable of such depravity, but—oh, perhaps there has been some very great mistake and Mr Wickham did not mean to say such awful things."

Elizabeth abandoned her hairbrush to the surface of her dressing table and turned about to face Jane, her expression sympathetic. "I am afraid so, dearest, for I have had it from Mr Darcy himself that Mr Wickham is not a man to be trusted. Based on what Mr Wickham relayed to me tonight—and without prompting too!—I suspect that Mr Darcy was entirely correct. The sad fact of the matter is that Mr Wickham is a lying blackguard who wishes to cast aspersions for some form of petty revenge against Mr Darcy, and all for things which are the fault of Mr Wickham himself. I am sorry to distress you, but so it is."

Elizabeth then swore Jane to the strictest of confidences—"Of course, Lizzy, you know I would never speak a word of whatever you tell me in secret"—and related to her all the offences that Mr Darcy had laid at Mr Wickham's door. Jane attempted to suggest again that both men had been deceived, that interested people had perhaps misrepresented one to the other, creating an alienation between them with no actual fault on either side, but any defence of Mr Wickham's character was abandoned as Elizabeth revealed his greatest crime. Holding Jane's hand within her own to support her against the idea that so much wickedness could exist in the whole race of mankind, much less within the soul of a single man, Elizabeth told her about Mr Wickham's predatory attempt upon Miss Darcy and her fortune.

"It is difficult indeed—it is distressing—one does not know what to think!" cried Jane, squeezing Elizabeth's hand tightly.

Elizabeth squeezed back and gently soothed, "I beg your pardon, but one knows exactly what to think. Mr Wickham is a man lacking in honour, morality, and goodness, and aims to injure an innocent man for perceived injustices against himself. The only positive I can say about Mr Wickham is that he is clever, indeed. His falsehoods were so close to the actual truth that one could not help but believe him were they in ignorance of the flaws in his character. I very well might have been tricked by his tales of woe had Mr Darcy not enlightened me prior to hearing them. I would admire his gift for gab were it not so malevolently applied."

Jane shook her head, a few wispy strands of hair that were too short to be tied into her braid brushing against her pale cheeks, and begged Elizabeth not to disturb her further with Mr Wickham's perfidy. Elizabeth acquiesced immediately, weary herself of all thoughts of such a treacherous man.

Averting the subject to one more palatable, though still close enough to the same theme so as not to come from nowhere, Jane raised her golden head and asked, "And what are your thoughts on Mr Darcy? You seem inclined to defend him against Mr Wickham's assertions, despite your former dislike of him. Does this mean your opinion of him improved since...?"

Elizabeth bit her lip in consternation and considered her answer, for it was not a simple one to give. Her former prejudice against Mr Darcy had been so strong that it was difficult to overcome, especially in such a short amount of time. Was her good opinion of Mr Darcy truly lost forever?

No, I am not so implacable in my resentment as Mr Darcy once professed. Indeed, the petulance she had been feeling over the circumstances in which they found themselves was melting away. Were she forced to be honest with herself—and it seemed that she must be at last—she would admit that the situation was not Mr Darcy's fault, nor had he behaved in any way that was less than honourable throughout the whole. At most, she could blame him for not being careful enough riding his wild steed, but even then, he could not have expected a bird to fly up and startle his mount at an inopportune moment; it had been an accident.

Afterwards, he had stood by his unnaturally elicited proposal when he could have taken her up on her offer of pretending it had not occurred at all; Jane and Mr Bingley would surely not have spread rumours, and Mr Darcy could have escaped unshackled, even without Elizabeth's blessing. But he had come to her, reiterated his words of adoration, answered all of her concerns, warned her against the potential trespasses of Mr Wickham at great cost to his family's reputation, and acquiesced to all of her subsequent demands to keep his pursuit private, whenever possible. *It says much about Mr Darcy that he is honest and honourable even when no one is there to witness it.*

But what of Mr Darcy's abominable pride? Mr Wickham might be at least partially correct about him disdaining those beneath him in consequence—Elizabeth had seen something of this tendency herself—but if this assertion were entirely true, then it followed Mr Darcy would not consider himself in love with a lowly country girl such as herself. Nor would he proclaim an intimate friendship with the son of a tradesman, now that she thought of it. How many of her former assumptions could she set aside?

"Lizzy?"

Elizabeth startled, having nearly forgot that her sister was in the room with her as she navigated the labyrinth of her feelings for Mr Darcy. "Forgive me, Jane. I had not meant to neglect you."

Jane observed her with a mixture of patience and pity. "There is nothing to forgive. You merely looked a bit...lost, and I was concerned."

Elizabeth emitted a single, humourless laugh at Jane's apt description. "Lost, indeed. Lost and with no compass to guide me! I usually have much faith in my own observations, but I have apparently been so wrong about Mr Darcy and his intentions that they are of no use to me in this instance."

"Surely you have formed some opinion of Mr Darcy based on what you have recently learnt? I cannot believe you unmoved by his declarations, nor his subsequent persistence."

"I admit that he was not what I had thought at first, but beyond that...it is all so much to consider, Jane. Even if he is not the awful man that Mr Wickham claims he is, I cannot say if I like Mr Darcy or not. I know him so little, and his first impression was so poor that his proposals, both of them, are as confusing to me now as they were when he first delivered them. Contrary to Mr Wickham, I know not what to think of Mr Darcy."

It was Jane's turn to soothe Elizabeth, and she pulled her younger sister into an affectionate embrace. A long moment later, after they had indulged in the comforting warmth of one another, Jane pulled back and offered her advice. "I think, dearest, that this is a matter you must sleep on. Everything will be clearer in the morning."

Elizabeth darted her eyes to the window where rain was, once again, lashing against the pane, and wind swirled and whistled beyond in the darkness. She laughed at Jane's unintentional jest. "Clearer than the weather, I hope. Though, I must admit, nature is reflecting my current state of mind very closely."

"Oh, Lizzy." Jane chuckled and hugged her sister again before standing. "Just promise me that you will be fair to Mr Darcy. He truly cares for you, I think, and it says much for his taste and good sense that he should feel so."

"I believe I must, for there is nothing else to be done," replied Elizabeth, smiling. "However," she nodded towards the weather-beaten window, "if the rain does not let up soon, I suspect that the point will be moot. He cannot come a-courting in such weather. Why, his boots would be six inches deep in mud!"

Both sisters laughed at this reference to Elizabeth's ruined petticoats and bid each other a final farewell for the night. Just as she was about to exit, Jane paused at the threshold of Elizabeth's room and turned back for a parting remark. It was said with equal measures of seriousness and affection. "I would not be surprised, Lizzy, if Mr Darcy were to brave six inches, or more, of mud just to see you again. Sleep well."

NINE

"You cannot be serious."

Darcy did not bother to lift his glare from the sodden landscape outside before he replied to Bingley's incredulity. "I am afraid so. It was all I could do to convince Elizabeth to consider my proposal rather than outright rejecting it. It seems that I was rather mistaken as to her opinion of me."

"I should say so," said Bingley, snorting. When Darcy turned halfway round to scowl at his friend, his grievances against the poor weather forgotten momentarily, Bingley shrank down in his chair and begged his pardon in a mumbling tone. "I had not thought her especially enamoured of you while she stayed with us, but I still would not have guessed that she would refuse such an eligible offer. Perhaps there has been some mistake?"

Darcy rolled his eyes and followed the direction of their arc to face the window again, putting Bingley's empty library shelves to his back. The last time he had been in this room, searching for a reprieve from temptation, only to be drawn closer to its maw instead, Elizabeth had been curled up in the same chair where Bingley now sat, reading a book. He had then thought her absentminded fidgeting with her curls to be designed as an enticement, her studied neglect of his presence some coy game, but she had truly been ambivalent. Perhaps even annoyed that he had intruded upon her solitude, no matter how relaxed she had seemed with her feet tucked beneath her and her head rested leisurely against the chair back. Far from desiring his attentions, Elizabeth had been blind to them. Though not nearly as blind as he had been regarding her interest.

"There have been some...misunderstandings," Darcy admitted, at length, to Bingley, who had fallen silent in anticipation of a reply to his last question. "Do you recall my behaviour at the assembly last month?"

"You were sullen and irritable as you usually are when dancing is the entertainment of the evening. Why?"

Darcy grimaced at the dim apparition of himself reflected in the windowpane, though he could hardly dispute Bingley's description. Elizabeth had said much the same and, besides, it was a truth he had accepted long before this stint into Hertfordshire. "It turns out that I insulted her without meaning to. Something about not being 'tolerable enough' to dance with, or some such. I do not recall the exact wording, but I can assure you that she does."

"No! Wait—I remember now. I was trying to encourage you to dance and—oh, Darcy, my most sincere apologies. I knew you were not inclined, and I provoked you into saying something unkind. I had not realised that Miss Elizabeth overheard us."

Darcy sighed, his breath fogging up the glass level with his face. "No need to apologise, my friend. You might have provoked me to it, but I knew better than to say something so incendiary in a public place. All the blame rests with me. I was, at least, able to make an apology and explain myself to Elizabeth, though I am unsure how effective it was. That slight alone is perhaps enough for her to dismiss me permanently. I had not behaved as a gentleman ought, and she was correct to take umbrage with me." Unclasping his hands from behind his back,

Darcy lifted one to rub at his eyes with a thumb and forefinger. His anxiety over Elizabeth's ultimate answer was beginning to fatigue him.

"I am sure that Miss Elizabeth will find it in her heart to forgive you," replied Bingley, his voice full of the sort of sunny optimism that Darcy found difficult to engender in himself. He was more inclined to brood when a situation was not to his liking, though it occasionally hampered his productivity. Today, it was merely the rain that did so, and Darcy was frustrated with it. "I am sure her resentment is not as implacable as yours."

Darcy lowered his hand, blinking away the black spots swimming before his vision, and then linked it with the other once more at his lower back. "Let us hope not."

"And there is still hope! Miss Elizabeth might very well accept you in the end, especially if you take steps to prove yourself in the meantime. With a little effort, she will come to see you as the decent, honourable fellow that you are."

"She will not today, that much is certain." Darcy nodded his head towards the window where the rolling hills and fields were being assaulted with precipitation. At least the rain had settled into more of a drizzle, though the ground would still be muddy and the day exceptionally cold—not conducive to paying visits upon one's neighbours at all.

Darcy felt a hearty slap upon his shoulder and jerked forwards slightly in the wake of the unexpected force. When Bingley spoke again, his voice was much closer. "The sun will come out again tomorrow, old chap. In the meantime, how about a toddy and a round of billiards?"

"'Tis better than standing here grousing at the clouds, I suppose. Lead the way, man."

Much as Elizabeth had predicted, Mr Darcy's intentions to visit had been stymied by the persistent rain and there was no sign of him at all on Thursday, same as Wednesday. More surprising was her disappointment that she had been right. Perhaps she had been counting on a chance to warn Mr Darcy about the perfidy of Mr Wickham, spouted so heedlessly in the midst of her aunt's card party the night before, or perhaps she was weary of being trapped inside the house after so many hours already of indoor activity. Then again, it could very well be that she was simply tired of the company which was trapped inside Longbourn with her.

"Cousin Elizabeth." Mr Collins's voice drew Elizabeth's gaze, most reluctantly, away from the rain-blurred landscape beyond the window of the family sitting room, and she forced herself to fix it upon his odious face instead. He was standing before her—hovering, more like, as if he were a gigantic, sweaty bat—and simpering. "Might I say that you are looking especially lovely on this gloomy day? You are truly a vibrant bloom against the grey sky."

As this praise was so prettily worded, Elizabeth suspected that it must be an example of one of those little elegant compliments which had been the effort of his previous study. Since it had been delivered so matter-of-factly, with none of the tenderness expected of a lover, Elizabeth decided that Mr Collins did, indeed, flatter himself if he thought he had successfully managed an air of spontaneity. Her lips threatened to twitch themselves into an inappropriate smirk at her cousin's expense, so she pursed them tightly together in a bid to make them behave. Mr Bennet would be much amused himself when she shared this anecdote with him later.

Once she had collected herself enough to reply with equanimity, she thanked him with politeness, if not warmth, and then picked up her previously abandoned book from her lap and opened it to a random page. Pretending to read, however, was not enough to dissuade her persistent suitor, and he took a seat so close to her as to encourage their knees to touch. Much irritated with this presumption, Elizabeth shifted further away from Mr Collins under the pretence of resettling herself. She had no choice but to give him her attention, but she would not stand for an imposition upon her person.

Mr Collins, either ignorant of his offence or eager to press his luck in spite of it, inched closer until his feet mingled with hers. Elizabeth moved again, prepared to make an excuse and scurry away entirely should he make yet another attempt, but thankfully he was now caught up in his own speech—"Lady Catherine proclaims that rain is most beneficial to us all, yes indeed. Why, it encourages plants to grow, keeps our bodies of water refreshed and..."—and remained in place.

Elizabeth could not help but remember a similar situation with Mr Darcy the last time she had seen him, and the contrast of her feelings then to now; she had been unsettled by the proximity, but not repulsed. Mr Darcy smelled better, for starters, and he had not followed when she had retreated. Comparatively, Mr Collins was a loathsome creature.

And this same said comparison did not end at gentlemanly comportment over a lady's personal space, either. Elizabeth did not like to consider herself shallow, but anyone with fully functioning vision would readily admit that Mr Darcy was the handsomer of the two. Still, Mr Collins could not help that he was unattractive to the eye, having no say in the way the Almighty had arranged his features and sculpted his form, and so Elizabeth did not hold this unduly against him. It was not his fault that his neck was fat, his stomach paunchy and his legs strangely too skinny; he looked like an overstuffed stork rather than a bat, now that she considered him more closely.

Mr Darcy was about as handsome as any man dared to be with his tall, muscular frame, strikingly angular features, and dark, curly hair that was just wild enough to be dashing. And those staring, probing eyes were imbued with an electrical intensity which could easily intimidate if their object were not inclined towards courage. Elizabeth had felt them fixed upon her frequently enough that she was intimately acquainted with their shape, their colour, and their movements, all of which followed her. She had genuinely thought that he had looked at her with disdain, but knowing that the converse was true made her feel...

Suddenly warm and flustered, Elizabeth dismissed all thoughts about Mr Darcy's eyes and how they prickled at her skin, and resumed her consideration of Mr Collins instead. It was more his personality of moronic servility which was truly against the parson. If he was capable of discussing any topic other than Lady Catherine de Bourgh, it would be a welcome change. Currently, he was expounding upon the finer qualities of her ladyship's opinions on the weather, and once more flattering himself that he was deserving of the grand dame's attentions at the same time.

Mr Darcy, she recalled, had had much to say on a variety of different subjects while she had still been at Netherfield tending Jane. Not all of them had been to her liking at the time—indeed, she had considered him boorish and haughty—but there had been greater variety to be discussed in their conversations, such as they were, and he had held her interest.

Looking back on what they had said to one another, Elizabeth was inclined to re-examine some of what had passed between them, much as she had his unwavering gaze. Mr Darcy's censure of unaccomplished ladies, for instance, might be open to greater interpretation than she had first allowed; it had been Miss Bingley who had crafted the long list of the skills a female must cultivate to achieve the title, and Mr Darcy had merely added his suggestion of improving her mind with extensive reading. Had he truly been agreeing with Miss Bingley's assessment, or slyly paying Elizabeth, who had recently settled herself with a book, a compliment? Her memory was imperfect, so she could not be sure, but Elizabeth acknowledged that the latter might be the case. He might have even been making a subtle jab at Miss Bingley's expense as the lady was, as revealed by her mean-spirited tease of Elizabeth's habits, not a great reader herself. Either scenario was possible, and both could very well be true.

Besides that one, there were other conversations which

required further consideration from hindsight. She had thought him to be vindictively teasing her at the time, but Elizabeth now recalled with a flush that he had asked her to dance with him one lazy evening. She had rebuffed him with a sparkling quip after he had asked a second time and then thought no more about it afterward. Now, of course, Elizabeth wondered if the invitation had been genuine.

With even greater heat infusing her cheeks, she further recalled Miss Bingley's ploy on a different evening to draw Mr Darcy's attention to herself by walking about the room, one which only succeeded after she had enjoined Elizabeth to do likewise. When pressed by Miss Bingley, Mr Darcy had declined to rise from his seat and proclaimed—*Oh!* Once Elizabeth could view Mr Darcy's words and behaviours through the lens of infatuation, so many strange encounters with him became clearer. He was absolutely in the right when he had accused her of wilfully misunderstanding him.

Elizabeth jumped when another touch by Mr Collins, this one from the tips of his spindly fingers to the back of her hand, jolted her thoughts back to the present. Seeming mightily pleased with himself for causing such a reaction, Mr Collins grinned unnervingly. "Forgive me, Cousin, for startling you. You look rather flushed. Shall we take a turn about the room together? Lady Catherine says—"

Elizabeth, discomposed further by the suggestion which mirrored Miss Bingley's from a week previously, leapt to her feet and dismissed herself with a hasty apology and fled the room.

"Are you well, dearest?" Jane's voice followed immediately on the heels of a soft knock upon the stillroom door, a warning that Elizabeth's privacy was about to be gently invaded.

Elizabeth, not minding the intrusion of her sister in the slightest, looked up and offered Jane a warbling smile. "Very well, indeed. I was just feeling a little hot, is all. We are all so crowded together in the parlour."

Jane came further into the room to where Elizabeth sat upon a stool and peered at her younger sister more closely, the curve of her lips arched downwards and her eyes narrowed as she conducted her inspection. Elizabeth's cheeks were already suffused with an uncomfortable amount of heat, and so she supposed that any increase in her colour would go unnoticed, but she could not help squirming under the scrutiny. Sometimes she almost suspected that Jane could read her mind, as her eldest sister was most astute about the feelings of others, and especially those she knew well. Elizabeth, closest to her in both age and companionship, could rarely hide anything from her.

"Tell me your troubles, Lizzy," insisted Jane as she settled herself upon the stool closest to Elizabeth. Though generally docile and always gentle, Jane was firm where she felt herself to be right or when she suspected that something was amiss with one of her loved ones.

Knowing the futility of resisting Jane's well-meaning entreaties, Elizabeth sighed and pressed her hands to her cheeks. The coolness of her palms soothed the burn of barely understood feelings somewhat. "I simply could not stand Mr Collins's attentions another minute. He insists on sitting too close and touching me, which I do not like at all. I know he was not born a gentleman, but surely any man can tell where his overtures are not wanted!"

"Mr Darcy could not."

Elizabeth dropped her gaze and her hands simultaneously, allowing her fingers to nervously fiddle with one another in her lap. "No, he could not, but I was unaware of his interest in me until he proposed. I might have done more to dissuade him had I known. He is not as stupid as Mr Collins and likely would have desisted had I hinted that his attentions were unpleasant to me."

Jane's hand appeared and covered both of Elizabeth's own,

encouraging the latter to look up where the former regarded her with sympathy. "Are his attentions still unpleasant to you?"

"I..." Elizabeth meant to launch into a denial of any positive feelings for Mr Darcy, or at least any positive enough to lead to acceptance of his hand, but found she could not. Her mouth snapped shut with a clatter of teeth colliding against one another.

"It seems," Jane continued, her tone patient and everything compassionate, "by what you have just said, that you are willing to concede that Mr Darcy is an honourable sort of gentleman who would not trespass where he is not wanted. Since you are delaying your ultimate response and allowing him to court you more properly, I wonder if perhaps you are not so decided against him as you once avowed. I have never known you to reconsider something of such import without acknowledging first that you were somehow in the wrong. And I have not forgotten how hotly you defended him against Mr Wickham's defamation last night, either."

"I...I admit that I was wrong, somewhat, about Mr Darcy," replied Elizabeth after taking some moments to collect her thoughts together into coherence. "He is still haughty and rude at times, but not so cold hearted as I had once thought."

One corner of Jane's mouth quirked upwards, and Elizabeth was tempted to call it a smirk. It certainly reminded her strongly of their father. "A fine concession. Yes, a man confessing his ardent love cannot be considered cold hearted, I think, especially to the object of his affections."

Elizabeth's blush, which had cooled somewhat, renewed itself in a flash of prickly heat. "I thought we were discussing Mr Collins?"

"I think Mr Collins is not at the heart of your discomposure, Lizzy," Jane countered. "If he is making you uncomfortable, ask Papa to have a talk with him. Perhaps he is unaware that his behaviour is causing you distress. A simple solution, one I am sure you have already considered. Mr Darcy, on the other hand, is a more complex issue, and you have been attempting to divert all discussion of him since I entered this room."

Elizabeth shook her hands free of Jane's and hopped down from her stool so that she could pace the room. After a circuit and a half round the long wooden table upon which she and her sisters performed their work, she turned back to Jane. "There is nothing about Mr Darcy to discuss."

"No?" One of Jane's brows lifted higher upon her forehead, again hearkening a comparison to Mr Bennet. "Then why are you so agitated?"

"Because...because..." Elizabeth faltered in her answer and resumed her steps. "Because I am stuck in the limbo of considering a proposal which I refused twice, and Mama is encouraging the match and...and..."

Jane got off her stool as well and rounded the table in the opposite direction as Elizabeth, meeting her younger sister when their paths collided. Placing both hands upon Elizabeth's shoulders, she halted them both. "Lizzy, Lizzy...all is well, there is nothing to fear." After Elizabeth had calmed herself somewhat, Jane continued, "No one will force you to make any decision that you do not desire, and I know that you can easily dismiss Mama's matchmaking if you wish to. I think you are in such a state because, contrary to what you tell yourself, you are undecided about Mr Darcy. I think you would be much more at ease if you knew which answer you wanted to give. And Mr Collins, perhaps, reminds you that there is another man out there seeking your favour, which makes you nervous. Is that not the case?"

Elizabeth giggled madly at the thought. "Nervous! No, say I am anything but that. I should hate to carry smelling salts about with me for fear of fainting at any moment."

Jane's mouth tightened with disapproval at the jest at their mother's expense, but Elizabeth could see one of her cheeks twitching as if she, too, longed to laugh. "That is unkind."

"But so very true."

"Oh, Lizzy..."

Laughing at herself settled Elizabeth somewhat, and the jittery palpitations of her conflicted heart eased. A deep inhale of breath through her nose and an exhale from her mouth helped further. With more composure, she said to Jane, "I cannot say if you are right or wrong in this instance, but I will admit to being unsure of what answer I should give Mr Darcy. If I ultimately reject him, I must live the rest of my life knowing that I have hurt a man who, based on my new information of his character, is honourable and good. If I accept him, I cannot say for sure whether he will not later come to resent me for not being well dowered or drowning in useful connexions. I should hate to end up like Mama and Papa."

"All you can do for now is try to get to know Mr Darcy better, as you already promised. You will know what to say to him when the time comes, I am sure of it."

Elizabeth wrinkled her nose and cast an impatient glare at the mist-frosted window at the end of the room. "If the weather does not let up soon, we may not have much of a chance of anything. I cannot make my decision based on what I currently know, and Mr Darcy certainly cannot come courting in a deluge. How am I supposed to get to know him better, give him a chance to reveal his character to me, if we cannot even be in one another's presence?"

"As I said to you last night, I think Mr Darcy will not let a little thing like poor weather keep him from visiting. If he loves you as he says he does—and I suspect that he has even understated his feelings somewhat—he will come."

Elizabeth sighed. "And if he does not, then I suppose I know my answer."

TEN

Darcy glared out at the spitting rain, his jaw tight with frustration, as he cursed the dismal weather which still kept him trapped at Netherfield when he should be attending Elizabeth. He had not been able to visit Longbourn yesterday, or the day before, and he was growing increasingly impatient to see her. He had practically begged her for leave to court her properly, and her acquiescence had been hard won; being stymied by something so banal as the weather was intolerable. At this rate, he would be unable to make his case at all before she arrived for the ball on Tuesday, and he did not doubt that her answer would be a resounding no as a result. He was much tempted to brave the wet and dirt any way, no matter how many inches deep in mud his attire became. An image of Elizabeth with dirty petticoats and flushed cheeks, her eyes brightened by exercise, flashed into his mind, and he smiled indulgently.

"Come away from the window and have some tea, Mr Darcy," whined the nasally tones of Miss Bingley from somewhere behind him. "You would not wish to take a chill!"

Darcy squeezed his eyes shut and prayed silently for patience before turning about. In the centre of the drawing room, the collection of Bingleys and Hursts were gathered in a semi-circle near the fire, a tea tray set before them on a low table. Miss Bingley, as hostess, was pouring for the party and parcelling out cups to her family with as much studied elegance as she could muster. He had no inclination to join them, especially since Miss Bingley always seemed to get his beverage wrong, but knew it would be impolite to neglect the others in the room with him. Elizabeth had chastised him for as much during the more acrimonious portions of his proposal. *Well, she had been complaining of how I treat her friends and neighbours, but her advice still applies more generally. I could be more present in company.*

With that wearying thought in mind, Darcy removed himself from the window and walked across the room to where the others had gathered themselves and accepted his cup of tea from Miss Bingley, which was delivered to him with a flourish and a coquettish simper. He took a sip and tamped down a grimace; much too sweet.

Miss Bingley, seated upon a fashionable and uncomfortable looking sofa, patted the stiff cushion next to herself as an encouragement for him to sit beside her. Darcy pretended not to see and took the chair adjacent to Bingley, who was smirking beyond the rim of his teacup.

Undeterred, Miss Bingley pivoted towards Darcy and rattled on, as some young ladies do, with false sympathy. "It is such a relief to see you looking so well, Mr Darcy. I was just saying to everyone how grateful we all are for the speed of your recovery. Was I not, Louisa?"

Mrs Hurst, caught somewhat by surprise at her sister's sudden comment, swallowed a gulp of tea which seemed to pain her. When she replied, her voice was rasped slightly. "Yes, indeed. We were all most concerned."

Miss Bingley took back the reins of the conversation once her sister had pointlessly agreed with her. "I was never more frightened than when I heard you had fallen from your horse! I was so overcome that I fainted dead away."

But not until she had gathered herself an audience, according to Bingley. The pretence of Miss Bingley's histrionics had been something of a joke between the two friends who doubted her sincerity upon all occasions. In this case, acting the role of distressed lover had been meant to fool Darcy into thinking she had deeper feelings for him than avarice, and she had been playing this same card since then. It was growing most tiresome, especially since Darcy could not escape her machinations by leaving the house. Miss Bingley made Darcy wish even more fervently for Elizabeth's company.

Truly, there was no comparison between the two women. Or none that would be flattering to Miss Bingley, at least. Though he had mistaken Elizabeth's sportive manner for flirting—and how humbling it was to realise that he had been taken in by his own wishful thinking—there was still no dispute that she was an intelligent, witty lady who was a pleasure to converse with. Miss Bingley might have her share of cleverness, but it was always wielded like a blade, cutting and slicing at those unfortunate enough to be on the sharp end of her disdain. Elizabeth used her powers more for kindness and setting others at ease. Even when she chose to be disparaging, she did so in a way which was so subtle that the object of her ire was often unaware of it—Darcy certainly had not recognised her barbs for what they were, though it seemed obvious to him now that she had merely tolerated his presence all this time.

Physically, Miss Bingley was not a chore to look at, but neither was she his preferred image of feminine beauty. She was tall, slender, and fair in both hair and skin tone, as well as fashionably attired on all occasions. Her face was a little thin for his tastes, but in no way hideous, though it would have been greatly improved by a more natural expression than the haughty airs that she had adopted. She would be some men's concept of perfection.

Elizabeth, by contrast, was all that was lovely to Darcy's eye. She was shorter than Miss Bingley by a significant amount, the top of her head coming up only an inch or so above Darcy's shoulder, and her body was much more...well, without descending into any lewd descriptions, Darcy would concede that Elizabeth was more plump in figure than Miss Bingley, though still light and pleasing. Her cheeks were round and plush, her skin browned lightly from her daily walks, and the epitome of natural beauty. Her expressions were delightfully arch when she was feeling playful, warm and soft when her affection was engaged, and full of enticing fire when riled, and it was a pleasure for Darcy to watch her features shift into these different formulations. He had not always been successful at reading her, but that only made him wish to watch her more closely to suss out more detail. With his newly evolved knowledge of her heart, no matter how painful, he might be more successful at detecting the nuances he had previously missed which indicated her true thoughts on a subject. It would be a fascinating project—if she would allow him to continue in her presence, that was. Darcy did not relish the thought of worshiping her from afar or, worse, in his memory alone.

"Mr Darcy?"

Darcy started and looked up from the depths of his teacup, abashed that he had, once again, fallen into his unsociable habits. He cleared his throat, apologised, and prompted, "I was not attending. Could you please repeat what you were saying?"

Miss Bingley simpered at him and teased him for wool-gathering before reiterating, "I was just remarking on how excellent it is to have you in good health again. It was really quite shocking to see you so unwell."

"Mm."

"I thought for one terrifying moment that you were no longer for this world," Miss Bingley continued, a hand pressed daintily to her slight bosom as if soothing herself, "or that you would become permanently addled. Promise me that you will take greater care in the future, sir, so that I shall not worry so again!"

Darcy would promise no such thing to Miss Bingley, as such would give her the wrong impression of her role in his life, but he muttered his thanks for her concern in vague terms. "I appreciate your sentiments, Miss Bingley, but I cannot say that I will never find myself in such straights again. I shall not give up riding, as to do so would be impractical, nor can I swear that I will not ever be distracted enough to be unseated again. Such are the vagaries of fate."

Miss Bingley resumed fussing over Darcy, flattering and scolding him by turns with teasing concern, until her brother bid her cease. "Enough, Caroline. It was an accident. It could have happened to anyone here, including you. We must simply count ourselves fortunate that Miss Elizabeth's quick thinking mitigated the damage done and leave it at that."

Miss Bingley straightened her back and sat taller upon her sofa cushion, her face drawn into a haughty scowl. "I suppose I must concede that Miss Eliza did well to raise the alarm, but really, Charles, anyone could have done the same. She hardly deserves a medal and, if anything, dear Jane was the hero of the hour in bringing all the men to Mr Darcy's aid."

Darcy's teeth squeaked against one another as he clenched them tight. Doing so prevented an angry outburst at his hostess, though he longed to let it loose. Who was Miss Bingley to denigrate Elizabeth? Even had she not been the daughter of a tradesman, and thus lower than Elizabeth, her cruel manner, impolitic jibes, and her preference for fashion above function would have made her ineligible as Darcy's bride. She had twenty thousand pounds to her name, but money was the least important factor in selecting a wife; money he had and did not need more of. He had such wealth that he could not possibly spend it all even in ten lifetimes. He needed something more than that, something which Elizabeth had in spades: integrity, honour, intelligence, and honesty. That silly list Miss Bingley had boasted as the qualities of a truly accomplished woman were all superficial nothings compared to what Elizabeth had to offer. He had not seen it at first, admittedly, but knowing that Elizabeth would not accept him for his fortune alone had opened his eyes to what was truly desirable in a spouse.

"I will not dispute that Miss Bennet performed her part

admirably," Bingley replied to his sister when Darcy remained stonily silent, pressing his lips together into a light frown. His cup clattered into its saucer with a touch more force than necessary as he pressed his point. "However, it was Miss Elizabeth who climbed over a hedge to tend to Darcy herself while she waited for help to arrive. In my opinion—and I am sure Darcy feels the same—Miss Elizabeth behaved with much bravery and concern for her fellow man. I cannot say whether or not she saved Darcy's life, precisely, but I have no doubt that he would have been in much danger had she not taken charge of the situation as she did. We must all be very thankful that it was Miss Elizabeth," here Bingley glared at his scoffing younger sister as if to imply that her presence would have not been nearly as helpful, "who witnessed the accident. Truly, it was the work of the divine that she was at the right place at the right time to assist."

Darcy was unsure whether or not Elizabeth had actually saved his life as Bingley had intimated, but it was certainly possible that she had. Had his fall not been witnessed, or had she frozen and dissolved into the same hysterics so fashionably mimicked by Miss Bingley, he might have been in severe trouble. Would anyone have spotted him buried in the tall grass before he expired, either from blood loss or the cold? Darcy was lucky, indeed, that Elizabeth was a hardy country weed and not some wilting hot house flower like Miss Bingley.

Sniffing, Miss Bingley countered, "I suppose all that traipsing about the countryside has made Miss Eliza Bennet into the type of lady who thinks nothing of taking so much manly work upon herself, no matter how undignified the escapade. It must have been nothing for her to scurry over the hedge to the rescue. Why, I am only surprised that she did not throw Mr Darcy over her shoulder and carry him back up to the house herself like some mule!" She tittered at her mean-spirited jest, and her sister joined in.

"Yes, I greatly admired her bravery," Darcy interjected, his temper finally overriding his control. He set down his cup and saucer upon the table with a clatter and turned the heat of his most disapproving glare upon the so-called ladies disparaging the great service his beloved Elizabeth had done for him. Miss Bingley and Mrs Hurst ceased their laughter, startled either by Darcy's tone or his abuse of their dishes. "It is why I proposed to her forthwith. If you will excuse me."

Darcy stood, bowed sharply, and stalked from the room, those he left behind palpably silent. Rain or no rain, he was going to call for his carriage and make for Longbourn; he could not stand the company at Netherfield another moment.

On Friday, much to Elizabeth's continuing annoyance, she awoke to yet more rain. Upon first renouncing her covers for the chill of her bedchamber, Elizabeth had scampered over to the window to peer outside only to be dismayed by the rivulets of water continuing to cascade down the glass on the other side. Vexed, she threw herself back upon her mattress, buried herself beneath her quilt and grumbled complaints into her pillow.

An hour or so after that, Elizabeth had reluctantly risen again and dressed for another day indoors. She had few expectations of pleasure in the morning and afternoon ahead, and so threw on one of her oldest and least flattering day gowns, the half-hearted aspiration of tempering Mr Collins's admiration floating about in her apathetic mind. Considering her cousin's continued ignorance of her intolerance for him, Elizabeth did not pin many such hopes upon the threadbare, mustard-coloured dress, but it was better than nothing, she supposed.

After breaking their fast, nothing was to be done by the ladies except to adjourn to the morning parlour as they had done for the past two days and take up their individual indoor pursuits. Jane worked on a complicated piece of embroidery which Elizabeth could never have attempted, Mary copied out extracts from a large tome of sermons, Kitty and Lydia squabbled over a partially trimmed bonnet and Mrs Bennet alternately lamented how dull everything was and scolded her youngest daughters for disturbing the peace. It was a homey cacophony of feminine activity and would have been comforting had Elizabeth not been subjected to it unceasingly for so many days together. Some variety was in order.

To distance herself as far from her family as possible and to give herself an activity with some measure of intellectual challenge, Elizabeth had seated herself at the writing desk with a small stack of letters which required a response. She had no sooner unfolded one to refresh her memory of its contents when she was interrupted by the arrival of their odious house guest.

Mr Collins entered the room with the pompous air of owning it and all else he surveyed. Elizabeth had known that her reprieve would be short lived, but she had hoped that their cousin might linger above stairs in his chambers a bit longer and leave his long-suffering relations to themselves. They were fortunate, Elizabeth supposed as she dropped her letter heavily into her lap, that Mr Collins apparently believed in sleeping late as much as filling his stomach; it gave them an hour or two daily without his looming presence.

After sweeping his eyes over the room and nodding at each of his cousins in turn, as if he were the Prince Regent bestowing favour upon his subjects, Mr Collins greeted them in the style to which they were accustomed from him. "Good morning, Cousins! You all look charming this fair morning, seated so elegantly about the room with your domestic pursuits. Why, Lady Catherine herself promotes elegant accomplishment in ladies, considering it their duty to care for their homes and families..."

Once he had summed up his blathering speech, the Bennet ladies each returned to her chosen 'elegant accomplishment' and proceeded to ignore Mr Collins as best as they could manage. To Elizabeth's great misfortune, though not her surprise, her loathsome cousin then bent his steps in her direction with the obvious intent of settling in next to her for the duration of this most tedious morning. He could not have done so in a more disruptive way, which made his presence all the more irksome. Not only was he again babbling endlessly about something or other—a topic which undoubtedly led back to his patroness—but the legs of his chair squealed unpleasantly against the floorboards as he dragged it nearer to his 'dear Cousin Elizabeth'. The noise drew scowls from about the room and thundered within Elizabeth's ears, causing her to wince.

"I see you are reading your letters, Cousin," he noted once he had slumped gracelessly into his commandeered seat. He maintained a more proper distance today, at least, and she could be grateful to her father for that. Mr Bennet's post-dinner chat with him the evening before had perhaps made something of an impact.

Elizabeth closed her eyes a moment, allowing her impatience to subside, before she folded her correspondence closed. "Yes, I was about to write to my aunt Gardiner in London." She wished to tell him to leave her to it in privacy but was not yet irritable enough to be rude. When it came to that point, it would be better to escape up to her room for a time instead.

"Ah, yes, your relations on your mother's side. I have heard of them. Perhaps someday soon I will have the right to correspond with them myself...but then nothing has been settled. Yet." Mr Collins beamed at her and reached out his hand as if to touch her knee, but then withdrew it quickly as if she had smacked it away. Mr Bennet's warning must have been fresh in his mind for him to beat such a hasty retreat, but Elizabeth could see from his unapologetic expression that he was liable to forget at any moment and take as many liberties as he could get away with. If only she could address the matter herself! She would make sure that Mr Collins was not tempted to try his luck again. "Might I say you look especially becoming today?"

In relation to his presumption of adopting her mother's relations as his own, Elizabeth did not bother to reply, suspecting that he would not be dissuaded even if she did. Nor did she acknowledge his misplaced compliment; clearly, a man so wilfully blinded by his own ambitions would not be dissuaded by an ugly yellow gown. Instead, she veered them onto another subject. “Have you written to her ladyship often since you have been away?”

As she had expected, Mr Collins then launched into a lengthy explanation of what he had written, the length of his letters, the quality of his penmanship, how much he disliked mending his pen, unnecessarily complimented her on the finely whittled point of her pen, what sorts of subjects he was intending to canvas in his upcoming sermons—subject to her ladyship’s approval, of course—and so on without cessation. Lady Catherine’s advice was sprinkled into his monologue liberally, as was Mr Collins’s sycophantic veneration of the grand dame.

Elizabeth felt comfortable only half-listening to her cousin, as he was unlikely to say anything even slightly interesting or worth while, though she did lament that she could not pursue another activity whilst he carried on. For whatever reason, it was not acceptable to fight rudeness with yet more rudeness and so Elizabeth was trapped giving all the politeness between them and receiving none of it. She nodded along occasionally as his speech lengthened, and disappeared into the depths of her thoughts where even Mr Collins could not reach her.

There, Elizabeth found the dashing figure of Mr Darcy lurking. He was staring at her with that sparking intensity she had become familiar with and looking every bit as handsome as his real-life counterpart. He stood perfectly still, allowing Elizabeth a thorough perusal of his person, and patiently allowed her to consider him with all his flaws and merits. Unfortunately, he remained as much an enigma as before, since all her newly acquired information regarding him was becoming as threadbare as her dress. No matter how long she pondered, Elizabeth was still no closer to knowing her mind about Mr Darcy.

Elizabeth startled when, of all things, there was a knock at the door. As she refocused her attention outward, she noticed that everyone else in the parlour was similarly taken aback by the unmistakable sounds of the front door opening, murmured voices in the vestibule, and footsteps treading the short length of the hall in their direction. Almost in unison, the Bennet ladies rushed to hide their pursuits and straightened themselves to greet the first non-resident of Longbourn that they had seen since Wednesday night.

Scant seconds after Elizabeth had tucked her letters securely into the drawer of the writing desk and resettled herself demurely into her chair, the door to the parlour opened, and Hill stepped inside, a sodden gentleman nipping closely at her heels.

Hill announced, "Mr Darcy."

ELEVEN

Everyone else in the room rose a beat before the stunned Elizabeth and so her curtsey was somewhat unbalanced in her scramble to aright herself. Mr Darcy's bow, by contrast, was delivered with quick precision and stoic formality.

"Oh! Mr Darcy, how good it is to see a friendly face after so much time cooped up indoors. But, dear me, you are soaking wet!" Mrs Bennet crowed, tempering her tone only at the last into one of simpering concern.

Indeed, Mrs Bennet was not exaggerating when she proclaimed Mr Darcy soaking wet. He stood just inside the threshold with his hair plastered to his face, his clothes moulded almost indecently to his body and steadily dripping water onto the floor about his feet. He had already gathered quite a puddle in the seconds he had been standing in that spot. Elizabeth flicked her eyes to the window, half expecting to see his wild black steed loitering in the drive, but through the heavy deluge she spotted a black carriage parked where she had thought his stallion would be. So wet only dashing from his equipage into the house? Elizabeth's lips bent in a smirk as she pondered whether the plagues of Egypt were upon them.

When she turned her attention back to the dripping Mr

Darcy, she found herself the object of the intense gaze she had only recently been considering within her imagination. His eyes fairly crackled with feeling, with purpose, and she felt the hairs upon her neck raise and a tingle race down the vertebrae of her spine.

In the background of this silent but heated moment between them, Mrs Bennet railed on about seeing to Mr Darcy's comfort. "Do sit by the fire, Mr Darcy—just there, yes. Lizzy, come here and keep Mr Darcy company while I call for tea. Hill!"

Before Elizabeth could move even a finger to follow her mother's directions, she found herself tugged by the wrist and corralled by Mrs Bennet across the room where a fire was blazing in the grate. Belatedly recalling the horrid nature of her dress, Elizabeth opened her mouth to protest that she should go upstairs and change into something less mortifying than an old, patched, mustard-coloured frock, but had no time before it was too late to do anything about it. Without any sort of hesitation or preamble, Elizabeth was thrust into one of the two armchairs which sat facing each other before the hearth, Mr Darcy seated across from her looking half-drowned and quite cheerful about it.

"Hill, do fetch a blanket and perhaps a change of clothes for Mr Darcy," said Mrs Bennet, an absolute flurry of movement and nervous orders. Poor Hill, who had only just left the room to fetch the tea from the kitchens, returned to the parlour moments after exiting it with a harried expression upon her weathered face. "Oh, but Mr Darcy is so tall." Mrs Bennet looked to their guest, sizing him up with her roving eyes. "I am not sure at all if Mr Bennet's things will fit him. Does John have anything clean? It will not be what Mr Darcy is used to, of course, but—"

"I thank you for your concern, Mrs Bennet," Mr Darcy broke in at a volume a level above that of his fluttering hostess, "but I am well enough as I am. If I could have a bit of towelling and some tea, I should be quite well."

"Oh, but—"

"Mama," said Elizabeth, ready to end this interlude—her mother was liable to injure herself if she continued to carry on so. "We are quite warm here by the fire. Send for the tea and towelling only as Mr Darcy suggests."

"If you are sure..." Mrs Bennet looked to Mr Darcy for reassurance which he provided with a simple nod. "Very well, but you absolutely must stay for a long visit, sir. I will not have it said that I turn my guests out in such awful weather! You will catch your death out there."

Mr Darcy's eyes swivelled back in Elizabeth's direction and fixed upon her. She felt herself flush warmly and hoped he would attribute the heightened colour in her cheeks to the fire. "I assure you that I am quite settled for the moment, madam."

"Good, good...Hill—!"

"Ahem."

The small party clustered about the fireplace turned their heads in the direction of Mr Collins, who was standing just beyond Mrs Bennet and looking rather put out. Elizabeth supposed he believed he had a right to be, as his chosen lady had been rather unceremoniously pulled from his company and placed into that of another gentleman, though she had not a whit of sympathy for his sense of entitlement.

"Oh, Mr Collins," said Mrs Bennet, her inflection implying that she had quite forgot about him in all the excitement. "There are only two chairs here. Look, there is a very comfortable spot next to Mary."

Mr Collins did not even bother to turn his gaze to the greater part of the room where all of Elizabeth's sisters were assembled as they had been prior to Mr Darcy's arrival, his face set in something of a haughty scowl. Beyond him, Elizabeth could see Mary tense in her chair. "My fair cousin Elizabeth and I were in the middle of a lovely chat before Mr Darcy graced us with his presence, and I had hoped to resume it. Perhaps she would be so kind as to adjourn to the sofa..."

Mrs Bennet began shaking her head before Mr Collins had

even completed his request and, in much the same manner as she had treated Elizabeth, began redirecting their house guest to another portion of the parlour. "No, oh no, sir. Lizzy is needed here to see to Mr Darcy's comfort. Come, come. I am sure Mary has found some fascinating extract or other in Fordyce."

As Mrs Bennet herded the sputtering Mr Collins away, she turned to give Elizabeth a wide-eyed stare, her lips pulled in a taut line of warning. Although she had said no actual words, it was impossible to interpret her look as anything other than 'Do not waste this opportunity, Elizabeth! Mr Darcy is worth ten thousand a year, very likely more, and his interest must be maintained!' To stifle the snorting laugh that threatened to burst from her mouth as she essentially read her mother's mind, Elizabeth bit her lips together so that nothing impolitic might escape them.

When she had curbed this impulse and regained something of her equanimity, Elizabeth turned back to Mr Darcy to find him similarly wrestling with his own amusement and had to look away again lest her defences crumble entirely. She pressed her fingertips against her quivering lips, closed her eyes tightly and breathed deeply through her nose to dispel the humour that yet threatened to overwhelm her.

After approximately half a minute or so of this, Elizabeth felt capable of behaving as she ought and resumed a more demure posture with her neck erect and her hands folded in her lap. There was still an irrepressible twitching at her lips, but she was no longer on the precipice of bubbling over with laughter. Mr Darcy seemed to have regained his own composure, likely more quickly than she had, but his eyes continued to spark with mirth. "Lovely weather today," she commented, her tone as bland as she could manage.

Mr Darcy's mouth bent for a moment at a precipitous angle and then smoothed back into a more polite curve. "Quite."

"I suppose that you must have your way in all things, even when it is raining," Elizabeth accused, though playfully.

"You did give me leave to call, Miss Elizabeth."

"So I did, sir, though I would not have insisted that you risk your health and safety in coming all this way just to pay a visit. Why, Miss Bingley must be beside herself with worry!"

Mr Darcy's upper lip hitched minutely in what Elizabeth read as disdain, though he most properly did not disparage his hostess further. "It was a mere sprinkle when I started out, I assure you. It only became a deluge the last quarter mile or so."

"And now you are stuck here with us until it lets up again!"

"I assure you, Elizabeth," Mr Darcy leant towards her, his voice low as a drop of rainwater lazily descended the slope of his face; Elizabeth shivered as the deep timbre of his words seemed to vibrate between them, "I am precisely where I wish to be."

They were interrupted a moment later by the arrival of Hill and their maid of all work, both of whom were loaded down with linens intended to dry out the sopping Mr Darcy. The gentleman himself leant back and accepted the burdens of the servants with quiet thanks and Elizabeth willed her heart to calm during this reprieve.

"I do not wish to disrupt our pleasant conversation with something distasteful, Mr Darcy, but I am afraid that I must say something."

Darcy glanced up at Elizabeth over the rim of his teacup—black and unsweetened, just the way he preferred it—as wariness began to build deep in his gut. He had been settled most comfortably by the Bennets' fireside for the past two hours, supplied liberally with refreshments and blankets, and he had thought that his discourse with Elizabeth had been going well. They had not argued, except in light-hearted fashion, since his arrival, and he had been building hopes that her opinion of him was shifting somewhat for the better. Now her expression was tense and her body language revealed discomfort as if she had something most disagreeable to say and it put him on his guard. *She is not about to dismiss me, is she?*

Darcy balanced his cup upon its saucer and set it aside. "Oh?"

Elizabeth had already finished her beverage and was fiddling absently with her dishware. "Yes, it is about Mr Wickham."

Well, at least his initial fears had not been realised, though Darcy suspected that what Elizabeth had to reveal would not be much more pleasant. "Has he imposed himself upon you?" Darcy asked, his voice a low murmur which would not carry to the others in the room.

Elizabeth shook her head initially, then seemed to reconsider and shrugged instead. "Yes, but not in the way that you suppose. He was a guest at my aunt Philips's card party on Wednesday night and had much to say about his acquaintance with you."

"I can see from your expression that he did not share happy boyhood exploits."

Elizabeth huffed a quiet, if humourless, laugh. "No, that he did not. It was all nothing but vicious lies, I am sure."

Darcy felt his pride swell at the implication that Elizabeth had believed his version of events over Wickham's.

"...But it was most disturbing. The bulk of his discourse was his contention that you had denied him the living your father intended for him, which of course I already knew to be patently false."

"Ah, that old chestnut." Darcy sank deeper into his chair and snorted with exasperation. "It has always been one of his favourites. What else did he say?"

"I suppose you most wish to know if he mentioned your sister." Elizabeth arched an eyebrow in Darcy's direction.

"You have seen through me, Elizabeth. Yes, I would be most interested to know what he is saying about Georgiana. Has he..."

Elizabeth shook her head and quickly glanced about the room. Darcy followed her example and determined that everyone else in the parlour with them, including that pesky buffoon Collins, was deeply involved in their own activities.

They returned their attention to one another after a few seconds of perusal. "You need not fear that he is spreading rumours about her, Mr Darcy, at least not the kind injurious to her reputation. He merely said that she was very proud, like yourself."

Darcy was relieved to hear that Wickham had enough wit and self-preservation to keep the sordid business of Georgiana's near-elopement to himself but was dismayed that Elizabeth still characterised him as 'proud'. It was at least partially true, he admitted silently, but it stung that she continued to consider him in negative terms. "I am glad he has some sense, though I will defend my sister further. She is not proud at all, but rather exceedingly shy. Some who feel inferior might consider her reticence as a sign of pride, but in truth she is merely uncomfortable amongst strangers."

"Ah, so very much like you then." Elizabeth's eyes were twinkling at him, their verdant green flickering different shades in the firelight, and her lips were stretched into an impish grin.

Darcy's returning one was more like a grimace. *Proud and shy. This is her estimation of me.* "I suppose so."

Feeling the whisper of a touch against his knee, Darcy looked down to see Elizabeth's fingers already drawing away from him. He glanced back up to see her pink and chagrined. "Forgive me, sir, I meant no offence. It seems that being out in society does not come easy for you, and I should not make fun."

"Not at all. There is nothing to forgive."

"Very gracious of you, sir. And do not despair, I am sure you can improve much with practise. Consider it as aspiring to an accomplishment."

"I shall take your suggestion under advisement." Elizabeth still seemed discomfited by the effects of her teasing, and Darcy quickly changed the subject. "As much as I am enjoying your company, I did come to Longbourn for another purpose. Is your father available?"

Elizabeth seemed to accept Darcy's shift of topics with some relief. "As we have all been housebound without exception since Wednesday, he should be in his study. I assume you wish to relate to him the information you imparted to me about Mr Wickham?"

"Amongst other things." Darcy was pleased to see a blush rise upon Elizabeth's cheeks and knew she understood his unspoken intention to request formal permission from Mr Bennet to pursue her. She made no outward objection, and her features were formed into a bashful configuration, so he dared to hope that she was not as opposed to the notion as she had been at their last meeting.

"I had intended to speak with him on the subject myself," she pressed on, not acknowledging Darcy's implication, "but I was unsure how much I was at liberty to reveal and so ultimately decided to say nothing. It seemed as if it could harm no one to remain silent so long as we remained trapped at Longbourn without any contact with Mr Wickham, in any case."

Darcy wished to reach out for her hand, but recalled how she had withdrawn from him on Tuesday and so clenched his fists in his lap instead. "I will take care of it. Can you tell me where your father's study is located?"

"Just down the hall, across from the breakfast room."

Darcy rose, discarded the quilt which had been warming his legs and bowed to Elizabeth. He was just stepping away from his chair when Mrs Bennet called out, "Oh, Mr Darcy! You are not headed back out into that dreadful weather, are you? I must insist that you remain where you are by the fire."

Turning towards the matron of the house where she was perched upon the edge of her own seat, her eyes darting accusingly towards Elizabeth, he assuaged her fears at once. "Not at all, madam. I thought to have a quick word with Mr Bennet."

Mrs Bennet perked up noticeably and her mouth spread wide with satisfaction. "Well, in that case, you may be about your business. Off with you!"

Mr Collins stood up quickly and began scurrying across the length of the room as he worried his hands together. "I should like to have a word with my cousin Bennet myself, yes indeed. I will just follow Mr Darcy—"

"Oh, no, Mr Collins." Mrs Bennet climbed quickly to her own feet to intercept her house guest. She did so most ably by planting herself in his path and forcing him to stop short lest he actually knock her down.

Recalling how Mr Collins had once nearly sent him sprawling, Darcy repressed a snicker. *At least he is more cautious with the ladies.*

Mrs Bennet continued, "I require your presence here to read to us. We are so very dull, and it would be just the thing."

The younger girls giggled behind their hands as Mrs Bennet redirected Mr Collins elsewhere in the room, settled him again beside the petulant Miss Mary and deposited her tome into his hands. Darcy took his opportunity to escape and, save for another quick bow to an amused Elizabeth, left to make his way to Mr Bennet.

"I do wish you would stay for dinner, Mr Darcy."

Elizabeth watched by the parlour door as her mother begged plaintively for their guest to remain to no avail. Mr Darcy, to his credit, was being patient with Mrs Bennet's machinations, either because he felt the true concern she was exhibiting for his health—Mrs Bennet would be genuinely dismayed were an eligible gentleman to die suddenly of a violent cold before marrying one of her daughters—or because he was simply growing used to her ways as the rest of them had. In either case, his manners were above reproach, despite the vulgar spectacle Mrs Bennet was making of herself, and Elizabeth admired his forbearance.

"I cannot delay any longer, as it will be dark in another hour and therefore unsafe for travel, but I will admit that I am loath to go." Mr Darcy's eyes darted in Elizabeth's direction and she looked away, suddenly shy of him. "I thank you for your hospitality."

"But...but...you can stay the night! Yes, and then you will not have to leave at—"

"Mama," Elizabeth broke in firmly. "We do not have a guest room available, and I am sure Mr Darcy will be more comfortable at Netherfield. Besides, think of how worried Mr Bingley will be if he does not return. Mr Darcy will visit again soon." *Or so I hope.*

"At the very next opportunity," he affirmed, and Elizabeth could still feel his eyes upon her, though she did not verify it as a fact by looking at him.

"Come, Mr Darcy, I shall see you out." Elizabeth nodded towards the door and then quickly thereafter crossed the threshold into the hall. Mr Darcy followed and allowed her to precede him to the entrance.

Once he had donned his caped greatcoat, dried and warm after spending so many hours in front of the kitchen fire, Mr Darcy waited only for Hill to leave them before facing Elizabeth. "Dare I hope that my presence today was not entirely irksome?"

Elizabeth's mouth curled impishly at either end and she shook her head. "Not entirely, no. I actually quite enjoyed our time together today, Mr Darcy. It was a welcome change from... well, I should not say more, but I was pleased with your company regardless. You can be quite the conversationalist when you put in the effort."

"With some people, it is not so difficult." Mr Darcy's eyebrows were raised with meaning, and Elizabeth felt that same shyness rising inside her again. "I greatly enjoyed myself today, as well. Might I hope to call again tomorrow?"

"If the weather is better?"

"It is something I hope for, but do not depend upon."

Elizabeth swallowed as she felt suddenly compelled to rewet her throat. "I shall look forward to it then."

Mr Darcy's face lit up with a natural grin and he was all the more handsome for it. So distracted by this rather flustering expression, Elizabeth noticed only belatedly that he had gently captured her hand within his and was slowly lifting it. Mr Darcy bent and pressed his lips to the backs of her fingers, his eyes still trained upon her face, and Elizabeth felt a fluttering deep within her breast. It was a strangely pleasant sensation. "As shall I. Good day, Miss Elizabeth."

Mr Darcy nodded at her a final time, released her hand with visible reluctance, and turned to exit the house into the drizzling rain. Elizabeth remained frozen in place, her recently kissed hand cradled against her chest, until long after his carriage could be heard rattling away.

"And here I had almost thought him to be pulling my leg when he asked permission to court you, Lizzy."

Elizabeth jerked and whipped about to face down the corridor where her father was approaching, mocking her agitation with a smirk. She scowled lightly in return. "You frightened me, Papa! Please do not sneak up on me like that."

"I was not sneaking," her father denied with a raspy chuckle. "I was walking down the hall, as is my right as master of the house. It was you who was lurking in the vestibule. In any event, I was hoping for a word with you before we dine. Care to join me in my book-room?"

Elizabeth acquiesced and proceeded ahead of him as the sweep of his hand indicated that she should. Once they were safely ensconced within his study, Mr Bennet settled himself into his desk chair and Elizabeth took up the seat by the window that was her favourite, waiting for her father to broach whatever topic it was he wished to discuss. It was hardly difficult to divine what that might be.

"So, this Mr Darcy," Mr Bennet began after he had comfortably reclined in his seat, "told me the most remarkable thing today. I suppose you know what that was?"

Elizabeth nodded warily, but did not say anything. Had Mr Darcy told her father about the proposal? She had thought it a secret between them—although she had told Jane and she presumed that Mr Bingley was also aware—and not to be divulged to others.

At length, Mr Bennet apparently decided that Elizabeth was not going to speak and so continued, "He said that he had been granted your permission to call upon you and asked for my blessing on the matter. I had thought you indifferent—or perhaps something even more unfavourable—to him and so had not considered him serious at first. He assured me, however, that it was the truth and, as a man in my position can hardly deny a man in Mr Darcy's anything he condescends to ask, I have granted him leave to pay his court to you. Be that as it may, if I am not mistaken about your feelings, if you are actually averse to Mr Darcy's attentions, I beg you to speak up now so that I might rescind my permission. What say you, my child?"

Elizabeth breathed in deeply and considered her answer. Her father was offering her the graceful exit from her predicament that she had been hoping for since Tuesday, but now she was unsure if she wished to take it. She could not, as yet, determine whether or not she was ready to accept Mr Darcy's offer of marriage, but today's visit had been pleasant, more than pleasant, and she felt unwilling to abandon the progress she had made in understanding her enigmatic suitor better. There was still so much to learn about Mr Darcy, and he would remain an incomplete puzzle if she ended their agreement now.

"I cannot say that I…that is, I find that my initial impression of Mr Darcy might have been incorrect. I do not yet know how I feel about him, or if our friendship will ever lead to anything more permanent, but for now I am interested in learning more about him and seeing if we are compatible. There is no need to deny his suit at the present time."

Mr Bennet observed her over his spectacles, his green gaze pensive, before he sighed and shook his head. "Very well, my dear, but if you ever need my assistance in dissuading Mr Darcy, if he ever behaves in anything other than a gentlemanly manner, you will let me know that I need to step in."

Elizabeth shook her head. "Mr Darcy would never force his attentions upon me. Not like Mr Collins."

Mr Bennet's expression darkened. "And has my cousin been behaving himself today?"

"A little better." Elizabeth found herself suddenly amused by an image of the constantly thwarted parson who had visibly pouted throughout Mr Darcy's visit. "Though he did not have much of a chance to overstep his bounds today."

"Good. I shall give him another reminder of proper decorum if necessary—just say the word."

"I shall. Oh, did I not tell you that I was the recipient of one of Mr Collins's studied compliments yesterday?" Mr Bennet guffawed, his mood lightened instantly, and motioned for her to proceed with her story. "I have no doubt that he spent several hours in crafting this particular bit of flattery. He said..."

Elizabeth and Mr Bennet laughed at Mr Collins's expense for some minutes as the former related her silly anecdote with much energy, lingering on the way her pompous suitor fluttered his eyelashes at her in a way which reminded her strongly of Kitty and Lydia, and how his wording might have been improved. They agreed that the adulation had been heavy handed, yet that was what made it so worth while to repeat.

After an absentminded glance at the clock, Mr Bennet shooed Elizabeth from his study so that she might dress for dinner, which would be called at any time now. His second and most favourite daughter kissed him along the edge of his receding hairline with affection and turned to leave.

With her hand on the doorknob, Mr Bennet called her back for another word. Elizabeth turned to regard him and found his expression once again serious. "One final thing, Lizzy. I would ask that you assist me in keeping your sisters away from Mr Wickham whilst he resides in Meryton. I cannot think that they are much of a temptation for him since they have little fortune, but there is no telling what a man of his ilk might do when the opportunity presents itself. I think I need not explain why."

"You need not," Elizabeth agreed, sobered. "I shall do my

best, but I think you should forbid them directly. Mary will not be tempted by such a man, but Kitty and Lydia are not always inclined to listen to my warnings, especially in regard to officers."

Mr Bennet waved impatiently towards the door. "Yes, yes, I was planning to bring it up at dinner this evening. Now get on with you before the meal is delayed and your mother comes looking for us."

Elizabeth kissed his forehead again and swept from the room to change out of her dreadful yellow frock. Just in case, she would be sure to wear something more flattering upon the morrow—although Mr Darcy had not minded it any more than had Mr Collins.

TWELVE

As had become her habit of late, Elizabeth checked the weather immediately upon waking on Saturday. For the first time in the greater part of a week, she felt some optimism that their precipitation-imposed confinement was lifting, and she bounced joyfully upon the balls of her feet. The sky was still overcast and the surrounding countryside remained rather slick with muck, but there was no rain actively falling. If the clouds would only break and let through some sunshine, Elizabeth would have nothing left to wish for.

Well, almost nothing. Elizabeth scampered over to her wardrobe and pulled it open. As she sorted through her collection of frocks, dismissing this one as too drab or that one as too old, she hummed a cheerful tune that was a favourite of hers to play for company. Elizabeth was feeling quite sunny, cloudy skies notwithstanding, as it seemed Mr Darcy's return would remain unhampered by the weather.

Elizabeth slowed her perusal as this thought occurred to her. *I am looking forward to Mr Darcy's call. What a notion.*

Startled from her realisation by a soft knock at the door, she bid her visitor to enter. As it almost always was, it was Jane on the other side and she came into Elizabeth's bedchamber still in her night rail and with her hair braided over one shoulder.

"You are up early," Elizabeth said before turning back to her task of searching out an acceptable frock for the day. *Perhaps the blue?*

Jane swept across the floor in slippered feet and joined Elizabeth at her wardrobe, reaching across her younger sister and pulling out a dusky rose-coloured dress. "Well, I could not allow you to dress as dreadfully as you did yesterday, and I knew that my advisement could not wait too long past sunrise. Put this one on." She lifted the pink day gown, shook it out and then held it up against Elizabeth's form thoughtfully. "Yes, you look stunning in this one. Mr Darcy will approve."

Snatching the garment from Jane, Elizabeth stuck her tongue out at her elder sister. "For your information, I wore that yellow thing for Mr Collins's sake, little though he seemed to notice it. I had no idea that Mr Darcy was going to come calling in the rain!"

"I warned you that he would, if you recall." Jane was looking rather smug, the same way Charlotte Lucas behaved whenever she was similarly fortunate. "Now, the pink one. It brings out your complexion."

Elizabeth huffed at Jane, but there was no true vexation within her. She laid the rose-coloured dress across her bedspread and began the simple process of removing her nightgown. "I suppose Mama put you up to this?"

"You are lucky she did not come to direct you herself," said Jane. "I am actually somewhat surprised that she did not send you upstairs directly to change yesterday when Mr Darcy arrived. That yellow gown is truly awful, Lizzy. Why do you still have it?"

Elizabeth tossed her nightgown onto the bed next to her selected frock and shrugged. "It is warm and good for walks in cool weather. I hardly ever wear it before company."

"I think you must say goodbye to it now. Mama will surely throw it into the rag pile at her first chance."

"Unless she burns it."

The sisters giggled over the terrible fate awaiting her much maligned mustard-yellow dress as Jane assisted Elizabeth into the preferred pink one. It was also appropriate for the Season, being constructed out of a fine velvet, and sported some minimal ornamentation of creamy ivory embroidery along the edge of the bodice, sleeves, and hem. It was not ostentatious, but certainly more flattering and fashionable than much of Elizabeth's secondhand wardrobe. It had been a Christmas gift from Aunt Gardiner, who was a much lighter touch with lace and ribbon than Mrs Bennet tended to be. The embroidery, however, had been a birthday surprise from Jane, who had decided to elevate an otherwise plain garment into something more special. It was still acceptable for daytime wear, even after the improvements, and Elizabeth wore it often in the colder months.

"Can I assume that you are looking more forward to Mr Darcy's visit today than before?" Jane asked as she buttoned the last tiny fastenings at Elizabeth's back.

Elizabeth felt her skin warm, its hue mimicking that of her gown. "You may," she admitted with a reluctant huff. "If nothing else, he is comparatively fresh company, and I am not yet weary of looking at him as I am all of you."

Jane swatted her sister lightly upon the shoulder. "Lizzy, do be serious."

"Very well, I am anticipating Mr Darcy's visit today with much pleasure. There, is that better?"

"Yes."

Elizabeth sat down at her dressing table and began unravelling her braid with practised fingers as she peered at herself in the looking glass. Jane picked up Elizabeth's hairbrush in anticipation of helping her younger sister style her wild locks into something more presentable to her handsome suitor.

Once Jane was industriously involved in taming Elizabeth's curls, the latter felt compelled to fill the silence with teasing. "Do you suppose Mr Darcy will bring Mr Bingley with him? If he does, we shall both have a handsome gentleman to—oh, Jane! Do be careful!"

"Forgive me." Jane's cheeks were awash in a blush which Elizabeth witnessed in the mirror. The brush she had been using slipped free of her fingers and clattered to the floor, where she bent to pick it up.

"I suppose I deserved that for timing my tease so ill," Elizabeth said ruefully. "Still, I do not think Mr Darcy will be impressed by bald spots, so I beg you to be gentler."

Jane pulled sharply on a loose curl and they both laughed.

"You look very well this morning, Lizzy!" Mrs Bennet said as her two eldest daughters took their places at the breakfast table. "Your gown would benefit from some more lace, but I will say you look very well, indeed. Mr Darcy will not be able to tear his eyes from you today!"

Elizabeth ignored the backhanded nature of her mother's compliment and pulled a jar of jam towards herself, scooping some of the contents out onto her plate for her toast. "Thank you, Mama."

"If you had worn something so flattering yesterday, I am sure Mr Darcy would not have left without securing your hand for more than a few dances. Oh! How you try my poor nerves."

At the opposite end of the table from Mrs Bennet, her husband sat with a newspaper opened up and erected as a wall between himself and the rest of the family. She could hear the pages rattling as if its owner were shaking with silent laughter behind it. Elizabeth shook her head with amusement and returned her focus to slathering jam on her toast.

Mr Collins, thankfully, had yet to descend the stairs and join them as it was his established habit to sleep late into the morning. Elizabeth rather wondered that Lady Catherine did not correct this tendency towards sloth, but supposed perhaps her ladyship was unaware of it. Either that or Mr Collins only dared to slumber past the cock's crow when his patroness was not about to direct him otherwise. An image of a haughty, ornamented lady standing atop the roof of a grand manor house crowing for the neighbourhood to wake and begin the day caused an impertinent curl of a smirk on Elizabeth's face.

All the rest of the Bennets were seated and enjoying their morning meal, however, and chattering about the usual topics. Elizabeth endured some teasing from Kitty and Lydia about Mr Darcy, further lamentations from Mrs Bennet about how she had failed to show herself to advantage the day before, and more hidden humour from her father. Aside from the references to Mr Darcy, the day was shaping up as usual at Longbourn.

Just as she had been about to rise and adjourn to the parlour—her mother had absolutely forbidden Elizabeth to take even a short turn in the garden lest she ruin the acceptable image Jane had crafted for her—a knock at the front door was heard and the party in the breakfast room stilled. The pause was only a short one for Mrs Bennet began to bounce in her chair with excitement. "It must be Mr Darcy! And so early! Eager to see my Lizzy! Straighten up! Smile, girl, smile. Thrust out your —oh, Mr Darcy, how wonderful to see you again! And Mr Bingley too!"

Elizabeth shot her elder sister a triumphant smirk as she rose out of her welcoming curtsey to the newly arrived gentlemen. Jane ignored her and affixed her usual expression of placidity onto her features, but Elizabeth could see a bit of colour in the apples of Jane's cheeks. Mr Bennet had bowed with the rest of them, offered a compulsory greeting and then disappeared once again behind his paper.

"I hope we have not arrived too soon and imposed upon your breakfast." Mr Bingley spoke for both himself and Mr Darcy as he beamed about the room. "I confess, we were so delighted by the sudden improvement in the weather that we could not sit still at Netherfield another moment! Though I understand Darcy managed to stir himself over here yesterday."

"He did, indeed." Mrs Bennet practically glowed over the prospect of not one, but two, eminently eligible suitors calling upon her daughters. "And we were most pleased to have his company, were we not, girls? Lizzy, especially, enjoyed having you here, sir."

Elizabeth was inclined to blush for her mother's transparent attempts to matchmake, but Mr Darcy bent his head in acknowledgment to Mrs Bennet and then affixed his gaze to the object of his interest. Elizabeth felt her face heat in earnest once he had done so. "It was, indeed, a most pleasurable visit."

"Come, come, let us all adjourn to the parlour then." Mrs Bennet rose and flapped her hands at the gentlemen, shooing them in the direction of the doorway. Mr Darcy and Mr Bingley fled before her down the hall as Mrs Bennet called over her shoulder, "Lizzy! Jane! Come make our guests comfortable."

Elizabeth glanced at her father's end of the table, but he merely turned the page in his vigorously shaking newspaper and did not deign to follow the rest of the party out of the breakfast room. She shook her head fondly at him and followed Jane into the corridor.

When she reached the parlour, Mr Darcy was standing beside the chair he had been ushered into the day before, waiting for her to be seated before him. He indicated the wing-back across from his with hope brimming in his eyes, and Elizabeth took pity on him by accepting it. Jane arranged herself demurely upon a sofa close to Elizabeth, and Mr Bingley followed her thither.

Once the couples had been arranged to Mrs Bennet's satisfaction, she settled herself in her preferred armchair in which she resided like a queen upon her throne. The rest of the Bennet daughters filtered into the room at their own pace and resumed their usual places and activities.

"So, Mr Bingley, how are the preparations for the ball coming along? I am sure your sister..."

Mrs Bennet's jabbering voice faded away into the background as Elizabeth turned to face Darcy, smiled brightly, and began speaking of books.

Elizabeth was especially lovely in her pink gown, which looked as if it would be pleasantly soft to the touch. Darcy could not exactly recall what she had been wearing the day before, consumed as he had been with the sparkle in his lady's eyes, but he was happy to admire the effect her current ensemble created. His sister had a few dresses which were pink, as most girls did, but not one the exact shade of Elizabeth's. It looked as if the material had been selected to exactly match the flush of her skin.

"Mr Darcy?"

Darcy straightened himself, cleared his throat and refocused his gaze upon Elizabeth's face, which sported an impishly raised brow. "Forgive me, I was wool-gathering. What were you saying?"

"I was enquiring, sir, whether you have done much travelling. I have not had the pleasure of venturing further than London and had hoped that you might describe the beauties of faraway lands to me. However, I had not realised that your mind had wandered away into the great wild yonder." Elizabeth's words were censorious, but her tone playful and not cutting. Her impertinent smirk further indicated that she was amused with him, and Darcy could not help but wonder if it were simply with his inattention or some vacant expression which might have overtaken his features as he stared at her. If he looked anything like Bingley when his friend was gazing upon the elder Miss Bennet, Darcy had no doubt that his besotted countenance was quite silly.

"Oh, yes, I was fortunate enough to travel in my youth, though perhaps not as much as I might have wished." When Elizabeth raised her second eyebrow and remained silent, Darcy realised that she expected him to elaborate. "Due to the war, of course, my grand tour was somewhat contracted, but I spent a year exploring Scotland and Ireland. Then I had to return to Pemberley when my father became ill. He died not long after, and I have not had much opportunity to go abroad since."

Elizabeth's face crumpled into a look of sympathetic concern. "I am very sorry for your loss, sir. Has your father been gone very long?"

"About five years now." Darcy said nothing for a long moment, allowing the longstanding grief little time to take hold of him, and returned to the previous subject. "Though I have been forced of necessity to remain in England, I have been to most of the northern counties, including the lakes. I assume you have never been?"

"No," Elizabeth said with a wistfulness in her voice. "I have not had that pleasure, though I have always longed to visit. More so since Mr Wordsworth has published his beautiful poetry."

"He is, indeed, very masterful."

A few more words about the great gifted wordsmith brought Elizabeth back to travel. "It seems that you have toured extensively in the north, but what of the south?"

Darcy shook his head, feeling a squirming in the pit of his stomach. "As you know, I paid a visit to Ramsgate last summer." Elizabeth looked rather embarrassed at the reminder of Georgiana's near-elopement, and Darcy moved on quickly. "And of course, my aunt, Lady Catherine, resides in Kent. I visit her every year in the spring."

"Of course, I had forgotten. Have you—"

"Lady Catherine?"

As a new voice sounded behind him, Darcy, whose admiring gaze was still fastened to Elizabeth's face, watched his conversation partner's expression tense into a subtle scowl. At first Darcy was alarmed that she was directing such a disapproving look at him, but then realised that her eyes were focused on something over his shoulder. Turning, he recognised the source of her displeasure immediately.

Mr Collins stood within the doorway, his face lit with unexpected delight, and stared at Darcy with an adoring expression. Rather sickened at the sight, Darcy leant away from the besotted-looking parson, eyeing him warily.

"Did I hear you correctly, Mr Darcy?" Mr Collins queried as he scampered closer with an unbecoming eagerness. "Did you say that your aunt is the right honourable Lady Catherine de Bourgh, the most beneficent and condescending lady in all the land?"

Darcy tensed as he realised what he had just unwittingly done. As Mr Collins had not been present either in the breakfast room or the parlour, Darcy had quite put the odious toad out of his mind until this most awkward moment. Naturally, Mr Collins would decide to make his presence known at the exact moment reference to Lady Catherine passed through her nephew's lips. It was almost as if Mr Collins were lured there by the invocation of his patroness's name.

Darcy tightened his features into as impassive a mask as he could manage and responded simply, "Yes."

"And so you must be—forgive me, sir for not realising the connexion immediately!" Mr Collins worried his hands together as he spoke, visibly horrified that he had not known through some divine intervention that one of Lady Catherine's relations was living amongst them. "And you hail from London?"

"Derbyshire."

"Derby—you are not the master of Pemberley?" Mr Collins's eyes somehow managed to widen further at Darcy's nod of acknowledgment. "Then you must be—oh, Mr Darcy, allow me to congratulate you on obtaining the hand of the fairest flower in all of England! Miss de Bourgh is everything perfect and lovely, and shall make you a splendid wife. Lady Catherine has said that you will be setting a date for the wedding soon, and I humbly wish to offer my services to you in any way possible for this most auspicious occasion. I would be most eager, I assure you, to preside over..."

As Mr Collins nattered on about the 'happy, happy day'

anticipated most keenly by his aunt, Darcy repressed his offence temporarily to gauge Elizabeth's reaction to it all. He had dutifully informed her that he was not in any way promised to Anne, but with her cousin speaking of the inevitability with such authority, Darcy worried that she might doubt—

She is laughing at me.

Far from looking concerned, Elizabeth's hand was cupped over her mouth and her shoulders were hunched and shaking. Occasionally, an endearing little snort would escape her, or she would convulse with silent humour. Well, that rather punctured Darcy's pride.

In hindsight, Darcy thought with a half-cocked smile and a huff, *I should have expected as much from her.* Mr Collins and his veneration of Lady Catherine was everything ridiculous, and Darcy's unintended revelation of his connexion to this supposed paragon would necessarily be remarkable to such a simple-minded sycophant. Mr Collins's expression of it, while irksome, Darcy was forced to admit would be entertaining to some who were inclined to laugh at life's foibles as Elizabeth was. He glowered at Elizabeth for her traitorous laughter at his expense, which only sent her into another paroxysm of mirth.

While Darcy was thus distracted by the charming picture Elizabeth presented, Mr Collins had drawn closer to the pair of them and pulled up a chair. Darcy only noticed once the hefty young man had lowered himself into the seat with a thump, his monologue ongoing without cessation. "It is not too late to read the banns for a Christmastide nuptial, Mr Darcy, and I would happily put my own affairs on hold to attend you. Just say the word, sir, and I shall start preparing directly—"

"Mr Collins," Darcy broke in, forcing the parson into a stuttering stop. With a firm expression and tone, he proceeded to disabuse Mr Collins of his erroneous assumptions. "While I thank you for your interest, you must know that I am not—"

"Not at liberty to discuss any particulars without Lady Catherine's advice."

Darcy whipped his head about at Elizabeth's interruption,

taken aback and hurt that she would be advocating his marriage to another woman, but she just smiled sweetly and gave him a subtle shake of her head. *What is she about?*

She then returned her attention to Mr Collins, who was gaping at her as if equally astonished. "I am certain that her ladyship is most attentive to all such details and would assuredly be put out to discover that anything had been determined without her."

At the suggestion of Lady Catherine's disapprobation, Mr Collins let out something like a howl of dismay and began blubbering about how he would never, on any account, wish to offend her ladyship in any way and thanked his 'dear Cousin Elizabeth' for her insight into the matter. "Your thoughtfulness does you great credit," he praised earnestly, his head bobbing up and down rapidly as if it were slightly unhinged, "and when our own happy day comes about—"

"Mr Collins!" Yet another interruption, this one far more welcome, came from the quarter of Mrs Bennet, who had belatedly noticed that Mr Collins was making himself a pest to Mr Darcy. She scurried over to the fireplace where the trio of Darcy, Elizabeth, and Collins were seated in a semicircle before the hearth, waving her lacy handkerchief about with nervous energy, and began tugging insistently on their house guest's arm at the crook of his elbow. "Come here, Mr Collins. You are wanted on a matter of great import, sir."

"But—but Mr Darcy—"

"Oh, Mr Darcy has Lizzy to entertain him," Mrs Bennet insisted and hustled Mr Collins to his feet. Seconds later, the parson was across the room and seated next to a frowning Miss Mary, both of whom appeared entirely bewildered as to how he had got there.

Darcy watched all of this happen with some befuddlement of his own. He was forced to admit that Mrs Bennet's methods, while uncouth, were mightily effective in their directness. She was not afraid to be meddlesome to get her way, and he must be grateful that she was prepared to be so on his behalf.

"My apologies, Mr Darcy." Darcy's attention returned to Elizabeth, who was bent forwards in her armchair and grinning somewhat sheepishly at him. It was a most becoming expression, and he was thoroughly charmed by it. "I did not wish to perpetuate your supposed engagement to Miss de Bourgh, but I thought it might be for the best at present."

Darcy stared at her, his brow furrowing downwards in confusion. "Whatever for?"

"You are concerned about my cousin revealing your interest in me to your aunt, are you not?" Elizabeth's eyes widened slightly as if she expected him to understand something beyond what she was saying. Still somewhat befuddled, however, Darcy could not catch her underlying meaning and so she elaborated. "If he believes you engaged elsewhere, he is not likely to suspect your attentions to me and so will not mention them in his inevitable letter to Lady Catherine. Instead, he will extol your virtues for several pages and not think to mention me at all. Well," she amended with a lyrical laugh, "perhaps in a postscript. He is set on marrying me, after all."

Darcy's expression eased as understanding set in. It was a brilliant manoeuvre, really, in all its simplicity. Elizabeth had not actually stated her belief in his engagement to Anne now that he considered her words more carefully. She had merely observed that Lady Catherine would prefer to partake in the planning of her daughter's wedding. With Mr Collins spouting reverent nonsense about her every waking hour, it would not be a leap for anyone at Longbourn, especially his clever Elizabeth, to assume as much.

Shaking his head slightly, Darcy joined her laughter with a chuckle of his own. "I should not have underestimated you, Elizabeth. I bow to your brilliance. Can I presume that you are protecting me for yourself?" The last was said as something of a jest, but with real hope infused therein.

Elizabeth's cheeks flushed, and she looked down at her lap where she was fiddling with one of the cuffs of her lovely matching pink gown. "Do not get so ahead of yourself, Mr Darcy. There are still three days until the ball."

In a conspiratorial whisper, Darcy asserted, "Three days to win your favour. Tell me, Elizabeth, do you prefer a winter wedding?"

THIRTEEN

Though Elizabeth was meant to be paying her undivided attention to Reverend Brown's sermon, she found she could not prevent it wavering across the aisle at frequent intervals throughout. There was nothing unique or especially mesmerising there which would also draw the eyes of her neighbours, only the Netherfield party in all their resplendent glory.

Mr Bingley sat directly in the centre, between his sisters, with his eyes locked on the parson but glazed over. Mrs Hurst, on his far side, did not bother to even so much as feign interest in the service, though she was at least polite enough to mask her yawns with her fan. Her husband was snoring beside her, occasionally audible even as far away as Elizabeth was seated.

Though this trio made an amusing tableau, Elizabeth could not keep her eyes trained on them. No, her focus was all for the gentleman at the end of the row closest to her own position, whose gaze frequently contacted hers.

After the past two days in Mr Darcy's company, Elizabeth would admit that her interest in him was increasing apace. They had sat at the fireside and spoken on so many different subjects that Elizabeth could not recall how many. Some of them were serious, such as what was to be done about Mr Wickham and his lies, while others were more light-hearted, but in each instance, he was a refreshing conversation partner. Neither dull nor threadbare, obsequious nor conceited, Mr Darcy had interesting things to say and listened raptly to her in return. Truly, Elizabeth felt that she had never been so well entertained by a gentleman's discourse before, not even her father's.

She also felt as if she had never known a gentleman so well before, despite having only a passable understanding of him since Tuesday last. Oh, there were certainly others she had been acquainted with longer, many of whom she was friendly with, but it was a rarity in society for young ladies and eligible gentlemen to sit down together and discuss topics deeper than the weather. It was almost unheard of prior to marriage unless the lady and gentleman in question were companions of long duration and their families intimate with one another. To meet someone and have their almost exclusive company to become acquainted on a greater than superficial level, however...well, Elizabeth considered herself fortunate, indeed, to have been granted the opportunity to familiarise herself thus with Mr Darcy. And was, amusingly, grateful to her meddling mother for enabling it.

Though familiarity often breeds contempt, Elizabeth found that the opposite was true in this instance. The more she got to know Mr Darcy, the more she found she wanted to know of him. They did not always agree—no two people were constantly capable of it—but he was not dismissive of her opinions, either. His own opinions were decided, though open to amendment when a proper argument was offered, and Elizabeth was learning a great deal from him on a range of topics. There was nothing quite like being taken seriously by so estimable a gentleman.

Yes, indeed, Elizabeth was becoming very fond of Mr Darcy and his unwavering attentions.

Attentions so unwavering that she was experiencing them that very moment as she caught a flash of silvery grey in her peripheral vision. Unable to resist, Elizabeth angled her regard towards Mr Darcy and their gazes locked. If the small upturn of his mouth was any indication, Mr Darcy was pleased to have solicited her notice. He verily glowed with it, and Elizabeth found his pride, in this instance, endearing. She reflected his smile back at him and fought the overwhelming urge to blush.

Their connexion was severed, however, an instant later when Mr Darcy's face jerked round to his other side. The pleasure on his countenance dissolved as he beheld Miss Bingley, who had commandeered his attention by reaching up to whisper intimately in his ear. As he hissed something inaudible in reply, Elizabeth turned away and redirected her observation to Mr Brown where it was meant to be. She bit her lip to contain the giggle that fought to escape.

Had the interloper been any woman other than Miss Bingley, or had Mr Darcy's impatience with her been less clear, Elizabeth might have been concerned at the level of familiarity between them. However, it was exceedingly obvious to everyone —save Miss Bingley herself—that the lady had not a prayer of turning Mr Darcy's head, and he was perfectly safe from her arts and allurements. Why she even bothered was a mystery to Elizabeth; had a man showed such pointed disinterest—nay, annoyance—in her, she would not have had the heart to continue her pursuit. But Miss Bingley, it seemed, was not to be deterred by something so paltry as Mr Darcy not liking her. *She is persistent, I will give her that.*

Amidst the hustle and bustle of the congregation leaving, en masse, Elizabeth lost track of Mr Darcy and his party. She deflated once she realised that he was already gone, having hoped throughout the service that she might be allowed a word with him before they each went their separate ways. She had already been authorised, if not commanded, to invite him and Mr Bingley to dine with them that evening and had secretly hoped that Mr Darcy would accept. If Elizabeth had to guess, Miss Bingley had hustled him from the building the moment Mr Brown said 'Amen' on the closing prayer to prevent this very event from occurring. *Alas...I suppose there is still the hope that he might visit Longbourn again tomorrow.*

In the meantime, their remaining guest was not a palatable exchange. Mr Collins, with his entitled claim upon her and his fawning attentions to Mr Darcy, was as irksome as he was homely. Thankfully, once Mrs Bennet had sensed Mr Darcy's intentions—and, truly, how had Elizabeth ever thought that she would not?—she had begun to interfere. Elizabeth felt sympathy for poor Mary, who was the unhappy lady forced to entertain Mr Collins in her stead, but it did not overwhelm her relief at the reprieve. She would make it up to her next younger sister one day.

As Elizabeth exited, she looked up to find Mr Darcy waiting for her in the churchyard and her heart skittered triumphantly in her chest. Miss Bingley was nowhere in evidence, though she could not be far, and her suitor stared at her with that intense longing she had once misconstrued.

When she reached him, he bowed to her. "Good morning, Miss Elizabeth."

Before Elizabeth could offer him more than a return greeting, she was jostled practically into his arms by her own mother. "Good morning, Mr Darcy! How lovely it is to see you this fine Sunday. Is it not, Lizzy?"

As Mr Darcy steadied Elizabeth, her hand clasped gently in his, she replied, "Indeed."

"I hope you are well, sir."

Mr Darcy inclined his head. "Quite. And yourself?"

"Oh! How kind of you to ask. You know how I suffer with my poor nerves...but enough of that. My Lizzy, as you can see, is quite well. Is she not particularly lovely today, Mr Darcy? So full of bloom and vigour?"

Elizabeth felt her face heat at Mrs Bennet's obvious ploy and opened her mouth to object to it, but Mr Darcy answered before she could. "Indeed, I had noticed."

Mr Darcy's response had been quiet, almost shy, and Elizabeth turned to look at him in amazement. That this powerful, often arrogant man could sound so...so bashful was astonishing and immensely gratifying to her vanity. And his expression, which was everything tender as he regarded her, made her tingle all over. "I thank you, sir."

"'Tis only the truth, Miss Elizabeth," he said with another bow.

Oh, I must be brighter red than a beet!

"Mr Darcy! How extremely fortunate it is to see you today, sir."

Any contentment Elizabeth might have felt at Mr Darcy's compliments fled as Mr Collins, a scowling Mary on his arm, introduced himself to the conversation. Irritation replaced it, an emotion she could see mirrored on Mrs Bennet's face.

"Mr Collins," said Mrs Bennet through her clenched teeth, her glare roving over to fix upon Mary, "I had thought you were escorting my other daughters back home. It still threatens rain, and it would not do for them to be drenched."

"I could not leave without my dear cousin Elizabeth," he said, though his adoring gaze was still riveted to Mr Darcy. "And, of course, I must pay my respects to my patroness's nephew before I depart. Lady Catherine—"

"Nonsense! Come, Mr Collins, we must away immediately."

"But Cousin Elizabeth—"

"She is very well where she is. Mr Darcy shall see her safely home, I am sure. Come now."

With a parting glare at her second eldest daughter, one which communicated much to Elizabeth, Mrs Bennet hustled Mr Collins and Mary away. Elizabeth was unsure if she should be more amused or mortified by her mother's transparent matchmaking, but shook her head at Mrs Bennet's back all the same.

"She is difficult to deny, your mother."

Elizabeth turned back to Mr Darcy at this observation, searching for any hint of derision in his countenance. She found none, only a chagrined fondness, and her initial offence melted away. "Difficult, but not impossible. There is a technique to it."

"Firmness?"

"Equal obstinacy."

Mr Darcy grinned at her jest and held out his arm. "Shall I escort you back to Longbourn?"

Elizabeth accepted without any trace of hesitation. "I would like that."

Darcy could hardly believe the marked improvement in Elizabeth's manner towards him. Not only was she treating him to friendly smiles and encouraging blushes, but she showed no reluctance in taking his arm as she had earlier in the week. Darcy felt as if he could float all the way to Longbourn, such was his elation.

It was punctured, however, when he felt someone else latch onto his unoccupied arm.

"Oh, Mr Darcy, there you are. Come, the carriage awaits."

Having halted unceremoniously at being thus accosted by Miss Bingley, Darcy turned towards her with impatience. She appeared unaffected by his ire, her features drawn into a mask of studied innocence.

Curses. Darcy had thought her disposed of in the carriage, having deposited her there himself a few minutes prior, but it seemed he would not escape her so easily. And it had truly been an escape; Miss Bingley had been intolerable company since he had unintentionally announced his attachment to Elizabeth on Friday. Sullen and wheedling by turns, she had been incessant in her attempts to get him to break it off. Blessedly, he had seen her but rarely while safely ensconced at Longbourn, warmed by its hearth and Elizabeth's presence.

When the banns had failed to be called by Mr Brown that morning, Miss Bingley had looked so positively triumphant Darcy thought he had seen the feathers in her headdress sit up a little straighter. No doubt she believed that there was still some small chance of her own success without an official announcement, hence her increasingly forward attempts to divide him from Elizabeth.

And now I must rid myself of her again. "I am escorting Miss Elizabeth home. You may feel free to leave without me."

Miss Bingley did not spare a glance for Elizabeth, who watched the other lady's presumption unfold with amused interest. "I am certain Miss Eliza knows the way from here. Look, there is her family, just ahead."

Aside from the rudeness required to simply abandon a lady in the middle of the road, Darcy was not inclined in the slightest to capitulate to Miss Bingley's whims. "Even so, I stand by my previous commitment. I shall see you back at Netherfield."

"But I require your attendance thither, sir." Miss Bingley flapped her lashes at him in what she must have believed to be a coquettish manner. Darcy thought it merely looked as if she had something in her eye. "And as Netherfield is much farther from here than Longbourn..."

Darcy was about to remind Miss Bingley that her own relations were available to see her home when Elizabeth spoke up. "I am afraid I must commandeer Mr Darcy for myself. He has already promised to dine with my family this evening."

Though Darcy was surprised by Elizabeth's appropriation, he was by no means inclined to object. Quite the opposite.

"And it appears that Jane has just finished proffering the same invitation to your brother." Elizabeth nodded down the lane where Bingley and Miss Bennet were, indeed, in some sort of confederation with one another. "You and the rest of your party are welcome to join us, of course. I am certain that my mother would be happy to add extra place settings."

Darcy could read the conflict writ across Miss Bingley's face. On the one hand, she would not wish to relinquish her prize to the keep of her rival. On the other, she despised the Bennets and their boisterous ways.

Miss Bingley, to Darcy's great relief, sneered at Elizabeth's solicitous offer. "As obliged as I am, I think not."

"Then I believe we must bid you farewell here. Have an excellent day."

So saying, Elizabeth tugged Darcy out of Miss Bingley's clutches and all but dragged him away. Darcy felt then the same sort of relief he imagined rescued damsels must experience as they were carted off on their brave knight's noble steed.

Mr Darcy had spent the remainder of Sunday and much of Monday at Longbourn, much to the approval of some and the consternation of others. Elizabeth considered herself solidly in the former group, little though she could explain how a mere week of understanding him better could so vastly improve her opinion of him. Regardless of how incredible she found the situation, bidding him farewell at the end of each evening became increasingly difficult for her.

As she led him to the front door after dinner on Monday, Elizabeth felt the now familiar pang of regret in saying her goodbyes to Mr Darcy and found herself lingering overlong in issuing them. "I suppose I shall not have the pleasure of your company tomorrow morning."

Mr Darcy, for his part, looked as reluctant to part as she was. "Unfortunately, not. I wish I could, but I am certain that your entire day will be consumed with ball preparations, and I would merely be under foot."

"Perhaps so, but your absence will be felt, good sir."

Mr Darcy's eyes widened only slightly, but even so, Elizabeth could still read the surprise in them. *Have I been too bold?*

"As will yours, Elizabeth."

Elizabeth dropped her chin, suddenly too bashful to look at him directly, and bit her lip. *Boldness has its rewards.*

As Mr Darcy collected her hand and raised it to his lips for a soft kiss, Elizabeth's face rose likewise and she witnessed a glowing warmth deep within his gaze, like lightning flashes behind a bank of clouds. She almost thought she felt it prickling along her arm from the point where his mouth had brushed against her fingers.

At length, he lowered her hand back down, but retained possession of it. "I look forward to seeing you tomorrow evening. For our dances and..."

The conversation died away as Mr Darcy's allusion hovered between them.

Though Elizabeth's heart palpated vigorously, she chose to ignore it and distracted them both with a jest, one carried over from their discourse at the dinner table. "I do hope you will oblige me in matching your waistcoat to my gown. We shall be all the rage if you do!"

"Whatever you command of me shall be done."

By the tone of his voice and the cast of his features, Elizabeth had no doubt this would prove to be true. *It would be best not to take advantage, unless...*

"Good evening, Elizabeth. I shall see you on the morrow."

"Yes, I am counting on it."

FOURTEEN

Darcy stood, fully attired in his evening costume, in the guest corridor outside his suite and stared out of an upper floor window which oversaw the long drive of Netherfield. In the dim glow of the setting sun, Darcy could see the black silhouettes of carriages coming towards his position like a fleet of encroaching ships, each no doubt filled with Bingley's uncouth neighbours all dressed in their finest, and he witnessed their approach with equal parts anticipation and trepidation. The festivities were only just about to begin, but based on the number of carriages outside already, it was guaranteed to be a crush. In his friend's zeal to make a good impression upon the area, it was clear that Bingley had offered up invitations to more than four-and-twenty families; likely a cadre of his other friends from town, as well as the quartered militia, would be present in addition to the minor gentry of Hertfordshire. A hellish prospect, truly.

Though it was hardly unusual for Darcy to feel anxious at the start of such an evening—one which promised to be loud, overly warm, and tedious—his ordinary complaints were far from his thoughts as he watched the revellers gather down below him. Rather than concerning himself with the unwashed hordes gathered to dance, drink, and make fools of themselves, Darcy was focused upon a single guest who would soon arrive with the answer to a question he had posed a week previously. Miss Elizabeth Bennet, the only woman he had ever glanced at more than once in interest, held his heart, throbbing with hope, in the cupped palms of her dainty hands. She had the power to either crush or enlarge it with her response; would she deny him? Or show benevolent mercy and accept him? Darcy could not be sure, though there was no question as to what he wished would be so.

Before doubt could consume him yet again, Darcy breathed deeply through his nose and reminded himself of his alternate plan. Should his beloved Elizabeth seem reluctant to give him an answer—or, worse, should she seem inclined to outright reject him for a second time—he would beg for another reprieve. Surely, given that the first half of the week his visits had been stymied by near constant rainfall, she would be so beneficent as to allow him additional time to woo her? Elizabeth, with her strong sense of fairness, could not deny him the chance he had bartered for. Unless she determined it would be kinder to release him immediately...Darcy shook his head sharply as that creeping uncertainty began to cloud the edges of his thoughts once more. The last few days, he reminded himself with overcompensating vehemence, had been very promising, despite all the obstacles between them. Elizabeth had welcomed him with increasing approval over the course of Friday, Saturday, and Sunday, and had even seemed to like him somewhat yesterday when he had seen her last.

On Monday evening, Elizabeth had teased him over dinner about colour coordinating their ball attire so that they might look well together as they danced; as a result, Darcy now wore his cream waistcoat shot with burgundy thread for the ball. And, when he had finally been forced to bid the Bennets adieu, Elizabeth had escorted him to the vestibule herself and lingered there some minutes over her goodbyes. He recalled the exact shade of her blush and the effervescent sparkle in her eyes as he had pressed his lips to the backs of her dainty fingers, and his heart squeezed within his breast. Was this not encouragement of his suit?

Alas, Darcy had so poorly understood her feelings at the beginning of their acquaintance that he lacked faith in his interpretations now. He might have had more confidence in his observations had Elizabeth fawned over him as Mr Collins now did, but just the thought of such a display unnerved him. The image of a leering, oily simper on Elizabeth's face which mimicked her cousin's toadying flattery caused Darcy a shudder of revulsion.

"Darcy! There you are."

Darcy turned his head fractionally so that he could see the approaching form of his friend. He nodded in acknowledgment as Bingley slapped him upon the shoulder and took up station next to Darcy so that he could admire the view from the same window.

"Shaping up to be quite an evening, eh?" Bingley's rhetorical query was accompanied by a fervent rubbing together of his hands, a signal of self-satisfaction. "Caroline will be pleased. Well, perhaps not pleased, but..."

Darcy grunted in response. Pleasure in the evening's events for him was contingent on one lady's charity, and no amount of merrymaking would compensate should he not receive it.

"Do not fret, old man." Bingley thumped Darcy upon the back again. "She seemed to like you just fine when I saw you together on Sunday. All will be well."

If only Darcy could take comfort from Bingley's encouragement, but he could not. He would feel no measure of peace until Elizabeth agreed to marry him, and all was as it should be. Darcy indulged a moment by closing his eyes and imagining what it would be like to bring her home to Pemberley as his wife; he could picture her quite clearly curled up in one of the library armchairs, much as she had done that fateful day here at Netherfield, with a book unfolded in her lap and her curls spilling loose about her face...enchanting. The fantasy was soothing to Darcy's tattered nerves and steadied him to face the evening ahead.

After another deep breath which he released in a calming rush, Darcy opened his eyes and peered out into the twilight. Down below, at the foot of the front steps, a carriage door was opening, and a coterie of hooded young ladies were being handed out by footmen. The last, following immediately on the hem of another, climbed down and tilted her head back to gaze upon the face of the house. Her head covering slipped from her crown and pooled upon her shoulders to reveal dark curls and a fine pair of shimmering eyes. She smiled up at whatever it was she saw, and Darcy's heart tripped over itself in a stuttering beat.

Without a single word to Bingley, Darcy pivoted on his heel and made quickly for the staircase.

As Elizabeth entered Netherfield upon the arm of Mr Collins—an unfortunate position she had been unable to decline—she looked round the vestibule with awe. Whatever Miss Bingley's faults of personality and character, she was clearly a gifted hostess with a flair for decoration. Some of the elements were a touch too gilded for Elizabeth's tastes, but she would admit that the general effect of the room was enchanting and that any criticisms she could think of would be of a nit-picking variety. Hundreds of wax candles were lit above her and along the walls, creating light enough that one would almost think it midday. Garlands and flowers, no doubt procured from a London hothouse, were draped strategically about, and their scent, heightened by the heat of the candle flames, wafted throughout and disguised the odour of too many bodies packed together. Up ahead, the ballroom doors were thrown wide open to reveal further splendour and the sounds of an orchestra warming up. This evening promised to be everything delightful for the residents of Meryton and its surrounding estates.

"Oh my, Lizzy…it is like fairyland!"

Elizabeth tore her eyes away from the glittering spectacle of Miss Bingley's arrangements to affectionately indulge in Jane's wonder. Her youngest sisters were already dispersing amongst the crowd to search for redcoats, heedless of anything aside from their own pleasure. Their father had similarly escaped, most likely to the card room, and their mother had stopped along the way to gossip with her gaggle of friends. Mary had disappeared to parts unknown to Elizabeth, perhaps to avoid the presence of Mr Collins as her elder sister could not manage. Jane, dearest Jane, remained steadfastly at Elizabeth's side to help alleviate the burden of entertaining their ridiculous cousin. "That it is, dearest. Miss Bingley has outdone herself."

"She certainly has!" Jane's agreement to the sentiment was not unexpected, but nor was it unworthily given in this instance.

"Most excellent arrangements, most excellent indeed," added Mr Collins, though neither sister had requested his opinion. "It is nothing to Rosings Park, of course, but I will do Miss Bingley the compliment of saying that she has done splendidly with what she had. Why, Lady Catherine herself…" And on he went as though his audience were enraptured by his self-important soliloquy about Lady Catherine and her magnificent home.

As the splendour of first impression abated and her cousin prattled on, Elizabeth began to surreptitiously glance about the room for signs of a tall, dark, and handsome gentleman whom she had expectations of meeting for the opening set.

Where is Mr Darcy?

Some of her anxiety from earlier in the day began to return as Elizabeth searched and failed to find the single person she sought. There were so many bodies crowded into the entrance hall that it was impossible to pick out an individual face from within the horde, and Elizabeth's nervousness rose another notch. She was confident that she would see Mr Darcy at some point this evening—there were dances promised between them, after all, and he would almost certainly come seeking something else altogether, as well—but she had been anticipating their moment of meeting for several hours together as she had prepared for the ball. Elizabeth was, to no one's surprise but her own, looking forward to seeing him.

And she finally had an answer to give him. It was still a bit tentative as a half-week's worth of visits could hardly make her sure of her own feelings, but Elizabeth was decidedly leaning towards offering Mr Darcy a yes in response to his proposal. She had a list as long as her arm which told her that Mr Darcy would make a fine husband, full of sterling practical qualities and endearing peccadilloes which set her heart to a stuttering beat. The one she had kept prior to his attempts at wooing, by contrast, was growing shorter as she crossed unsavoury items off it, causing the scale of Elizabeth's rational considerations to tilt strongly in a more positive direction.

However, it was not this system of checks and balances which made Elizabeth inclined to accept Mr Darcy, but rather a feeling. A feeling that, regardless of the contents of any list and the obvious mercenary benefits to her family, made her wish to be in his company always. As an intelligent, thoughtful man, Mr Darcy would make an excellent companion in her future life, and she could see them being content with one another for many years. More than content, even.

Elizabeth's heart skipped about in her chest as if the dancing had already begun, and she had no doubt that its partner was beating within Mr Darcy. It was this feeling which made Elizabeth determine she could do nothing other than accept him. She hoped he would be pleased.

"Ahem." Mr Collins, perhaps belatedly realising that their attention had wandered, interrupted Elizabeth's solitary musings with a condescending little cough and drew his cousins' eyes to himself. Jane presented her gaze with patience and indulgence whereas Elizabeth's was bestowed by barely concealed reluctance. "I believe the dancing will start soon,

Cousin Elizabeth. Shall I lead you into the ballroom so that we might be well placed to begin?"

Elizabeth forced her features into a neutral expression before reminding him, with equally forced fortitude, "You forget, sir, that Mr Darcy has claim to my first set. However, I would be pleased to search for him in the ballroom."

"You cannot hold him to such a promise, dearest Cousin!" Mr Collins tittered in the same fashion of Kitty and Lydia in the presence of a handsome officer. Elizabeth, having only just a moment before been in the throes of considering the matter of another, more important promise regarding Mr Darcy, felt annoyance prickle at the back of her neck. "Mr Darcy is all that is magnanimous and condescending, but you must not expect him to show you particular favour, especially when he has a lovely betrothed of his own awaiting him in Kent. But worry not, I am perfectly happy to fill his vacancy." This last declaration was accompanied by a smug little smirk which Mr Collins must have thought charming, but was decidedly the opposite.

"And Mary?" She would not bother to correct Mr Collins on the subject of promises to Mr Darcy, but the slight to her younger sister must not go unchallenged. Jane, to her side, looked slightly dismayed at the thoughtlessness being played out before her, but said nothing and allowed Elizabeth to take lead in this confrontation.

Mr Collins blinked stupidly at them both. "Miss Mary?"

"Yes, Mary. She is your assigned partner for the first set, sir. It was arranged so Tuesday last."

Mr Collins looked discomfited for a moment, but then regained his sense of importance immediately. "I am certain that Cousin Mary will not be offended and I shall make sure to save her a set later in the evening. Now, shall we—?"

"Good evening, Miss Bennet!" Mr Bingley inserted himself into their conversation with no consciousness of what he had walked into the middle of. He beamed about at them all as bows and curtsies were exchanged, though his eyes remained locked upon Jane. "And Miss Elizabeth and Mr Collins, of course. It is lovely to see you this evening, and I must thank you for attending our humble gathering. Forgive me for not being there to greet you in the welcome line with my sisters. I was attending to a small matter above stairs when you arrived."

With Mr Bingley before them, Elizabeth could not but wonder at the absence of his friend who had obviously not accompanied him. Again, her thoughts turned to Mr Darcy with nervous anticipation—*Where is he?* She was tempted to enquire as to his whereabouts from their host, but she loathed to interject herself into her sister's felicity for the evening. Jane and Mr Bingley were gazing longingly at one another, and it would be sinful to interrupt them.

Jane demurely responded for their collected party. "Not at all, Mr Bingley. We are very pleased to be here and grateful for your hospitality."

"Oh! Yes, so very grateful, Mr Bingley. As I was telling my fair cousins last week, I am by no means of the opinion, I assure you, that a ball of this kind, given by a young man of character, to respectable people, can have any evil tendency..."

"Yes, well..." Mr Bingley, at length, interrupted Mr Collins's unnecessary speech as the orchestra within the ballroom began to play the warning opening strains which alerted the guests that the dancing was about to begin. "It seems that the main festivities are starting. Miss Bennet?" Mr Bingley offered his pointed elbow for Jane's acceptance, and she shyly placed her hand upon his forearm.

"Oh, but Lizzy..." Jane paused to look back over her shoulder to the spot where Elizabeth remained with Mr Collins.

Elizabeth shook her head and made a shooing motion with her free hand. "Go on, Jane. I shall be along shortly, and your partner needs to attend his hosting duties."

"Are you sure?" Jane's eyes darted meaningfully to Mr Collins before she retrained them on Elizabeth.

Elizabeth appreciated her sister's reluctance to leave her in irksome company—it was certainly more thoughtfulness than the rest of her family had displayed—but in no way wished to encroach upon Jane's pleasures. "I am. Go, Mr Darcy will come to collect me shortly, I am sure, and we will join you in the line."

Jane made no further protests, though her expression was still mildly troubled, and allowed Mr Bingley to lead her in the direction of the ballroom.

As the more fortunate pair were threading their way through the diminished crowd ahead of them, Elizabeth remained in place where she was, searching more frantically about the emptying room for Mr Darcy. Where could he possibly be? The dancing was about to start, and Elizabeth did not wish to be trapped on the arm of Mr Collins when it did. Perhaps Mary would not really feel the slight of being abandoned for an elder sister, as she had shown no inclination towards opening the ball with their cousin, but Elizabeth was conscious of the degradation to them both should she be forced to capitulate and dance the first with Mr Collins. She could always refuse to stand up with him on principle, but the harsh rules of society would then demand she sit out for the rest of the evening and not be allowed to later accept Mr Darcy's hand for a set. Even in defence of another woman's claim, it must be so, or so her mother would insist.

As Elizabeth fruitlessly searched the great hall for Mr Darcy, her discomfiture increased. *He has not...could not...would not change his mind! Would he?*

"Come, Cousin."

Her thoughts fluttered about the absent Mr Darcy and whether they would find one another in time for the first dances—as well as the more alarming, panicked suspicions that Mr Darcy had for some reason decided to avoid her—and Elizabeth found herself suddenly unbalanced by a sharp jerk upon the arm which was attached to Mr Collins. She staggered an inch or so before righting her balance and casting a reprimanding glare at her cousin.

Mr Collins, however, was paying Elizabeth absolutely no heed as he directed her through the throngs of people flowing in the direction of the ballroom, grinning at everyone in that smarmy, conceited way she found so contemptable. He seemed to be silently bragging as he paraded her about like some exquisite ornament, a bauble he expected others to admire and envy. No doubt he was full of self-aggrandising speeches to unleash upon anyone who dared speak to him over the course of the ball. Elizabeth staggered slightly along in his wake, feeling as she had little choice but to allow Mr Collins's continued escort.

Perhaps Mr Darcy is waiting inside the ballroom and is, even now, looking for me. The thought calmed her more outrageous concerns and she plodded onward towards their destination.

"It seems that we shall be opening the dancing together after all." Mr Collins's tone, far too close to her ear for comfort, was irksomely boastful. He had got what he wanted and was happy to lord it over her.

Elizabeth rolled her eyes and followed their arc away from the disgusting spectacle that was the puffed-up Mr Collins. When they rested in a new direction, she felt her heart startle into a momentary stop before resuming its beat at an increased pace. Mr Darcy was coming towards them, weaving his way through the crowd as expeditiously as he could manage, and his gaze was trained fixedly upon her. The relief at spotting Mr Darcy's handsome face, at last, amongst the crowd of revellers was great to Elizabeth. He had not abandoned her or their dances and was, quite to the contrary, coming to claim both away from Mr Collins.

Elizabeth halted in place to allow him time to catch up, and it was perhaps this which ultimately alerted her other suitor to Mr Darcy's presence. She could feel Mr Collins tugging insistently on her arm but would not oblige him by moving, and so he bent down to hiss in her ear, "My dear cousin, the ballroom is this way—Oh! Mr Darcy!" The last was exclaimed at a louder volume which reverberated within Elizabeth's ear most uncomfortably.

Before Mr Darcy could come to them, Mr Collins took it upon himself to change their direction so that they might meet his patroness's most esteemed nephew along his course. Elizabeth found herself whipped about and practically dragged across the marble floor, Mr Collins shouldering other guests out of his way with rude efficiency. Elizabeth longed to release herself from her cousin and his mortifying behaviour, but he kept a firm hold on the arm within his possession. At least Mr Collins was taking her to Mr Darcy instead of away, as before.

Perhaps seeing her distress, Mr Darcy increased the speed at which he approached and only halted when she and Mr Collins were within proper proximity for a greeting. Finally, Mr Collins saw fit to release Elizabeth and, in doing so, sent her sprawling as she fought to compensate for the sudden lack of his momentum.

Mr Collins noticed nothing of this, however, as he was bent very nearly at a right angle in a deep bow to the object greater in his affections. "Mr Darcy! Good evening, sir. I am most honoured, I can tell you, to be at the same event as yourself."

Mr Darcy's eyes flickered only an instant in Mr Collins's direction—a flinty cold glare—before offering Elizabeth his own assistance. His white-gloved hands reached out to steady her by the points of her elbows, and she grasped at his forearms to regain her balance.

As Mr Collins continued babbling in the background, Mr Darcy leant closer to murmur a concerned question directly into Elizabeth's ear. "Are you well? Are you injured?"

Elizabeth, feeling a flood of embarrassment heat her face and neck, nodded quickly. "I am well, sir. No harm done."

Mr Darcy helped Elizabeth stand erect and then took her arm for himself in a proprietary gesture. Elizabeth might have been irritated a week before at his high-handedness, but instead could not complain that he was protecting her from further bumbling abuse from Mr Collins.

"Mr Collins." Mr Darcy interrupted the routine of bowing and scraping the parson seemed fond of with a barking command. "You have a very unpalatable habit of knocking people down. I think an apology is in order."

This scold put Elizabeth suddenly in mind of the day Mr Darcy had renewed his proposal, more specifically the meeting of their parties in Meryton where she had turned her back on him and Mr Collins had followed. At the time, she had felt a certain amount of cruel glee that her clumsy cousin had nearly knocked Mr Darcy down into the dirt, but now...well, it was still rather funny, though Elizabeth did not consider the scene with meanness of spirit any longer.

After a long stretch of silence in which the parson considered Mr Darcy's words with some confusion, he seemed to recollect this very same incident with horrified mortification. "Oh! Mr Darcy, I must apologise for the very great offence I committed on Tuesday last in nearly oversetting your very estimable person—"

"No, I meant your callous disregard to a lady's welfare. You have nearly felled your cousin in your haste to come pay your respects to me, and I would have you apologise to her."

Mr Collins glanced over at Elizabeth, espying her now on Mr Darcy's arm where she was clutched protectively to his side, before returning his eyes to the nephew of his beloved patroness. He then began begging forgiveness anew, though the object of his simpering remorse had not changed. "I beg your most humble forgiveness, sir, it shall never happen again. I am quite mortified to have behaved in such a manner and—"

Mr Darcy, perhaps realising at this belated point that no proper apology would ever be forthcoming from such a dullard, side stepped Mr Collins and more gently led Elizabeth in the direction of the open ballroom. Her cousin nipped along just behind at Mr Darcy's heels but, most thankfully, found he could not keep up with the more fit man's stride and fell behind not long after they had crossed the threshold.

With one final glance at the diminishing form of Mr Collins, Elizabeth refocused her attention upon her escort. "I suspect any day now, Mr Collins will be announcing his engagement to you rather than me. He is quite enamoured of your greatness, sir."

Mr Darcy's nose crinkled in a grimace, and Elizabeth laughed heartily at the sight. This seemed to restore Mr Darcy's good humour, for his features eased into the more natural expression she had come to expect from him over the past few days. He then returned her tease in like measure. "I assure you, Miss Elizabeth," he said with an air of mock gravity, "that my affections are not engaged by your cousin. If there is to be an announcement of that sort in the next few days, I have high hopes that I will be connected to another."

Elizabeth felt her cheeks burn anew as Mr Darcy's jest transformed into something more sincere and earnest. She met his gaze, though her bashful inclination was to look away from the shining intensity of it, and said with not a trace of humour, "Let us both hope so."

As Darcy led Elizabeth to the long line of dancers eagerly waiting to commence the first set, he could feel his heart leaping as if for joy within his chest. He had been struck positively dumb by his beloved's last pronouncement, one which had seemed extremely promising to his pretensions towards gaining her hand for something more permanent than a country dance. *Could Elizabeth be intending to say yes when I ask her again?* Just the idea made him giddy with hope.

A man who had felt less might have been capable of making conversation with the object of his desires, but Darcy remained mute until well after their positions in the line had been assumed and the first steps of a minuet had been taken.

In the meantime, Darcy drank in the vision of loveliness his Elizabeth presented in her ballgown. She might have been teasing him yesterday evening at Longbourn about coordinating their clothing for the ball, but she had been accurate in what she had told him of her ensemble, and Darcy was glad that he had worn the cream and burgundy waistcoat upon that chance.

Elizabeth was enshrouded in ivory satin which assumed the hue of candlelight in the glow of the myriad flames which enlightened the room. The edges of her sleeves, the lower hem of her gown and the tantalising edge of her bodice—at which Darcy only allowed himself a glance, as a gentleman never ogles a lady in company—were embroidered with swoops and whorls in delicate golden thread to complement the sheer overlay of deepest wine red. If Jane Bennet was an angel, Elizabeth was a goddess walking amongst them.

At length, the heavenly body that was his Elizabeth playfully insisted upon something being said between them. "We must have some conversation, Mr Darcy."

"Whatever you wish me to say shall be said, Miss Elizabeth."

"Very well, that reply will do for the present, though I must wonder at your tardiness this evening. I had thought you quite eager to take up all my dances for yourself?"

"I was—am," Darcy amended as he reached for her hand, a fortunate consequence of the dance. "In fact, I had been on my way to collect on the promised first set and found myself waylaid by Miss Bingley. After tolerating the distraction for some minutes, I was finally forced to be rude and leave her behind so that I could come find you. Had I realised that you were being treated so roughly by your cousin," Darcy's lip lifted into a sneer without conscious intention, "I would have shaken her sooner. Forgive me."

"Do not berate yourself on that score, sir, as that was an effect of your arrival. Mr Collins fancies himself in love with one or the other of us, and I am no longer convinced that it is myself who can claim the compliment."

Darcy scoffed at Elizabeth's jest and was rewarded by an amused giggle from that quarter. His face eased into a pleased smile; it felt good to banter with her so casually. So good, in fact, that most of his anxiety had melted into nothing.

Most, though not quite all. There was still a faint feeling of nervous anticipation buzzing along his skin and churning within his innards, but at least he no longer felt ill as a result. Elizabeth's presence and encouraging words had done much to quell the worst of his fears.

They danced in relative silence for the rest of the first set, commenting only here or there in an arch manner—it was not acceptable to discuss books in a ballroom, apparently, though the size of the room and number of couples were of great import according to Elizabeth's whimsical rules of conversation—but Darcy considered it a comfortable lack.

As they assumed their positions for the second, however, his complacency began to transform into impatience. Not with Elizabeth herself, but in regard to the discussion they were due to have sometime over the course of the evening which would settle their futures either together or apart. As this anxiety set in, the quiet between them became more stifling.

Elizabeth, perhaps cowed by Darcy's shift in mood, had not offered up any witticisms for some time and pranced through the movements without the joyful spring in her step which had characterised their first set.

Seeing her unhappiness and knowing himself to be the cause, Darcy waited for the pattern to take them as far as possible from the other pairs dancing about them and made his apologies. "Forgive me, Elizabeth, for being so dull. I was merely thinking…" he trailed off as a turn in the dance brought them closer in proximity to another couple.

Once they resumed their relative privacy again, thanks in large measure to being forced to remain in one place and await their turn to skip down the length of the line, Elizabeth prodded him to continue. "Yes?"

"I was thinking, since our time together was interrupted by the dismal weather early in the week," Darcy swallowed, attempting to force his heart from his throat and back into its usual position, "if you are not ready to give me your answer, I would beg an extension to court you more properly."

Elizabeth, after ascertaining with skittish glances that they had not been overheard, looked at him with the same sincerity of her earlier promising statement. "I do not require more time, sir."

"Oh...?"

"Indeed, I know exactly what I shall say when you ask me... what you wish to ask me." Elizabeth's cheeks were flushed brightly, though Darcy could not say whether from their conversation or the demands of the dance. His pulse quickened sharply as he waited for her to say more. "And—"

At that moment, Sir William Lucas appeared close to them, meaning to pass through the set to the other side of room; but on perceiving Mr Darcy, he stopped with a bow of superior courtesy to compliment him on his dancing and his partner.

And so their conversation was deferred yet again. Darcy despised balls.

FIFTEEN

Darcy's second partner of the evening was not so palatable as his first. Cornered, he had reluctantly secured Miss Bingley for the second set, though he took no pleasure in enduring her continued petulance. Ever since he had implied an engagement between himself and Elizabeth—a recollection which caused him to squirm with guilt—Miss Bingley had been even more insufferable than was her general wont. She had never been his preference of company, but desperation had made Miss Bingley bitter and single-minded, which was reflected in the sharp escalation of her forward behaviour.

Since his revelation on Friday, Miss Bingley seemed to be coming apart somewhat, putting her not only in conflict with others but also herself. At times she would simper and praise him with the same coquettish attentions which had always characterised their interactions, albeit with a manic glint in her eyes which had not been present before, while at others she would be sullen and short with him. Sometimes Miss Bingley would openly plead with Darcy to abandon his understanding with Elizabeth, but more frequently she would try to tempt him away with increasingly determined arts and allurements. Miss Bingley had also argued daily against him going to Longbourn to pay his visits upon the insistence that conditions were too dangerous for travel, even as the weather had improved day by day. In the next breath, she would attempt to entice him out into the sodden rose garden for a private stroll. Had he not known what she was about, Darcy would have been amazed at Miss Bingley's willingness to muddy her hems by venturing outside.

Miss Bingley had obviously not given up her pursuit of him, but it was becoming progressively clear by her erratic behaviour that she was coming to comprehend that all her former pretensions were for naught. Darcy presumed it was only denial which kept her from abandoning her hopes completely.

Darcy might have felt some pity for Miss Bingley if he had believed her interest in him were anything other than mercenary, but her constant praise of Pemberley belied any romantic sentiments she espoused. Much like her brother, Miss Bingley's every action was entirely transparent, her motives no mystery. Thus, all her final attempts at luring him into an engagement to herself had done nothing but frustrate Darcy and sap away any potential for compassion. He dearly hoped, for more than one reason, that Elizabeth would accept his hand tonight and take him off the marriage mart for good. Perhaps then he would feel more secure in leaving his bedchamber door unlocked at night.

In the meantime, Darcy had warned Bingley that, regardless of how Elizabeth ultimately answered his proposal, he would never consider himself beholden to Miss Bingley or her schemes. He hoped that Bingley had informed his sister of this fact, just in case the lady had been considering a move even more desperate than what she had yet attempted.

This evening Miss Bingley's behaviour had been of a piece of what he had experienced over the last few days in that she had done her utmost to keep him apart from Elizabeth while simultaneously putting herself forwards to his notice. When he had descended the main staircase, anticipating that he would meet Elizabeth as she walked into Netherfield and could assign himself her escort at the earliest opportunity, Darcy had found his path blocked by a somewhat flustered Miss Bingley.

"Oh, Mr Darcy!" Miss Bingley had exclaimed upon his arrival to the lower floor, disengaging herself immediately from the welcome line to come to him. In her stead, she left only the Hursts to greet the influx of guests, for Darcy had left her brother in the upstairs hall only a few minutes prior. "I am absolutely desolate for your opinion on a most important matter. Come with me."

She had then latched herself onto his arm like a clinging barnacle and led him away from the great hall where, over his shoulder, his love had just entered with her coterie of sisters. Darcy's eyes had lingered upon Elizabeth as she consigned her cloak to a servant, looking lovely in her warmly hued ballgown and shrinking every second as he was led away.

Darcy, unwilling to make a scene in the midst of a crush of people, had allowed himself to be commandeered by Miss Bingley and her flimsy pretext. But he had not tolerated this possessive treatment for long; as soon as Miss Bingley had drawn him away from the melee of revellers into the relatively empty card room, he had planted his feet firmly in the carpet and refused to move further, compelling her to stop likewise. His patience with her antics was decidedly at an end.

"Miss Bingley," he said, his words mangled through his gritted teeth, "whatever advice you require can surely be given by someone more adept at offering it than myself. You must excuse me."

"Oh, but—"

Darcy cut off Miss Bingley's sputtering with a raised palm. "You do not fool me, madam, with this guise of requiring my opinion. I think it best that we part ways here before you embarrass yourself further." So saying, he disentangled himself from Miss Bingley's clutches, prising her clinging fingers from the fabric of his jacket sleeve.

As he turned to leave, having nothing left to say to the woman, Miss Bingley called him back with an exasperated outburst which drew the eye of a pair of elderly gentlemen already seated at one of the tables. The hand which one of them had been dealing lay before them upon the green baize in half-distributed limbo as Miss Bingley began to unleash words which could only be termed unwise.

"I suppose you are off to greet your adventuress? Well, I am not surprised. You have long been led astray by her fine eyes, so it is little wonder you have found yourself entrapped by her."

Darcy turned back to her at a three-quarters position and glared at her with all the disdain that he felt. "Were I you, I would be cautious about slandering the good name of an honourable lady. I will not always be so forgiving of these lapses."

Miss Bingley opened her mouth as if to press her luck by saying more, but then her expression smoothed back into its usual placid hauteur and she closed it, having apparently come to her senses. The gentlemen in the corner, ignoring their cards entirely, were watching the scene unfold before them with undisguised interest.

Moderating her tone, Miss Bingley said, "I shall expect your escort for the first set."

"It is promised elsewhere. However, my second is still free."

Miss Bingley accepted this pronouncement with the small amount of grace she had remaining. "Very well."

With a final nod, and a quick glare at the eavesdroppers—the two gentlemen hastily took up their hands and began perusing their cards—Darcy had left Miss Bingley standing there in all her disgruntlement with the intention of finding Elizabeth. Unfortunately, by the time Darcy had freed himself from Miss Bingley and her schemes and returned to the hall where he had last seen his beloved, she and her family had already gone through the welcome line—with only the Hursts there to greet them, it could not have taken long—and been absorbed into the surrounding crowd. Darcy had then gone on the hunt.

Now, as Darcy turned about the floor with the disgruntled

Miss Bingley, he glared at Mr Collins's back as he led Elizabeth, limping, towards the chairs placed against the far wall. It was well for the parson that looks were not incendiary for, if they had been, Mr Collins would surely have gone up in flame in the heat of Darcy's displeasure. Almost as if he could feel Darcy's eyes burning into the back of his coat, Mr Collins quickly bowed to Elizabeth and scampered away.

Darcy was preparing himself to make apologies to Miss Bingley and go see to Elizabeth's comfort when his beloved, upon catching his eye, smiled placatingly and shook her head. Though it was still tempting to abandon his partner and her cold silence, Darcy sighed and remained where he was, though his attention remained divided between the demands of the pattern and his dearest, loveliest Elizabeth.

"Now that it seems Eliza will survive her injuries," Miss Bingley's waspish tones interrupted Darcy's more pleasant thoughts of Elizabeth, drawing his focus back to her, "perhaps you might attend to your partner? Regardless of what you have promised her, I am engaged to you for this set and require your full concentration."

"My apologies," Darcy replied without any real sincerity. As Miss Bingley was technically correct, he forced his gaze away from where Elizabeth sat with a friend dressed in blue. He would not bother to converse without first being spoken to, however.

Miss Bingley, as he could generally expect from her, did not require Darcy's share of the conversation to carry on a tête-à-tête. No matter her habit of falsely agreeing with him or fawning over his every monosyllable, Miss Bingley truly had no interest in hearing aught but her own voice on any occasion. "Of course, I would have died from humiliation after partnering that oaf. He is her cousin, I understand, and part and parcel with the rest of them, it seems. I can only wonder that you were so willing to tolerate his company just to visit with your dear Eliza and her fine eyes."

Darcy wanted to respond that Mr Collins was no more

vexing company than Miss Bingley herself but held his tongue. Even he would not say something so impolitic directly to a person's face in the middle of a crowded dance floor.

"But then, they are to be your family soon enough, so I suppose you must accustom yourself to their ridiculous ways. Of course, as I have yet to hear an announcement, perhaps you are reconsidering this foolishness...?" Miss Bingley looked at Darcy through her periphery expectantly.

"No, indeed."

Miss Bingley sniffed and they pranced down the line while she radiated discontent.

When their set was blessedly over, Darcy led Miss Bingley to where her sister stood along the perimeter of the room and abandoned her there with a stiff bow. Without any hesitation at all, he turned and made for where he had last seen Elizabeth seated next to Miss Lucas. Much to his dismay, however, he arrived just as a red coated lieutenant—one which looked vaguely familiar, but whom Darcy could not definitively place—was leading his beloved towards the dance floor for the third set. Darcy's shoulders slumped with disappointment.

As she passed him, however, Elizabeth reached out and discreetly touched the cuff of his sleeve and offered him a shy smile. His heart danced a little reel within his chest as she moved away, visibly disappointed at their growing distance. It seemed that, save for their predetermined sets, they were destined to be always watching the other from afar.

Instead of begging for the hand of another lady, Darcy determined to follow the steps of his heart and watched as Elizabeth took her place in the line. If he could not partner her himself, he would observe.

As Mr Collins assisted her in hobbling over to the chairs against the wall where Elizabeth could sit out for the remainder of their set, he babbled apologies at her. "My dear cousin, I am most sincerely apologetic for the injuries you have suffered. The pattern seemed simple enough at first and I am sure that Mr Lucas was meant to go the other way—"

"You are forgiven, sir. Please, do not make yourself uneasy on my account." Elizabeth cut off Mr Collins before he could elaborate any further on how very sorry he was or how he had thought he had been up to the challenges of the dance when, apparently, he was not. Should she allow him his head, Mr Collins would undoubtedly be prattling on without cessation throughout the rest of the ball, and Elizabeth had not the patience for it. Further, Mr Collins was already unpardonably tardy in introducing Lady Catherine's opinion into the matter and Elizabeth would spare herself the grand dame's unsolicited advice if she could.

Dropping down into the most conveniently close seat available, Elizabeth sighed at the relief experienced by her poor abused toes. She stretched them out within her slippers and wiggled them to determine if there was any lasting injury. There was soreness, of course, but it was fading and all her digits were functioning as they should; they would likely be interesting shades of blue and purple in the morning, but Elizabeth suspected that they were otherwise no worse for wear thanks to her cousin's clownish dancing. With some rest, it was likely that she would be prepared for her next partner.

"Can I bring you anything for your present comfort, Cousin Elizabeth?"

Elizabeth at first intended to issue a curt negation to Mr Collins's offer, but it then occurred to her the next instant that sending him on an errand would at least have the benefit of freeing herself from his company temporarily. He would come back as she could not possibly be so fortunate for him to stay away, but any reprieve would be welcome.

"A glass of lemonade would be most appreciated."

"Then I shall go fetch you one!" Mr Collins said and, after a long stream of unnecessary words and a deep bow following this benevolent proclamation, scampered off to do just that.

Once Mr Collins was out of sight, the line of dancers became visible to Elizabeth again. She smiled and chuckled to herself as she realised that a tall dark figure of a man who was proceeding down the dance as the partner of Miss Bingley kept glancing in her direction, an inquisitive scowl upon his face. Mr Darcy, wholly ignoring the petulant lady promenading at his side, raised a single eyebrow as if to ask if Elizabeth required his assistance. Elizabeth smiled at him and shook her head, and he remained where he was, though he seemed disappointed to not be of service to her. Or perhaps he had been looking for an escape from Miss Bingley; either motive would have been sufficient to inspire the sullen cast of his features.

While Elizabeth was indulging in her amusement and watching Mr Darcy skip about with Miss Bingley, she felt the air next to her unsettle and heard the soft thump of another body descend into the chair to her right. Elizabeth pivoted her head, wary at first of seeing Mr Collins there, and then smiled with real pleasure when she discovered her good friend instead. "Charlotte!"

Charlotte leant forwards and the two ladies exchanged kisses to each cheek before settling back into their chairs. "Lizzy, when I saw you sitting over here, I had to come and congratulate you on your triumph! To open the ball with Mr Darcy is a coup, indeed. Ten thousand a year, and very likely more. Your mother must be beside herself."

"A 'coup'? Oh, Charlotte..."

Playfully swatting Elizabeth with her fan, Charlotte said, "Do not look at me that way. You know that I was only teasing. And, in any case, it is true. Can I assume, however, that your opinion of Mr Darcy has altered for the better?"

Any offence at Charlotte's first implication was superseded by warm embarrassment and the quickened flutter of her pulse as her revised opinion of Mr Darcy came to the fore. Ducking her head with sudden bashfulness, Elizabeth focused on the fine weave of ivory satin across her lap. "You may."

"May I also ask what brought about this revolution in your feelings?"

"I am not at liberty to divulge everything here in the middle of a crowded ballroom." Beside her, Charlotte straightened, and Elizabeth could almost feel interest radiating from her. "Suffice to say that events occurred in the past week which induced me to get to know Mr Darcy better. He has been calling upon me at Longbourn."

Charlotte captured Elizabeth's gaze, her vividly blue eyes—Charlotte's most striking feature by far—searching the green depths of her friend's for sincerity. Apparently finding it, Charlotte covered her mouth in astonishment and sat back in her chair. "Truly?"

Elizabeth, her courage risen again, sat erect and replied, "Truly."

"In the rain?"

"Yes."

"Lizzy," Charlotte paused to gasp, "he must be in love with you!"

"That is what he tells me, yes." Elizabeth wished to laugh at the deepening shock upon Charlotte's face, finding amusement in her typically unflappable and ever practical friend being so taken aback, but withheld it. "Before you say anything, yes, I acknowledge that you had the right of it a few weeks ago when you claimed Mr Darcy looked at me other than to find fault."

Charlotte's hand dropped back into her lap where it rested upon the deep navy velvet of her own gown. "I admire your willingness to admit my perspicacity, Lizzy. But tell me, has Mr Darcy proposed? Should I expect an announcement forthwith?"

Elizabeth, though inclined to be open with her friend, recognised that in the middle of a crowded ballroom surrounded by inveterate gossips was not the place to do so. Her intentions to accept Mr Darcy's offer notwithstanding, it was not in the nature of either Elizabeth or her suitor to make a spectacle of themselves, and so it was best, at the present time, to be circumspect. Charlotte would not spread any news which Elizabeth asked her to conceal, but as Elizabeth watched Mary King skip by on the arm of an unknown redcoat and Mrs Long take a seat at the end of their row of chairs next to Mrs Goulding, it was apparent that being overheard was a genuine risk. Elizabeth felt she had already said too much considering the revelry ongoing about them.

Charlotte, following Elizabeth's gaze, apparently recognised this for herself. Without awaiting her friend's polite demurral, Charlotte deferred her request for more information. "On second thought, I believe I shall come by Longbourn tomorrow and we can discuss this at greater length then. I must ask now, however, as to the intentions of your second partner, whom I understand to be your cousin and heir to your father's estate. He seemed most...eager during your dance."

"Mr Collins. I have been trying to dissuade him from his attentions since almost the moment he arrived and have yet to shake him. Even Mr Darcy's presence has not encouraged him to look elsewhere!"

"Why not?"

As she sought out Mr Darcy on the dance floor, still moving stiffly alongside Miss Bingley, she smiled faintly at the expression of long suffering upon his face. He did not see Elizabeth watching him and so an air of tense discomfort hovered about him as they swirled through the pattern. *Poor man. So uncomfortable in company and also shackled to the likes of Miss Bingley.*

Distantly, Elizabeth responded to Charlotte. "He believes Mr Darcy engaged to his cousin, the daughter of his beloved patroness. Should you make Mr Collins's acquaintance yourself, be prepared to hear all about Lady Catherine de Bourgh, her daughter, her estate, her condescension...and so on. I know far more about the people of Kent than I ever expected to after a week of Mr Collins in residence at Longbourn."

"And I suppose Mr Darcy is not engaged to Miss de Bourgh?"

"Not at all."

"And Mr Collins does not suspect otherwise, even when Mr Darcy is paying court to you?"

Elizabeth at long last tore her attention away from Mr Darcy and refocused it upon Charlotte with an irreverent tilt to her mouth. "I think it is inconceivable to Mr Collins that any gentleman would throw over a Miss Anne de Bourgh for a Miss Elizabeth Bennet. I cannot, in all fairness, blame him there, though it is true."

"Oh, Lizzy..."

"You are beginning to sound like Jane!"

"Or rather Jane is beginning to sound like me! I have long felt much exasperation for your ways, Eliza."

"Oh dear, I am always in the very deepest of trouble when you call me 'Eliza.'"

The two dear friends broke into quiet laughter at Elizabeth's expense, neither of them truly annoyed with the other's insincere insults, and were caught up in it when a sweaty Mr Collins finally returned with a half-full glass of lemonade. He presented it to a startled Elizabeth with wheezy gallantry. "Here is...your lemonade...Cousin."

For the first time in Elizabeth's experience, Mr Collins seemed to be finished speaking after these few words. She accepted the glass, though she did not drink from it under the suspicion that Mr Collins already had, and said, "I had begun to wonder where you had gone, Mr Collins."

Mr Collins slumped into the chair on the left side of Elizabeth and rested his balding head against the wallpaper behind him. After a stretch of time in which he panted heavily, he replied, "It was madness, Cousin! I was on my way to fetch your lemonade when..."

And on he went to tell a strangely convoluted tale of somehow finding himself tangled in the line of dancers at the other end of the room, which then forced him into another chamber which had been set up for cards, where he had caused a ruckus by knocking over a vingt-et-un table and invoked the ire of the players, who then thrust him out into the entry hall where a footman unceremoniously shunted back into the ballroom. At that point, of course, Mr Collins had belatedly realised that he had not yet procured Elizabeth's beverage, and so had doubled back the way he had come—from the hall, through the hostile card room and then skimming along the wall behind the dancers—to where he had thought the refreshments were located, only to be informed that they were set up in a chamber location off the entrance hall opposite to the card room.

Even Elizabeth, despite her disgruntlement against this man and his pretensions, could not help but feel sympathy for his bumbling ineptitude. Mr Collins had, after all, been in pursuit of her comfort at the time and so she resolved not to laugh at him. Though she would be sure to share this anecdote with her father in private at a later time.

When Mr Collins had exhausted his tale, Elizabeth then performed the service of introduction between him and Charlotte, the latter of whom acquired another name on her dance card as a consequence. Elizabeth whispered a swift apology to Charlotte for this unfortunate circumstance as the second set ended, the third began, and she was approached by her partner.

Mr Denny awaited her patiently as Elizabeth expressed her concerns to her dear friend in a hissing whisper behind her fan. Mr Collins, who had promised himself to Jane for the third set, was thankfully not present to overhear in any case. "Guard your toes, Charlotte. Mr Collins seems to be only passingly familiar with dancing, and my own feet will likely be feeling the results tomorrow. I apologise again for not being able to spare you from this."

"Do not concern yourself," Charlotte said, a neutral smile spreading across her lips. "Go dance."

After a handful of additional dances and an equal number of partners, Elizabeth was pleased to be upon Mr Darcy's arm again, despite the whispers which followed them mercilessly throughout the room. It was quite something to her neighbours to not only see the stern, unsociable gentleman from Derbyshire dancing with someone other than his own party, but something else entirely to see him stand up with the same lady more than once—and for significant sets. That this lady was one of their own confounded and thrilled them in equal measure. Elizabeth found herself greatly amused at all the fingers pointing in her direction as she went down the line and could not but tease Mr Darcy for shocking the populace with his superior dancing.

"If you are not cautious, sir, some of the more delicate ladies in attendance will surely faint from such a magnificent display."

Mr Darcy had shaken his head and then smiled at her. "Then it is perhaps well that our acceptable number of sets have been exhausted for the evening. I would not wish to inadvertently create pandemonium. To prevent public unrest, I shall be sure to sit out for the remainder."

"Most considerate of you."

None of the other partners Elizabeth had stood up with could compare to Mr Darcy's 'superior dancing' either in regard to the actual performance of the steps or interesting conversation. Mr Samuel Goulding, with whom she had danced the fourth, had spent the duration hinting about wishing to know more about the nature of her relationship with Mr Darcy. Elizabeth had played innocent and pretended not to understand his aims, as it was widely known about Meryton that Mr Samuel Goulding was an even bigger gossip than his dear mama. Further, it was none of his business in any case. After that, Elizabeth had endured much the same from Mr John Lucas during the fifth and Mr Percy Purvis for the sixth. Not that she had expected any great pleasure from anyone aside from Mr Darcy this evening, but the other gentlemen were unusually tiresome without even suffering from comparison to her beau.

Only her third partner, Lieutenant Denny, had provided

any sort of variety of conversation, though Elizabeth found herself happier to endure the drudgery of nosiness over Mr Denny's veiled accusations against Mr Darcy.

"Mr Wickham wished me to convey his particular regrets that he could not be here this evening, Miss Bennet," said Mr Denny, his expression coloured with sympathy for what he must have assumed to be Elizabeth's great disappointment not to have the company of his loathsome friend. "He was forced to go to London yesterday on some matter of business for the regiment and has not yet returned."

Elizabeth, having not thought once about Mr Wickham since informing Mr Darcy of the vile slander the scoundrel had peddled to her, had startled at the mention of his name. "I am sure that it is a great misfortune for Mr Wickham to miss out on such an event."

Instead of leaving the topic at that, Mr Denny would prod at it as he turned her round in the dance. "I do not imagine his business would have called him away just now if he had not wanted to avoid a certain gentleman here." Mr Denny had then inclined his head to his left where a line of chairs was set up against the wall.

Elizabeth had looked that direction and saw Mr Darcy prowling about the perimeter of the room, his narrowed eyes following her progress down the dance with the lieutenant. Mr Darcy had been frowning, and Elizabeth had had no doubt that he was suspicious of Mr Denny, who was widely known to be a friend of Mr Wickham's. Considering this, she could not blame him for being displeased at seeing her dance with this particular officer. Not that he need worry about her head being turned by any of Mr Wickham's lies by proxy, something she intended remind Mr Darcy of at some later point.

Turning back to Mr Denny, Elizabeth had cooled her tone and remarked, "I recall Mr Wickham telling me once that he would not be driven away by Mr Darcy as he had nothing to be ashamed of. I wonder, then, at his absence tonight."

"Um, well..." Mr Denny's gaze then darted away and his

expression became befuddled. Eventually, his eyes had brightened as if something had occurred to him. "I suppose he did not wish to discomfit his host if certain scenes should arise unpleasant to more than himself."

"Then I suppose we must thank him for his very great sacrifice," Elizabeth replied, unwilling to disguise the sarcasm in her tone. "I will only say this, and then I will have done with Mr Wickham for the evening. Remember that there are two sides to every tale, and you have only heard one."

She said no more as they went down the other dance and parted in silence, on each side dissatisfied. It was difficult to say which was most pleased to withdraw from the other's company, though neither could lament the distance between them.

Aside from the unpleasant scene between herself and Mr Denny, the worst Elizabeth could complain of her other partners was that they were all a bit tedious in comparison to Mr Darcy. However, now that the dancing was on intermission and he was leading her in to supper, Elizabeth was once again most content with her lot. She clung to his elbow and laughed at his wry quips and very generally enjoyed his company.

Mr Darcy deposited her into a seat near the host's end of the table next to Jane while he and Mr Bingley left to fill their plates. As this would likely be her only opportunity to speak to her dearest sister for the remainder of the ball, knowing that Jane would likely be otherwise occupied with Mr Bingley afterward, Elizabeth discreetly teased her about the stir she was causing as the lady of the evening.

"Me!" Jane exclaimed with a soft laugh. "I think you have greatly underestimated the interest you have garnered as Mr Darcy's particular companion of the evening."

Elizabeth waved a hand in dismissal. "Not at all. As the favourite of our host, I believe you must be the preferred object of gossip."

As they were pleasantly bantering back and forth and awaiting their suitors' return, Elizabeth found herself jolted forwards in her chair. She started and turned round to locate the source of the sudden disturbance and witnessed the back of Miss Bingley's gown moving away from her towards the other end of the table. Her dinner companion, a gentleman that Elizabeth did not recognise but who dressed as if he hailed from London, seated her in the hostess's chair almost as far from the Bennet sisters as possible where she presided with a haughty air. After settling herself like a queen upon her throne, Miss Bingley cast a sour glare in Elizabeth's direction and then made a great display of cutting her rival by turning her face away.

Elizabeth might have been annoyed had Miss Bingley not looked entirely ridiculous. With amusement tugging at her lips, Elizabeth turned back to agree complacently with her sister that she was sure Miss Bingley had not meant to bump her chair. *No, of course not.*

The gentlemen soon returned with their plates and the conversation amongst their group of four broke up into the obvious pairs; Jane was absorbed with Mr Bingley on her opposite side while Elizabeth had attention only for Mr Darcy and his endearingly subtle charm. Over his shoulder, however, Elizabeth could not help but notice that Miss Bingley was imbibing rather heavily from her wine glass. It seemed that her dining companion was refilling it at an unusual frequency and, despite Elizabeth's dislike of the other woman, she could not help but feel concerned.

"Miss Bingley does not appear to be enjoying the success of her evening," she noted to Mr Darcy, a non sequitur that seemed to confuse him a moment.

Mr Darcy turned his head to glance over his shoulder at the other end of the table and, upon noting Miss Bingley and her spirit-soaked gloom, pivoted back to Elizabeth just as quickly. His voice was low so as not to carry across to the other guests when he said, "I suspect she is unhappy that I am showing you such attention. She has long held the desire to receive the same for herself."

"That much I had guessed. However, I do wonder that she is not attempting to insert herself between us. I have not known her long, but, in hindsight, she seemed to have that tendency while I was staying here to care for Jane a fortnight ago. She appears to have given up."

Then, much to Elizabeth's quiet astonishment, Mr Darcy looked away from her and began squirming upon his chair cushion as if it had suddenly sprouted thorns. "That is likely my fault. You see, on Friday, before I came to Longbourn, I may have...that is, I *did* announce to her and the rest of the Netherfield party that I had proposed to you. Now Miss Bingley presumes us engaged."

Elizabeth blinked at Mr Darcy, nonplussed at this revelation. Then she frowned at him, vaguely annoyed that he had, yet again, ignored her pleas for discretion, and this time without the excuse of inevitability at his disposal. "I see."

Mr Darcy scooted his chair closer to hers and, with panicked contrition characterising his features, lowered his voice further to apologise in a rumbling murmur. "I am more sorry than I can say, Elizabeth. I swear that I did not intend to say any such thing without your express permission, but I found myself caught up in the moment and spoke impulsively. It is no excuse, but so it is."

"I see," Elizabeth said again, her ire unabated.

"Truly, I had not meant to speak of it, but I felt compelled to defend your honour. Miss Bingley was insulting you terribly, and I could not allow it to stand. Please," Mr Darcy tentatively reached out and, beneath the cover of the table cloth, took her hand in his. "Forgive me."

The soft, downy quality of Mr Darcy's grey eyes implored Elizabeth to absolve him and, against her inclinations otherwise, she felt her anger melting under their power. With a sigh that released the remainder of her irritation at his mistake, she admitted to herself that what Mr Darcy had done was not so very bad; it was not as if he had stood up before the congregation at church on Sunday and called the banns himself. At worst, he had been impetuous and spoken hastily, a fault which Elizabeth could attribute to herself from time to time. Further,

Miss Bingley—and, by extension, the Hursts—would be the last person to spread rumours which would hurt her own chances at becoming Mr Darcy's bride, so it was unlikely that word of the 'understanding' between them had extended beyond Netherfield. *And it is not as if I am still wavering over whether or not to accept him.*

"Very well, sir," she said, squeezing the hand Mr Darcy had placed within hers, "you are forgiven. Though, really, you must learn to control yourself."

After the tautness in his shoulders had relaxed in relief, Mr Darcy smiled wryly at her. "When it comes to you, Elizabeth, I can promise nothing of the sort. But I shall try." The effect of his words was felt in the heat tingling in Elizabeth's cheeks.

Quite of a sudden, the moment between them was shattered by a shrill exclamation. "Ten *thousand* a year, and very likely more! I knew my Lizzy could not be so clever for nothing!"

SIXTEEN

Elizabeth cringed as her mother's excessively loud voice pitched itself high above the general murmur of conversation throughout the room. Of course, seated only across the table and two down from Mrs Bennet, Elizabeth and her suitor were in close enough proximity to have heard her clearly, even had she not been gloating at the top of her voice. Her hand, still captured within Mr Darcy's, clenched his fingers tightly as she began to feel the upheaval of mortification within her chest.

Mrs Bennet, never particularly circumspect even in her day-to-day life, became excessively loud and loquacious after imbibing more than a single glass of wine at dinner. At social events where the punch flowed freely and the claret was refilled whenever her cup dipped below the half empty mark, she was almost guaranteed to make some sort of ridiculous scene. All their neighbours were quite used to the phenomenon and were even known to make sly comments about Mrs Bennet's propensities amongst themselves. It was treated as a harmless community joke, one which Mr Bennet himself perpetuated with good humour.

Amongst strangers, however, Mrs Bennet's behaviour was a source of great embarrassment to her children, and the eldest two in particular. Elizabeth glanced to Jane who was blessedly insensible of the commotion their mother was making; her attention was riveted to Mr Bingley, who was similarly unaware.

Her eyes then shifted to Mr Darcy, and Elizabeth swallowed deeply. It was clear by the stony cast of his expression that he was perfectly cognisant of Mrs Bennet's display. Elizabeth squeezed her eyes shut tightly and prayed for her mother to move on to a different subject.

"Can you not imagine the carriages, the jewels, the fine clothes my Lizzy will have as Mrs Darcy? And the pin money! She will be able to purchase absolutely anything that she fancies with no consideration of the cost at all. The only shame is that she will be living so far from her family after she marries,"

"Does Mr Darcy not have a house in town?" Elizabeth could hear Lady Lucas ask. She silently cursed Charlotte's equally silly mother for provoking the subject further.

"I had not considered that! Naturally, he will live somewhere in Mayfair. Perhaps Grosvenor Square, or Brook Street."

Elizabeth slowly removed her hand from Mr Darcy's keeping and returned it to her own lap where it joined her other in twisting knots into her linen napkin. The churning shame in her stomach was beginning to make her feel ill.

"And I have yet to tell you the best part!"

"Indeed?"

"According to Mr Collins—he has taken quite a shine to my Mary, you know. Not as illustrious a match as her elder sisters, but at least Longbourn will remain in the family. Well, in any case, Mr Darcy is related to the nobility!"

"No!"

"Yes, indeed! As you know, Mr Collins owes his living to Lady Catherine de Bourgh, who just so happens to be Mr Darcy's aunt..."

Elizabeth reached for her own wine glass and imbibed deeply from within, simultaneously doing her utmost to block out her mother's continuing monologue on Mr Darcy's most superficial merits. The gentleman himself sat stiffly beside her without saying anything, and she had no doubt that he was deeply offended by Mrs Bennet and her increasingly loud bragging.

"And with Mr Bingley paying Jane so much attention,"—Jane and Mr Bingley, upon hearing their names referenced, looked up—"I expect we shall be planning a double wedding this Christmastide."

Elizabeth set her wine glass upon the tablecloth with more force than necessary, causing the deep red liquid within to slosh up against the sides of its crystal cup. "For heaven's sake, madam," she said, her face no doubt the same colour as her drink, "speak lower. The entire room can hear you."

Mrs Bennet turned her bleary eyes in her second daughter's direction and blinked slowly. By her expression, Elizabeth guessed that she had only just realised that the object of her monologue was seated so near to her. "And what have I said that is so offensive, pray? Has Mr Darcy not been calling upon you this week? Did he not dance with you twice?"

Elizabeth's response was forced through pursed lips. "He did, but there is no cause to humiliate him over it. I beg you, speak of something else."

Mrs Bennet then glanced to Elizabeth's right where Mr Darcy was seated—Elizabeth could not bring herself to do the same, fearful of the disdain she would find upon her suitor's features should she dare—and her expression eased from haughty offence to belated introspection. Mrs Bennet was not a clever woman, but she was always cognisant of keeping the marital prospects of her daughters happy.

"Very well." Mrs Bennet hiccoughed, reached for her wine, and then turned away to face Lady Lucas again. The matrons' conversation continued at a less objectionable volume as Mrs Bennet's topic shifted to grumbling complaints. "You see? Not even married yet, and she acts as if she is so far above us..."

Without looking in his direction, Elizabeth began mumbling an apology to her dining companion. "Mr Darcy, I beg you would excuse my mother's poor behaviour. I believe she has forgotten herself in the excitement of an evening out."

"Not at all—"

The calm rumble of Mr Darcy's voice was again overwhelmed by a cacophony of unpleasant sound, this time from the direction of the pianoforte at the other end of the room. The dirge which cut off Mr Darcy's sentence began with a loud boom as if the pianist had brought their fingers down with crashing intensity, causing more than one guest to jump in their chair.

Elizabeth, and most of the rest of the room besides, swivelled in her seat to observe the source of the sudden commotion. When she discovered her sister Mary seated at the instrument with a pedantic air of self-assurance, she bit her lip to prevent herself from groaning aloud. As if it were not bad enough that her mother had already created a most mortifying scene, it appeared that Mary, with her inappropriately dour song choice, was prepared to do the same. As Mary began to tinkle out the subsequent notes to her unexpected opening, Elizabeth began to fervently pray that her sister would not feel compelled to sing.

Unfortunately, much as He had when Elizabeth had begged for intervention during her mother's mortifying speech, God apparently was not inclined to heed her wishes. No sooner had the thought crossed her mind than Mary opened her mouth and a screeching, warbling sound came out of it, causing many of the room's occupants to involuntarily flinch. Mary projected her weak voice loudly until the bitter end of the song and accepted the lukewarm applause with a haughty expression that suggested it was only her due. Then, without even awaiting entreaty for an encore, Mary turned to another lengthy concerto and began again. Her audience settled in to listen with grudging politeness.

Since the Almighty would not listen, Elizabeth searched the length of the table for a different authority. Spotting him only three seats down from herself on the other side of her mother,

Elizabeth leant forwards and surreptitiously called to Mr Bennet. In doing so, Elizabeth was forced to bow round Mr Darcy, who silently sat back and allowed her egress into his personal space, but she did her best to ignore his proximity. "Papa!"

Mr Bennet dragged his eyes away from where his middle daughter was performing to look at his second eldest. There was a twinkle in his eye as if he expected Elizabeth to share in his enjoyment of the excruciating display unfolding before them.

Instead of the amusement her father was expecting, Elizabeth pressed her lips into a thin line and glared at him. This seemed to only increase Mr Bennet's humour, and his shoulders shook with silent laughter. However, Elizabeth persisted, raising her eyebrows expectantly, and at length he relented by shrugging his shoulders and nodding. From there, Elizabeth could only settle back in her chair, avoid Mr Darcy's scrutiny, and wait for the end of Mary's interminable display.

Eventually, at the end of an eternity of humiliation, the final notes of the song faded away and again polite smatterings of applause rippled about the dining room. While their doting mother praised Mary's performance—"So accomplished! Eminently befitting for a parson's wife."—their father interrupted the unwilling acclamation by speaking above it. "That will do extremely well, child. You have delighted us long enough. Let the other young ladies have time to exhibit."

Mary, though pretending not to hear, was somewhat disconcerted; and Elizabeth, sorry for her, and sorry for her father's speech which had not lessened her mortification but increased it, was afraid her anxiety had done no good. Others of the party were now applied to.

"If I," said Mr Collins from where he stood at his place next to the befuddled Sir William, "were so fortunate as to be able to sing, I should have great pleasure, I am sure, in obliging the company with an air, for I consider music..."

And on he went in an awkwardly pedantic style to describe how music was perfectly compatible to his position as a clergyman—just in case anyone had ever, for some reason, considered it an evil pastime—and further reassurance that he did not partake of it to an unhealthy degree. No, no, not when there were sermons to be written, parish duties to be attended to and, naturally, fair tithes to be charged without either impoverishing himself or offending his patron. When Mr Collins got to the point of his monologue at which he advocated grovelling to one's illustrious betters and their families, complete with a simpering look to Mr Darcy, Elizabeth covered her face with her hands and wished fervently that she might fade into the pattern of her chair. She could endure no more!

"Mr Collins is a remarkably clever, good kind of young man," said her mother from across the table. Elizabeth lowered her hands and stared at Mrs Bennet with an expression which could not help being incredulous. "He favoured my Jane at first—with her beauty and grace, who would not? And then Lizzy, but Mr Darcy has staked his claim there. Mary shall make him an excellent wife."

Further humiliation from that quarter was drowned out by a new source; Lydia, holding an officer's sabre above her head, was darting out of the reach of her dinner companion and laughing uproariously at his expense. The young lieutenant was chasing her with little chagrin and much playfulness, swatting at her with no real attempt to reclaim his property. "If you want it back, you shall have to kiss me!" Lydia threatened at the top of her voice.

"In that case..." Mr Saunderson made another lunge, this one with more intent than the ones that had come before it, but Lydia danced quickly out of reach and scampered away towards the open doors which would lead back into the entry hall.

Kitty, though not explicitly part of this vulgar display, was sitting in a group of other neighbourhood girls giggling and squealing over it. Once Lieutenant Saunderson had followed Lydia out of the room, Kitty grabbed hold of Maria Lucas and dragged her from her seat so that they might follow. The rest of the girls jumped up likewise and scampered after all the rest.

At least Lydia would not be alone with Lieutenant Saunderson, though Elizabeth did not feel as if she would be properly chaperoned. She was just about to get up and follow herself when she spotted several other concerned parties—mothers of some of the girls, all of them apparently more sensible than her own parents—rise and dismiss themselves from the table with a sense of urgency. Mrs Bennet remained largely insensible of the ruckus while Mr Bennet poorly stifled his laughter with a fist pressed against his quivering lips.

To Elizabeth it appeared that had her family made an agreement to expose themselves as much as they could during the evening, it would have been impossible for them to play their parts with more spirit or finer success. Jane and Mr Bingley, after conversation about them in particular had shifted to something else, resumed speaking only to one another and seemed largely insensible of what was going on about them. Elizabeth was happy for Jane but could not help wishing that she had someone to share in her misery besides Mr Darcy. As the evening had progressed from enjoyable to embarrassing, his discomfiture had become increasingly obvious and she had witnessed it evolve into disdain with mounting dread; the cold offence which emanated from him raised gooseflesh on Elizabeth's bare arms. He would certainly be withdrawing his offer now that the Bennets, far from behaving with the decorum of gentlefolk, had exposed themselves as vulgar, ridiculous, and unforgivably improper.

Elizabeth clenched her fists tightly within her lap and swallowed the thickness which was building in her throat. The tears collecting in her eyes were beginning to blur the candlelight, and she blinked rapidly to banish them; she would not make a spectacle of herself in company as the rest of her family had. She would be strong and control her emotions until she attained the privacy of her bedchamber at Longbourn later in the evening. Until then, she would meditate on how to relieve Mr Darcy of his obligations to her while still preserving some small amount of dignity for herself.

Her heart clenched most painfully as she internally debated the best words to knit together for this purpose. Only a week ago—less than, even—it would not have been so difficult to calmly and intelligently refuse Mr Darcy's offer of marriage, but now that she had come to understand him better, it was inexpressibly agonising to even consider it. Elizabeth had been ready to accept him, to admit truthfully that her feelings had shifted most decidedly in his favour, to tell him that she was falling in love with him...but her family had ruined it all. Elizabeth cared too much for Mr Darcy's happiness to saddle him with such ill-bred relations and so she must, to be kind, release him permanently. He would likely see the necessity of it, which only made it all so much worse, but Elizabeth was confident that he would be a gentleman about it and do nothing to increase her shame. No, Mr Darcy would respond gently, express his great sorrow, and only silently exult in his near escape. And then he would very likely leave Netherfield and she would never see him again.

Elizabeth jumped, startled in the middle of her miserable musings by a delicate touch to the back of one of her tightly fisted hands. She looked in the direction from whence the invasion had come and found Mr Darcy gazing at her steadily, his features solid and unreadable. "Come," he said quietly once he had achieved Elizabeth's attention, "it is quite warm in here." He stood abruptly and offered his hand for her to take.

Instead of doing so immediately, Elizabeth blinked at his proffered assistance, frozen in her chair. She knew without him saying so that he was prepared to have their long-awaited conversation, to put the matter of their tentative arrangement to rest. Even though Elizabeth had spent the past several minutes acclimating herself to the idea of releasing him and composing a speech for the purpose, she found herself unprepared now that the moment had come.

Her heart threatened to choke her and her lashes were wet but, at length, Elizabeth nodded, placed her hand within his and allowed him to steady her rise as she reluctantly climbed to her feet.

Mr Darcy firmly tucked Elizabeth's hand into the crook of his elbow and steered her away from the table towards the door which exited into the hall. Both were grave and silent as they walked the length of the table where the guests continued to eat and chat with one another, snide and mean-spirited whispers erupting here and there along the line. Mrs Bennet could be heard above them all, crowing about the good fortune of having three daughters well settled, while her smirking husband glanced about the room and chuckled at the folly of his family and neighbours. Mr Collins, having been denied the opportunity to sing by a quick-thinking Mrs Hurst, was seated again next to Sir William, each blabbering to one another without thought as to what the other was saying. Mary sat sullenly amongst the crowd and picked at her half-empty plate, looking up only occasionally to glower at the newly occupied pianoforte or her father. Kitty and Lydia brushed past them, arm in arm, as they reentered the room, their heads bent together in giggling confederation. There was no sign of an illicitly obtained weapon between them, and Elizabeth dimly wondered if Lydia had, in fact, traded it for a kiss. The thought made her burn with further humiliation.

The last person Elizabeth noted as she crossed the threshold was Miss Bingley, seated close to the door in the mistress's position, ironically toasting her as she passed by on Mr Darcy's arm. *Well, at least one person will be cheerful in the morning.*

Elizabeth dragged in a deep, shuddering breath and followed Mr Darcy out of the dining room.

As Darcy led Elizabeth away, his insecurities began to rise once more. She had not looked at him for the past half an hour, at least, whilst her family had made fools of themselves amidst the company. It had been a humiliating spectacle, and Darcy would be untruthful if he said that he had not been at least slightly disgusted by their behaviour, but he should have hidden it better; he was sure that Elizabeth had witnessed the disdain on his face and was now disinclined to accept him. What use was all his vaunted self-control if he could not show himself to better advantage in front of his beloved?

Darcy threaded his way through the diluted crowd lingering in the vestibule, Elizabeth trailing along beside him with her hand clenched tightly upon his arm, and made his way down the long hall which led to the retiring rooms. Instead of taking her there, however, he bypassed the one set up for ladies and proceeded farther into the house with a different destination in mind. At the end of the corridor, he paused at a set of frequently forgotten double doors and silently turned one of the knobs.

Beyond these doors was the place it had all begun, the place where his resolve to forget Elizabeth had unravelled into nothing and left him vulnerable to blurting out his feelings so recklessly. Here he would receive his answer, even if that meant the end to his hopes. Darcy's heart thudded restlessly in his chest as he crossed the threshold into his destiny.

"The library?"

Elizabeth's whispered question startled Darcy, who had become accustomed to her silence, and he jumped. "Yes, I thought this would be the best place for a private conversation."

Indeed, Darcy had planned ahead for this moment earlier in the day, expecting that they would require a respite from the festivities if they were to discuss their future in any detail. With this thought in mind, he had assigned a servant to the task of making sure that a fire was lit in the grate against the wall and that a couple of lamps were ready to be ignited at a moment's notice. Further, he had requested a decanter of fine wine in case there was cause to celebrate in the wake of Elizabeth's response. He suspected now that this particular preparation would not be used.

Though he was reluctant to do so, cognisant as he was that he might be denied other chances in the future, Darcy released Elizabeth's hand and proceeded over to the fireplace to stoke the flames higher. Neglected for so many hours, the fire had dimmed down to its embers and so Darcy threw a fresh log into the grate to prolong its life. Really, he was prolonging the minutes until he would be forced to face Elizabeth and what he suspected she was going to say.

When he could occupy himself with his menial task no longer, Darcy turned to face Elizabeth. She was standing where he had left her in the middle of the room, her eyes downcast to the carpet, and had said nothing beyond her initial surprised query as to their location.

After a deep swallow, an attempt to force down his rising dread, Darcy said, "I presume you know why I have brought you here."

Elizabeth still would not look at him. "I do."

"Before you give me your answer," Darcy began twisting the signet ring bearing his family crest round and round his little finger, a nervous habit which contradicted the strength in his voice, "I must beg your forgiveness. And possibly your mercy."

Her eyes widening with surprise, Elizabeth raised her head properly for the first time since her mother's exclamations at dinner and looked at him. Her jaw was slackened and, as a result, her mouth gaped as she regarded him with confusion. "My forgiveness? Whatever can you mean, sir?"

"I was not as circumspect about my feelings over your family's...enthusiasm as I should have been, and I have made you uncomfortable. I apologise."

"What?"

Darcy pressed on lest he lose his momentum. "I can assure you, that I will behave better in the future. I beg you not to allow my momentary lapse to affect your answer. Or," a sudden thought struck him which might preserve the tentative understanding that they already had, "if you would grant me the extension I requested of you earlier to prove myself to you. I swear it, I will overcome the pride which so disgusts you and become the sort of man to deserve your affections. I will make it my life's ambition to make you happy, Elizabeth, if you will but allow me another chance."

Elizabeth continued to stare at him as if he had gone entirely mad. At length, she blinked, shook her head as if to clear away the cobwebs of confusion from her mind, and finally spoke. "I…you still wish to marry me?"

"Of course I still wish to marry you!" It was Darcy's turn to stare at Elizabeth in bafflement. "Elizabeth, I love you."

"Even after that horrid display by my family?" Elizabeth's words became strangled as her eyes glossed over with a sheen of tears. She blinked rapidly as if to keep them at bay, but in doing so, the moisture overflowed and escaped the grasping of her lashes to scale down her cheeks. She swiped at the trails left behind as she continued, "How can you possibly wish to align yourself with me? It would be better if we both pretend that your proposal—either of them—never occurred."

Darcy, his previous hesitation forgotten, was across the room and in front of Elizabeth before she had even completed her miserable speech. With similar impetuosity, he reached out and gathered her into his arms so that he could trap her against him where she could not so easily escape. "Do not say such things, Elizabeth!"

"But it is the truth," she said around a bursting sob, pressing closer to him and burying her face in the folds of his cravat. "I scolded you for what you said against them, but you were right. They are crass, inappropriate, and entirely mortifying. I cannot allow you, or any respectable man, to connect yourself to them."

Darcy tightened his grip about her and buried his nose within her carefully styled coiffure. After breathing in her scent, an intoxicating mixture of lavender and the essence of Elizabeth herself, he felt calm enough to respond. With his cheek pressed against the top of her head, he said, "You are too generous to trifle with me. If your feelings are still what they were when I last asked for your hand, tell me so at once. My affections and wishes, regardless of the behaviour of others, are unchanged, but one word from you will silence me on this subject forever. However, if you think yourself one day capable of loving me, or even developing a comfortable fondness, my offer of marriage stands."

During the course of his speech, Elizabeth had stilled within the circle of his arms where her face remained hidden against his chest. At its cessation, however, she stirred and began to pull away. Darcy allowed it with some trepidation and awaited what she would say in response.

Elizabeth moved only enough so that she could look up at him, the sheen of her eyes bright in the firelight. "You truly do not mind taking on my family as your own? Even considering how mortifying they can be? You could never invite them to town, or introduce them to anyone, or—"

"I was a fool to say that before. While I will concede that, perhaps, a few measures must be taken before your mother makes her curtsey before the queen, I cannot see how this would greatly affect our happiness. What are a few vulgar relations to that?"

Elizabeth tittered a laugh in response to Darcy's surprisingly witty tease about Mrs Bennet being presented at court. No doubt she would come out of the experience with the same pomposity as Sir William. "Says the man with irreproachable connexions."

"I believe Lady Catherine's reputation precedes her," Darcy retorted, earning another laugh. More seriously, he begged her, "Please, Elizabeth, do not allow your mortification of tonight lead you to reject me. I have many flaws," he cringed slightly as he considered her list of them, "and I can accept it if these are insurmountable to your better feelings, but I would rather fail on my own merits than give you up because you would spare me embarrassment. Such is a noble but empty sentiment. With this in mind, I will ask again—will you marry me?"

The green in Elizabeth's eyes seemed to flicker in time with the firelight which cast a dull glow about the room. He could read some lingering indecision therein for a moment before her expression eased out of its crumple of melancholy. Her lips parted, she breathed deeply and replied, "I will."

"You will?"

"Yes, Fitzwilliam, I shall marry you if you truly wish it. After all, I...I love you too."

In the next moment, Darcy had groaned and covered her smiling mouth with his own. There was a small squeal of surprise from Elizabeth, but she did nothing to pull away or otherwise dissuade him from kissing her. Indeed, after an additional moment of hesitation, she angled her head to one side and her mouth softened beneath his. Darcy responded in kind to Elizabeth's encouragement by dipping his head in the opposite direction and sliding his hands up the length of her spine to rest them at her jawline where his fingers could luxuriate in the texture of her hair. Her own were balled into fists between them, clinging tightly to the lapels of his coat, and she made a tiny sigh of satisfaction as their embrace progressed.

When Darcy realised that he was on the cusp of taking their embrace too far, he reluctantly peeled his lips from Elizabeth's and swallowed deeply. He refused to release her entirely, however, and rested his forehead against his beloved's where he could continue to revel in the intimacy of the moment. "Dearest, loveliest Elizabeth..."

Darcy lifted the veil of his eyes to find Elizabeth beaming at him, her gaze full of sparkle and adoration. "My Fitzwilliam."

"Yours, always."

Darcy could not help himself. He kissed her again.

SEVENTEEN

Darcy could not recall being in a better mood. Of course, he had never experienced the euphoria of becoming an engaged man before, no matter how smugly confident he had been about Elizabeth's initial response to his offer the previous Monday. Now he exulted in the thrill of successfully obtaining not only his beloved's hand, but also her affections, both of which she had previously denied him. Was there any greater feeling?

The only thing which depressed his spirits even slightly was the interminable wait he must suffer before galloping over to Longbourn to request Mr Bennet's permission to marry Elizabeth. It was already half past ten, and Darcy longed to be off, but he had bowed to the convention of not paying early calls to his neighbours after a late night of revelry. The Bennets, and no doubt Elizabeth herself, were likely still abed after returning from the ball in the wee morning hours and so Darcy must exercise patience. How desperately he wished for a glimpse of Elizabeth's fine, teasing eyes!

Not that Darcy had got much sleep himself. When the last of the guests—the Bennets, incidentally, who had lingered thanks to a manoeuvre of Mrs Bennet's—had departed at two o'clock, he had dutifully floated up the staircase and laid down in his bed but had failed to actually achieve any repose for an additional hour after that. His head was so full of felicitous thoughts of his future with Elizabeth as his wife that Darcy had been unable to quiet his mind. Eventually he had drifted off but had woken again at eight in the wake of a blissful—and rather amorous—dream featuring his newly betrothed along the banks of Pemberley's lake. Darcy had tried to sink back into the vision but had achieved nothing greater than a doze before giving up, and rising for the day.

Since then, Darcy had primarily spent his time grinning like a besotted idiot and glancing at the clock repeatedly to determine if he could leave for Longbourn and see his dearest, loveliest Elizabeth. All attempts to distract himself with some other activity were felled by a blissful disinclination and so he paced about the half empty library, reliving every moment of similar longing between himself and Elizabeth which had taken place there.

Elizabeth had been so beautiful in the firelight the evening before, so stunning even in her initial melancholy, that Darcy was enraptured by his memories of her. She had fit so perfectly within his arms, her head tucked beneath his chin, pressed against his heart. Darcy sighed like a green boy with his first *tendre* as the sensation of kissing Elizabeth rose up into his conscious thoughts.

He was in the midst of recalling the sweet flavour and soft texture of his beloved's lips when he was dragged from his reverie by the staggering entrance of Bingley. It was the opening of the door which first alerted Darcy to his friend's presence, but the clumsy jostling of furniture which drew his eyes to where Bingley stood straightening a small end table. As Darcy had already been grinning continuously since Elizabeth had granted him her hand the night before, his expression did not change upon beholding Bingley in all his ungainly magnificence.

"You are up early," Darcy said in an uncommonly jovial fashion.

Bingley stared at Darcy as if surprised to see him there. "As are you! Well, I suppose that is not unusual, but..."

Darcy guffawed. "I could not sleep. But why are you up? I had not expected to see you until past noon, at least."

"Caroline," replied Bingley. "She woke in a dither about an hour ago and barged into my room to demand that we all adjourn to London as soon as possible. I sent her back to bed to finish sleeping off all that wine she drank last evening. After that, I could not get back to sleep myself, so I wandered downstairs hoping that one of my guests was awake. I suppose I should not be surprised to find you up and about."

The thought of a foxed Caroline Bingley barging into his rooms to make a spectacle of herself was both amusing and disturbing to Darcy. He rather wondered if she had not stopped at his bedchamber first and then, upon discovering him absent from his bed, sought out her brother instead. It would not surprise him if it were so, but it was unfair to conjecture such behaviour of a lady.

"You could not really expect your friends from town to be awake just yet," Darcy said, avoiding any commentary on Miss Bingley. "In my experience, they tend to stay abed until the next debauchery is about to begin."

Bingley laughed and stumbled over to seat himself in front of the fireplace. Darcy joined him there, taking up the chair which Elizabeth had preferred during her stint at Netherfield when her sister had been ill.

After a long moment of wearily rubbing the corners of his eyes with a thumb and forefinger, Bingley said, "Can I suppose by the ridiculous grin on your face that Miss Elizabeth has given you a better response to your most recent proposal than the last?"

"You may," replied Darcy, unrepentantly smug. "After dinner last evening, in this very room. I am to be married."

Bingley dropped his hand to his lap, blinked a few times and then grinned broadly at his long-time friend. "Congratulations, man. I know you will be very happy with Miss Elizabeth as your wife."

"I most certainly will."

"Now I must beg you for my own congratulations," said Bingley, sitting up and practically bouncing upon his chair cushion, "for I have made my own proposals to your lady's elder sister and, I am proud to say, she has accepted me. We are to be brothers!"

Darcy stretched his hand out to Bingley and the two men shook hands vigorously, each furthering the manly sentiment by patting one another upon the shoulder as well.

"Congratulations. Miss Bennet is a charming lady, even if she is nothing to my Elizabeth, and will make you a very happy man."

"Nothing to your Elizabeth, eh?" Bingley shot back with a chuckle, taking no true offence at Darcy's jest. "I beg to differ there, old boy. My Jane is everything a lady should be and, as lovely as her sister certainly is, has no equal. She is an angel!"

"I stand by my assessment! An angel is nothing to a goddess."

And so Darcy and Bingley continued on with their good-natured dispute, each boasting to have claimed the hand of the best Bennet sister of the bunch while dismissing the biased view of the other, until it was finally time to depart for Longbourn.

As Darcy and Bingley approached Longbourn together, Darcy astride the spirited stallion who had brought about his current happiness and Bingley plodding along atop his more gentle grey mare, they discussed what they might anticipate from a meeting with Mr Bennet. Darcy, who had already spoken to him in regard to his intentions towards Elizabeth earlier in the week, warned his friend that their future father-in-law would likely find much pleasure in toying with them before ultimately granting his consent, such was his sardonic nature.

"When I spoke to him on Friday, he danced about the question until I was ready to demand an answer," Darcy cautioned his friend with a wry smile. "I would expect no less for you."

"But he would not deny his consent, would he?" There was something of a whine in Bingley's voice which indicated how nervous he was to be at Mr Bennet's mercy.

Darcy wished to laugh at his friend's expense, but it had not been so very long that his own suit had been rather tenuous and he restrained himself. "If he did, you can be assured that Mrs Bennet would convince him otherwise. But, in all seriousness, I cannot think that you have much to worry about. Mr Bennet is perhaps a little too inclined to laugh at the follies of others, but he would not deny his daughters anything that would bring them happiness. If you are Miss Bennet's choice, then he will undoubtedly give you his blessing."

"Are you certain?"

"As certain as it is possible to be," Darcy replied with much solemnity. "Elizabeth thinks highly of him, and he was receptive to my overtures earlier in the week. Now, stop fretting like an old woman or you will hardly be able to speak to Mr Bennet when the time comes."

Bingley grimaced and then quieted, almost sulking atop his saddle. Darcy was not as sanguine as he had intimated to his old friend about facing Mr Bennet—he recalled perfectly well the wary look upon the elder man's face when he had requested the honour of calling upon Elizabeth with the eventual goal of marriage—but he felt secure enough that he would not be refused consent. It had been Elizabeth's esteem which had been difficult to achieve and, now that he had, Darcy was filled with the confidence that all would be right in the end. Elizabeth wanted him for her husband, and nothing would deter him from meeting her at the altar in a few weeks' time.

The pair of gentlemen rode down the main street of Meryton in contemplative silence, nodding occasionally to a familiar face as they passed through the town, and proceeded down the lane which led to Longbourn in the same fashion. Bingley persisted in twitching nervously while Darcy was calmly introspective. They approached their futures in manners suited to their individual personalities.

While they were dismounting from their horses some minutes later, they both jumped at a shrill cry which had suddenly sounded from within the manor house. It had been one of dismay, or perhaps rage, and had raised the small hairs on the back of Darcy's neck. Before he and Bingley could do more than glance at each other with alarm, the front door burst open and a pair of young ladies exited the domicile with some haste, one still tying the bow of her bonnet beneath her chin and the other pulling on a glove as if they had barely paused long enough to gather their outdoor things before thrusting themselves into the cold November weather.

"Elizabeth!" Darcy cried out in some surprise, his eyes wide and brows raised high.

Elizabeth looked up from where she had been straightening her glove and her eyes found him directly. The next instant she smiled so broadly and so brightly that Darcy's heart gave a great leap and then began to stutter.

"Fitzwilliam!" was her joyful response as she quickened her steps in his direction.

Darcy passed Blackthorne's reins on to a servant and hastened to meet her halfway. When they reached one another, she held out her hands and he claimed them for his own, lifting them up so that he could place kisses upon the backs of each. Elizabeth's cheeks reddened bashfully, but she did not protest the affectionate gesture.

She looked fresh and lovely in a deeply green gown that reflected the verdant shade of her eyes. She had paired it with a richly yellow, almost golden in tone, spencer with a high collar which enhanced the hint of tan which lingered upon Elizabeth's skin even so long after summer had concluded. She looked as if she belonged amongst the changing trees which backed the house—or, better yet, at Pemberley, where tall oaks flourished and set the landscape aflame every autumn.

"Ahem."

Tearing his eyes away from Elizabeth for the first time since seeing her, Darcy looked up to determine the origin of the disdainful cough which had interrupted him. Miss Mary stood a few yards away with her eyes narrowed and her lips turned down at the corners in a disapproving frown. To her right, Bingley was approaching to join their party.

Darcy straightened, embarrassed to have been rebuked for publicly showering his newly betrothed with adulation, and bowed his head in the other lady's direction. No matter his discomfort, however, he maintained his grip upon Elizabeth's fingers and she did not bother to pull them away. "My apologies. Good morning, Miss Mary."

"Mr Darcy." The perfunctory greeting was accompanied by a sniff which might have been subtle if Miss Mary had not accompanied it with a toss of her head. She then turned her attention to her elder sister. "Lizzy, I think it best that we take our walk now."

Another loud noise, this one deeper and more thunderous, emanated from within the house and both sisters flinched visibly. In the wake of this, Elizabeth said, "I think you are right. Fitz...ah, Mr Darcy, would you please provide me your escort?"

Darcy glanced towards Miss Mary, discovered her actively watching them and bent his head to whisper in Elizabeth's ear. "I had come to speak to your father this morning."

"I think it best that you not go inside at just this time, sir," Elizabeth said, indicating Longbourn with a nod. Inside, the shrill exclamations from Darcy's arrival could again be heard and were now formed into barely decipherable words. The thunderous explosions continued as well and the combination created such a cacophony of sound as to disturb a flock of birds nesting in the nearby trees. It was clear that a turbulent row was ongoing somewhere within.

Thankfully, Elizabeth was already outside with him and so

Darcy had no worries that she would come to harm, but he was still concerned about the combatants and the potential for attendant damage from their battle. "Should I offer my assistance?"

Elizabeth shook her head and began tugging him in the direction of Longbourn's back garden. "No, that will not be necessary. 'Tis just Mama and Mr Collins, and Papa will step in if necessary. Come, I wish to show you the hermitage."

"I see." Darcy allowed himself to be led away from the front of the house a few steps but then, recalling Bingley, stopped and turned back a moment. "Bingley," he called to his friend who was eyeing the house warily, "you may feel free to speak to Mr Bennet first. Inform him that I shall be up directly to make my own petition."

Bingley shot Darcy an alarmed look, darted his eyes again at the face of the house and then nodded with some resignation. He marched up to the front door, knocked, and awaited a servant to let him in.

Darcy turned away and offered his arm to Elizabeth. She took it, shifted as close to him as she could while still allowing them to walk, and they ambled in tandem in the direction Elizabeth indicated. Miss Mary was a short distance ahead of them, waiting and scowling. She surely meant to be a most diligent chaperon.

"You said that your mother and Mr Collins are having a disagreement?"

Elizabeth shook her head, but her eyes sparkled with some mischievous amusement. "I think 'disagreement' is an understatement but, yes, they are not best pleased with one another."

"Might I ask why?"

Elizabeth lifted an impertinent eyebrow at him and a smirk formed on her kissable lips. Darcy was tempted to lean down and taste them as he had last night, but Miss Mary would not have stood for it, and he owed his beloved the courtesy of listening to her reply.

She gave it with a healthy measure of teasing. "Can you not guess?"

He shook his head, though he had his suspicions. Undoubtedly Mr Collins had learnt something of Darcy's ultimate intentions towards Elizabeth and, combined with the lingering effects of strong drink from the ball, might have become belligerent over them. As for Mrs Bennet, Darcy could detect little difference in the volume or timbre of her voice at all.

"Then I shall tell you all about it. It all started when I came down for breakfast this morning..."

Earlier...

It was only seven o'clock in the morning, but Elizabeth could not lie abed any longer. She kicked herself free of her covers and practically sprung from her mattress with an exuberance that belied her lack of rest from the night before.

They had come home from the Netherfield Ball in the earliest hours of the morning, but Elizabeth, full of bursting joy and anticipation for the following day, had been able to manage no more than a doze when she had finally retired for sleep. *I am engaged!* was her constant mental refrain. *To Mr Darcy, my sweet Fitzwilliam.* Better yet, he had still wanted her despite her family's detestable behaviour, so wantonly displayed at the ball, indicating that his feelings for her ran deeper than the thin inclination she had accused him of earlier in the week. Only the very deepest of love could overcome the faults and follies of the Bennets in all their dubious glory.

Elizabeth only dimly noted the cold floor beneath her toes as she skipped over to her wardrobe and began rifling through it for something appropriate to wear. *The mustard yellow gown is definitely out,* she decided with a chuckle to herself, *and the pink velvet requires laundering, but perhaps the blue? Or the green? What would Fitzwilliam prefer?*

At length, Elizabeth had determined that the green one would do and she dressed herself carefully, feeling that she ought to take as much time as possible at her toilette as no one else was likely to be up and about so early today. She donned her dress without assistance from either sister or maid and then turned her focus to her hair, something which she had never shown much promising talent in arranging herself. Elizabeth piled it up as neatly as she could and hoped that either Jane or Kitty would be awake before Darcy arrived to speak to Papa; they were both deft hands at taming her curls into something flattering, with Kitty perhaps boasting the most fashionable eye amongst the Bennet ladies.

When Elizabeth had dressed and coiffed herself to the best of her limited abilities, she rose from her dressing table and, after quickly donning her slippers—she would not walk out this morning for fear of being away when Darcy called—left her room to seek the warmth of the parlour where a fire was most likely to have been set.

A mere hour after leaving her room, right about half past eight, Elizabeth was startled from gazing steadily out the parlour window—she found herself equally too lethargic and distracted to concentrate on any activity requiring more industry than daydreaming—by the entrance of another person into the room. Her head pivoted in the direction of the door and she found, to her pleasant surprise, that Jane was up. She looked as amazed as Elizabeth felt to find anyone besides herself out of bed.

"Lizzy! I had thought you still asleep," Jane said as she came nearer and took a seat across from her dearest sister.

Elizabeth, who had taken up the wingback chair by the fireplace out of sentiment as much as a desire for the warmth of the hearth, welcomed her. "I had thought the same of you! I have been down here an hour or more. I could not stay abed."

With no one else about, the eldest Bennet sisters lounged in the unladylike fashion of their early youths with their feet tucked warmly beneath them and their elbows propped against the armrests. Elizabeth smiled as she recollected how she had once taunted Darcy in the library at Netherfield with her hoydenish ways by sitting in a remarkably similar fashion; she had intended to shock him, and was almost certain that she had succeeded at her aim, for he spent no more than half an hour in her company before abandoning her there alone.

To go riding. Elizabeth's smile shifted to a grimace for a moment before she shook off the more awkward remembrances of that day, reminding herself that all had turned out well in the end.

"I could not either," said Jane as her eyes travelled the length of the room to the window Elizabeth had been pondering for some time.

"Oh?" Thoughts of her dear Darcy wiped from Elizabeth's mind for the moment. He would be back soon, she was sure, but in the meantime, she was eager to hear what had disturbed Jane's repose. Had it something to do with Mr Bingley? The flush creeping slowly into her sister's cheeks told her as much. "Do you have something to tell your most favourite sister, Jane?"

Jane turned back to Elizabeth and, with an unconvincing display of passivity, countered, "Do *you*, Lizzy?"

Elizabeth felt her own cheeks warm, but more from happiness than embarrassment. Darcy, as she had expected, had sauntered right back into the forefront of her mind where he rightfully belonged. "As a matter of fact, I do. Fitzwilliam…that is, Mr Darcy and I spoke last night and…we are engaged."

"Oh, Lizzy!" Jane lurched forwards and grabbed her younger sister round her shoulders in a hug. Elizabeth returned it by twining her own arms about Jane's back, laughing joyfully at the reaction she had received. Pulling back after a lingering embrace, Jane continued, more spiritedly than many thought her capable, "I just knew you would accept him in the end! I knew he could not be so in love with you for nothing!"

Elizabeth laughed again, finding that she was afflicted with the impulse most grievously this morning. Ever since accepting

Darcy, now that she thought of it. She had never been in such an excellent mood before this—or at least she could not think of another time when her joy had overflowed so much.

"Yes, I rather suspected that you were on his side all along."

"No, I was always on your side," Jane said with a fond shake of her head. "I admit that I had hopes for his success, but only because I could see how very much he cared for you. You deserve a husband who loves you deeply, and I could not allow your stubborn prejudices to deny you the opportunity to have one. Mr Darcy is just the sort of man who would love a woman forever, and he had the exceptionally good sense to fall for you."

"Literally!" Elizabeth exclaimed, reminding them both of the mishap which had instigated Darcy's first offer of marriage. Jane, after a short moment of puzzlement, joined Elizabeth in expressing her merriment in fits of giggles.

At length, when their mirth had subsided and they had caught their breath, Elizabeth turned the conversation back to Jane and her beau. "And I will ask you again, do you have any news to share?"

Jane bowed her head as shy pleasure overcame her. "Last night, while we were all waiting for the carriages, Mr Bingley asked for my hand. I said yes."

It was Elizabeth's turn to throw her arms about Jane for an exuberant hug of congratulations. "You will be a very happy woman, Jane! I cannot say how delighted I am that you will marry the man that you love."

"And can I congratulate you on the same?" Jane asked, settling back into her chair as they separated again. "It was less than a week ago that you felt very differently about Mr Darcy. Are you sure of your happiness with him now?"

"I thought you were in favour of my match with him?"

"I am, for Mr Darcy is an honourable man who loves you dearly, I believe, but I would know that you are content with your choice and do not feel persuaded into it. Forgive the question—are you quite certain that you can be happy with him?"

"There can be no doubt of that. It is settled between us already that we are to be the happiest couple in the world."

"Do be serious."

"Very well, I shall make an attempt." Elizabeth breathed deeply, exhaled, and began speaking of what she had only come to understand in hindsight. "I found, much to my embarrassment, that my policy of believing in first impressions is not as infallible as I had once thought. It turns out that I have long misunderstood Fitzwilliam and that, once my prejudices against him had been wiped away, a good man was left behind, a man I can respect and love more than any other. Truly, Jane, I cannot imagine marrying anyone else! He has such steadiness of character, such intelligence, so much loyalty and affection...what more could any woman ask for in her husband? Other than to be handsome and very, very rich, of course, which he already is."

Jane laughingly entreated Elizabeth to be serious again and so she obliged by adopting as much sombreness as her elevated mood would allow.

"Honestly, I have learnt more about my future husband sitting before this fire," Elizabeth nodded to the cheerily flickering hearth, a fond smile creasing her lips, "than I have about any other gentleman of my acquaintance, no matter how long known to me. We spoke of everything, of nothings, of whatever occurred to us in the moment, and he actually listened when I spoke. He did not talk down to me or dismiss my opinions, but sought to understand them. Further, he has shown great trust in me by revealing certain things which ought to be kept secret wherever possible. That faith was inspiring. Most of all, however, I think no woman can be insensible of the very great compliment of a worthy gentleman being in love with her. I think knowing that Fitzwilliam felt so strongly inspired my own feelings at first—little though I was willing to admit to them at the time—and from there they have grown into a very great affection for him and all his many strengths and flaws, all the things which make him into the man he is. I am even fond of his pomposity!"

Elizabeth chuckled shakily and blinked away the slight sting which was the harbinger for a surge of tears. She also swallowed against a certain tightness in her throat which threatened to shut down her ability for further speech. "We are very different creatures, he and I, but we are also so much the same that I think it was inevitable that we fall in love with one another. Indeed, I have come to comprehend that he is exactly the man who, in disposition and talents, would most suit me. His understanding and temper, though unlike my own, will answer all my wishes. It is a union that must be to the advantage of both of us. By my ease and liveliness, his mind will undoubtedly be softened—indeed, his manners are already improved. And from his judgment, information, and knowledge of the world, I will receive the benefit of greater importance. In short, yes, Jane, I think we will do very well together."

Jane grasped Elizabeth's hand within hers, squeezing it lightly. "I congratulate you. We shall both be incredibly happy."

Breakfast was delayed at Longbourn after the late night at Netherfield and so the Bennets did not gather round the table until nearly eleven. Even then, both Kitty and Lydia were absent and Mary, who was unused to staying up into the early hours, could not stop yawning into her napkin. Mrs Bennet sat at the end of the table rubbing at her temple with one hand and disdaining the food set before them while her husband, seated at the head, hid behind his newspaper and chuckled at the rest of them.

Elizabeth and Jane sat next to one another and spoke quietly in deference to their mother's headache and Mary's bleariness, though they avoided any topics even tangentially related to their newly acquired betrotheds. It would not be right to discuss their engagements without the gentlemen first acquiring Mr Bennet's explicit consent and, further, Elizabeth did not wish to incite an uproar—even a happy one—

until it was absolutely necessary. Then there was Mr Collins and his ambitions for a Bennet bride to consider; surely, it was best to remain mum on the subject of Elizabeth's betrothal to Darcy until it was absolutely necessary to reveal it.

"Well, I am off to my study," Mr Bennet said in his usual off-handed manner as he folded up his newspaper and tossed it upon the table cloth. So saying, he rose, stretched out his back and then trundled from the room.

"Shall we adjourn back to the parlour, Lizzy?" Jane asked, daintily dabbing the last crumbs of her meal from the corners of her lips.

"We shall."

Just as Elizabeth was setting down her cup after her final gulp of tea and preparing herself to stand, their pompous house guest made his first appearance of the day. With great solemnity, he bowed to them all and bid them a good morning. The collected Bennets responded with returning sentiments, disharmoniously expressed at different times, and Mrs Bennet prompted Mr Collins to come in and seat himself to partake of the meal.

"I thank you, madam." Mr Collins bowed specifically in Mrs Bennet's direction before straightening as tall as his hunched shoulders would allow him. His gaze then travelled to Elizabeth. "However, I have a particular matter of business I should like to conduct first which, I flatter myself, will be of a happy nature to us all. May I hope for your interest with your fair daughter Elizabeth when I solicit for the honour of a private audience with her in the course of this morning?"

Had Elizabeth been holding anything, she surely would have dropped it with much loud fanfare. Instead, her teacup, which she had yet to release after depositing it upon its saucer, rattled against its matching china. She let it go quickly and tucked her hand into her lap.

Mrs Bennet, who had been drooping in her chair, perked up and looked at Mr Collins with more interest as he hovered in the doorway, awaiting her answer. "Elizabeth?" she repeated, her eyes darting in the direction of her second daughter.

Elizabeth, taking advantage of Mrs Bennet's attention, shook her head quickly from side to side and prayed that her mother would take the hint. Mrs Bennet narrowed her eyes while Elizabeth widened hers, silently communicating her plea to disallow Mr Collins his way.

After an extended few seconds of observing Elizabeth with some suspicion, Mrs Bennet nodded once and turned back to Mr Collins. "My apologies, sir, but Elizabeth is not available to you this morning. However, my daughter Mary is at leisure to receive you."

A startled clatter from across the table drew Elizabeth's eye to where Mary was sitting, looking horrified at the very suggestion of being 'at leisure to receive' their cousin. Elizabeth could understand the sentiment perfectly and projected sympathy towards her younger sister.

Elizabeth turned back to gauge Mr Collins's thoughts on her mother's suggestion and discovered that his smugness was only lightly tainted by confusion. "Miss Mary? No, no, you misunderstand me, Mrs Bennet. I wish to speak to Miss Elizabeth."

"I have not misunderstood anything, sir," Mrs Bennet said, somewhat testily; her headache really should have kept her above stairs this morning, but her daughters knew that she would not miss out on an opportunity to visit with neighbours after a grand event such as a ball. "Elizabeth is not available to you. Mary would be happy to hear whatever it is you wish to say."

With his application rejected a second time, Mr Collins began to sputter. "Miss Mary? No, no, forgive me. Cousin Elizabeth—"

"And what is wrong with Mary?" Mrs Bennet's ire was so hot and caustic that it astounded the entire room into silence. Mary, her mouth agape in a way which usually would have earned her a scolding, seemed the most shocked of them all.

Elizabeth, thinking back to Mrs Bennet's coldness towards Darcy in the immediate wake of the insult they had all believed intended for Elizabeth, felt a smile threatening at the corners of her mouth. Mrs Bennet might be full of criticisms for her offspring—for her second and middle daughters, in particular—but woe betide the person who dared to disdain them in their mother's hearing.

"Nothing!" Mr Collins's voice was pitched into a squeal which reminded Elizabeth of a frightened pig. "She is...um, lovely, but you must have noticed that my delicate attentions were all for your second daughter. I would not wish to be a matter of discord between two sisters, however..."

Mrs Bennet scoffed and Elizabeth found her feelings, for once, in accord with her mother's. To think that Mr Collins considered himself so worthy a suitor as to be the object of two ladies at once! Mary was glaring heatedly in Mr Collins's direction and seemed equally offended by his presumption. Or perhaps his awkward rejection of her; it was hard to say for certain. Jane, poor Jane, sat to Elizabeth's left with her hand cupped over her mouth in dismay at what was unfolding before her.

Rising from her chair with her nose pointed decidedly into the air and a haughty mien which would have done Miss Bingley proud, Mrs Bennet sniffed at Mr Collins. "I am afraid, good sir, that your *delicate attentions* are not wanted here. My Lizzy is on the point of an engagement with Mr Darcy, as you must have realised yourself days ago."

Mr Collins stiffened in affront, his face suddenly flushed with the same emotion. "That is impossible, madam, for I have it on good authority that Mr Darcy is engaged to Miss Anne de Bourgh, the lovely, noble daughter of my patroness. Forgive me, but a Miss Elizabeth Bennet is not exalted enough for a gentleman such as Mr Darcy of Pemberley."

"Why I never—!" Mrs Bennet gasped at Mr Collins's audacity. To suggest that one of her daughters was unworthy in any way was the greatest offence she could fathom, and to say so outright might as well be a hanging crime as far as she was concerned.

Elizabeth darted her gaze nervously about the room and found that her sisters had each formed the same concerns as she, if their widened eyes and palpable silence were to be judged in that way. With a suddenness that startled even her, Elizabeth leapt up from her chair and, in a voice louder than intended, suggested hastily, "I think I will take a walk while the weather continues so fair! Would you like to join me Jane? Mary?"

Mary nodded fervently and scrabbled upright, but Jane, still frozen from the shock brought on by the acrimony of the room, remained in her chair. Elizabeth tugged on her arm to encourage her to her feet and then she and Mary hustled her out of the breakfast room.

Behind them, Mrs Bennet found her voice at last. "You have some nerve..."

Elizabeth smiled somewhat grimly at Darcy as she concluded her tale at the point where he had arrived on the scene, afflicted by a strange mixture of amusement, chagrin and annoyance as well as a dose of affection for her vulgar, but loving, mother.

"And so I suspect that they will be at it for some time yet, unless my father can stir himself from his book-room to intervene." At Darcy's expression shifting to alarm, Elizabeth laughed at him and said, "I would not worry for my mother, sir. She can easily handle a man such as Mr Collins. Your aunt might receive her parson back in pieces, however, if he continues to press her much longer."

"And is Miss Bennet well? She did not come out with you and Miss Mary."

"The argument has discomposed her, I am afraid, and she went upstairs to lie down for a while. Do not worry, she will be well. Jane despises discord more than any person I know."

"Then she is truly a perfect match for Bingley."

Elizabeth thought back to the time that Mr Bingley had, in the midst of her debate with Darcy regarding whether it was better to sway to the persuasion of a friend or remain resolute to one's previously arranged plans, put an end to their argument with some awkwardly interjected jesting. She chuckled and leant her head against Darcy's shoulder, the memory a fond one in hindsight.

"Yes, they are particularly well matched, are they not? The only wonder is how they will ever achieve anything between them since they will constantly defer to the other's wishes!"

Darcy placed his free hand over the one Elizabeth was using to grip his sleeve and squeezed it. "I am sure Miss Bingley will be happy to decide things for them."

As the couple rounded the corner of the house, having wandered their way back to the front, they were in time to see Charlotte approaching Longbourn on foot along the gravel drive. She waved upon recognising them from a distance and bent her steps in their direction, meeting Elizabeth and Darcy only a few yards from the entrance.

The ladies exchanged quick kisses to each other's cheeks and Charlotte then greeted Darcy with less familiar politeness, which he returned in kind with a bow of his head. Mary nodded to Charlotte with her usual gravity and, perhaps seeing an easy escape from the duty of chaperoning her elder sister, bid them all a quick adieu and wandered away in search of much deserved solitude.

Once all the social niceties were completed, Charlotte looked to Elizabeth and asked, "Am I the first to offer you congratulations, then?"

Elizabeth felt the tingle of a blush in her cheeks. "You are premature, I am afraid."

Darcy snorted. "By only half an hour, I suspect."

Smacking him lightly upon the arm with her free hand, Elizabeth playfully began to scold him. "I shall tell Papa what you have just said and he will make you regret it. Now you will be in his book-room for at least an hour!"

"Well, Miss Bennet—"

Whatever sally Darcy was about to offer in response was cut to the quick as the front door of the manor house burst open and collided with the outer wall with a loud bang. Elizabeth, Darcy, and Charlotte each turned their attention quickly to the disturbance and witnessed Mr Collins stomping across the threshold in high dudgeon. He tripped upon the front step, caught his balance clumsily and then continued marching away from the estate which had been entailed upon him. From within, Mrs Bennet's screeches could be heard with sharp clarity, banishing Mr Collins from her presence. "Go, go! Out! Out with you! Hill! Bring me my smelling salts!"

With a great show of dignity, Mr Collins tipped his nose up into the air and proceeded to put some distance between himself and his overwrought hostess, his face a study in pique. His steps halted, however, when he noticed that he was being observed by the very people who were at the source of his calamity. Mr Collins's eyes widened to apoplectic proportions and he changed his course, rushing in their direction.

"Cousin Elizabeth! Have you no shame? Mr Darcy is an engaged man! No matter what nonsense your mother has filled your head with, you cannot hope to aspire to the exalted circles in which Mr Darcy resides. No, no, come with me—yes, we shall have our discussion and then go see your father. Surely he will see sense, even if your mother will not. As a man, he is much more suited to deciding these things, in any case. Come, Cousin."

As Mr Collins reached out to grasp Elizabeth's free arm, Darcy held more tightly to the one he already possessed and turned them in such a way that she was placed out of Mr Collins's range. His scowl was already thunderous, but became darker when the bumbling oaf attempted another lunge, and Darcy was forced to parry him a second time by stepping back and guiding Elizabeth away.

"Mr Collins!" Darcy shouted to gain his so-called rival's attention. Mr Collins finally looked up at Darcy and, perhaps seeing the storm gathering behind Darcy's eyes, flinched back. "I have warned you before to treat ladies more gently, and now you attempt to grab at your cousin? I have never seen such ungentlemanly behaviour, and I shall be certain to inform my aunt of what I have witnessed and your refusal to accept correction."

Mr Collins's face did not pale entirely, but instead only in uneven patches, which left several spots of red behind that looked to Elizabeth like some sort of angry rash. "Bu-But, Mr Darcy! You cannot possibly know the very great danger you are in. The so-called 'ladies' of this household are scheming Jezebels, seeking to entrap you—"

"And you now compound your sins with these slanderous accusations?" Darcy's voice was now at little less than a roar. Mr Collins stumbled backwards in fright and nearly fell to the ground. "How dare you! I will have you know that you have just insulted the woman who is to become my wife. Apologise, sir, or we meet at dawn."

Mr Collins turned his head in Elizabeth's direction and his mouth dropped open, his flabby cheeks quivering in indignation. With an accusing finger, he pointed at his cousin and shrieked, "Temptress! Harlot! You have turned the head of a man belonging to another with your arts and allurements!"

Darcy released Elizabeth's arm and advanced so that he might tower over Mr Collins directly, bearing down upon him with disdain and outrage. The parson was by no means a short man, but he verily shrunk in the shade of Darcy's ire. "You will not say another word, Collins. Not one word. Speak against Elizabeth again, even to comment upon the colour of her dress, and my aunt will be the least of your worries. Am I clear?"

"Bu-bu-but Mr Darcy—Miss Anne de Bourgh—your engagement—"

"I am not, nor have I ever been, engaged to my cousin, much as you are not engaged to yours. Now, apologise to Elizabeth and be gone from my sight."

Elizabeth and Charlotte stood together and watched Darcy

overwhelm Mr Collins with his inherent authority, and it was a sight to behold. Elizabeth shivered slightly at the cold look of utter contempt in her betrothed's eyes as he glared down at Mr Collins; to think she had once believed that Darcy had looked at her to find fault. In hindsight, the contrast between the warmth of that gaze and the chill of the one he bestowed now upon her hapless cousin was imminently clear.

"I apologise, dear cousin, if I have offended you. Do forgive me."

Elizabeth did not respond immediately to Mr Collins, frozen in place with no small degree of shock, but came to herself when Charlotte nudged her discreetly in the side. Spurred into action, she hastily stepped in and placed her hand gently upon Darcy's shoulder in a manner which she hoped was placating. To her relief and satisfaction, she felt him calm beneath her touch.

"I accept your apology. Now, perhaps you had better take yourself on a walk for the nonce."

Mr Collins bobbed his head up and down in rapid agreement and carefully backed away from the still-scowling Darcy.

"Perhaps you would like to spend the day at Lucas Lodge, Mr Collins?" said Charlotte, surprising them all. She was studiously looking away from Elizabeth and Darcy as she presented her suggestion. "I know my father would be pleased for your company."

Mr Collins continued to back away from Darcy as he responded to her. "Yes, that sounds most delightful, Miss Lucas."

Elizabeth wished she could intervene and rescue Charlotte from what would certainly be a tedious and lengthy visit from her cousin, but could not think of any polite way to extricate her from an invitation she had offered herself. Instead, with reciprocal looks full of meaning and confusion, the ladies bid one another farewell and Charlotte led the way back down the lane with Mr Collins trotting along beside her.

"I shall have to purchase her something very fine for this

service, I dare say," Elizabeth said with a sigh as she finished waving off her friend and dropped her hand back down to her side.

Darcy grunted. "I suspect she knew what she was doing, though I cannot account for her taste in this instance."

"What?" Elizabeth looked up at Darcy, searching his face for some clarification as to his meaning.

He shrugged and turned away from the shrinking forms of Charlotte and Mr Collins to offer his arm to Elizabeth once again. "Let us go speak to your father before we suffer another interruption. I believe Bingley will be finished with his own application by now."

Forgetting all about Charlotte and Mr Collins, Elizabeth smiled broadly and accepted his escort by slipping her hand back into the bend of his elbow. "You mean it is time to go rescue him from Papa's teasing. Quite right, my love, I would not wish such a fine gentleman as Mr Bingley to suffer unduly. It would not be kind."

"No, indeed."

They walked into the comparatively quiet house entwined together.

EIGHTEEN

Three incomparable weeks after making their engagement official, Darcy lamentably found himself bidding his bride a temporary farewell in the denuded gardens about Longbourn. "I should only be gone two or three days at most," he promised. "I shall return well before your aunt and uncle arrive for Christmas."

Elizabeth responded with a tiny sigh and leant her head against his shoulder as they ambled through the crumbling roses. "I know, but I shall miss you terribly. Are you absolutely certain that you must go to London?"

"Sadly, yes. There are documents which must be drawn up, a few errands to run, and I really should retrieve Georgiana myself. My cousin Colonel Richard Fitzwilliam, her other guardian, is occupied with his regiment at the moment, and I would not wish to entrust her safety to servants alone." *Especially since Ramsgate.*

Georgiana had been invited to stay with him at Netherfield until the wedding, an affair jointly arranged with Bingley and Miss Bennet—or Jane, as he was privileged to call her now that they were to be brother and sister. Darcy had a few remaining reservations about Georgiana residing in the same neighbourhood as Wickham, but he could not deny her the opportunity to bond with her future family because of that reprobate. Darcy would simply have to remain on alert in case Wickham proved stupid enough to make any fresh attempts at mischief.

"I know, but I selfishly wish to keep you with me always." Darcy could not help the smug grin which split his face at this announcement.

On seeing it, Elizabeth laughed and tweaked his nose for it. "If you continue to be so abominably proud, sir, I shall change my mind and find myself happy to be rid of you!"

"Ah, but it is much too late for that, dearest. You are quite stuck with me now."

"Oh dear, what have I done?" she playfully lamented.

"Marry in haste, repent at leisure, and all that."

Sighing again, this time with more exasperation than melancholy, Elizabeth said, "I fear that shall be Charlotte's experience."

Darcy rather agreed with his betrothed on this point; Miss Lucas, sensible girl that she seemed to be, had made a rather foolish choice a day after they had announced their own engagement. Mr Collins had turned his fickle affections from his cousin to her friend—either out of spite or desperation, although quite possibly a mixture of both—and asked Miss Lucas for her hand. Against every notion of better feeling and, as Elizabeth argued, good sense, Miss Lucas had accepted him and they were to be married just after the new year.

Still, Darcy could not entirely fault a lady of seven-and-twenty pursuing perhaps her only opportunity at being the mistress of her own household; no doubt Miss Lucas's chances of marriage dwindled every year. One might wish for better than Mr Collins, who had been petulant and sanctimonious until the last, but beggars could not be choosers.

He had said as much to Elizabeth before, but his beloved stubbornly adhered to her opinion that her friend had made an ill-advised alliance. She might become more sanguine on the matter in time, but at the present, Elizabeth's affection for Miss

Lucas prevented her from seeing the possible good in the situation. For the nonce, Darcy would comfort his bride and encourage her to focus upon their own felicity.

Elizabeth shook her head mournfully and returned to their previous subject. "I truly shall miss you whilst you are away. I very much look forward to the day that you can take me with you without inciting a terrible scandal."

Darcy stopped, pulled her behind a most conveniently placed hedge, and dipped his hand into his coat pocket where a velvet bag resided. "As do I, my love. In the meanwhile, I have a small token for you. I hope you shall look upon it and remember me fondly during our separation."

"Oh?" Elizabeth's eyes followed his movement as he retrieved her gift. "You do not have to give me anything. I do not require baubles to miss you properly."

"Perhaps not, but I have been wishing to give this to you since I first proposed; I sent to Pemberley for it almost as soon as Bingley informed me of my addled offer. I was rather too optimistic at the time, of course, but held onto it with the intention of giving it to you if I could convince you to accept me." With a wry chuckle, he opened the drawstring and poured the contents into his palm—a ruby ring with a band of braided gold. "It was my grandmother Darcy's. She and my grandfather shared a rare love match, and he gifted this to her on their wedding day. They led a long and happy life together, and I had hoped that it might bring us the same luck."

Elizabeth's lips puckered into a soft and silent 'oh' of surprise as she regarded the simple, if elegantly rendered, jewellery in his palm. When she continued to stare at it for some length of time, Darcy began to worry that he had chosen his token of affection ill. "If it is not to your taste, there are many other pieces amongst my family collection you might like better. I can check the vault in London and—"

Darcy's stammering was abruptly disrupted by Elizabeth's lips upon his. She teetered on the tips of her toes to reach them and leant into his chest for balance, forcing him to quickly reach out and steady her with his hands at her waist. It was something of a miracle that he did not drop the ring during their hasty rearrangement, but Darcy was not inclined to complain.

Indeed, he was as far from complaining as it was possible to be. Once he had overcome his astonishment at Elizabeth's boldness, Darcy became an eager participant in their embrace. Whilst the hand which was gripping the ring remained at Elizabeth's waist, the other ascended the steep slopes of her body until it came to rest along her jawline. He then encouraged her to dip her head more acutely in one direction whilst his went the other, intensifying their kiss as their mouths naturally fell open. With this invitation, Darcy's tongue made egress and swiped against hers. Elizabeth responded, tentatively, in kind, encouraging him to moan and delve deeper.

Sensible that they were on the precipice of allowing their passions to tempt them too far, Darcy peeled his lips from Elizabeth's with a reluctant groan. To placate them both—for Elizabeth attempted to follow and resume their embrace—he pressed them repeatedly to her cheek and temple as he fought to regulate his laboured breathing. "Good God, Elizabeth...how I wish we were already married!"

Elizabeth pressed her forehead against his shoulder as she, too, struggled to regain her equanimity. "As do I. It is agony to wait."

"I do not suppose there any chance we might convince your mother to allow us to marry at Christmas?"

"I am afraid not." Elizabeth replied with a throaty chuckle. She slowly descended the length of his body, the material of her pelisse rasping against that of his greatcoat, until she was standing flat-footed once more. Darcy bit his lip to contain the ungentlemanly sound which threatened at this newest test to his restraint. "Mama is determined that our wedding will be the grandest event that the country has ever seen and insists she requires six months, at least, to pull it off."

The chilling effect of this pronouncement severely dampened Darcy's ardour. Aghast, he croaked, "Six months?"

"Fear not," Elizabeth said around a chuckle. "She has been reasoned down to a more acceptable three, though she remains unhappy about it. I am sure she will mention it a dozen times before you leave. However, Jane and I were quite firm—we shall marry in March."

"That is still too long from now, in my opinion."

"But much sooner than summer."

"Precisely. Here, before I become distracted again." Darcy once more presented the ring to Elizabeth's notice, offered to her freely upon the bed of his open palm.

Elizabeth hastily removed the glove from her left hand and held her bare fingers out to him. Taking the hint, Darcy slid the ring onto her fourth finger, luxuriating in the rightness of the gesture. To their mutual pleasure, the ring fit her almost perfectly, though it was somewhat loose. No doubt it would sit just right on her hand once her fingers were plumped by warmth.

"It is so lovely. Thank you."

"It is nothing to what you deserve, but I am glad that you like it."

"I adore it." Elizabeth placed both of her hands upon the sides of his face and pulled him down for another kiss. The ring he had placed on her finger was cold upon his cheek and he grinned against her lips. Elizabeth was well and truly his.

When they broke apart some minutes later, they were enshrouded by a cloud of their mingled breath and rasping on the frigid winter air. Elizabeth held his face close to hers, their foreheads together, and Darcy was no less possessive in the way he clutched at her waist. How he had lived his entire life without her in his arms, Darcy did not know, but the next few days away from her would be agony. Would it truly be so terrible if he took her with him and they married from London? It would be nothing to get a licence and engage the services of his parish rector at short notice. Her family might even follow and stay in Cheapside with Mrs Bennet's brother.

"Now, now, Lizzy, he is not going off to war. No need for such a maudlin farewell."

Darcy and Elizabeth leapt away from each other with some alarm at the unexpected interruption by Mr Bennet, who stood a few yards away staring at them over the rim of his spectacles. He seemed equal parts amused and perturbed at the sight of his daughter and her betrothed kissing behind a rose bush.

"Forgive me, sir, I—"

"Papa!" Elizabeth cut him off with a scolding tone. "You gave us quite a fright!"

Mr Bennet's returning smirk was wry. "Just be glad it was me and not Mary who discovered you, or you would both be in for a month's worth of moralising. In any event, I have been instructed to bring you both inside for some tea before Darcy here takes his leave. Any chance Jane and Bingley are hiding behind the next bush?"

"No, they walked in the direction of the hermitage." Bingley, who had much nuptial business of his own to conduct, was following Darcy's example and travelling to London as well. He was, no doubt, making use of the fashionable ruins to say his own private farewells to Jane.

"Of course they did. Go on now, or I really will send Mary to chaperon you."

Three days later, Elizabeth returned to the rose garden despite the forlorn late December weather. The sky was overcast and the scenery about her was a uniform shade of dull brown, but she could not remain quietly within the parlour another moment longer. She expected Darcy back at any moment, and it was miserable to wait.

Mrs Bennet's constant talk of wedding frippery only made the anticipation worse. Instead of being allowed to distract herself with a book or commonplace tittle-tattle with her sisters, Elizabeth was made to endure endless lists of what must be accomplished before the wedding, whining laments that her mother had not enough time to do it all, and fits of nerves when Mrs Bennet could control them no more. This had gone on in a repetitive loop the entire morning, and Elizabeth was feeling as frazzled as her mother claimed to be. Hence her muddy, cold, unpleasant constitutional in the gardens.

Forgetting that she was wearing gloves, Elizabeth moved to twist her ruby ring round the fourth finger of her left hand, a recently acquired habit since Darcy had given it to her earlier in the week. She chuckled at her absentmindedness and turned her eyes up the lane. No sign of a carriage yet.

Elizabeth sighed, equal parts disappointed and exasperated. She understood that, even if Darcy returned from London that very day, he would probably head straight to Netherfield and visit Longbourn on the morrow, but she missed him so. *How is it possible that Fitzwilliam has become so necessary to my happiness in such a short time? I do hope he returns soon...*

At this maudlin thought, Elizabeth huffed at herself. Honestly, she was being ridiculous, pining after a man she had seen a mere three days ago. It was no wonder Mr Bennet was finding such amusement at her expense if she was acting like such a lovelorn ninny. Kitty and Lydia considered it tragically romantic and commended Elizabeth for her suffering, but that was all the more reason to rally her optimism and recall that which she had to be thankful for. She was beloved by an honourable man, she was to be wed alongside her dearest sister in a matter of weeks, and she no longer need endure the pomposity of Mr Collins, who had returned to Kent after much sullen complaining. Aside from Darcy's temporary absence, Elizabeth had nothing for which to repine.

Enough. Darcy would return as quickly as he was able and they would be reunited, probably with more fanfare than such a short separation deserved. Elizabeth rolled her eyes at her own foolishness and turned back to the house.

Almost at the same instant, Elizabeth detected the subtle sounds which heralded the approach of a carriage. It came round the bend and into view, and she recognised it as belonging to Mr Bingley, which only heightened her jubilation.

She scurried to the drive just as her mother and sisters came flooding out the front door, wrapped in warm shawls and bouncing excitedly on their toes. Lydia squealed as she tugged on Jane's arm with one hand and pointed rudely at the approaching equipage with the other. "He is come back!"

Jane smiled serenely and merely nodded in response, but Elizabeth could see the enthusiasm bubbling beneath the surface of her placidity. They exchanged looks of utmost rapture as the carriage finally came to a stop before them.

It seemed an age before the door opened and Mr Bingley stepped out, but in all likelihood, it was only a few seconds. "Good day, sisters. Jane."

Jane rushed forwards and held her hand out to Mr Bingley, the only sign of affection she could offer before such an irreverent audience. Elizabeth knew not how Jane maintained her equanimity with Lydia and Kitty mocking their reunion with sloppy wet kissing noises. "Welcome back, sir. I am glad to see you."

Mr Bingley grinned and regarded Jane with glowing warmth, equally insensible of the silly girls in their midst. "And I you."

As thrilled for Jane as she was, Elizabeth impatiently craned her neck so that she might see behind Mr Bingley and into the loitering carriage. Why did he not move aside for Darcy? Why had Darcy not likewise sprung out to greet her? She had only received one letter from him, announcing his safe arrival in town, but it had been full of longing effusions only two days ago. Surely, he was as eager to see her as she was to see him.

"Oh, forgive me, Lizzy." Startled to be addressed by Mr Bingley—or Charles, as he had insisted she call him as her future brother—Elizabeth tore her eyes away from the open carriage door. "Darcy has charged me to tell you that he has been delayed in town for several days. Some sort of family emergency has him detained."

Elizabeth gripped at the solid lump beneath her glove, fingers itching to twist her ring round and round. "Is someone ill? Is it his sister?"

"I wish I could tell you more," and Bingley truly looked as if he did, "but Darcy sent a note round this morning telling me to go on to Hertfordshire without him and there were no details about what sort of emergency it was. He promised, however, to send a longer letter explaining everything within a day or two."

Elizabeth could feel her elation diminishing, crushed by the anxiety which rose up to beat it down. "I see."

"Mr Darcy is not returning?" Mrs Bennet's shrill exclamation rent the cold air like a hot blade. Elizabeth winced at the sheer volume of it and the precognition that her mother was about to unravel into an inconsolable fit of nerves. "He has jilted our Lizzy?"

Bingley, perhaps well acquainted enough with the Bennets to scent danger in the air, rushed to reassure Mrs Bennet. "No, no! Not at all, he has merely been delayed. He will be back by Christmas, mark my words. I am sure his letter on the morrow will explain everything."

It was far too late, however, to curtail her mother's fit. Despite Bingley's placating speech, Mrs Bennet wailed piteously and continued on as if he had not spoken at all. "We are all ruined! I knew this would happen, I knew Lizzy would not be able to maintain his interest for long. I insisted that they marry as soon as possible, but did anyone listen to me? No! None of you ever think of my poor nerves!"

As Mrs Bennet dissolved into hysterics, all but Elizabeth rushed to assist her into the house where she might be medicated with tea and mollycoddling. Elizabeth herself remained standing on the drive, frozen and staring after the empty carriage as the servants took it away.

NINETEEN

It was Christmas Eve, four days since Darcy was meant to return from London, and Elizabeth felt no inclination to be merry, despite the revelry which surrounded her. She would have much preferred to remain at home where she might quietly sulk in her room, away from the noise and busyness of the season, but her mother—rather unfeelingly—would not hear of her snubbing the Lucases. It was a tradition to attend the party at Lucas Lodge on Christmas Eve, and attend it she must lest she set Mrs Bennet off on yet another diatribe—easily done these days. Never mind that Elizabeth herself grew increasingly troubled as the days stretched on without word from Darcy.

While not as anxious as her mother, at least outwardly, it did not necessarily follow that Elizabeth was indifferent. It was not her way to be so demonstrative with her woes, but she still felt Darcy's absence acutely. Since Bingley had arrived sans his friend, Mrs Bennet had tormented them all with an unceasing flood of tears and wailing complaints of ill-use by Elizabeth, Darcy, and Elizabeth again; not only had her second daughter rebuffed Mr Collins, but she had apparently frightened away

Darcy by some unknown means, dooming them all to the hedgerows. Her ridiculous premonitions of doom might have been amusing had Elizabeth not been at the centre of some supposed conspiracy to destroy the family with her heartless, hoydenish ways. More than that, though, Mrs Bennet's lamentations poked directly at the heart of Elizabeth's fears—what if Darcy truly was not coming back?

Elizabeth might have been content, or at least less fearful, if Darcy's promised letter of explanation had arrived in his stead. However, they had not received a single word, either in person or by post, from her betrothed regarding his continued absence. Not one to sit idly and wait, Elizabeth had sent her own letter to Darcy at his London address two days ago, but she had yet to receive a response to it. What could that mean? Even if he was busy attending to his family emergency, surely he could find time to write and explain the situation, if not to her then to Bingley or her father. Evidently not. No one in Hertfordshire had gotten so much as a note from Darcy since the intended day of his arrival.

Elizabeth sighed as she absently fiddled with her ring and watched her younger sisters skip about the room with their dance partners. Sir William had called for an impromptu reel, not uncommon at one of his parties, and enlisted Mary to play for them. Jane and Bingley were part of the set and appeared to be having a jolly time, albeit with more decorum than Kitty and Lydia displayed. Elizabeth had deftly avoided their host when he had come round looking for dancers and tucked herself away into a forgotten corner with Charlotte—who had since abandoned her to attend to some charge of Lady Lucas's—where she might indulge her worries without interruption.

She had chosen her spot well, it transpired, because those in the room seemed to have forgotten her presence entirely. Silly as her neighbours could occasionally be, they were at least more circumspect in spreading rumours within the presence of the object of them, yet Elizabeth heard more than one murmur speculating over Darcy's absence. Mary King was of the opinion that Darcy had been prevented from returning because of his family's violent disapproval over his match. Mrs Long agreed with this conjecture and reminded everyone she spoke to that Mr Collins had informed her that Darcy was already betrothed to Miss de Bourgh. Undoubtedly, his family had pressured him to throw over Elizabeth for this far more eligible bride. Her aunt Philips could be heard postulating to the entire room that Darcy was merely injured horribly, or possibly dead, thus making it entirely reasonable that he might have abandoned Elizabeth through no fault of her own. Strangely, Elizabeth herself was not comforted by this defence.

The authority behind much of the gossip, Charlotte had informed her, was apparently Miss Bingley. She had painted herself as Darcy's intimate friend of many years and was, therefore, supposedly knowledgeable about his private affairs. Despite Miss Bingley's veneer of unconvincing sympathy, Elizabeth was not surprised in the slightest by this revelation, nor could she even drudge up enough spare emotion to be angered over it; Miss Bingley was a jealous cow. It made no difference that Darcy had never once considered her for his bride—as he had once confided to Elizabeth when they had spoken of Miss Bingley and her machinations—she apparently felt entitled to the position of Mrs Darcy and would avail herself of every opportunity to achieve it. A futile endeavour, but Elizabeth admired her persistence. Somewhat.

Well, it mattered not what Miss Bingley or any of the others thought; Darcy would return and they would be married, Elizabeth was certain. None of them knew Darcy the way she did, none of them had heard the words of adulation and devotion he had whispered to her, none of them could know how hard he had fought to convince her to accept his hand. If they wanted tangible proof of Darcy's intent, all she need do was show them his grandmother's ring which resided on her finger. A gentleman did not give away family heirlooms to every passing flirtation; Elizabeth was distinguished by the glinting jewel she wore.

"You appear most contemplative, Miss Elizabeth. Are you well?"

Elizabeth startled at being so suddenly addressed, having not noticed the approach of Mr Wickham. He stood at her shoulder, smiling down at her as if he commiserated with her pain, and she felt her hackles rise. "Quite well, I thank you." So saying, she turned her face away and pretended to observe the dancing.

Mr Wickham, as immune to her hints as ever, took a seat next to her and mimicked her false interest in the festive display. "If you are not truly well, you need not pretend with me. If you recall, I know what it is like to be favoured by the Darcys and then thrown away. I understand your feelings perfectly."

Outraged, Elizabeth whipped her head round to regard Mr Wickham with widened eyes. "How dare you presume to know anything about my engagement! Whatever you might have heard from ill-natured gossip, I can assure you that it is all unfounded. Once Mr Darcy has attended to whatever emergency keeps him in town, he will return here at the earliest possible moment."

With another smile, one Elizabeth felt to be mocking her, Mr Wickham replied, "Of course, I am sure you are correct. However, I would caution you to prepare yourself in case..."

"In case nothing. Mr Darcy shall be back at my side imminently."

"Can you really be sure? His pride, which you yourself have called 'abominable,' directs his every move. You are a lovely young woman, one whom any man would be fortunate to call his own, but Darcy's family will not embrace you for your beauty or cleverness. To them, only fortune and connexions matter, and Darcy has always been eager to please them."

Riled beyond measure at Mr Wickham's presumption, Elizabeth thrust her left hand before him and presented Grandmother Darcy's ring. It winked at them both in the firelight, cheekily aware of its worth. "He will return. A man does not give his grandmother's ring to just anyone."

Wickham observed the ring with some shock, but it was quickly masked by a more overt display of false compassion. "I cannot agree more, however..."

Elizabeth refused to take his bait and glared at him in silence.

"However," he continued, after a pause, "I have seen this ring before, and not amidst the family jewels. I dare say it looks very similar to one belonging to another young woman—one who was even less worthy of the Darcys' exalted notice than you —whom I knew in my youth at Pemberley. It was said that she and the young master...well, I should say no more in mixed company."

"You lie!" Elizabeth hissed, jumping to her feet. "He would never..."

Mr Wickham observed her with so much apparent pity that Elizabeth was tempted to spit in his face. Only years of proper deportment prevented her from doing so. "Forgive me if I have offended your sensibilities, but I could not sit idly by and say nothing. Darcy's behaviour has always been selfish and disdainful of the feelings of others, but now it truly sickens me. I hope you will not be too distressed if..." He allowed his words to trail off meaningfully.

Having listened to more than enough of Mr Wickham's self-serving falsehoods, Elizabeth turned on her heel and marched away from him without bothering to take leave of him. Hopefully, this cut would dissuade him from pursuing her company again in the future.

Elizabeth waded through the crowd of revellers in pursuit of the refreshment table; she could do with a glass of wine to settle her temper. Upon reaching it and obtaining her drink, from which she took a deep draught, she looked round for another hidden corner which was not so infested with snakes.

Before she could make a new selection, her aunt Gardiner approached and placed a hand on her arm. It was the first act of genuine care she had experienced all night. "There you are, my dear. I have been looking for you this past quarter of an hour."

"Forgive me, I am not very good company tonight."

"I cannot blame you," said Mrs Gardiner, her brow folded with concern, "but you mustn't let the tittle-tattle of others depress your spirits. I may not know your Mr Darcy personally, but I grew up not five miles from Pemberley, where his family is very well regarded. He would not tarnish his sterling reputation by breaking an engagement."

Elizabeth swallowed more wine, a moderate sip this time. "I know you are right, Aunt, but—"

"...not only has she refused Mr Collins, leaving him to that grasping, scheming Charlotte Lucas, but now she has frightened away Mr Darcy! Oh, Sister, what am I to do with Lizzy? If she keeps on like this, we shall all end up in the hedgerows before Mr Bennet is cold in his grave! But does she care? My only comfort is that Mr Bingley is remaining loyal to Jane despite his friend's capriciousness. I have urged them to marry straight away, but they insist upon vexing me by awaiting Mr Darcy's return—as if anyone expects him at this point! Gone nearly a week and without a single word..."

Elizabeth inhaled deeply, determined to remain calm in the face of her mother's inappropriate and extremely loud philippic. If she made a scene, it would only heighten the scurrilous talk and wound her already tattered reputation further.

A gentle hand on her arm brought Elizabeth back to herself and she regarded Mrs Gardiner with gratitude. She was a most excellent woman, so supportive and understanding, unlike... well. It was probably best not to follow that train of thought.

"Why not come back to Gracechurch Street with us after Christmas?" Mrs Gardiner suggested. "It might be good to come away." Her gaze flicked momentarily to where Mrs Bennet spoke to Mrs Philips across the room.

Elizabeth embraced her aunt. "I thank you, but I ought to remain here. Mr Darcy will either send word or arrive himself soon, and I would not wish to be out of reach."

"Of course. If you change your mind, or something... happens, remember that we are not to leave until after Twelfth Night. Our invitation stands until then."

"I shall remember." Although nothing would drag her from Hertfordshire until all hope was extinguished.

TWENTY

Though it was not in Darcy's nature to fidget, he fought against the impulse as his valet dressed him for an evening out. He was less anxious for the evening to begin than he was for it to end; only adoration for his sister could compel him to procure theatre tickets when his mood was so black. At least he might spend a few hours away from his disagreeable house guests, though he would rather have gone to his club for that purpose and avoided the swarming crowds. Still, Georgiana insisted that he required distraction from his woes, and he was not so overcome by his foul temper as to disappoint her efforts.

At last, Bailey finished the knot in his cravat and stepped away. "Will there be anything else, sir?"

"Not at the moment. I shall return as early as possible."

"Very good, sir." With a bow, Bailey took his leave through the dressing room.

Once his valet was gone, Darcy unleashed a weary sigh and threw himself into an armchair by the fireplace. With his forehead cupped in his hand, he closed his eyes and concentrated on the image of his beloved Elizabeth's face. Just recalling the sloping lines of her cheekbones, the warm tint to her skin and the thick fan of her lashes comforted him, but it also provoked a deeper longing. He had not looked upon her fair countenance in over a month—exactly thirty-five days—and he felt the lack down to his bones.

He might have borne the deprivation better had he a stack of correspondence from Elizabeth to lovingly peruse, but he had only received a single letter the entire time they had been apart, in spite of the twenty or so he had sent off to Hertfordshire. The one note he had received, full of loving sentiments and entreaties for him to come back to her as soon as possible, he kept in his possession at all times, now threadbare from much handling. It resided that moment in his breast pocket, and Darcy soothed himself by touching his fingers to it through the fabric, something within him loosening at the responding crinkle. It was the only tangible representation of Elizabeth's love, the only piece of her he had with him on this doomed escapade to London.

Had he angered Elizabeth in some way? He had thought his explanation for his absence sufficient in the first report he had sent to her—and to Bingley and Mr Bennet, besides—but perhaps she was displeased by the extension of his sojourn. He had promised to return to her in two or three days, but surely the circumstances spoke for themselves, and Elizabeth, who herself had remained at a neighbour's house for the better part of a week to nurse her sister's cold, could appreciate his predicament. Alas, he was trapped in purgatory; unable to go to her, yet equally unable to stay away.

If Lady Catherine had only controlled her temper...but no, that was an unworthy thought. It was not his aunt's fault that she had been stricken down by an apoplexy at an inopportune moment, it was *his*.

Several weeks earlier...

"Where is my nephew? I demand to see him this moment!"

Darcy looked up from the piles of correspondence he was sorting with a sense of inevitable doom. The strident tones seeping into his study around the seams of the door foretold a visit from Lady Catherine de Bourgh, his vexing aunt and self-elected mother-in-law. He surmised by this unexpected call that she was unsatisfied by his response to her last letter in which he had firmly, but respectfully, refused to break off his engagement to Elizabeth. Collins, that worm, had brought the news back with him to Kent and stirred up a hornet's nest of consequences for them all.

Darcy settled back in his chair and awaited Lady Catherine's entrance with his fingers steepled against his chest. He wanted to begin in a position of power when she barged in and started demanding the unreasonable—nay, the impossible. Darcy would never bend so far as to give Elizabeth up, no matter what was due to his family. If Lord Matlock could resign himself to the match, so could his sister.

It was no more than a minute since he first heard her haranguing shrieks before Lady Catherine burst into his private sanctum, his harried-looking butler nipping at her heels. "What are you thinking, Darcy? Setting aside Anne for some nobody adventuress from the wilds of Hertfordshire? It is not to be borne!"

Darcy leant to one side and addressed his butler. "Thank you, Clarence, you may return to your duties."

Clarence bowed and beat a hasty exit, closing the door behind him. At least Darcy's servants could appreciate the notion of privacy, even when his own family ignored it.

Once the door had been securely sealed, Darcy returned his attention to his aunt and greeted her sarcastically, "Good morning, Lady Catherine. To what do I owe your visit this fine day?"

Lady Catherine stalked forwards and slapped her hand upon his desk, sending a few stray papers fluttering out of place. "Do not toy with me, boy, you know exactly why I am here. I have come to put a stop to this travesty of an engagement. It is not enough that you insult Anne by breaking your promise to her, but that the woman of your choice should be the cousin of my very own rector—what could you be thinking?"

Up close, Darcy could see the signs of Lady Catherine's recent illness—reported to be a trifling cold in her last missive, albeit one which kept her abed some weeks—in her features. Her skin and eyes appeared somewhat feverish, her face was thinner than usual, and she should attend to her nose with her handkerchief soon. More than that, he could hear a slight wheeze with each irascible proclamation, which concerned him.

Witnessing her comparative frailty softened Darcy's response. "Do sit down. I would not wish for you to faint."

Lady Catherine grumbled at his impertinence, but slumped into a chair in front of his desk, sniffling. She seemed somewhat relieved to be off her feet.

"As to your reason for coming," Darcy continued once she had settled, "I feel I must remind you that I have made no promises to Anne; if she believed so, it was all your own doing. I believe I made my disinclination for our supposed 'betrothal' clear on several occasions, as did my father before his death."

"But your mother wanted it!" countered Lady Catherine, then coughed into her handkerchief. When she had recovered, she said, "From your infancy, you have been intended for each other. It was a favourite wish of your mother, as well as of hers. From your cradles we planned the union, and now—"

Lady Catherine was interrupted by another fit of coughing, though Darcy hardly needed to hear more. It was the same tripe she had been peddling for years, to no avail, and he was quite sick of it. Her arguments had not swayed his father, nor would they sway Darcy himself, even if Lady Anne had promoted the match. Honestly, had his mother seen the sickly creature her namesake had become, she very likely would have withdrawn her own approval; Anne de Bourgh was fit to be no man's wife.

When Lady Catherine once again gained control of herself, she persisted, wheezily, "Obstinate, headstrong boy! I am ashamed of you! Throwing away the expectations of your family for some penniless bit of muslin is the height of ingratitude. Is there nothing due to me, due to Anne, on that score?"

"As I have already said—"

"I will not be interrupted!" Lady Catherine screeched, her face deepening in colour. "And now, at the moment when the wishes of both sisters would be accomplished, to be prevented by a young woman of inferior birth, of no importance in the world—"

"That is quite—"

"—and wholly unallied to the family! Do you pay no regard to the wishes of your friends? To your elders? Have her arts and allurements blinded you to every feeling of propriety and delicacy? I can only imagine how she has worked upon you—"

"Enough!"

Darcy's exclamation was loud enough to finally silence Lady Catherine and left a subtle ringing reverberating about the room. His temper, which he had kept in check in deference to how unwell his aunt appeared, was inflamed beyond endurance by the slanderous nature of Lady Catherine's speech, and he was done allowing her any say. It was time that he had his.

"While I am sympathetic to your dashed hopes for Anne, I reiterate, I have never been engaged to her. Further, I never intended to be so, which I have dutifully informed you of on several occasions. I am sorry that you must brook disappointment, but in this you will be forced to submit to the whims of others. I will not rescind my proposal to Elizabeth Bennet, nor is there any method or argument you could make which would compel me to do so. Not only have I given my word to her and her family, thus engaging my honour, but I have not even the slightest inclination to dissolve our understanding. You must reconcile yourself to this conclusion for, short of being dismissed by Elizabeth herself, it is unalterable. I will marry her at the earliest opportunity, and you will treat her with the respect that is due my wife."

Lady Catherine stared at him in utter astonishment. "And this is your final resolve?"

Darcy nodded, a short, sharp gesture. “It is.”

For a few moments, Lady Catherine’s eyes narrowed shrewdly and she opened her mouth as if to render another objection, but only a strangled sound emerged. She gurgled, choked, and sputtered, but formed no intelligible words as her countenance grew increasingly blotchy. She grasped at her throat, cast him a final accusatory glare, and fell from her chair to the floor.

The hours following Lady Catherine’s collapse from an apparent apoplexy were a confused flurry of activity, from summoning the servants to assist his aunt to a vacant bedchamber to calling, at her insistence, the physician who treated Anne whenever they came to town. In the midst of this upheaval, Darcy had had just enough time to jot down a note for Bingley, imploring him to go on to Hertfordshire without him and promising more information when it was available.

The following morning, after Mr Nicholson had delivered his stuttering diagnosis—an acute apoplexy, as they had suspected—Darcy had found the opportunity to write lengthy missives each to Bingley, Mr Bennet and, most especially, Elizabeth detailing the cause for his delayed return. Darcy had also written to Anne, informing her of her mother’s sudden turn, and inviting her to come to Darcy House. He had left them with the other post going out and then turned to more immediately urgent business.

Days had gone by without any reply from Hertfordshire, though Anne had arrived on his doorstep in a timely fashion and made herself quite at home directing the servants and appropriating one of the grander saloons for her exclusive use. Darcy had known it would happen, as Anne had always been a demanding creature, though he had hoped that much of her time might have been spent above stairs in her mother’s bedchamber, at least in the pretence of nursing the invalid.

Instead, she sat in the gold saloon with Mrs Jenkinson and, occasionally, Georgiana—who felt obligated to apply herself to her studies more rigorously than ever before—and sending Darcy messages for his attendance near constantly. It was maddening.

Darcy had sent another letter to Elizabeth and the others before the week was out, fearing that the missives had somehow gone astray, but there was no response to any of those either. Three days later, he had sent another. Then another. Then yet more letters to Elizabeth as time wore on without any word from her, each increasing in desperation as he began to fear that she was resentful of his neglect. About a week ago, Darcy had abandoned the endeavour, feeling by that point that anything he sent was likely being consigned to the fire, unopened.

Had Elizabeth changed her mind? It was not difficult to imagine, considering how Darcy had laboured to garner her acceptance. Had time apart, far from making her heart grow fonder, made her regret their engagement? It was this idea, combined with missing Elizabeth dreadfully, which kept Darcy awake at night. He would behave as a gentleman and release her from her promise if it came to that, but...no, even to think about such a devastating scenario caused his gut to clench painfully. He would put it from his mind.

Darcy longed to go to her and clear up whatever misunderstanding beset them, but with Lady Catherine in an indifferent state of health and her doctor cautioning him that any further agitation of her spirits could lead to another episode, it was impossible. It had been implied, if not outright stated, that Lady Catherine's disappointment—and Darcy's harsh handling of it—had led to the initial incident, and that her body could not take a repetition of the same. Therefore, until his aunt was strong enough to accept his engagement, Darcy was required to avoid all mention of it and remain in London to oversee her care. He only hoped that this situation had not caused irreparable damage to his understanding with Elizabeth, although that hope was an extraordinary one in the face of her continued silence.

The clock in the hall struck the hour, and Darcy reluctantly stood from his chair. Georgiana had proclaimed a great desire to see this particular play, one of Darcy's long affirmed favourites, and he meant to indulge her, even if it was a transparent ploy to cheer him. At least he could leave the de Bourghs behind for the night; Lady Catherine remained abed, and Anne detested evening engagements.

Perhaps he might forget his troubles for a short while, even if he could not prevent himself from searching out Elizabeth's face in the crowd.

TWENTY-ONE

"I thank you for bringing me to the theatre. *Macbeth* is an old favourite of mine."

"Yes, I recall you telling me so once or twice," said Uncle Gardiner with an indulgent chuckle. "When the opportunity arose to get tickets for this performance, I jumped at the chance."

Meaning, I have been unbearably melancholy of late, and my uncle, dear man that he is, wanted to cheer me. Elizabeth was grateful to him for this small act, and many others besides, of kindness. To her aunt, as well, who had taken it upon herself to soothe Elizabeth's wounded heart with various excursions, treats, and boisterous distraction from the children since she had come to London with them after Christmas. The Gardiners need not have exerted themselves so much—taking her away from Mrs Bennet's vociferous grievances had been more than enough—but their care warmed Elizabeth and took some of the sting out of Darcy's abandonment.

Elizabeth bit back a sigh, exasperated. She had promised herself not to think of him this evening, to put his fickle notions of love from her mind, but it seemed he was never far from her thoughts. It was no wonder because, despite his callous treatment, she was as much in love with him as before. Wretched, foolish heart.

Determined to banish her faithless beau to the recesses of her mind where he belonged, Elizabeth swivelled her head about to observe the people filing into the theatre about them. Though she and her relations were down on the main floor in the more affordable seats, she had an excellent view of the boxes above which held persons of more distinguished rank. Their insufferable conceit amused her, as did the outlandish head-dresses and foppishly bold waistcoat patterns some of them wore. Altogether, they looked like a flock of tropical birds with their pointed beaks jutted into the air.

Just as Elizabeth was about to point out a particularly absurd arrangement of feathers sprouting from the top of one lady's head, her eye caught upon a painfully familiar figure dressed in a classically rendered suit. Even were his face not clearly visible to her, his upright bearing and broad shoulders declared it to be him. Darcy.

Upon his arm, dressed entirely in white, in perfect contrast to Darcy's black tailcoat, was a young lady. Elizabeth did not recognise her, of course, but she was tall, on a larger scale than Elizabeth herself, and her appearance in general was everything womanly and graceful. Was this mysterious lady the reason Darcy had failed to return to Hertfordshire? They certainly seemed intimate, considering how they leant in close to whisper to one another.

Could she even be—Elizabeth pressed her fingers to her lips to contain her dismay—the honourable Miss Anne de Bourgh?

Overcome, Elizabeth abruptly turned away from Darcy and whomever the lady was and focused her wavering gaze upon the empty stage. She blinked rapidly to discourage the tears which threatened to embarrass her at any moment and breathed deeply to restore her equanimity.

"Lizzy? What is the matter?"

Swallowing against the tightness in her throat, Elizabeth

replied, "It is nothing, Aunt. I am merely looking forward to the performance."

"You cannot fool me. What has upset you so?"

Reflexively, Elizabeth glanced up at Darcy and his guest—holding hands! And he, supposedly still engaged to another—and quickly looked away again. "Nothing, I am well."

But Elizabeth's moment of weakness must have informed her aunt where the source of her distress lay. There was a slight gasp and Elizabeth felt a squeeze of her hand. "Is that who I think it is?"

Elizabeth nodded. Her throat was too clustered with emotion to speak.

"Should we leave? I hate to let that man ruin our evening, but if he distresses you so..."

Not wishing to draw attention to herself as the performance was about to begin—how mortified she would be if Darcy spotted her fleeing from his presence—Elizabeth chose instead to preserve her dignity. At intermission, when their movements could be covered by the throng, she would beg to return to Gracechurch Street. "I thank you, but I am well enough. Let us enjoy the play."

Though Georgiana assured him that the play was performed ably by the company, Darcy had hardly paid attention to what was happening onstage. He had, at first, believed the figure of his dear Elizabeth seated down below to be a mere illusion conjured up by his yearning heart, but the more he stared at the woman in question, the more convinced he was that it was she. Somehow, and without any word to him, Elizabeth was in London.

Upon accepting that she was real and not a figment of his longing, Darcy had intended to go to her immediately, only to be forestalled by his sister's whispering entreaty. "You must not cause a scene!" she had hissed in his ear. "Wait until intermission."

Annoyed as he was by Georgiana's advice, Darcy was forced to admit that it was sound. A crowded theatre just before the start of a performance was not the place to reunite with Elizabeth; too many judging eyes and curious ears would become privy to a conversation which should, and must, occur in private.

And so Darcy waited with impatience for the first act to conclude, his knee bouncing with agitation all the while, and leapt up from his seat the instant the curtains drew closed. He waited only until the lights came up so that he could note Elizabeth's position amidst the masses—she was rising and following a fashionable couple up the centre aisle—so that he might pursue her with greater accuracy. His sister wished him luck, and he was gone.

Down below, Darcy searched for a glimpse of Elizabeth's yellow gown, a beacon in the sea of drab neutrals he waded through. His height gave him an advantage, but there were so many people, several of whom sought to actively block him with fawning greetings, that it took him some time to locate her.

Finally, just as he was losing hope, he spotted her standing near the front doors next to a woman several years his senior. The aunt from Cheapside, he presumed, as he struggled in their direction. They were outfitted in cloaks with their backs turned to him, peering out into the night, and apparently waiting for something. A carriage if he had to guess; she was leaving.

"Elizabeth!" Darcy called once he was within range for her to hear him. To his dismay, he saw her shoulders stiffen before she slowly, reluctantly, rotated to face him. When he saw her expression, so blank and cold, something wrenched within his gut.

Elizabeth dipped into a slight curtsey and greeted him in a formal tone in counterpoint to his more familiar address. "Mr Darcy."

Though in appearance, she was much as he had left her a month ago, there was a palpable shift in the way she regarded him now, as if with suspicion. Elizabeth was so lovely in her yellow gown, what he could see of it beneath her cloak. It was the radiant colour of candlelight in a dark room, but all the warmth of her ensemble was dulled by the coolness of her air. Darcy glanced to where her left hand should be in search of his grandmother's ring, hoping for the comfort of seeing it there, but it was impossible to tell whether she was wearing it underneath her many layers.

Though there was much he was wild to say to Elizabeth, Darcy struggled to speak. "I...would you introduce me to your friend?"

"Mr Darcy, my aunt, Mrs Gardiner. I have lately been staying with her and my uncle in Cheapside. Aunt, this is the Mr Darcy I have spoken of."

The mistrustful sweep of Mrs Gardiner's eyes informed him that whatever Elizabeth had told her about him had not been complimentary. *Blast it!*

After muttering some nonsense about being glad to make Mrs Gardiner's acquaintance, Darcy returned his focus to Elizabeth. "I can see you are about to depart, but would you and your party like to join me in my box for the second half of the performance? I would like to speak to you in more comfortable surroundings." As if to prove his point, Darcy was jostled from behind by a passing gentleman who appeared to be well within his cups.

"I thank you, no," replied Elizabeth, frostily. "I find myself stricken with a headache. Besides, we would not wish to intrude upon you and your...guest."

So she had already seen him, and he had caught her in the act of avoiding his company. Darcy's dread deepened. "I assure you, it would be no intrusion at all. Georgiana has been eager to meet you."

"Your sister?"

"Yes. She would be most disappointed if I failed to bring you back with me."

Elizabeth observed him warily. Had she believed him parading another eligible woman about town? It wounded Darcy that she might think so poorly of him.

"Forgive me, Mr Darcy, but my husband has just arrived with the carriage," Mrs Gardiner interrupted, nodding out the window where a gentleman was approaching. "I believe we must abide by our original plan and be on our way. Lizzy?"

Elizabeth glanced between Darcy and her aunt, almost as if undecided. Her answer, when it came, was a disappointment. "Yes, I am quite fatigued. It was good to see you again, sir."

As Elizabeth turned to follow Mrs Gardiner, Darcy fumblingly grasped at her arm and halted her progress. "Wait!" She stopped, glaring pointedly at where Darcy's hand trespassed upon her person, and he let go hastily. "We must speak. If you will not come back to my box, then tell me the time and place and I shall be there. We cannot leave it like this."

Sighing with apparent defeat, Elizabeth agreed, "You are right, of course, we must speak at some point. You may call upon me at my uncle's house at number twelve Gracechurch Street."

"I shall be there upon the morrow."

"Very well. Goodnight, Mr Darcy."

With this final dismissal, she hurried after her aunt. Darcy watched disconsolately as her uncle helped her into the waiting carriage.

TWENTY-TWO

Elizabeth discreetly disguised a yawn by hiding it behind her teacup. After the emotionally wrenching events of last evening and a night spent tossing more than sleeping, it was no wonder that she was utterly exhausted this morning. She only hoped she did not look it; Darcy was expected sometime during the course of the day, and she had rather present a show of strength than weakness.

The reminder of this dreaded call sent Elizabeth's fingers scrambling for the ring she wore about her neck—his ring. Though she had removed it from her finger weeks ago, once she had accepted the truth that her lover was not returning, she had been unable to banish it entirely from her person. She had made the attempt to secure it in her jewellery box and put it out of her mind, but her lingering, unwanted feelings for Darcy kept her coming back to the one token he had given her. After several days of pointless struggle, she had attached it to a long length of red ribbon and taken to wearing it about her neck instead, keeping the ring itself hidden beneath her bodice where it could not aggravate her mother's nerves. Even in Gracechurch Street, though, it was best kept hidden away with her more tender sentiments.

A warm hand descended upon the arm which fiddled with her trinket, calling Elizabeth's attention. Seated next to her at the breakfast table, her aunt regarded her with compassion. "All will be well, my dear. Simply have your say, return the ring to him, and it shall be done with. Then you may set your heart to falling in love with a worthier young man."

Elizabeth nodded and offered Mrs Gardiner a tight smile. The solution sounded so simple, yet it felt like the most difficult task she had ever set herself. However, it must be done, and it would be done for the best; she could not continue on as she had, caught in a limbo of uncertainty and hurt.

"Of course, you are right, but I dread seeing him. The last time..." Elizabeth shook her head sharply, absolutely refusing to allow her threatening tears to form. Though that remembrance brought her much pleasure, it was of the bittersweet variety. "I will be relieved when it is done."

Mrs Gardiner squeezed her arm. "Naturally. Once it is, you may have yourself a good cry and purge yourself of this experience. If this business is concluded early enough in the day, I shall take you to Gunter's for an ice, how does that sound?"

"Very well, indeed, Aunt." And it did. As delightful as indulging in an uncommon treat sounded, it was her aunt's consideration which provided the greatest balm to her wounded feelings.

After a final silent exchange of commiserating expressions, the ladies resumed consumption of their meal. Elizabeth had taken only a single bite of her toast when there was a knock at the door, causing her to choke on it.

As Elizabeth cleared away the obstruction with a needed gulp of tea, she could hear the deep, vibrating tones of a man speaking to the housekeeper down the hall. It was Darcy, and he had arrived far too early for a polite call.

Elizabeth regarded Mrs Gardiner with wide-eyed terror; she had not expected him to come so soon. Mrs Gardiner patted her on the hand, reasserted that all would be well, and rose from her chair. Elizabeth followed and they both adjourned to the front parlour where Darcy was waiting.

When they entered, they found Darcy pacing back and forth before the fireplace, his head bowed and his fingers busy toying with the signet ring on his right hand. Elizabeth was inclined to smile at their shared habit of fiddling with jewellery when they were nervous, but quashed it; this was not to be a happy meeting.

Darcy halted at their entrance and bowed deeply. "Mrs Gardiner, Miss Bennet, forgive me for coming so early, but I felt our business was pressing. I hope I find you well."

Elizabeth left it to Mrs Gardiner to exchange the obligatory pleasantries as she was in no mood to make the man before her feel at ease. She took a chair at the far point of the room simply to disoblige him.

Once the necessary business of greeting was out of the way, Mrs Gardiner announced, "I know that the two of you have much to discuss and that my presence would only hamper you. I shall be in the breakfast room should I be needed, and I expect this door," she indicated the one which created easement between the two rooms, "to remain open." She then left, leaving the door in question ajar several inches.

Mrs Gardiner's exit seemed to have sucked all conversation out of the room with her. Elizabeth sat, Darcy hovered in the centre of the parlour and both were palpably silent.

At length, and with much apparent effort, Darcy broke it. "I had not realised you intended to come to London," he said in an awkward mimicry of small talk. "Why did you not write to inform me? I should have been happy to send a carriage for you."

Elizabeth's huffed at him, offended by his pretended ignorance. "I had not thought you interested in my comings and goings any longer, sir. However, I did write to you of my intentions, amongst my other communications which went unanswered."

Darcy looked convincingly puzzled. "I do not understand you."

"Though I suppose that letter must have gone the way of the others, and you have ignored it. Had you bothered to read them, you would have known that I fled from my own home to escape the humiliation of being jilted."

Jilted! What on earth can she mean? Darcy's stomach heaved violently and he thought he might be sick. Fortunately, he had not been able to take breakfast, so only intemperate, horrified words spewed forth. "What do you mean, 'jilted'? I always meant to come back!"

Elizabeth's reply, in harmony with his own, was little less than a shout. "Then you ought to have said as much! I sent you letter after letter only to receive nothing in return. After weeks of this, a lady begins to understand. You were not gone a month when I realised the sort of man I had agreed to marry."

Darcy's alarm was growing apace, and he stepped nearer to Elizabeth and knelt down before her. He reached out for her hand, but she snatched it away from him. "I have no notion what you are talking of. I have received only one communication from you since I arrived in town." He almost thought he felt Elizabeth's note heating in his breast pocket as he alluded to it.

"Nonsense," she scoffed, tossing her magnificent head. "I sent you above a dozen different letters."

"And I have sent at least twenty to you! All without any sort of response. I thought you angry with me for staying in town beyond the two or three days originally promised, though I could not fathom why you should be so under the circumstances. Are you saying that you never received a single letter explaining what happened?"

"No, not one." Elizabeth eyed him warily, her voice

wavering in uncertainty. "And you claim that you never received any of mine, either?"

"No, none of them. Yet I know the post has been operating as usual, because I have received various other letters from my steward, friends, business associates...why should only yours go astray?"

"I am sure I do not know, but you might have tried writing to my father, or Mr Bingley, if you did not hear from me."

"I did! Numerous times. Nothing from Hertfordshire ever came across my desk."

Elizabeth's suspicion seemed to be melting into simple perplexity. "Why should only communication from Hertfordshire be affected? And why did you not simply come back to Longbourn?"

"Because..." Darcy's mind stuttered to a stop as it collided headlong with the answer to their confounding mystery. "Lady Catherine."

"I beg your pardon?"

"Lady Catherine! She has done this!" Darcy, in his agitation, jumped to his feet and paced away from Elizabeth, grumbling to himself as the pieces fell into place and resolved into a full picture of what must have happened. After Lady Catherine had collapsed—and, considering what he was now putting together, Darcy also wondered at the convenient timing of her sudden attack—she must have orchestrated with someone in the household to steal any post either to or from Hertfordshire, thus fabricating a breach between himself and Elizabeth. It all made perfect, if foolhardy, sense; desperate for Darcy to make an alliance with Anne, Lady Catherine had attempted to sever his engagement to Elizabeth. *That scheming, underhanded...*

Elizabeth's impatient cry recalled Darcy to his surroundings. "What do you mean? What has Lady Catherine to do with anything?"

Darcy stalked back to where she remained seated and resumed his kneeling position beside her chair. "My love, we have both been the victim of her unpardonable scheming.

There was never any rift between us other than the one she manufactured. I beg you, listen to me, for what I say is the absolute truth—I always meant to come back to you, and only a calamity of the greatest import could have prevented me."

"What sort of calamity?"

"The day I was to depart for Hertfordshire with Bingley, Lady Catherine called upon me. I am sure you can guess the purport of her visit, knowing as you do her expectations that I would marry my cousin Anne, but I refused to kowtow to any of her demands to break off my engagement to you. Then—in a manoeuvre I now regard as highly suspect—she collapsed on the floor of my study with an apparent apoplexy. I called for her doctor, and he seemed to confirm it, no doubt for a hefty sum. I have been hosting her at Darcy House since then, believing her an invalid, and writing to you almost daily begging for some word. Now I learn that your letters—and, presumably, also those of your father and Bingley—have gone astray by mysterious means. I am positive that my meddling aunt is at the centre of this."

Elizabeth's posture, which had been stiff and unyielding at the start of their conversation, had eased into a more natural air. Similarly, the taut lines of her face had loosened and she regarded him with limpid eyes brimming with hope. "Truly? You always meant to come back?"

Darcy reached for her hand again and was rewarded by no resistance from Elizabeth. He did absently note, however, that her ring finger was bare. "Always. I love you beyond measure, and nothing could keep me from you for long. I was plotting my next course of action when I happened upon you at the theatre last evening."

"I do not suppose your aunt has made any sort of miraculous recovery in the last few hours," Elizabeth commented wryly. "Were you intending to abandon her and hope for the best?"

"Ideally, no, but I could have sent a carriage to collect you and bring you to London, or a persistent servant who would not leave without obtaining a response to my letter. I might have done either before, but Lady Catherine and Anne have kept me quite busy with their complaints this past month."

"I can well imagine! If it was Lady Catherine's aim to disrupt our betrothal, she could not have you sitting idle and plotting your return to my side."

"I am so sorry that I let her come between us, my love." Darcy kissed her hands with apologetic fervency. "I have always known her to be resistant to brooking disappointment, but she carries her point too far! Once I return to Darcy House, I shall roust her from my home and send her back to Kent. After that, I am through with her."

"Though I am hardly a great defender of Lady Catherine at this moment, I would not have you cause a breach in your family because of me."

"You are magnanimous to offer her any sort of absolution, my dearest, but do not take so much upon yourself. You might have been at the heart of the matter, but you would not be the cause of the breach; that dubious honour falls to my aunt. I cannot tolerate a person who would descend to such duplicitous means to get her way, nor should I. I abhor deceit in every form, and Lady Catherine's actions have been the worst kind: malicious, selfish, and of long duration. For your sake, mine, Georgiana's, and any children we may be blessed with, I cannot allow her influence in our household."

"I suppose you are right." Elizabeth's eyes fell closed and she emitted a shuddering sigh. "I am so thankful that this misunderstanding has been cleared up between us. I had thought...I had feared that you were regretting your proposal and wishing to dissolve our alliance."

Darcy tugged at Elizabeth and pulled her, somewhat awkwardly, into his lap. Once they were seated on the floor, he applied himself to kissing every inch of her beloved face, proclaiming between them, "Never, my love, never. After so much effort spent on convincing you to accept me, how could you believe that I would throw you away?"

"I resisted it as long as I could, but after so many weeks..." Elizabeth allowed her sorrowful statement to trail away as she responded to his ardour.

Darcy cursed Lady Catherine and her interference for shaking Elizabeth's confidence in him. He could not blame her, for had he not worried the same about her? That she had regretted accepting him and wanted to pretend their betrothal had never happened?

Elizabeth pulled back only enough to bury her face in his neck. "You cannot know how overwhelming it was to be surrounded by people who doubted your intentions. Only Jane and Mr Bingley believed you would come back, and everyone else either looked upon me with pity or derision."

"There are no words to express how sorry I am that you were subjected to their scorn. It will all be put to rights, I swear it." He held her tighter to his chest and pressed his lips to her hair.

With a weak semblance of her usual sportiveness, Elizabeth sat up and quipped, "By the by, Miss Bingley has everyone half-convinced that you really were engaged to your cousin, as Mr Collins said, and you had gone off to marry her in my place. I mention it because you will have more than just me and my family to convince upon your return."

Another presumptuous female I must strike from my acquaintance. "I hope that saying my vows to you before God will quash that particular rumour."

"And Mr Wickham..."

Darcy unclenched his jaw to ask, "What has that miscreant said now?"

"Well, he perpetuated Miss Bingley's theory that you were actually engaged to Miss de Bourgh," Elizabeth paused and withdrew her eyes from his, "and claimed that you had given me a piece of costume jewellery in place of an actual heirloom. I did not believe it at first, but once I thought I had been abandoned..."

Tilting Elizabeth's chin up with the crook of his finger,

Darcy placed a delicate kiss upon her lips. “I understand, my love. Wickham is persuasive, even in average circumstances, and he has a particular talent for sensing vulnerability in his dupes. Had Lady Catherine not meddled where she was not wanted, I am positive that you would have given him no more credence than a barking dog. I can assure you, however, that your ring did, indeed, belong to my grandmother Darcy; whilst you are still in town, I can show you a portrait of her wearing it at Darcy House. It hangs just outside the mistress’s chambers.”

After pressing another, more lingering kiss to his mouth, Elizabeth said, “I would very much like to see it. In the meantime...”

From the depths of her bodice—and Darcy could not help but stare as she revealed it—the ring in question was withdrawn, twinkling gold and crimson in the daylight streaming in from the far window. It dangled at the end of a long length of matching red ribbon and was warm in his palm from where it had rested against her heart. It pleased Darcy mightily that, even in the midst of their great division, she had kept a token of him so close to her.

Darcy took the liberty of untying the ribbon and freeing the ring. He then placed it upon the fourth finger of her left hand, where it belonged.

TWENTY-THREE

Darcy marched up the steps of his town house with purpose, filled with grim determination to confront his duplicitous aunt and evict her from his life. In the name of his newly repaired relationship with Elizabeth, his own sense of justice, and their shared future happiness free of Lady Catherine's venomous influence, it had to be done, and without delay.

Inside, he shed his overcoat, gloves, hat, and walking stick with impatient motions and then made for the staircase, only to stop with his foot on the first step. The strident tones of Lady Catherine were close, far too near for a woman supposedly confined to her bed. Though her voice often carried, especially when it took on that hysterical pitch, it seemed to be coming from just down the hall rather than the family wing above. *How well she has recovered*, Darcy thought with a sneer.

Changing course, Darcy headed directly for the gold saloon where he suspected Lady Catherine was cloistered with her daughter to discuss their ongoing intrigues.

As he approached, the doors to the saloon flew open and a footman rushed out. His expression was admirably stoic, but the quickness of his feet and the jerkiness of his motions indicated that he was rather flustered. Lady Catherine's demanding voice followed the poor fellow out. "Honestly! The servants today...Anne, when you are mistress here, I expect you will take a firmer hand with them. Darcy has obviously been too soft, and standards are slipping."

Darcy loitered in the corridor, breathing deeply in an attempt to rein in his temper, while she continued on, sounding no more strained by ailing health than she ever had. "You are spending time with your cousin, are you not? He cannot appreciate your charms if you hide yourself away in here all day."

Peevishly, Anne replied, "I see him at meals and call upon him to attend me several times a day, but he is often working, Lord knows on what. What more can I do?"

"Go to his precious study and wait upon him there!"

"His study?" Anne said this as if it left a vile taste upon her tongue. "What ever would I be doing there?"

"Ask to borrow a book, say that you are overcome with worry for your dear mama's condition and require his consolation. Use your imagination, girl!"

"Why can you not arrange it all for me?" This came out as little less than a whine. "I have not the constitution for all this conspiracy."

Lady Catherine emitted an exasperated huff and Darcy heard a thump which he suspected was her fist hitting the arm of her chair—a frequent habit of hers when she was especially frustrated. "I have done more than my fair share! Now that I have set you up here, it is up to you to prove yourself an able mistress and desirable lover. I cannot do it all!"

"But, Mama..."

Far from cooling his outrage, Darcy's delayed entrance had only heightened it. He burst through the door, left slightly ajar by the fleeing footman, and made his presence known to the ladies within with much clamour. They both jumped and Anne shrieked, which was perhaps the most impassioned thing he had ever seen her do.

"Darcy! What on earth possessed you to come marching in

here like that?" Lady Catherine objected, her bejewelled hand pressed against her chest. "Explain yourself!"

"It is not I who need explain myself, but you." Darcy fixed her with the withering glare for which he was famous, and his aunt shrank back. Anne, though she never seemed to have much colour to lose, paled to a ghastly pallor. "I see you are looking well."

Lady Catherine, as if suddenly recalling that she was meant to be ill, swooned in her chair. "I was feeling a little better until you came storming in here and frightened me half to death! Oh...Anne, call for a footman, I must return to my rooms before—"

"Save your histrionics for someone who might believe them. You cannot fool me any longer."

Lady Catherine, abruptly cured of her swoon, gaped at him. "I know not what you mean, Nephew."

Darcy snorted. "I think you do. I have just come from seeing Elizabeth and discovered some unnerving intelligence. Would you like to hear it?"

Sitting up straight on her cushion, Lady Catherine hissed at the mention of Elizabeth's name. "Whatever that little adventuress says has no merit with me, nor should it with you. What can she have to accuse me of?"

"It is not Elizabeth who accuses you, but rather speaking with her has made your behaviour more transparent to me. Can you explain to me how the post might run with its regular efficiency, yet I have received no correspondence from Hertfordshire over the past month?"

"Certainly," Lady Catherine paused to scoff, "no one there has anything to say to you. When you are not immediately before them, they cease to consider you as anything other than a hefty purse."

"Even were that the case, surely they would wish to keep their fatted calf well fed. Why, then, should my betrothed, her family and my dear friend fail to write?"

Lady Catherine opened her mouth to respond, exchanged a

terrified look with Anne, and said, "I am sure I do not know. Who could guess at the way simple, grasping minds work?"

"I can tell you why." Darcy's restraint was weakening as he arrived at the most salient point, his voice trembling with fury. "Because I have been betrayed in the worst way possible by someone I once trusted, by family. You have meddled where you were not wanted, Lady Catherine."

"Outrageous!"

"I concur, what you have done is outrageous. Stealing my correspondence, preventing it from being either sent or received—how dare you? You have no right!"

"I have every right!" Lady Catherine's fist descended upon the arm of her chair, as it had before. She must truly be riled. "I was defending my daughter's place in this household. You are the one who threw her over, disappointed all her hopes, by engaging yourself to that...that..."

"Tread carefully, madam. Any insult to my future wife will result in your expulsion from my sight all the faster."

"You see? You see what she has done to you? Pitting you against your own family! I am almost the nearest relation you have in the world, and I am entitled to your respect—nay, your obedience!"

"Georgiana is my nearest relation, and I have never owed you any sort of submission," Darcy countered, all but baring his teeth at his arrogant relation. Her presumption was astounding. "Respect, yes, but my will is my own and you have no right to compel me against my inclinations. If there is no other objection to my marrying where I choose, I shall certainly not be kept from it by knowing that you, and you alone, wished for it."

"Your mother—"

"My mother has been dead these many years and would never have taken part in such unconscionable deceit to force my hand. Stop invoking her name to your cause, for I will not have it!"

Lady Catherine sputtered and reared back at the vehemence of Darcy's exclamation. She had not been silenced by it, however, and tried another approach. "Then I shall speak to the earl, and he will support me."

"Lord Matlock has already blessed my union with Elizabeth." Blessed was perhaps too strong a word, but Darcy had demanded and received his approbation. "He will not stand in my way because he understands, as you apparently do not, that I am my own man and will be dictated to by no one. Further, once I tell him the lengths to which you were willing to descend in order to have your way, you shall be lucky if he does not consign you to Bedlam."

"The only madness here is that you would tie yourself to a penniless nobody. I might have enlisted a maid to interrupt your correspondence, but it was all done for the best, you must see that."

Darcy lifted an incredulous eyebrow. "And your supposed 'apoplexy'?"

Lady Catherine had the temerity to look affronted. "What do you accuse me of?"

"Of misleading me in regard to the state of your health. Once I deduced that you were interfering with my post, the timing of your collapse began to seem awfully convenient. I presume you insisted upon calling in Mr Nicholson to corroborate your concocted malady?"

"Nonsense, I have been very ill—"

"Do not insult my intelligence, madam. Your condition here today proves that you were never in any danger."

Lady Catherine huffed and threw up her hands in surrender. "I only meant to save you from making a horrible mistake, Darcy. You cannot fault me for that."

"Can I not? I think we both know your motives were entirely selfish. I doubt even Anne, aside from her role as your pawn, entered into your thoughts as you schemed to defraud me of my happiness. I tell you now, Lady Catherine, that your machinations would never have borne fruit; even had you succeeded in dividing me from Elizabeth—and, for your sake, be glad that you did not, for my wrath would have been all the more terrible if you had—it would not have made a marriage between myself and your daughter at all more probable. I would never bestow my hand upon so unworthy an object, particularly when she is attached to you."

Lady Catherine launched from her seat and strode over to Darcy where she poked him, hard, in the chest. "How dare you speak to me that way? I deserve more consideration than—"

Darcy snatched her hand away from himself and restrained it. "You deserve nothing! You have deceived me into believing you on your deathbed in order to enact a conspiracy contrary to my wishes, using underhanded means to part me from the only woman in the world I could possibly marry. I am disgusted with you."

"I had to do something!" Lady Catherine screeched and stamped her foot, reminding Darcy very much of Lydia Bennet in all her childish petulance. "You were about to ruin everything, decades of planning—wasted! Overthrown by the pretensions of a young woman without family, connexions, or fortune. It is not to be endured! If you were sensible of your own good, you would not wish to elevate an undeserving wretch from the muck in which she was brought up."

Darcy thrust Lady Catherine's hand away from himself and took a step back, lip curled in distaste. "In marrying Elizabeth, I should not consider myself 'elevating her from the muck,' as you so inelegantly suggest, but rather uniting two people of similar feeling and understanding. I am a gentleman; she is a gentleman's daughter. So far, we are equal and, frankly, far above you. I cannot express how repulsed I am by your behaviour—it reeks of the mercenary stratagems you accuse Elizabeth of."

Lady Catherine shrieked in one long, shrill note which quavered on the air. With her eyes wild and her hair coming free of its pins, she looked every inch the madwoman. From the sofa behind her, Anne watched her mother unravel in abject horror. Darcy stood his ground, unwilling to be intimidated by her tantrum.

"You refuse, then, to oblige me?" Lady Catherine wagged her finger just under the tip of Darcy's nose. "You refuse to obey the claims of duty, honour, and gratitude. You are determined to ruin us all and make us the contempt of the world, for the sake of some harlot not of our sphere?"

Darcy straightened his waistcoat and stretched to his full, impressive height. "The only one in danger of making us the contempt of the world is you. Good day, Lady Catherine; I shall see that your trunks are packed and your carriage brought round within the hour."

TWENTY-FOUR

A week after being reunited with Darcy, he escorted Elizabeth home to Longbourn. This was, according to him, done quite deliberately, so that her friends and neighbours would see them together as they passed through Meryton and spread word that their engagement remained as intact as it ever was.

The Gardiners—who, once the misunderstanding had been explained to them, had quite warmed to Darcy—sadly were not able to accompany them due to Mr Gardiner's business obligations, but they both promised to attend the wedding in March. Instead, Georgiana and Mrs Annesley played the role of chaperon during the journey.

How relieved Elizabeth had been to discover that the mysterious, elegant lady on Darcy's arm that night at the theatre had only been his younger sister. Up close, Georgiana Darcy was more shy and awkward than Elizabeth had imagined from afar, and quite obviously not yet out. She might have looked old enough to tempt a man of Darcy's age and stature, but only a few minutes in her company assured Elizabeth that she had been wholly mistaken in the essentials of Miss Darcy's allure—her status as his sister notwithstanding. She was a sweet thing, eager to please and be known to her new sister, and they spent much of the carriage ride chattering on about things amusing to adolescent girls. She would be an excellent friend to Mary, Elizabeth believed, considering their mutual interest in music.

A letter each to Mr Bennet and Jane—as well as one to Mr Bingley, from Darcy—heralded their return and so the Bennets were well aware of the state of affairs between the betrothed couple. Elizabeth had been explicit in her missives about the cause of their temporary division, but cautioned that her mother and younger sisters should only be told the barest details; it was best to keep the full scope of Lady Catherine's calumny as quiet as possible. Instead, it was to be explained in the simplest terms: Darcy's aunt had fallen unexpectedly ill and there had been a problem with the post. It would not take a great deal of ingenuity to question these events, but then no one save the involved parties really knew what had happened in London. It was as good a story as any, particularly since it was, essentially, the truth.

A warm hand enveloped hers, covering the ring it bore. One which distinctly resembled one worn by Grandmother Darcy in a portrait loftily hung in Darcy House—just outside her future bedchambers. "Are you well, my love?"

Elizabeth shed her pensiveness and smiled warmly at Darcy. "Quite well, only recalling some of our recent tribulations. I am more glad than I can say that they have resolved themselves in a happy manner."

"Did you not recently caution me to remember the past only as it brings me pleasure?"

"How unfair of you to triumph over me with my own words! Badly done, sir."

Darcy chuckled at her easy playfulness even as Georgiana, from the forward-facing seat, goggled at their exchange. "I shall not apologise for repeating a piece of excellent advice, no matter the source. We have achieved our felicity, despite all the trials we have faced, and it is only right that we now focus upon that."

"Very true, though you must admit we have suffered more than our fair share of difficulties in coming to this happy conclusion. Though I do not wish to dwell upon them, I am inclined to laugh."

"I suppose that can be allowed. Some portions were rather amusing."

An impish grin spread across Elizabeth's face. "Such as your first proposal when you fainted dead away?"

Miss Darcy interjected here, her expression the picture of astonishment. "He fainted?"

"Oh, yes. Did he not tell you?" Miss Darcy shook her head. "Then I shall take it upon myself to relate the tale—no, no, Fitzwilliam, she must hear—because it will thrill you more than any novel. It all began when your brother fell off his horse..."

The story of Darcy's first proposal—told with much spirit and far less gravity than it possibly deserved—carried them the rest of the way to Longbourn and they halted there in the drive in a cloud of mutual laughter.

"She did not!" Miss Darcy's giggles were muffled behind her cupped hands.

"Indeed, she did!" insisted Elizabeth, the back of her hand pressed to her forehead in an affected manner. "Swooned right into Mr Bingley's arms, none the wiser that your brother had just asked me to marry him. I understand she was dismayed to learn the truth later."

At Elizabeth's sly sideways glance, Darcy returned a pained smile. "You might say that."

The door was opened a moment later and Darcy was ushered out by their laughter, which the ladies quickly subdued at a severe look from Mrs Annesley who herself appeared to be fighting the inclination. Darcy then handed each of them out himself, where they were properly presented to the contingent of Bennets—plus Bingley—waiting in the drive.

"Oh, Mr Darcy!" Mrs Bennet exclaimed after the introductions to Miss Darcy and Mrs Annesley were concluded. "How happy I am to see you again! I just knew you would come back, I never doubted it for an instant. Did I not say so, girls? I am sure I repeated it often enough. I do hope your dear aunt is much improved."

Darcy responded to Mrs Bennet's effusions stiffly, in concurrence with his attitude of late whenever Lady Catherine was mentioned. It was also probable that he had not entirely forgiven Mrs Bennet for her role in Elizabeth's disgraced flight to London, either. "She is, I thank you. I beg you would forgive me for my unintended silence these many weeks, there were some...problems with the post which have now been sorted out."

"Think nothing of it, sir! I am sure it was not your fault, and these things do happen. Come in, come in and have a spot of tea as you used to do. I have saved your chair by the fire." Mrs Bennet then whirled about and disappeared into the house with her younger daughters trailing behind her like a line of ducks, Bingley and Jane bringing up the rear. Mr Bennet lingered a moment longer, fixed Darcy with a cold stare, and followed.

Elizabeth was torn between amusement and vexation at her mother's sudden reversal of opinion on Darcy's constancy; would that she had shown as much confidence in his return a month ago. As for her father's coolness, that was to be expected on behalf of his favourite daughter, and it would pass soon enough once she reassured him that the schism was honestly not Darcy's fault. Ah, to be home.

Once they were all assembled in the parlour, with Elizabeth and Darcy in their matching chairs at Mrs Bennet's insistence, they were allowed a certain semblance of private conversation under the noise of the room. "I can see that your father is still somewhat suspicious of me."

"Yes, I noticed that, as well," said Elizabeth. "I would not let it worry you overmuch. I explained everything in my letter, but no doubt he wishes to hear it from me directly. Fear not, I shall assure him that it is all true and that you are not to blame for what happened. In the end, I suspect he shall be vastly amused by it. It is rather ridiculous when you think about it."

Darcy's nose wrinkled in a slight grimace. "I feel that I bear some of the responsibility, Elizabeth."

Elizabeth shook her head. "Nonsense, you were duped by your own aunt, a woman you have trusted since childhood, so you cannot be faulted for falling victim to her machinations."

"I knew she was desperate and angry," Darcy countered with a challenging set to his jaw. "I should not have trusted any of her actions implicitly."

"But who would suspect another of pretending an apoplexy? Really, you take too much upon yourself."

Darcy lifted her hand and, with an indulgent quirk of his lips, kissed the backs of her fingers. "It must be so when you put it like that. At least she and her conspirators have been purged from our lives, and we need not fear the same sort of farce again."

"I take it you discovered the maid who had been helping her?"

"I did." Darcy's mien shifted to a more severe aspect. "She has been dismissed without reference, of course. She might try her luck at Rosings, but I doubt even Lady Catherine will have her, considering her plan never came to fruition."

"Were there any others in collusion with her?"

"Not that I could find, and she identified no one else. Just in case, I have Mrs Hawthorne interviewing all the female servants and Mr Clarence the male. If there is any more treachery afoot, they will ferret it out. You need not fear any disloyalty from them as Mrs Darcy."

Mrs Bennet's voice rose above the fray, addressing Bingley. "And where is Miss Bingley? Did she not receive my invitation to dine with us today?"

Bingley glanced at Jane uneasily, clearing his throat. "Alas, my sister claims the headache today, otherwise I am sure she would be here. She is very sorry to have missed Darcy and Lizzy's homecoming."

Elizabeth bit her lip and struggled not to snicker at Bingley's hint. It surprised her not at all that Miss Bingley would not wish to be present at this occasion, which represented the bitter end to her own intentions of keeping Elizabeth and Darcy apart. No doubt she was not best pleased to learn that Darcy would be returning to Hertfordshire as engaged as ever to Elizabeth, despite his promising absence. Instead, she was left to all the satisfaction of having alienated those who might ease her way into the best society, for she would never again be invited to Pemberley or Darcy House. Elizabeth might have felt some sympathy for Miss Bingley but for the fact she had brought it upon herself.

"Now, Mr Darcy," Mrs Bennet turned her attention to her other impending son-in-law, "do tell us about your time in town. Your aunt suffered an apoplexy, you said?"

"Ah...we thought it was, at first, but a second opinion determined that it had merely been a fit of nerves. Lady Catherine has always been rather...excitable."

"My goodness! How horrible, yet how fortunate that it was nothing worse. You see, Mr Bennet? You see how low a nervous condition can bring someone?"

Darcy did his best to explain his absence to the collected party—and, by extension, the neighbourhood at large—how a series of unfortunate coincidences led to the misunderstanding of his intentions. He, too, had been concerned by the lack of word from Elizabeth, he certainly always meant to come back, etcetera. Thankfully, he and Elizabeth had found one another in London and it was all cleared up. Mrs Bennet and those not already in on the secret were satisfied and the conversation moved on to wedding planning.

EPILOGUE

Two Years Later...

"At least someone sleeps well in the carriage," said Darcy, though there was no underlying asperity in his tone. Quite to the contrary, he spoke with great affection as he smiled softly down upon the dark curly head resting against his wife's bosom.

Elizabeth's attention was similarly riveted as she tugged a knit blanket higher so that it better shaded the tiny face, blocking the autumn sunlight leaking through the curtains. The little girl snuffled softly in her sleep, rubbed a chubby fist briefly against her cheek and settled more deeply into her dreams. "If it must be one of us, I am glad that it is Nell."

"Fair enough, though it would do you some good to rest if you can. You were up half the night." Darcy's suggestion—more of an admonishment, really—was followed by a tender kiss to Elizabeth's temple, the only part of his wife he could reach without disturbing their babe.

Elizabeth leant into her husband's side, the infant shifting with her, and sighed with a mix of exhaustion and contentment. It was a strange combination, to be sure, but one which the relatively new parents had learnt to embrace over the past twelvemonth since little Penelope Anne, named for her Great-Grandmama Darcy, had come into the world. They had much help in caring for their firstborn in the form of various servants and relatives, but their decidedly opinionated Nell would only tolerate others besides her dear mama on a limited basis. When discontent or otherwise needy, only Elizabeth's attendance would do, and she would cry most piteously until reunited with her mother who would then affectionately cuddle and pamper Nell to her satisfaction. Even her devoted papa was no substitute.

The night previous, Nell had woken sometime before midnight for reasons unknown, bawling for Elizabeth's particular brand of attention. Elizabeth had been woken by the night nurse when all other efforts to calm Nell had failed. The child had instantly calmed once she had been deposited into her mother's arms, which meant that most of the household had been allowed to go back to sleep, but that the mistress herself lost a few precious hours of repose which otherwise would have done her a world of good. However, once Nell had settled between her doting parents and fallen back into the embrace of Morpheus at roughly two o'clock, the peace had resumed. Until dawn, at least.

Elizabeth nuzzled the fine curls upon the crown of her child's head and breathed deeply. There was nothing more soothing to her frazzled nerves than Nell's scent; all else paled by comparison. Darcy's tender, affectionate treatment came close, but Nell was a piece of her, a perfect amalgamation of herself and her dear husband. She was a physical manifestation of a love which had endured much and remained strong in the face of tribulation. To Elizabeth, her daughter was perfect, despite her imperfections. Perhaps even because of them.

After a reverent kiss to Nell's forehead, Elizabeth rested her cheek upon the soft bed of her child's hair and emitted another sigh. "There is not much point in attempting sleep for such a short trip. If we were on our way to Pemberley, I would bow to your wise advice, but we shall be at Longbourn within the hour. Any sleep achieved would only be interrupted."

Darcy shifted his arm so that it rested behind Elizabeth, wrapped loosely about her waist. His palm cupped the crest of her hip and settled there most comfortably. "Even a little might help."

"No, if there is anything I have learnt since Nell was born, it is that I am only more tired when woken half an hour after falling asleep. I think it best to stay awake for the nonce," Elizabeth said, scooting deeper into her husband's embrace. She felt him squeeze her tightly for a moment in response.

"Very well. Are you looking forward to seeing your parents again? It has been quite a while since they were all at Pemberley, not since the spring for Mary's wedding."

Elizabeth quirked a smile as she recalled the last time her nearest and dearest had all descended upon Pemberley to celebrate the nuptials of her middle sister, Mary, to the current incumbent of Kympton. Mr Winthrop was the man to whom Darcy had presented the parish living and was a much better choice than the man once intended for it. He was a gentle, pious soul with unassuming manners, full of forgiveness and Christian charity which he spread amongst his parishioners without even an ounce of prejudice. Mary had learnt much from him about what it meant to be truly devout and, as a result, she had made fewer and fewer pedantic speeches to them all since being introduced to and ultimately falling in love with him. For his part, Mr Winthrop, at a full ten years Mary's senior, had never expected to marry, so devoted was he to the felicity of everyone else. However, meeting a young lady with desires so well aligned with his own had changed his opinion of what was possible, and he had proposed to Mary less than six months after meeting her. They were currently too involved in their charitable duties to travel south with the Darcys on this particular visit to Longbourn, but sent along their best wishes to the Bennets in their stead.

"I am excited to see Papa, but Mama..." Elizabeth huffed

and Nell stirred against her chest. Once assured that the babe had drifted back into deeper sleep, she continued, "I am not looking forward to more advice on begetting you a son. Mama's letters have been full of nothing else now that Nell is a year old, and I am not at all eager to hear about it in person."

Elizabeth felt Darcy's chuckle more than she heard it as she was tucked up against his side and the offering had been quiet. "If it appeases you, I have no complaints regarding your...efforts."

"You..." Elizabeth lightly elbowed her husband in his side, though she dared not do more for fear of waking Nell. "I am serious, you should hear some of the things she suggests! Special teas, diets, health regimens, positions..."

"Positions?"

The elevated interest in Darcy's voice amused Elizabeth and she snickered, quietly, at him. "Nothing which would tempt you, dearest. These positions are meant to be performed after you have done your part."

"Oh, well, in that case."

Elizabeth shook her head at her husband. "Regardless, I have grown quite tired of Mama's 'advice'. It is all stuff and nonsense."

"What makes you say that?"

"I have four sisters."

"Indeed."

"It would not bother me so much if she would simply contain herself after a few comments, but she must bring it up over and over again." Elizabeth's ire at her mother's well-meant but mortifying instruction was growing with each complaint, and her voice was tight as a result. "Papa, at least, contents himself with a single quip about being surrounded by women and leaves it at that. I love Mama dearly, but I tire of her bemoaning something which I cannot help."

Darcy kissed Elizabeth's temple again and nuzzled the same spot affectionately. "It is a good thing we are staying at Netherfield, then."

"Yes." Elizabeth tilted her head back to offer her lips to her husband. Darcy met them with his own and they shared a brief kiss before resettling into their former positions. "I shall be very happy to see Jane with no qualifications whatsoever. I will also say that, for her sake, I hope she is carrying a boy. If not, Mama will be entirely unbearable until they are able to leave for Derbyshire."

Jane, the eldest and most sweet natured of all the Bennet sisters, had married her Mr Bingley at the same time as Elizabeth and Darcy. Despite their wedding dates being identical, Jane had not fallen with child as quickly as Elizabeth, which had caused much histrionic concern in Mrs Bennet. Fortunately, she and Bingley had finally been blessed some seven months ago, and now awaited the arrival of their firstborn before they could move to an estate they had purchased less than thirty miles from Pemberley. They expected to be able to pack up and leave Hertfordshire for their more permanent residence in the early spring, after Jane had gone through her confinement; the Darcys were eagerly anticipating having the Bingleys as closer neighbours, as were the Winthrops. The Bennets of Longbourn were mostly resigned to the change, except for Mrs Bennet who persisted in begging the Bingleys to change their minds and remain at Netherfield. Such wheedling likely only made her eldest daughter and son-in-law more eager to be away, but such an idea had never occurred to Mrs Bennet, and she kept at it in the hopes of eventual success—after all, it seemed to work well enough on Mr Bennet.

"So long as Mrs Cole is not in residence, I shall be happy enough," Darcy said with a grumble.

Mrs Caroline Cole—formerly Miss Caroline Bingley—had not much improved upon her marriage other than to be successfully out of sight and mind of her brother and sister-in-law. Of course, as she was only lately married, perhaps she had simply not had enough time to benefit from the state for such improvements to be apparent. Immediately after the double ceremony which had united the Bingleys and Darcys, Miss

Bingley had removed from her brother's care and been resigned to that of the Hursts, desirous of putting some distance between herself and the happy couples.

Truthfully, after her appalling behaviour to Elizabeth, she was not especially wanted in any case; even dear Jane was not so magnanimous as to wish for her company, though she did frequently remark that it was a 'great pity' that her sister-by-marriage should be so sadly overcome by her disappointment. It was Jane's opinion that Miss Bingley's temperament suffered from the blow of losing the man she preferred to any other and that she would, in time, come to accept it, and her spirits—and, therefore, her conduct—would improve. This was far more charitable a notion than Elizabeth was prepared to grant, but she would not quibble about it.

Miss Bingley had remained in her sister's household for another year before, upon the frustrated insistence of Mr Hurst, she had been turned out and set up in her own establishment. No one would admit to a specific cause for this breach, but whispers about town had it that Miss Bingley's newly acquired habit of overindulging in drink might have had something to do with it. Elizabeth rather doubted that this was the entire truth, however, as she could not see Mr Hurst begrudging a fellow lush room and board. Were it the case, Elizabeth did not want to imagine what sort of slovenly behaviour would make Miss Bingley unwelcome at the Hursts; it would have to have been quite shocking, indeed.

Regardless of the imperfectly known details regarding the former Miss Bingley's expulsion from her sister's home, at five-and-twenty, with her prospects, beauty, and fortune steadily dwindling, she had been forced to lower her standards for potential husbands and admit the attentions of gentlemen who would be more willing to consider her for a wife. In the end, only Mr Cole, a purveyor of fine carriages with the aim of expanding his business, had been interested enough to make her an offer, and Miss Bingley had accepted him. It was not the high society match that she had hoped for, but Mrs Cole at least had the advantage of living in London as she had always preferred, even if she resided almost—but not quite—in view of her husband's warehouses.

"No, Mrs Cole has not set foot in Hertfordshire in the past two years, and I doubt that she ever will again. For myself, I am only glad that there is no militia stationed in Meryton!"

"Hmph," was Darcy's agreement.

After the neighbourhood's dire pronouncements over the state of their engagement had proved wholly unfounded, Elizabeth had noted to Darcy that Mr Wickham had quite suddenly found a distaste for social occasions amongst the gentrified citizens of Meryton and its environs. Although, according to many of the shopkeepers, he had not been shy in running up debts with them. It had not been a stretch of imagination from there to assume that the libellous lieutenant had, much as he had done for the Netherfield Ball, fled from the presence of his former friend. No doubt Mr Wickham had realised that his tall tales had not prospered in the way he had intended if Darcy had, against all expectations to the contrary, come back to wed Elizabeth. Darcy's increasing popularity amongst the neighbourhood in the wake of his triumphant return had also thwarted any plans he might have had to spread his lies further; no one would believe a word said against the handsome, honourable, heroically romantic Mr Darcy. Miss Darcy, thankfully, never saw hide nor hair of her former beau whilst she resided at Netherfield, a circumstance which Elizabeth attributed to Mr Wickham's strong sense of self-preservation.

Later that summer, after the Darcys and Bennets had retired to Pemberley and the militia had marched on to Brighton for training, word had reached Hertfordshire and then been forwarded on to Derbyshire via letters from Elizabeth's gossiping Aunt Philips that Mr Wickham was in a great deal of trouble. It seemed that, after amassing a rather staggering pile of debts amongst the merchants of Brighton and his fellow officers, Mr Wickham had fled his commission. This would have been bad enough, but he had had the further temerity to take the wife of his commanding officer with him when he had escaped into the night, presumably as his 'special companion' for the journey. Mrs Forster had left behind a note alleging that she and Mr Wickham were headed for the Scottish border with an apparent unconcern for the fact that she was already, in fact, married and that any union between herself and the wayward lieutenant could in no way be considered valid by the laws of either God or man.

Many months later, Mrs Philips had confided the resolution of the sorry tale to Elizabeth in yet another letter on the subject. Running away from his regiment during a time of war had been a great enough offence, but Colonel Forster had made it his personal mission to bring Mr Wickham to justice, one must presume on behalf of his own injured honour. Instead of being consigned to the stockades or a stint in Marshalsea, Colonel Forster had pulled a few strings and sent Mr Wickham to the gallows once he had been apprehended. It had greatly disturbed Elizabeth to hear this much as, despite her own poor opinion of Mr Wickham and his slander, she had not considered him evil enough to swing. However, she had to admit that he had brought it upon himself with his own foolishness; imagine, running off with the colonel's wife and expecting no retribution from the army. Mr Wickham likely would have made it away clean had he only escaped by himself, but he would press his luck.

Mrs Forster, for her part, had been found more than two months prior to Mr Wickham's arrest, alone and stranded in the darkest parts of London. Though the details were, naturally, not privy to the public, one had to assume that Mrs Forster had eventually reached out to her cuckolded husband for salvation and then been reluctantly rescued from her self-inflicted folly. Mrs Philips's information did not spread quite so far as to say what had happened to her after this, but she had not been seen in the company of Colonel Forster since immediately after her recovery and was, most likely, set up in some forgotten cottage in a far-flung location to live out the rest of her days in shame.

Elizabeth felt sorry for Mrs Forster, remembering her as a flighty thing and a great friend of her youngest sister, but was more than grateful that Lydia's invitation to attend the militia to Brighton in her company had been politely rejected in favour of spending the summer at Pemberley instead. Had Lydia placed herself in the chaperonage of Mrs Forster, there was no telling what sort of scandal might have befallen her family as a result; even such a long period of time later, Elizabeth had to suppress a shudder at the thought.

"Are you cold, dearest?"

Elizabeth looked up at her darling husband and shook her head. "Not at all. If anything, Nell is keeping me overly warm."

Darcy's head tilted to one side inquisitively. "Then why did you shiver?"

"I was just thinking about Mr Wickham...and Mrs Forster. What might have happened had we not married when we did? Lydia might have been allowed to go off to Brighton, and we all could have been ruined by proxy. It was a near miss, I think." Elizabeth shuddered again as she always did whenever her thoughts turned towards the subject.

"I am grateful for many reasons that we married, but I am also glad that our union has had so many unforeseen benefits to others. I concur, it would have been potentially injurious to your family had Lydia been permitted to travel with Mrs Forster, but as she was not, I believe that to dwell upon disasters averted is an exercise in frustration. Remember your own philosophy and recall the past only as it brings you pleasure."

Elizabeth chuckled. "Well, when you put it like that, I suppose I must bow to your excellent advice."

The Darcys shared another kiss between them and resettled themselves comfortably. At length, after Elizabeth had accustomed herself to the quiet, Darcy startled her by venturing tentatively, "While we are on the subject of your younger sisters..."

When Elizabeth huffed in exasperation, it rustled the downy curls which covered the crown of Nell's head. "Mr Darcy, you really must stop fretting. Kitty and Lydia have improved so much in the past two years that you cannot have any real concerns in regard to their behaviour now. They will be, if not perfectly ladylike, certainly as close to it as one can expect from girls of their age. Further, Georgiana depends upon their attendance during her Season. She has threatened not to come out at all if she has not Kitty and Lydia at hand to give her confidence. You really must accustom yourself to the inevitable."

It was Darcy's turn to express his irritation with a hastily expelled puff of air. "'Mr Darcy,' am I?"

"When you are being insufferable, yes."

"It is not unreasonable—"

"For you to be unreasonable?"

"It is not unreasonable," Darcy persisted, nudging Elizabeth with his hip in admonition, "for a guardian to wish his charge the best possible beginning when coming out into society for the first time. You must admit that your youngest sisters have not always been the most..."

As Darcy trailed off, undoubtedly searching for a suitable euphemism which would not entirely offend his already prickly wife, Elizabeth pulled slightly away from him to glare more directly at his face. It was a silent dare to complete his sentence in a way which would not be haughty and insulting.

"You know very well what I mean. You recall that we discussed this before we were married."

"You discussed it, not I. During your first so-called proposal which, if you recall, I initially rejected."

"Technically, it was the second proposal."

Elizabeth scoffed at her husband. "The technicalities aside, I will remind you that I did not agree to your stipulations regarding my family's introduction to London society. However, you will further recall that, until now, I have not pressed you to invite them to town during the Season in deference to your opinion on the subject. You will not always get your way in this. Further, Mrs Annesley has assured you, repeatedly, that Kitty and Lydia are ready to be released into the world alongside Georgiana. And, of course, she will be there to chaperon in addition to ourselves. Finally, you would not disappoint them all by rescinding your permission to join us in town, would you?"

"I suppose not. I merely worry that they are not ready. Society might seem all that is fashionable and romantic, but there is ugliness in it, as well. I would not subject any young lady to the dangers therein if I could help it." Darcy's face tightened with consternation and displeasure as he tipped his head back onto the seat cushions, his gaze now averted to the ceiling of their equipage.

"Ah, so that is it," Elizabeth replied, realisation dawning. "You are concerned that the girls will be led astray as Georgiana was by Mr Wickham. Well, I will not deny that there are unscrupulous people in town—as there are everywhere, I might add—but you cannot put this off forever. The girls must venture out from under your protection at some point and find their own happiness. Showing a lack of confidence in them will only hurt them. You really must learn to acclimate yourself to this."

"Must I?"

"I am afraid so."

Darcy's head pivoted in her direction. "If you say it, it must be so," he conceded with a tone of defeat in his voice, "but I am not required to like it."

"I shall not demand it of you."

"Very magnanimous of you, Mrs Darcy."

Elizabeth laughed. "Oh, so I am 'Mrs Darcy' now that you must grudgingly admit that I am right?"

"Only so long as I am still 'Mr Darcy'."

"Of course, Mr Darcy."

"Mrs Darcy."

The air between them now sufficiently cleared of animus, Elizabeth resettled herself into Darcy's side, the dreaming Nell nuzzling likewise closer to her mother's bosom at the same time. "Let us discuss something more pleasant."

"Such as?"

A sudden thought sparking within her brain, Elizabeth smirked and queried, in as nonchalant a tone as she could conjure, "Have you heard from Lady Catherine recently?"

Darcy groaned so loudly in response that Nell stirred with a whimper, requiring Elizabeth to shush her daughter back into peaceful repose. She supposed that, considering their history with Darcy's quarrelsome aunt and her toadying parson, it was really her own fault that he had nearly woken their babe; he was always reluctant to discuss Lady Catherine and her unreasonable demands. They had tentatively reconciled with her, per the urging of Lord Matlock—a truly lovely man; he reminded Elizabeth greatly of her own father—who only wanted peace within the family. And ever since Anne had married his younger son—an arrangement put in place and enforced by Lord Matlock the same spring Elizabeth and Darcy had wed—Lady Catherine had become somewhat more bearable.

The rapprochement between the Darcys and de Bourghs was still relatively new, having been effected at Easter. Had the olive branch not been offered by Fitzwilliam and Anne, Elizabeth was certain her husband would have simply ignored it, for his disgust with Lady Catherine and her scheming persisted. For the sake of his favourite cousin and his wife, however, Darcy bent his neck and agreed to a short trip to Rosings Park to make the attempt. Lady Catherine had been relegated to the dower house upon her daughter's marriage and, in Darcy's estimation, the estate had been greatly improved by the change in management. Elizabeth had hardly been surprised to hear that Lady Catherine had once ruled her domain with meddling officiousness and supposed that any change must have been a cause for celebration throughout Hunsford.

Lady Catherine had not submitted quietly to her banishment to the dower house, but had been forced to capitulate in the end when her brother had threatened far greater deprivations. Lord Matlock had not gone so far as to suggest Bedlam, but there were a great many cottages in Scotland and Ireland—

or even Canada, as Darcy had semi-seriously suggested—available to their cause should she persist in her intransigence. Between a comfortable dower house near her daughter and an unknown, presumably draughty cottage cast out into the wilds of nowhere, the choice was a simple one.

"Unfortunately, yes, and I had opened the letter before realising who it was from," Darcy said once Nell had quieted. He had lowered his voice lest he disturb their daughter again. "Her latest accusation, if you can call it such, was to suggest that you are incapable of bearing me an heir."

"And that her daughter, of course, would have presented you with a son within a year of marrying you?" Elizabeth guessed with no little amusement at the absurdity of such a notion. It was unlikely that weak, sickly Anne would ever be healthy enough to bear a child at all, much less the greatly anticipated heir to the Darcy fortune. Fitzwilliam was not demanding it of her, and Rosings was now his to dispense with as he saw fit. Already he had promised it to a second son of Darcy's, should they have one. "No, an heir and a spare. As we both know, Anne would be a true proficient at anything she set her mind and talents to."

"How did you know?" Darcy's tone was heavily laden with the sarcasm which often characterised his father-in-law's communications.

"I am, as ever, most perspicacious."

"While we are on the subject of Lady Catherine, I might as well enquire whether you have heard from your cousin Collins of late." Darcy's voice was now infused with the mischievous humour of his wife; he had certainly expanded his witticisms since marrying into the Bennet clan.

Elizabeth's nose wrinkled at the thought of Mr Collins and his various presumptions—both prior to and following her marriage—of intimacy. He had been, perhaps, the most shocked of anyone upon the announcement of Elizabeth's pending nuptials to Darcy two autumns prior, both because of his own aspirations to his 'dear Cousin Elizabeth's' hand and his misguided assumptions about Darcy's supposed betrothal to his own cousin. Much to everyone's surprise, however, Mr Collins proved himself more sagacious than his beloved patroness in accepting the inevitable and applied himself to maintaining a good standing with the Darcys. What was less surprising to Elizabeth was that this reversal of opinion occurred shortly after the demotion of Lady Catherine and the elevation of Fitzwilliam as Hunsford's patron; it was not more than a month after this event that an olive branch was extended from the Collinses to their Derbyshire cousins.

To her husband's great good fortune, Mr Collins was not quite so daring as to attempt a direct correspondence between them—likely due to lingering fear of Darcy's temper, if Elizabeth had to guess—but Mr Collins managed to add his long winded well wishes to the end of each of Charlotte's letters, thereby flattering the object of his affections from afar. Elizabeth took great pleasure in reading each of Mr Collins's 'delicate compliments' to her husband whenever she happened to receive them and revelled in the inevitable roll of Darcy's eyes in response.

Fitzwilliam, for his part, filled his letters with complaints that Mr Collins would not be deterred from slobbering on his boots, but reported that Anne seemed pleased by the parson's overzealous attentions. She showed the makings of another Lady Catherine—albeit one who was less involved in the business of others, an activity in which she could not be bothered—in the way she enjoyed his fawning. Lady Catherine considered herself sadly neglected by this shift, even if Mr Collins still visited the dower house regularly.

At length, Elizabeth replied to Darcy's saucy enquiry. "I have not had a letter from Charlotte since we came away from Pemberley last month, but I have no doubt that Mr Collins will have something to add for you when I do receive her next. Do you think he will praise your greatness this time? Or will he be more direct and expound upon how very fine your eyes are?"

"Minx."

Not a quarter hour after this playful exchange, the carriage shuddered to a stop upon the gravel drive of Elizabeth's childhood home. Peeking out from between curtains of the window on her side, Elizabeth could see her parents and two unmarried sisters waiting impatiently upon the front steps of the family abode, and she breathed deeply to steady herself for what was to come.

Elizabeth looked first to Darcy, whose expression indicated that he, too, was girding himself to greet the exuberant Bennets, and then to Nell, whose peaceful sleep was about to be interrupted most rudely. She released her last inhalation with more contentment than she had taken it in.

"Come, my loves," she said to them both, readjusting her hold upon the bundle which was her daughter. "The sooner we pay our visit, the sooner we can continue on to Netherfield to see the Bingleys."

Darcy pressed his lips to Elizabeth's temple a final time, relishing the last moments of quiet with his eyes closed. "And then a rest."

"Of course, dearest. As you wish."

The End

GET A FREE EBOOK

A THANK YOU FROM THE AUTHOR & PUBLISHER

The authors and Quills & Quartos Publishing thank you for choosing this book. The favor of your rating or review would be greatly appreciated.

You can receive a free collection of short stories by signing up for the Quills & Quartos mailing list! This collection is not sold in stores and is available only to subscribers.

Get your copy HERE. Quills & Quartos will never spam you or sell your information to others. Thank you!

ACKNOWLEDGMENTS

I would like to offer my deepest, most heartfelt gratitude to everyone and anyone who assisted me in bringing this novel to completion. Firstly, my husband, who did his level best to watch the kids and let me work as often as possible; thank you for keeping them occupied—I know it wasn't easy. Secondly, to Cat Andrews and RYM who both gave me thoughtful feedback before I submitted this story to my publishers; I greatly appreciate you ladies taking the time to do so. Special thanks also belong to Debra Anne Watson, who helped me bring this story up to snuff with her incredible editing skills and deep well of regency knowledge. Thirdly, to all my readers on Fanfiction.net, A Happy Assembly, and Darcy and Lizzy forums who provided their thoughts, assistance and encouragement throughout the posting of my first draft, as well as understanding and patience when I had to put it on hiatus due to a death in the family. Thank you so much for your kind words of condolence during that sad time.

Finally, I would very much like to thank Quills & Quartos Publishing, as well as Amy D'Orazio and Jan Ashton specifically, for continuing to believe in me and my writing. I am exceedingly grateful to be part of this publishing house and can hardly believe my good fortune most days.

ABOUT MARY SMYTHE

Mary Smythe is a homemaker living in South Carolina with a rather useless BA in English collecting dust in a closet somewhere. Mrs Smythe discovered the works of Jane Austen as a teenager thanks to the 1995 BBC *Pride and Prejudice* miniseries featuring Colin Firth and Jennifer Ehle, and has since gone on to read everything written by Miss Austen at least once yearly, always wishing that there were more. She has been writing since 2001, but only discovered Jane Austen fanfiction in the summer of 2018.

facebook.com/mary.smythe.754

bookbub.com/authors/mary-smythe

goodreads.com/mrsmarysmythe

ALSO BY
MARY SMYTHE

A Faithful Narrative

Darcy's own name leapt at him from the page and his treacherous eyes could not withstand the temptation drawing them downward. What had Elizabeth written about him?

FITZWILLIAM DARCY IS ON THE VERGE of proposing to Miss Elizabeth Bennet when he happens upon her diary in a field of bluebells. Though he knows he should not, he gives in to the temptation to read it and discovers a perspective of himself he had never before considered. Not only does Elizabeth not reciprocate his love, she considers him arrogant, insulting and disdainful. Her reasons, to his shame, are not entirely unfounded. Properly humbled, Darcy must decide what to do —walk away from his beloved forever or make the effort to please a woman worthy of being pleased.

ELIZABETH BENNET IS A FIRM BELIEVER in the value of first impressions. Mr Darcy made a poor one and his subsequent behaviour did little to improve upon it. Worse yet, he has had the audacity to read her personal diary without permission.

NEVERTHELESS, MR DARCY'S VIOLATION of her privacy forces Elizabeth to reconsider many of her former prejudices against him. As a result, she comes to know herself, and him, better. Can Elizabeth forgive Mr Darcy all his trespasses and give him an opportunity to redeem himself?

Dare to Refuse Such a Man

"He is the kind of man, indeed, to whom I should never dare refuse anything which he condescended to ask."– Mr Bennet, Pride and Prejudice Volume III, Chapter 17

IT HAD NEVER OCCURRED TO FITZWILLIAM DARCY that once he had chosen a bride, her father might dare to refuse his consent. When his dearest, loveliest Elizabeth is taken from him with only a curt note of explanation, he determines that, far from accepting her father's rejection of his suit, he must instead find her again and make his case. After all, a woman worthy of being pleased is also worth fighting for.

SEVERAL MONTHS SHY OF HER MAJORITY, it is not so simple a thing to defy Mr Bennet's will, but Elizabeth, for the sake of her future happiness, must try. With various allies in her corner, as well as foes standing against her, Elizabeth's courage must rise against all attempts at intimidation. Even from her own, much beloved father.

Welcome Home

Outside the walls of the carriage, the wind screeched and howled in warning to anyone stupid enough to be out of doors in such weather. Darcy heard the shout of his coachman just as the carriage jerked hard, sending him sliding across the slick leather seat beneath him. His gloves lost their grip and...

HAVING LEFT ELIZABETH BENNET behind in Hertfordshire, Fitzwilliam Darcy is amazed to arrive at Pemberley and find her residing there as his wife, the mistress of both his home and his heart. Crushed to find that it was a fever dream resulting from his carriage accident, Darcy decides that it must have been a Christmas miracle, sent to show him the happiness he might have if only he could put his reservations about her aside.

SO RESOLVED, HE RETURNS to Hertfordshire, wishing to show her the man he is and the life they might have together but the spite of old rivals remains there, determined to keep them apart. Will their love prevail at last within the joys of Christmas?

Welcome Home is a Pride & Prejudice Variation.

Multi-Author Collections

'Tis the Season

A collection of Christmas-themed stories based on the beloved characters of Jane Austen.

Made in the USA
Columbia, SC
26 September 2022

67948389R00167